Christie RIDGWAY

AN OFFER HE CAN'T REFUSE

AVON BOOKS

An Imprint of HarperCollinsPublishers

AVON BOOKS
An Imprint of HarperCollins*Publishers*
10 East 53rd Street
New York, New York 10022-5299

Copyright © 2005 by Christie Ridgway
Excerpts from *Return of the Warrior* copyright © 2005 by Sherrilyn Kenyon; "Lost and Found" copyright © 2005 by Savdek Management Proprietory Ltd.; "The Matchmaker's Bargain" copyright © 2005 by Elizabeth Boyle; "The Third Suitor" copyright © 2005 by Christina Dodd; *A Perfect Hero* copyright © 2005 by Sandra Kleinschmit; *An Offer He Can't Refuse* copyright © 2005 by Christie Ridgway
ISBN: 0-06-076348-5
www.avonromance.com

First Avon Books paperback printing: August 2005

Avon Trademark Reg. U.S. Pat. Off. and in Other Countries, Marca Registrada, Hecho en U.S.A.
HarperCollins® is a registered trademark of HarperCollins Publishers Inc.

Printed in the U.S.A.

10 9 8 7 6 5 4 3 2 1

For Cynthia De Nardi,
who read my first romance stories
before we needed bras,
before we could wear makeup,
before we knew the first thing about boys.
Here's to us, old friend.

One

"Begin the Beguine"
Frank Sinatra
Frank Sinatra Story in Music (1946)

Téa Caruso had once been very, very bad. During a morning spent closeted in the perfume-saturated powder room of Mr. and Mrs. William Duncan's Spanish-Italian-Renaissance-inspired Palm Springs home, discussing Baby Jesus and the Holy Mother, she wondered if today was the day she started paying for it. Toward noon, she emerged from the clouds—both heavenly and olfactory—with a Chanel No. 5 hangover and fingernail creases in her palms as deep as the Duncans' quarter-mile lap pool.

Standing on the pillowed-limestone terrace outside, she allowed herself a sixty-second pause for fresh air, yet still managed to multitask the moment by completing a quick appearance-check as well. Even someone with less artistic training than Téa would know that her Mediterranean coloring and generous curves were made for low necklines and gypsy shades, but her Mandarin-collared, dove-gray linen dress was devised to button-up, smooth-out, tuck away. Though she could never feel completely innocent, she preferred to at least look that way.

The reflection in her hand-mirror presented no jarring surprises. The sun leant an apricot cast to her olive skin. Tilted brown eyes, a slightly patrician nose, cheekbones and jawline now defined after years of counting calories instead of chowing down on cookies. Assured that her buttons were tight, her mascara unsmudged, and her hair still controlled in its long, dark sweep, she snapped the compact shut. Then, setting off in the direction of her car, she swapped mirror for cell phone and speed-dialed her interior design firm, Inner Life.

"She's still insisting on Him," she told her assistant when she answered. "Find out who can hand-paint a Rembrandt-styled Infant Jesus in the bottom of a porcelain sink."

Continuing her forward march, she checked her watch. "Any messages? I have lunch with my sisters up next."

"Nikki O'Neal phoned and mentioned a redo of her dining room," her assistant replied. "Something about a mural depicting the Ascension."

The Ascension?

Téa's steps faltered, slowed. "No," she groaned. "That means Mrs. D. has spilled her plans. Now we'll be hearing from every one of her group at Our Lady of Mink."

A segment of Téa's client list—members of the St. Brigit's Guild at the posh Our Lady of Mercy Catholic Church—cultivated their competitive spirits as well as their Holy Spirit during their weekly meetings. One woman would share a new idea for home decor, prompting the next to take the same theme to even greater—more ostentatious—heights.

Three years before it had been everything vineyard, then sea life turned all the rage, and now . . . good God.

"The *Ascension*?" Téa muttered. "These women must be out of their minds."

But could she really blame them? Palm Springs, California, had a grand tradition of the grandiose, after all. Walt Disney had owned a home here. Elvis. Liberace.

It was just that when she'd opened her business, filled with high artistic aspirations and a zealous determination to make over the notorious Caruso name, she hadn't foreseen the pitfalls. Like how the ceaseless influx of rent and utility bills and the unsteady-trickle-and-occasional-torrent that was her cash flow meant she couldn't be picky when it came to choosing design jobs.

Like how *that* could result in gaining woeful renown as designer of all things overdone. She groaned again.

"Oh, and Téa . . . " Her assistant's voice rose in an expectant lilt. "His Huskiness called."

Her stomach lurched, pity party forgotten. "What? *Who?*"

"Johnny Magee."

Of course, Johnny Magee. Her assistant referred to the man they'd never met by an ever-expanding lexicon of nicknames that ranged from the overrated to the out-and-out ridiculous. To Téa, he was simply her One Chance, her Answered Prayers, her Belief in Miracles.

"Why didn't you forward it to my cell?" she demanded, her footsteps regaining speed. Between assistants and electronics, not once had she exchanged information with him voice-to-voice.

"And miss out on having the Love Machine rumble in my ear? No way. His 'hello' makes me horny. Besides, you don't like interruptions when meeting with a client."

Unless it was *him*! Sure, if she bagged Johnny Magee's project and their contact progressed beyond fax and e-mail, then the man would most likely prove a major disappointment. But from the instant she'd read "generous budget" and "complete redesign in mid-century modern" on his first communication, she'd decided theirs was the perfect relationship.

"I swear," her assistant continued with all the fervor of a former Catholic schoolgirl, "just the word 'bedroom' in that raspy voice of his makes me dream of dark nights, dark passion, and dark velvet stroking over my skin."

"Dark velvet," Téa echoed, as in her mind a more practical brand of fantasy burst to life. "Dark velvet and all other materials billed at forty percent over cost."

What a fantasy it was. Not only would winning this job mean a measure of financial relief, it meant so much beyond that. Respect in the industry. A more sophisticated portfolio to show prospective clients. All of which added up to a future free from marble-cherubed parlors, Venus de Milo verandahs, and Samson-and-Delilah–inspired dressing rooms.

But then—*beep*—Téa's wristwatch alarm snapped her back to reality. With her car now in sight, she doubled her pace. "I'm late. If he calls again, put him through."

"There's one more thing."

The reluctance in Rachele's voice caused Téa to slow again. "What is it?"

"Well, uh, an invitation came for you in the mail today. Engraved, heavy manila paper, it feels like the handmade stuff that—"

"An invitation to what?"

A hesitation. A hitch in her assistant's breath. "You believe in that whole 'don't shoot the messenger' thing, right?"

"Rachele—"

"Given your family's history, can you blame me for asking?"

"*Rachele*—"

"Okay, fine." Words tumbled out. "An invitation to a birthday party, a really big one, I'm guessing, at the Desert Star resort at the end of the month. My father's been invited, I've been invited. And, of course, you. It's . . . it's . . . it's your grandfather's eightieth birthday party."

Téa's feet lost their purchase, making an ineffective scrabble against the ground's uneven surface. As she swung out an arm to steady herself against the roof of her car, her briefcase clubbed the side window with a heavy thunk.

I was kidding about this being the day to start paying! was her first thought.

What kind of booby trap is this? was the second.

She ended the call with clumsy fingers, then slid into the driver's seat to join the slow-moving parade of Hummers, Caddies, and golf carts that cruised the Coachella Valley floor. *An invitation.*

Navigating on autopilot, she traveled along Bob Hope Drive, to Frank Sinatra Drive, to Country Club Drive. Packed into the congested midday traffic, her car inched past luxurious homes in stark bone-white and lush gardens colored in vibrant bougainvillea pinks and show-me-the money greens. *An invitation to his birthday party.*

In summer, the sun bore down with such ruthless intensity that structures, sky, and landscape paled from the heat, and even the edges of the well-watered golf courses curled up like dry sponges. The wealthy fled. But now it was autumn in Palm Springs, meaning the surroundings were stunning, the temperature was in the pleasant low-eighties, and if the cars around her were any judge, all the Hollywood hotties and megacorp magnates who had run away in May were back in full force, believing themselves safe from the ugly side of the desert.

The ugly, dangerous side her grandfather knew so well.

An invitation to his birthday party, she thought once again, nerves fluttering in her belly. *Why would Cosimo set a snare for her now?*

Finally, she reached the Café Azul. Avoiding the eye of the hovering valet, she parked her Volvo wagon in what she termed the "self-help" section of the lot and took the time to swipe a brush through her hair, a wet pinkie along each eyebrow arch, and clear gloss over her long-lasting lipcolor. Then, finger-ironing the seatbelt wrinkles from her dress, she hurried toward the café's entrance.

Still mulling over the unexpected invitation, she was halfway across the parking lot when her heel caught in a crack and she found herself stumbling again. Without a car to catch her this time, she landed hard on the opposite leg. Maybe it was the jolt to her knee, maybe it was her quick gasp of air, but suddenly her common sense kicked in.

An invitation to his birthday party. So what? Big whoop. It wasn't a royal decree or a legal summons. As a matter of fact, it was probably a mistake.

Hadn't she successfully avoided her grandfather and all those who surrounded him for years?

There was no reason to think that would change now.

Even the shivery sixty-seven degrees of the restaurant's foyer couldn't cool her more upbeat mood, nor did having to wait to speak to the harried hostess. "The rest of my party hasn't arrived," she said, when it was her turn. "But we have a reservation for Caruso."

"Caruso!" a voice echoed from behind her.

Startled, Téa glanced over her shoulder, but didn't recognize the forty-something brunette in a shantung silk suit the color of lemon sherbet.

"I'm sorry," the woman continued loudly. "But did you say your last name was *Caruso*?"

Téa tightened her grip on the strap of her purse. Usually, strangers never dared more than whisper about her family behind her back. She managed a stiff turn anyway. "Excuse me?"

The woman smiled. "My maiden name is Caputo. Caruso, so similar, leaped right out at me."

Téa's clenching hand relaxed.

"You're right," she replied. Noting again the woman's expensive outfit, she considered her current tower of bills and her ever-present need to drum up business. The smile she tacked on was full of warm good will. "The names *are* very much alike."

"Not only that." Apparently encouraged, the woman

stepped closer. "But ever since we moved to Palm Springs I've been hearing story after story about the infamous Carusos."

Téa's smile dropped away. Heat washed across her skin. "I'm not—I don't . . . " *We're an ordinary family!* All her life she'd wanted to say that.

Since she was twelve years old and her father had gone missing, presumed dead, she'd been unable to believe it.

The woman waved her hand. "Oh, no need explaining to me! I understand perfectly. People think if your last name ends in a vowel, then you're automatically in the Mafia. Ridiculous, right?"

Ridiculous, right. Women were supposed to be kept well clear of the illegal activities, and could never be members of *La Cosa Nostra.* The secret she kept hidden, the things she'd done, weren't that usual, even for a mob boss's daughter.

The stranger warmed to her subject. "The idea that an organization of brutish Italian thugs has power in this city, let alone the state, why that's television, not . . . " Her voice petered out as her attention strayed somewhere over Téa's shoulder.

The entire restaurant went quiet too, voices stilling, silverware and ice cubes ceasing to rattle. Through the glass entry doors in front of her, Téa saw a gleaming black limousine slither up to the front entrance.

Hadn't she successfully avoided her grandfather and all those who surrounded him for years?

The question mocked her now as instinct commanded she sidle closer to the foyer wall. The action provided no real protection. As they approached from behind her—presumably from the restaurant's private room in the rear—their scent reached her on a rustle of the air. The faint yet distinct scent of expensive colognes. The citrus tang of shaving soap bladed away with a straightedged razor.

When they drew nearer, she swore she could even smell the silk of their subtly patterned ties and the tropical-weight cashmere of their suits—never black, never gray, but putty or khaki or even celery, as if the lighter colors could disguise their dark reputation. The soles of their shoes—Italian leather, of course—murmured like rumors against the parquet floor.

Her father's memory came to her, unbidden, unwelcome. Unresolved.

Passing Téa, her grandfather and his cadre pretended not to see her, though she knew very well they did, realized they would have been told of her presence the instant her slingback pump stepped through the restaurant's doors. But they followed her wishes, and she followed the six of them with her gaze as they exited.

"Who was that?" The other woman found her voice just as the limo crept away.

The men of my family. My ordinary family. As if anyone, upon seeing them, would believe that.

Though they weren't your stereotypical organization of brutish Italian thugs, either. As head of a successful gourmet food company, the legitimate part of the world had crowned her grandfather the Sun-Dried Tomato King. To its underbelly he was known as the Cudgel. But to Téa's mind, he and the others were much more like stilettos. Elegant, sharp, lethal.

They were the ones she'd been successfully avoiding for years. The ones who, until this moment, she'd believed she could continue successfully avoiding for years to come.

They were the Carusos . . . a.k.a. the California Mafia.

Two

"Luck Be a Lady"
Frank Sinatra
Guys and Dolls (1963)

Johnny Magee reached for the phone on his desk, paused, then drew back his hand. "Who said 'revenge is a dish best served cold'?" he asked idly.

With the rest of the tech team at lunch, the only other person in the large Las Vegas penthouse office was Johnny's right-hand geek, twenty-five-year-old Calvin "The Calculator" Kazarsky. Cal continued peering at one of the three computer monitors crowded onto his desk. "Eaten cold. Ricardo Montalban to William Shatner, *Star Trek II: The Wrath of Khan.*"

Johnny frowned. "Not Shakespeare?"

"Then there's a line in *Les Liaisons Dangereuses.* French novel, written in 1782. *'La vengeance est un plat qui se mange froid.' Mange froid.* Eaten cold."

No doubt Cal's French accent was Parisian perfect, but it

sounded damn fishy—and swishy—to Johnny. "I could have sworn it was Shakespeare," he murmured. And served cold.

"Is that why we're changing bases?" Cal looked up, and the sun streaming through the fortieth-floor windows caught in the lenses of his thick-framed glasses.

Johnny blinked against the glare. Until this moment he hadn't been sure the other man actually grasped the fact that they were relocating the brains of the business from Nevada to Palm Springs, California. "Is *what* why we're changing bases?"

"Revenge."

Out of Cal's mouth, the word sounded harmless enough. But Johnny avoided answering by reaching for the stack of sports pages on his desk. He didn't have time for this conversation because he was a busy man. Of course, they'd already invested the organization's money on the Monday night game playing later that evening, but there were dozens of college and NFL events to consider for the upcoming weekend.

He could feel Cal's four eyes aimed his way, but Johnny ignored them to focus on the *Los Angeles Times*. It led with a weekend roundup of college football injuries. Stanford's defensive tackle had sprained a knee and would sit out the next two games. During the fourth quarter on Saturday, the Bruins freshman cornerback was carted off the field with a possible concussion. On the next page, Phil Campbell's gossipy column hinted at major marriage trouble between the Raiders QB and his very pregnant wife.

Mentally filing the details away, Johnny set the *Times* aside and pulled another sports section forward. Other gambling syndicate managers didn't bother with the papers, relying solely on computers to analyze past performances and then crystal-ball future results, but not him. His full-time crew of handicappers and tech-heads punched up daily statistical reports, hell yes, but it was his job to handicap the handicappers—which meant knowing how and when the public would bet a particular game. And the public read the papers.

From the 42-inch plasma TV on the wall across the room came the familiar trumpeting fanfare of KVBC, the local NBC affiliate. Then LaDonna Carew's high cheekbones and hooker mouth blazed on the screen, bigger than life. In Vegas, even the midday news anchor looked like she was noon-lighting from a midnight floor show at the MGM Grand.

Johnny used the remote to mute the sound, but when her mouth moved he could still hear LaDonna's voice. Not relating the latest story of alleged City Hall corruption, though; instead it was a replay of the last words she'd spoken to him eight months before. "The problem is, Johnny, you're too good at this. You've got style and you burn me up in bed, but for such a sophisticated guy you obviously only want shallow relationships."

As he'd watched her fine figure stalk out his door for the very last time that day, he'd merely felt relief—and a little twinge of guilt for never before noticing that she was smarter than she looked.

He turned the TV off completely. Then, aware that Cal was still studying him from his seat three desks away, Johnny made a big play of opening the *Kansas City Star*. But he found he couldn't concentrate on the vertical columns of black and white, damn it. The other man's continued silence was blaring louder than the combined hum of the room's desert-duty air-conditioning vents and the cooling fans of seventeen CPUs.

Johnny swallowed an irritated sigh. On the rare occasion when The Calculator swam up to breathe the air of the real world, he had an annoying tendency to remain at the surface for far too long.

The heavy quiet continued for another few moments, until Johnny gave up. "Fine," he said, wishing he could slap the paper shut, but settling for a controlled fold instead. "You want to know why we're leaving? It's because we've attracted too much attention lately."

"*We* didn't win a bracelet two years running. *You* did."

The championship bracelets weren't the problem. It was ESPN and the other cable channels that had made Texas Hold 'Em and the World Series of Poker hot.

After the first victory Johnny had felt hot too, juiced-up, invincible. But following the second win last May, he'd fielded one too many reporters' questions about his background and his day job. And started to worry. He owed discretion to the dozen other investors in the syndicate.

The only thing he took seriously—as money-making was just one game after another and women just something to do between games—was his responsibility to those who trusted him. You could bring the boy to the land of high-rollers and long-gammed showgirls, but you couldn't take the stolid, solid, Magee Main Street values out of the boy. No matter that he was a Magee in name only.

"The fact that it's my bad doesn't change a thing," he told Cal. "The business will be more secure away from the casinos' radar. And hey, you'll like Palm Springs. It's green there."

Cal shrugged. "I don't go outside much."

Hence the sickly neon-tube tan, Johnny mused. He pushed back his leather chair to prop his feet on top of his desk and then cross his ankles, conveying the image of a man in complete control of his business, his emotions, his world. Which, of course, he was.

"You need to get out more, Cal. Take up tennis or golf. The place I bought has a sweet three-hole practice course right outside the front doors of the guest bungalows. You'll enjoy the course, the exercise, the whole setup."

Cal appeared to consider the idea, the sunlight winking in his glasses as he slowly nodded his head. "That's what I thought. This move has something to do with that house."

"No!"

"You've been checking the real estate listings for almost a year. You snapped up that address the nanosecond it went on the market."

"How did you—" Johnny slammed his feet to the floor. "Have you been hacking into my files?"

"Exactly what kind of friend do you think I am? I haven't touched your computer files." Cal had the nerve to look offended, even though Johnny knew for a fact that the younger man's fingertips should be registered as weapons lethal to privacy laws. "I've been eavesdropping on your half of your telephone calls."

"Damn it, Cal—" Johnny started, then broke off, forcing himself to take a breath. Where the hell was his poker face when he needed it? Sucking in more air, he reminded himself of his cover story. He'd prepared it weeks ago, and there was no reason not to trot it out now.

"Look, I chose Palms Springs because of my brother. I told you he works near there and that he just got married. I'd like to be closer to him and his new wife."

Cal kept looking back. Then one brow rose above eyeglass frame to take skeptical refuge beneath a shaggy fringe of hair.

Johnny frowned. "Besides, there's the syndicate. . . . You know I'm right about that. The sports books won't take our action if they get wind of who we are and what we're doing."

It wasn't that their business was illegal, but the Nevada casinos were like any buck-ninety-nine, all-you-can-eat buffet on the Strip—they had the right to refuse service to anyone. And they didn't like to service consistent, very consistent and very big, winners. As it was, the syndicate had to avert attention by constantly rotating those who marched up to the windows at the casinos' sports books to physically place the bets.

"So the move's about Palm Springs."

Johnny shrugged. "Didn't I just say that?"

"And that house." Outside their windows an airplane flew

by, its tiny reflection mirrored in Cal's lenses. "That specific house. Don't bother denying it."

So Johnny shrugged again, aware that the microprocessor inside his friend's skull was busy decoding and analyzing all input data. To preclude providing anything further, he looked down at his desk and faked an interest in the Kansas City paper again.

"What I can't figure is what it has to do with that woman. That Téa Caruso."

Johnny kept his gaze on the front page photo from the Chiefs-Texans matchup without really seeing it. Téa Caruso. He'd never laid eyes on her outside of two fuzzy stills he'd found in the newspaper archives on the web—and even then she'd been no more than a smudge of a face in a crowd. But he had a feeling that . . .

Searching for a way to describe it, he looked up, his glance happening to land on the clock atop one of the lunching tech-heads' desks. 1:09:09.

Shit. Shit shit shit. He ground his teeth against the icy-blade sensation that the simple series of numbers sent scraping down his back.

That's why he was moving to Palm Springs, to the house where his father had lived sixteen years before. Because those same numbers had been plaguing him since his last birthday, showing up out of nowhere to unearth memories and emotions that had no place in his don't-wanna-scratch-the-surface life. He was so effing tired of looking up from his desk or waking up from a deep sleep to find it was 1:09:09, the exact time on the face of his digital watch when he'd heard the gunshots that had killed his father.

Months ago, Johnny had packed his Rolex away. Most nights he didn't close his eyes before 2:00 A.M. But damned if he still didn't find those numbers everywhere he looked.

He reached for the phone again. He needed to get on with it. Today. Now. Without further delay.

In Palm Springs, in that house, back at the scene of the crime, he was betting he'd put an end to this torture-by-numbers by puzzling out the answers behind his father's unsolved murder.

As for revenge . . . he didn't know why that had come to mind. His return to California had nothing to do with vengeance—well, at least not against Téa Caruso. But her last name meant she was a glimmer of possibility, a potential advantage, that's all. Professional gamblers like himself didn't bet on anything unless they had an edge.

And he had a hunch that Téa Caruso was his.

Three

"The Man That Got Away"
Judy Garland
A Star is Born (1958)

Following the brush with her grandfather, Téa escaped from the restaurant foyer to a corner booth. She grabbed up one of the waiting glasses of ice water and swallowed the liquid down, intent on drowning the sudden disquiet churning inside of her. The back of her neck prickled, and her gaze jumped across the room, catching the Caputo-Caruso woman casting her a nervous look over her lemon-sherbet shoulder.

Maybe she *should* have changed her last name, Téa thought. She'd considered it dozens of times. But years ago she'd vowed not to allow any more deceit into her life.

It was a promise made in response to her father's abrupt disappearance and her sudden understanding of the trouble he'd brought them. Both explained her need to always know exactly where she stood. Both were why she never wanted a man to surprise, shame, shock, or betray her ever again.

So she hadn't run away from her last name and she hadn't

run away from Palm Springs either. Instead, she'd cut her ties to her grandfather. And those ties were still cut, she assured herself, forcing down another swallow of water. *Still cut.*

Her mother and sisters were all the family she wanted. All the family she needed. The only people she truly trusted.

So where were they now?

She held the cold, sweating glass to her cheek, then checked her watch again, telling herself that three minutes tardy didn't really mean twenty-three minutes late.

It only felt that way. It only felt that way to *her.*

At least that's what her mother and sisters claimed. They teased her, claiming that along with a priggish appearance she was punctual to the point of compulsion.

What was it, exactly, that made a woman's closest female relatives feel entitled to identify her most serious character flaws? Not that they were wrong about Téa's—the four of them knew each other just that well.

The product, she supposed, of having their hearts broken by the same man.

The thought sent uneasiness churning inside her again until her two sisters finally walked through the restaurant doors. Younger by less than a year, Téa's half-sister, Eve, was dressed in a slinky, pearl-colored wrap dress. As usual, heads turned. With her golden-blonde hair and pouty mouth, she was the reincarnation of some sophisticated young starlet who'd spent her cocktail hours poolside in the Palm Springs of the 1950s. Beside her, in pipestem black pants, youngest sister, Joey, was oblivious to the attention. She pulled an impatient hand through the pieced-out chunks of her short hairstyle, further disordering its trendy disorder.

Téa blinked, and the years dropped away. *Once upon a time there were three little princesses . . .*

She saw them in her mind's eye. Towheaded Eve, wearing a stiff pink tutu, spinning dizzying, show-offy circles while chattering Joey monkeyed up the back of their father's chair.

Plump Téa sat on his lap as it if were her throne, serene in her position as the oldest princess, the smart one.

She blinked again and the image vanished, leaving behind the grown women her sisters had become.

Her sisters.

Of course!

Her sisters were the solution. She could count on them to make sure their grandfather understood her position hadn't changed, eighty birthday candles or no. Her sisters would help her maintain the safe distance she'd kept for all these years.

She waved to catch their attention. Their gazes found her, and all at once identical expressions dawned across their very different faces. Téa froze, cemented to the chair just as her shoes used to stick to the floor of the bathroom they'd shared as teenagers. But it wasn't a heavy layer of hair overspray that was gluing her down now.

Oh, hell! she thought, parochial-school guilt tacking on an automatic *pardon my French.*

But *oh, hell!* Eve and Joey were beaming smiles her way. Nice, fake, "Hello, sucker-sister" smiles.

Téa smiled back; there was no other choice. Anything less and they'd sense weakness—or even worse, willingness. And she was definitely not willing, because whatever it was they wanted, it had to be something terrible, very terrible, if it required those NutraSweet grins.

The party sprang to mind. They wouldn't . . . no. *No.* It couldn't be that.

But it had to be *something.* Thinking quickly, Téa pushed menus into their hands the instant they sat down. "Hello, hello! How are you?"

Without another weapon available, she whipped open her own menu, using it and a torrent of talk as a shield until she could get a bead on what they were after. "Do you know what you want? I'm starving. What a morning! My early meeting ran late. A rug I ordered weeks ago is missing and needs to be tracked down. I have two appointments this afternoon and then a slew of paperwork to get through back at the office. Oh yes, and Mrs. Duncan . . . "

She risked a glance over the top of the menu to gauge how her spur-of-the-moment plan of distraction was working. Her sisters were staring at her, Eve's blue eyes wide and Joey's narrowed into slices of bittersweet chocolate. If the two weren't derailed from whatever they wanted as she'd hoped, they were at least disconcerted by the way she was rattling on about her day. No surprise there, because as the ever-responsible big sister she usually encouraged *them* to talk about *their* days—probing for problems and doling out advice, all the while trying to inconspicuously nudge their water goblets away from their elbows or the table edge.

A balding waiter glided up.

"Are you ready to place your order?" he asked Eve.

Téa's sister started, then turned to him, sliding right into her regular routine: wiggling her butt, wetting her lips, waiting the second it took for the poor guy's tongue to hang out. During the past sixteen years, each sister had developed her own way of handling the Caruso connection. Like her mother, Téa pretended it didn't exist. Her sister Joey clung so closely to the Caruso's legitimate side—the gourmet food company, La Vita Buona—that she was blind to the other.

Eve diverted attention from who she was by how she looked.

Long accustomed to the process, Téa let her gaze drop from Eve's face to the glass of water in her hand and the bright crimson lipstick print along its rim. The last time they'd been out together, Eve's latest escort—a tennis star named Alex, or was it a rock star named André?—anyway, the guy had caught Eve's eye then shared her drink, turning it to sip from her raspberry-vodka martini right over the mark of her scarlet-tinged kiss. Téa had never witnessed anything so subtle yet so steamy in her life.

But felt not the slightest pang that even though she wore EverPerfect, the lipstick that claimed to be "flawless, 24/7," no date of hers had ever so much as picked up her smearless glass. Apparently the men who asked her out harbored a lingering, elementary-school fear that even grown-up girls had cooties, or perhaps her conservative attire made it clear she wasn't in the market for hot-blooded passion. Anything that uncontrollable was dangerous to a woman harboring her kind of secrets.

"And for you?" the waiter asked Téa. She requested her usual, the raw salad with the balsamic-lemon vinaigrette on the side. Then he took Joey's order.

As the man moved off, Téa's sisters glanced at each other, took a collective breath, then shared another glance. Téa opened her mouth to put them off again, but Eve beat her to it.

"Your hair looks wonderful," she gushed in synthetically warm tones. "A new style?"

Now it was Téa's turn to stare. "I've worn my hair like this for months. Mom calls it my Malibu Barbie look, remember?" And without her daughter-discount at the spa, she couldn't afford the Japanese straightening process that flattened out her waves, not to mention the delicate bronze highlights that had been woven into her half-yard of dark hair.

Joey jumped in, gesturing. "New dress, then. Nice."

The same tailored sheath her youngest sister had disparaged as "a cross between a nurse's uniform and a nun's habit" the last time she wore it in her company.

The compliments only underlined Téa's growing concern and she sighed. Clearly there was no point in putting this off.

"All right, what's this all about?" she asked. "Your phone message said you wanted a 'sit-down.' " A sit-down was their code for a not-to-be-missed meeting. She tensed as her sisters exchanged another speaking look. "And you said—"

"Family business," Eve interjected. "It's family business."

Téa slumped back against her chair. Well. Foreboding substantiated. Sham smiles explained. *Family business* was a code phrase too. For their paternal family. She took a breath then folded her arms over her chest. "You know I don't get involved in family business."

Joey rolled her eyes again. "You haven't spoken to Nonno or any of the rest in years. But the time's come for you to stop blaming him for . . . for whatever happened to Dad."

"It's *not*—" Téa swallowed her comeback. The reason she distanced herself wasn't something she could explain to her sisters without talking about other things she'd always protected them from. "Look, if this is about the invitation, it already arrived. I'm sure it was sent in error, but in any case I'm counting on you to make my excuses for me."

"Well, this *is* about that invitation," Eve said, then hesitated, sliding another glance Joey's way. "But you should also know that Grandpa is preparing to step down—retiring from all the family businesses. He's announcing it shortly after his birthday party."

"Preparing to step down?" Téa's heart skipped. Their father's disappearance sixteen years before had set off a small war on the urban streets of California—it was described in graphic detail at www.mafiatales.com. It had taken their grandfather's iron fist to rein in the criminal chaos that had erupted then and he'd remained in complete control since.

Then Joey released her own shocking dart. "And Nonno has just one birthday wish—he wants *you* at the party. He said to tell you he won't take no for an answer."

Now Téa's heart seized. To get it beating again she had to cough, the sound so harsh it caused the waiter, arriving with their meals, to tear his gaze off Eve a moment. But by the time the man had set down their plates and moved away again, Téa managed to form actual words.

"Why?" She tried not to let panic color her voice, but what

could be their grandfather's motive for trying to reel her back after all these years? "Even if he really is retiring—which I find hard to believe—why does he need me at his birthday bash when he has you two? You're the party girl, Eve. And Joey, you work for him."

Eve shrugged one slender shoulder. "Because you're the oldest grandchild."

The oldest grandchild. The oldest child of his only child, the latter presumed dead, the former who pretended the family was dead to her. If Cosimo was truly planning to pass on the family leadership to someone else, was this his way of demonstrating the prodigal granddaughter was still under his protection?

But he had no reason to believe she needed protecting. He didn't know her secret. No one did.

"You know I won't come," she said aloud.

Joey scowled. "Téa—"

"I won't." She picked up her fork and toyed with her salad, assuming a calm she didn't feel. "For one thing, there'll be too many of them. A party like that means people from the families all over California. The second cousins will fly in from New Jersey. The others from New York. Not to mention that sleazy Miami group."

Just the idea of seeing the large web of mobsters, of looking into faces that might suspect what she'd kept hidden all these years, made the skin along her spine shiver and sweat at the same time.

"The guest list's at three hundred," Joey admitted. "So far."

Shaking her head, Téa stared down at the mix of greens on her plate. Great, just great. Even if she kept well clear of it, an event as big as that, for someone as powerful as their grandfather, would be news. The story would make the California society pieces like Eve wrote as well as the Mob-watch columns in the Eastern papers. Remaking the Caruso name, let alone living it down, would only prove that much more difficult.

Her head jerked up and she held her sisters' gazes. "I don't care that he's retiring. You two will make him understand I'm not coming. He won't miss me. I haven't done more than glimpse him from afar in years, except for today, when—"

The sudden guilt on their faces explained that odd little "coincidence."

"I can't believe this," Tea said, slowly. "You told him where we were meeting." Meaning his appearance at the restaurant had been pure emotional blackmail—which shouldn't surprise her, given the other type he was so expert at.

Still, her right hand strangled her fork, while the other, in her lap, curled into a defensive fist. This wasn't right. *This wasn't fair!* She'd made a bargain—she was never quite sure if it was with God or with her guilty conscience—that went like this: She would stay away from trouble, and God—or her guilty conscience—would let her get away with her crime.

"Come on, Téa," Eve urged. "We could be a family again. That's all we want. That's all Grandpa wants. Remember that after Daddy . . . left, he was like a father to us. Do it for that. Do it for him because he loves you and wants you near again."

Or he wanted what she'd kept hidden all these years.

Joey scooted her chair closer. "Hey, do it for Eve and me." She sent Téa a grin that made her look ten years old instead of twenty-six. "We swore a blood oath to Nonno that we'd get you to agree."

Téa stared at their two entreating faces. Oh, but they were good, her sisters. *We swore a blood oath.* Joey counted on changing Téa's mind by counting on her big-sister sense of loyalty.

Do it for him because he loves you and wants you near again. Eve would know that in her secret heart of hearts Téa longed for the impossible—to be able to trust some man enough to get close to him.

But it wasn't need or duty that was building inside her now. It was a growing mix of anger and dismay that no longer fit into any of the compartments she'd built to contain the past. She tried tamping it down, but still it oozed around the edges to fill her again.

Forgetting the goody-goody image she worked so hard to maintain, she slammed down her fork and leaned forward to grip the table edge with both hands, temper heating her skin. "Listen to me—"

The ring of her cell phone interrupted. Glaring at her purse, she dared it to chirp at her again. It did. Frustration shooting higher, she pushed through the disorganized mess inside her purse, determined to get rid of the caller and get back to compelling her sisters to convince their grandfather that she couldn't be manipulated. That she was through with the past and she was through with that part of the family. For good.

She jerked the phone to her ear. "Yes?" she snapped out, sending Eve and Joey a narrow-eyed look, letting them know she was going to get off and get back to the matter at hand, no matter what, no matter—

"Ah." A raspy male tone vibrated against her ear. "We speak at last."

—who. Oh God. Who it had to be, with that low purr of a voice, was unmistakable.

"Johnny Magee?" she asked, hoping, hoping she was wrong.

"Yes. Have I called at a bad time? Your assistant put me through."

She flushed hotter. "No, no. It's not a bad time at all." Of course it was a bad time. She needed Eve and Joey on her side, but confessing she'd been about to berate her sisters over salads wasn't the image she wanted to project to her most important prospective client. She forced in a calming breath. "I was, uh, preoccupied with some furniture catalogs that came in today."

Across the table, Joey snorted.

Tea sent her a dirty look and hoped he'd mistaken the sound for the burp of a water cooler. "Can I help you with something, Mr. Magee? Answer a question about my bid?"

"Johnny," he said. "Call me Johnny."

The vibrations of his deep voice quivered like a caress across her skin. Whoa. Her assistant was right, Téa thought, the man should narrate erotic bedtime stories. She could imagine it now, something sizzling yet romantic in that get-naked-for-me voice.

Firelight flickered over the gypsy girl's bare skin, warming her shoulders, her collarbone, the full mounds of flesh below that ached for his touch. Ached for—

"Johnny." She said the name aloud and only then remembered that's who she was talking to. Her face burned again. "Yes. Right. Johnny. What can I do for you?"

"Meet me."

"Meet you?" Her business instincts perking, she sat straighter in her chair. "Certainly I'll meet you."

She'd have to wear exactly the right outfit—her IBM-blue suit, she decided. Two days before their appointment, she'd book a fruit-acid facial, then have her nails done the next. Going to her purse, she dug through it again for her PDA. "How about the end of the week, or—"

"Meet me today. Later this afternoon."

"This *afternoon*?" In the wrinkly linen dress? And she was pretty sure there was a chip in the polish on her right big toe. Yes, she was wearing closed-toe shoes, but still—

"I know it's short notice, but I've already arranged for a private flight from Las Vegas to Palm Springs and I want to make my decision about a designer as soon as possible."

Did that mean he wanted to make his decision *today*? Today, when she was wearing her worst lingerie, the scratchy bra and the panties that—good God, what did her under-clothing matter? She had bigger worries.

Today, *today*, Johnny Magee wanted to meet with her. To-day when everything had gone wrong. Today when it was im-perative she make certain Eve and Joey understood she wouldn't involve herself with the Carusos or their ilk ever again.

"Of course, if it's impossible . . . " he started.

"No!" Nothing was impossible when it came to winning this job—it was the only thing more important than winning over her sisters. "What time did you have in mind?"

As they finalized the details, Téa found her anxiety easing and her hope rising. Maybe it was due to Johnny Magee's be-guiling, bedtime voice. Maybe it was because her bargain seemed to be working out after all. Sure, the day had had its unpleasant moments, and she'd have to leave things unfin-ished with her sisters, but if she bagged this design job, then what had started out wrong might end up very, very right.

"Now," he finally said. "What can I bring you by way of apology?"

Leaning against the back of her chair, she discovered she was smiling. "Apology?"

"For the trouble I'm certain to cause you."

"You won't cause me any trouble," she scoffed.

"You might be surprised," he warned.

But she didn't take him seriously. Not when the worst trou-ble a design job had ever thrown her way was finding a foun-tain in the shape of a mammoth-sized sea urchin. She knew real trouble. She'd seen it, smelled it, been a part of it. "I'll take my chances."

"Then you sound like my kind of woman. Still, is there something special you'd like from Las Vegas as thanks for the last-minute meeting?"

"I wouldn't know what to ask for," she answered. "I've never been to Las Vegas."

"Never?" He sounded shocked.

"Never. My father cautioned me against gambling and gamblers a long time ago."

There was a little pause. Then he laughed. It was low and intimate and the warm sound of it only added to Téa's certainty. Things were finally turning around for her. Not just for today, not just for her career. But for her *life*.

Four

"Ain't That a Kick in the Head"
Dean Martin
Return to Me (1956–61)

Whistling the cheery opening of a TVLand Andy Griffith episode, Téa reached Johnny Magee's newly purchased property on El Deseo Drive. Its street frontage, two city blocks long, was screened by a twelve-foot-high wall of concrete block, the fencing material of choice in a climate that brutalized wood. He needed to contract with a landscaper as well, she noted. The intricate pattern created by the grainy, modular pieces was designed not only for beauty but for a practical flow of air, a purpose thwarted by the volunteer Mexican palms growing in profusion behind the wall. Their spiny fans thrust through the openings in the block as if to keep prying eyes out and dirty secrets in.

Secrets.

Her pursed lips sounded a sour note as the word crawled down her back. She couldn't help but think of her grandfather again. Or rather, she thought of that engraved invitation he'd sent. When she'd swung by the office to pick up the Magee portfolio, it had seemed to hiss at her from its place in her inbox.

To drown out the memory, she took up whistling again, louder, and pressed her foot to the gas. Nothing was going to ruin this meeting, she promised herself. Checking her watch, she was pleased to see she was still early, as planned. That would give her a few minutes alone to polish the collected, capable first impression she intended to make on Johnny Magee.

She turned into the driveway, following it past a tangle of overgrown vegetation and around a curve. Her foot shifted to the brake, slowing the Volvo as the drive dead-ended in front of a six-car garage. Other vehicles had beat her to the circular parking area, a gleaming Jag, a nondescript sedan, and a taxi-yellow moving van, its back gate lifted and ramp folded down. It appeared half-full of furniture.

So much for a few minutes alone.

Disappointed, yet curious all the same, she parked her car alongside the moving van then stepped around to its yawning opening to take a peek inside.

From the dim interior came a feminine voice. "Téa?"

She hid her guilty start by reaching for her sunglasses and sliding them down to squint toward the sound of her name. "Yes?"

"Téa Caruso, what on *earth* are you doing here?" From out of the shadows, a woman strolled down the ramp of the truck as if it were a fashion runway, placing one strappy sandal in front of the other, heel-to-toe, heel-to-toe. "You're the last person I expected to see here."

Téa pushed her sunglasses back and forced herself not to fidget. Lois Olmstead, she of the frosted-blonde hair, delicate features, and wrinkle-free wardrobe of a model for St. John resort wear, never ceased to make Téa feel rumpled and blowsy.

It wasn't the other woman's fault, but one look from her and it was seventh grade all over again, the year Téa had gone from smug and chubby Mafia princess to a missing felon's fat daughter. In all the years since, no low-carb diet, no hair-straightening process, no figure-diminishing foundation garment, or moustache-removal technique had made over the misery of that year when her father's vanishing act coincided with the acute self-consciousness and peer-awareness of preteenhood.

She sucked her navel toward her spine. "Hello, Lois. I didn't expect to see you here either."

And then it hit her, the reason the other woman was at the house. She was Téa's competition for the design job. *No.* The moving van must mean Lois was already the winner.

Warmth crawling up her neck, Téa began backwalking toward her car. Seventh grade had also taught her the importance of hiding her feelings—including humiliation. "I was just, uh . . . " Her thighs made contact with the heated metal of the Volvo's rear bumper.

"You were just what?" Lois asked, coming closer. The skin of her forehead was an alabaster that didn't wrinkle when she frowned.

"I must have misunderstood." Téa pretended a casual shrug, replaying the earlier phone conversation in her head. "I thought I had a meeting."

"With *Johnny Magee?*" Lois's eyes widened in disbelief.

Téa shrugged again, trying to slough off the blow. It had always been a long shot, she knew that. As a matter of fact, from the first she'd wondered if he'd contacted her by mistake. If she hadn't done her senior project on modern design, she wouldn't have dared preparing the bid. "But I see the job is yours."

"The *design job?*"

Téa clutched her car keys tighter and trudged toward the driver's side. "Good to see you, Lois."

"I'm not here for the design job," Lois said. She glanced over her shoulder as two beefy young men came toward the van carrying a portrait-sized mirror between them. "That's it, then. Twenty mirrors. We're done."

She looked back at Téa. "I did the staging."

The *home*-staging, Téa deduced. It was a growing trend—paying to have homes professionally de-cluttered or empty homes filled with furniture while they were on the market. "I didn't know you were into that now."

"The money's good. We take out tacky and bring in good taste, not to mention mirrors and more mirrors. The trick is to make prospective buyers see themselves in every room."

And apparently Johnny Magee had seen something that made him want to purchase this place. Téa's mood-meter took a return swing toward optimism. If the other woman wasn't here for the design job, then she hadn't missed out on winning it herself, at least not yet. She stepped back toward the rear of the Volvo. "I'm sure you're a big success, Lois."

"As a matter of fact, I just prepared a house for selling that you designed in the Movie Colony," the other woman replied. "Now *there* was a challenge."

Téa's fingers reached down to press against the wrinkles in her dress. "Oh?"

"The Hartman house."

"Oh." Her fingers stilled. What more could she say? The Hartmans, who had purchased a home in the part of Palm Springs first settled by movie stars in the 1930s, loved hearts. Demanded hearts. So there were hearts on the handpainted ceilings, hearts as part of the gold- and bronze-leaf-painted moldings, hearts in the pattern of the fabric on the tufted walls. There was even a kitschy heart motif in the side-by-side fur and luggage storage rooms.

The thought of that project, the thought of more of those types of projects in her future, made her sag against the back bumper.

"But now you think you're going to go from clients like the Hartmans to a man like Johnny Magee. That's quite a leap, isn't it?"

Knowing Lois's reaction would be shared by the desert's entire design community didn't soften the sting or silence any of Téa's own doubts.

So she turned to open the rear door of the Volvo, preparing to avoid further conversation by busying herself with the materials she'd brought along. After all, she consoled herself, Lois really didn't know any more than she did about "a man like Johnny Magee."

. . . or did she?

Téa spun back. "Were you around for the showing of the house?" she asked, nodding toward the rooftop that she could see in the distance.

"No."

But the glint in Lois's eyes hinted that she knew something more than the single word indicated and Téa wanted to know that something more, desperately. Anything she gleaned about Johnny Magee might help her cinch the job. Glancing at the other cars and then at her watch, she decided there wasn't time for subtlety.

"A massage at my mother's spa for what you know, Lois," she said quickly, before her pride got in the way of practicality. "On me."

Lois's eyes sparkled brighter. "With Erik."

"With Erik?" Erik was the most popular massage therapist at the spa and wedging in an appointment with him would cost her big in the daughter-duty department. She sighed. "Fine, with Erik. Now, what do you know about Johnny, Lois? Have you met him?"

"I don't *know* him," Lois said. "But on a visit to Las Vegas a couple of years back, a mutual acquaintance introduced us."

Téa frowned. "That's it?"

"That's all it took for me to recognize a bad boy."

A bad boy? Less than impressed, Téa reached inside her car for her purse, portfolio, and briefcase. "That little insight isn't worth a pedicure, let alone a massage with the legendary Erik, Lois." She elbowed shut the door and brushed past the other woman. She'd find the man and make her own estimation.

"I'm trying to tell you he's dangerous, Téa."

That made her hesitate. Hadn't he warned her about the trouble he'd cause? But she tossed the idea away and tossed her hair over her shoulders as she set off toward a path that led through more overgrown vegetation in the direction of the house. "I'm pretty sure I can handle him."

With her family history, who could doubt it?

But Lois wouldn't allow her the last word. "Don't misunderstand me or underestimate him, Téa," she called back. "Just remember that a real bad boy isn't any kind of boy at all."

The grounds of the Magee property could have benefited from a gardener's staging services or at the very least some simple pruning, Téa thought, making her way through unruly hibiscus plants and overgrown oleanders. She knew from the simple layout she'd been faxed that a three-hole golf course separated the main residence from the guest bungalows on the east side, and that on the south, between the stand-alone garage and the house, was a man-made lagoon.

So when she stepped into a clearing, she wasn't surprised to see the large body of water ahead of her.

It was the figure sitting on the wall of half-tumbled, large river rocks surrounding it that caught her off guard.

His long, thin legs bent like a grasshopper's, he was hunched over a computer on his lap while another was teeter-tottering on the ledge beside him. He wore crinkled khakis, black canvas high-tops, and a ratty bowling shirt not even a mother could kindly call "vintage."

No, Lois. Johnny Magee wasn't a bad boy.

He was a bad dresser.

And the other woman had merely been yanking Téa's chain. Unless . . . unless this wasn't him. Johnny hadn't sounded like this man looked.

Yet who else would it be?

And hadn't she known from the beginning he'd be a disappointment?

That didn't change what had to happen next, however. She sucked in a determined breath, then shook back her hair, pressed her lips together to even their color, and finally gave a little shimmy of her hips to straighten out the fall of her skirt. With her appearance the best it could be, she pasted on her most professional smile and continued her approach.

"Hello," she said, as she neared him. "I'm Téa Caruso."

"Yes, I've been waiting for you," he said, without looking up.

It was Johnny Magee, all right.

His fingers continued to race over the keyboard of his laptop. "Could you sit down a minute?" Apparently aware of the precarious balance of the notebook computer beside him, he lifted it up in one hand.

"Oh, uh, of course," she replied, eyeing the vacant spot he'd created and the murky depths of the lagoon beyond it. An odd frisson of distaste edged down her back, but she strode forward anyway. Then she set down her portfolio and briefcase and bent her knees to poise just the minimum of her weight and her behind onto the uneven surface of the rock wall.

Without a word or warning, the man plopped the computer he was holding onto her lap. To give it an adequate resting place, she was forced to settle more fully on the ledge. As her weight shifted, she slid backward along the slick surface and had to dig her heels into the soft ground to keep her seat. *Ewww.* She felt dampness penetrating the fabric of her dress. A slimy coating of moss covered the rock wall, she realized, and now the backside of her dress as well.

She grimaced, but her companion didn't seem to notice her discomfort. As a matter of fact, he didn't seem to notice anything beyond the contents of the two computers. He shifted the one on her lap to more fully face him and with a hand on each keyboard, proceeded to play them like a virtuoso.

"I hope you had a good flight," she ventured after a few moments of uninterrupted tapping.

He nodded, but whether it was at her or the numbers rolling by on the dual screens, she didn't know.

"I have several mock-ups of my designs I'd like to present to you," she tried again. "I'm looking forward to it. I have a great affinity for mid-century modern."

His fingers stilled and his head came up, his eyes magnified by heavy-framed glasses. The thick lenses along with his unkempt hair made it difficult to assess his age, but he was definitely younger than she expected.

"What is that, anyway?" he asked.

"Affinity?"

"Mid-century modern."

She blinked. Johnny Magee had seemed settled on the style from the beginning, so she could only assume this was some sort of test. Swallowing, she pressed her knees together and tried for a concise answer. "It refers to post–World War II domestic architecture. At that time, Palm Springs was becoming a luxury resort for the rich, and architects used experimental materials and technologies to create homes for people who wanted something more daring than a cozy cottage with a picket fence."

His gaze shifted back to the screens and his fingers returned to clicking the keyboards. "Psychedelic posters and bean bag chairs?"

"Um, no, not really. That was a bit later. The heyday of mid-century modern was in the 1940s and 50s, when this property was originally developed. The style is characterized by light, flowing interiors and a strong indoor-outdoor relationship."

He shrugged. "Too bad. I like bean bag chairs and psyche-delic posters."

"Well, um, I . . . " Téa's voice petered out as the implica-tions of his comment sank in. Bean bag chairs and psyche-delic posters were Budweiser and Kool-Aid to the martinis and highballs that symbolized sophisticated mid-century modern design. But nobody knew better than Téa that if the client wanted beer and soft drinks, then that's what she would give him.

Her shoulders sagged. All the concern over her appear-ance and the attempts to impress him had come to nothing more than this. She exhaled a small sigh, but that was the only sign of discouragement she allowed herself before set-ting about retooling her plans on the fly.

Shag carpet, she thought. The colors of lime and orange. Pet rocks. Okay, so it wasn't going to revamp her reputation as a designer, but it was probably no worse than the animal-print-everything Saharan sitting room she'd done for Mr. and Mrs. Finkelstein last spring.

She closed her eyes, hoping to envision a new look for the Magee residence. From what she knew of the house, it was made for the simple, clean lines of mid-century modern. But now, instead of Eames sofas and sunburst clocks, she'd have . . .

"Maybe a beanbag sofa in an Andy Warhol–inspired fab-ric," she mentioned aloud, trying to picture red-and-white can after red-and-white can of Campbell's soup without cringing. It made her squirm instead, setting her slime-stained dress to sliding against the slime-covered rock again.

"What's that?" a voice prompted.

"Bean bag furniture. Maybe a Twister-inspired area rug. What do you think of a lava lamp or two?"

"Personally? I'm not inspired by any of them, except, per-haps, the interesting possibilities of that Twister area rug."

The voice to her left was deeper now, sexier, more like it had sounded on the phone. Wait—the voice to her *left*? The man she sat beside was on her right. Her eyes popped open.

And there he was, another man, a different man, standing to her slight left, one polished loafer propped on the rock beside her. A man approaching his mid-thirties. With broad shoulders, lean hips, and dark blond hair, he was an adult version of the public high school boys who had forever fascinated her as a parochial prep school teenager.

Speechless, she let her gaze wander over him. His navy blue slacks had a knife-edge pleat and his sports jacket was a tiny blue-and-white check. Beneath it he wore an open-collared shirt in goldenrod that matched his impeccably cut hair. His eyes were sea-blue.

A natural athlete, he would have headed the varsity squad, Téa thought. She could tell, because he had the same look of every boy that Eve had dated, every boy that Joey had palled around with, every boy that Téa had lusted for from the safe distance of a party-size bag of potato chips.

His eyes narrowed when he looked amused and now they cut from her face to the man seated beside her. "Were you planning on bringing me my designer anytime soon, Cal?"

Cal. She'd been wrong. The glasses guy was Cal. And this . . . this . . . All-American god of a man was—had to be—Johnny Magee.

His designer, he'd said. *His.* The word danced down her spine, and if she didn't know full well that scary men came dark-haired, dark-eyed, and Italian, then she *would* consider him dangerous.

His focus switched back as his hand extended toward her. "Téa Caruso?" He smiled.

Okay. Here she is, and more beautiful than I bargained for.

The voice in her head and the outstretched hand had her rising from her seat without thinking, her palm shooting out as quickly as the goose bumps that his white smile sent speeding along her skin. The computer on her lap slipped, and Cal grabbed for it, Johnny grabbed for it, and probably she would have grabbed for it too, except that she recalled the stain on her dress and instead made a hasty drop back to the rocks.

But she'd forgotten the slimy moss. Her thighs slid, her feet found no purchase on the slick grass, and in her belated efforts to save the computer, she tumbled into the murky pond behind her with an ugly, undignified, bad-first-impression big splash.

The laptop suffered mere drops.

Her ego suffered much worse.

Not that she hadn't experienced a similar sort of humiliation—self-sabotage?—before. At fifteen, she'd been delegated family photographer when basketball star Rick Richardson had invited her younger sister Eve to the big public high school's senior prom. Trying to appear invisible behind the tiny Kodak camera, Téa had backed farther away from the posing couple and then farther, and then backed right into the sofa . . . and over it.

Rick Richardson hadn't known what to do.

Johnny Magee did. Though when her handsome varsity captain of a client hauled her out of the shallow depths—she, whose only captain had heretofore been Captain Crunch—Téa found herself as tongue-tied and knock-kneed as only an overweight teen in a twenty-eight-year-old, dripping-wet body could be.

"I . . . well . . . uh . . . perhaps we should do this another . . . " Hyperaware of her sodden skirt and her soggy hair, she ran out of words. Then, because she still had all the savoir faire of fifteen, she mumbled an apology, grabbed her purse, and fled.

Five

"What'll I Do"
Julie London
Lonely Girl (1956)

Johnny followed the designer home. He didn't have much choice, not after promising himself that today he'd make progress on his plan. Once he'd pulled her from the water, she'd hightailed it for her car, leaving behind her briefcase and a portfolio. He wanted to return them to her.

He couldn't let her get away.

It was because of that hunch he'd had about her from the beginning, he told himself, as he watched her steer onto a narrow lane and then park in the driveway of a small patio home. She was a key to the puzzle of his father's death, he knew it. He pulled alongside the curb across the street as she climbed out of her car, her shoes in hand.

Not that her wet, barefoot contessa look wasn't . . . compelling all on its own. He'd only made a brief observation of Téa Caruso dry, but he figured she couldn't be more attractive than she was right now, her damp dark hair rippling in wild waves down her back, her clothes plastered against her hourglass body to flaunt a small waist that flared into an eat-your-heart-out-J.Lo ass.

He let her get inside, counted to lucky number seven, then strolled to her front door. She answered on the first knock.

And couldn't hide her surprise. She pushed at her unruly hair with her hands, then swiped her forefingers beneath the bottom lashes of her sloe eyes. "I—well—I . . . What are you doing here?"

Lifting his excuse, her belongings, he smiled. "I thought you might want these."

"Oh." Their fingers brushed during the transfer and a rush of color washed up her neck. "Thank you."

She set the items down then looked at him, making it obvious she expected—hoped—he'd leave. Instead, he lingered in the doorway, still smiling. An awkward silence descended. As heartless as it was of him, he let it grow.

Her naked toes curled against the tiled entry. "I suppose I should have stayed long enough to reschedule," she finally offered.

He nodded. "We need to do that."

Silence drew out again, and again he did nothing to prevent it. The Texas Hold 'Em table had made him expert at the Buddha-like wait, but he suspected she'd had no such special training.

He was right. Ten seconds later she capitulated to his unspoken pressure. Her spine lost a little of its starch and she shuffled back, her toes still curled inward. "Would you like to come in?"

More than he wanted her to know. So he hid his satisfaction behind his poker face and crossed over the threshold. Even if she wasn't aware of it, she was an opponent of sorts, and he made it his business to study the particular "tells" of the people he played against. Invariably, through dress, body language, environment, or all three, other players gave the essence of themselves away.

Knowing more about Téa might give him an advantage he could possibly use at some time later in the game.

Yet in the five steps it took him to reach the living room, he saw that Téa Caruso's surroundings surrendered very little that looked useful. The neutrality of the pale gray walls and darker gray upholstered furniture was only broken by a collection of hand-painted Italian pottery lined like brightly uniformed *soldati* along the mantelpiece. The overall lack of color and embellishment surprised him, given the contessa's own exotic, dark-haired and dreamy-eyed looks. It was a cool, controlled sort of room, and the mystery of the contradiction between it and the woman drew his gaze back her way.

She shuffled. "Please sit down," she said, plucking at the skirt of her damp dress, as if trying to ease its plastic-wrap fit. "Would you like something to drink?"

"I don't want to put you to any trouble." Really, he didn't. However, after months of near-sleepless nights his needs were stronger than his scruples.

"It's no trouble. Iced tea? Coffee?"

But that polite yet halfhearted try at hospitality dealt him a painful, guilty pinch anyway. Damn, he thought with an inward grimace. Was this what he had come to? It was never his way to force his company on unwilling women.

"No, thanks. Nothing." He shoved one hand in his pocket, feeling for his keys. There was no pressing reason for him to push her so fast, so soon. It probably wasn't even smart. "On second thought, I won't hold you up any longer."

"Oh." She blinked those dreamy dark eyes. "All right."

And if she considered him crazy for traipsing in then traipsing right back out, she didn't comment upon it further as she followed him back to her tiny foyer. He paused in the open front doorway, his gaze on his car, parked at the curb of the home across the street. "We'll talk—"

Sunlight glinted against the brass numbers nailed on the side of that house. The address. 10909.

In a blink it altered, blazing across his brain like the numbers on a digital watch. 1:09:09.

The world altered too.

Darkness.

Night.

The sharp snap of gunfire.

Pop.

Pop. Pop.

Pop. Pop. Pop.

The past grabbed for him with its powerful claws.

Resisting with everything he had, Johnny gulped a breath, then spun around. He gripped the doorjamb to anchor himself in present reality before the tires could squeal in his head, before his heart could start jackhammering at his chest wall, before his senses were flooded by the stain and the smell of fresh blood.

The woman standing before him stared, and he stared back, cataloging every detail of her face to keep from falling into the flashback. He took in the smooth skin of her wide forehead, the exotic tilt of her eyes, the lock of hair that wiggled across one olive-toned cheek to catch in the corner of her full mouth. She hooked it away with her pinky and he counted out its three-second float to the join the rest of the wavy, vital mass.

God, she was gorgeous.

"Are you okay?" she asked.

No. His hands were icy and his breathing shallow and he realized that somewhere between his father's former house and here, ghosts had clambered aboard his back. Jesus. *Jesus.* Upon his arrival today at the El Deseo property, though he'd avoided entering the house itself, he'd made a quick tour of the grounds. He'd felt nothing there.

Now, though, now it was as if damp, dead breath was crawling down his neck.

He twitched his shoulders and focused on the contessa again. It wasn't a hardship. She looked so warm and so filled with energy in her wrinkled dress and with her mussed, wild hair that he had to dig his fingers into the jamb instead of digging them into the lush curves of her figure to remind himself he was still of this world.

He was almost grateful when his cock stirred. The response was inconvenient, but at least he knew that one part of him was alive, well, and apparently quite willing to function.

"Are you okay?" she asked again.

"Go out for a drink with me," he heard himself say.

She gave him a it's-a-full-moon-and-you-just-grew-fangs look. "What?"

"Go out for a drink with me." Okay, so he was as surprised as she was by his abrupt request, but right now he didn't want to be alone and he did want to be with her.

So he cleared his throat, forced his arms to drop to his sides, and tried to appear as slick and easy as he'd felt for all the years of his adult life until this last one. "We can talk."

"But I . . ."

He could tell she was searching for an excuse, but he wouldn't let her discomfort or his own guilt deter him this time. After this little episode in her doorway, it was clear once again that he had things to do. Demons to exorcise. "But what?" he pressed.

Her hands fluttered around her hips, in a gesture as uncertain as her obvious mood. "I . . . I'd need to change."

Letting out a silent breath, he took a step inside, crowding her backward. "No problem. I'll wait."

She went along with it. Redesigning the house must be that much of a prize, he figured, because his strange behavior during the past few minutes must have made it perfectly clear that he wasn't. She disappeared down a hallway and he heard a door close, lock.

Good for you, Contessa. Keep your guard up.

Minutes ticked by, and the ghosts riding his shoulders disappeared. His own guard relaxed. Remembering why he'd forced himself into her place to begin with, he ambled around Téa's living room, looking for more clues to her and her father's family. The only photo she displayed, however, was of three females. The oldest in it had to be Téa's mother, while beside her stood a twenty-something blonde, and then beside her was another brunette with an engaging grin.

He was still studying the picture when he heard Téa come into the room behind him. "Beautiful women," he offered as he turned, expecting to see another one.

But this . . . this *lady*, well, it wasn't that she wasn't beautiful. It was that she wasn't . . . well, she *was* Téa, but she wasn't the same wet and curvy contessa who'd barefooted it home.

He stared. She wore a neck-high, knee-length navy blue suit that would put even a born-again accountant to sleep. Matching pumps with medium heels were locked about her ankles with sturdy straps. Her natural plum lip color was muted to something barely there, and the lips themselves were as tightly clasped as her fingers.

Most changed of all was her hair. The glorious tumble that had rippled with life after her dunking in the pond was now tamed into strands as straight as a Young Republican. She'd clipped them behind her head in a no-nonsense, no-fun style.

"Are you ready?" she asked.

No. But he resisted the urge to tell her that truth, because no matter what, it *was* time to go forward. Getting close to her, and through her, close to her family, was his plan, after all. By buying the house and making contact with the designer, he'd anted-in. The game was already under way.

It didn't change a thing that he had the sudden, disturbing idea that Téa Caruso might have even more secrets than he.

Six

"Quiet Village"
Martin Denny
Exotica (1957)

By some stroke of luck, Téa had a second chance to make a good first impression and this time she wasn't going to blow it. As she walked with Johnny through the dusk to her car—it seemed more businesslike for her to chauffeur the potential client than the other way around—she glanced over at him. He was awfully quiet.

"Would you prefer to go back to your house for our meeting?" she asked.

His steps faltered, his sudden stillness reminding her of that odd moment in her doorway a few minutes before. Then he shook his head. "I'd rather save that for daylight."

When chances were slimmer that she'd end up in an open body of water and make a further fool of herself, Téa finished for him, stifling a sigh. The man must have serious doubts about her now. He had to be wondering just what kind of woman he'd approached for the design job.

But by the time they finished their drinks he would know, she promised herself. He'd see her as a cool, consummate professional, because she'd make sure she acted like one.

Inside the confines of her car, however, doubts washed over her again. She drew in a breath, but that only drew in *him,* his heat, his scent, the maleness that was so . . . so other to her. Of course, that was only natural, right? Though she'd grown out of her adolescent puppy-love for beautiful boy jocks, in her line of work she didn't often deal with straight men. If roped into a meeting by his wife, a male client would make it brief. He wanted to be assured of only two things: one, that the designer wouldn't go over budget, and two, that she wouldn't undersize the couches and the chairs.

"Téa?"

She started, realizing they were still in her driveway. "I'm sorry," she said, with a hasty turn of the key, "I was lost in my own thoughts."

"Not second thoughts, I hope. It occurs to me I might have interrupted plans you already had for the evening."

"Oh, no." She reversed the car then put it in forward gear for the short drive to Stellar, the restaurant/bar she'd decided upon. "This is fine."

"No date with a boyfriend?"

"No." Not that she'd share it with him, but dates and boyfriends were rare in her life, again, to some degree, because of the very few eligible men she met in the design business. Of course, her clients could never resist fixing her up. But that pool of potentials was filled by sons, grandsons, and great-nephews whose prevailing characteristic was their inability to say "no" to the female relatives in their lives.

It might sound like a wonderful quality until you understood that it also meant they were the kind of men who trusted older women to make so many of their decisions for them. They tended to wear Arnold Palmer golf sweaters in

Easter egg colors and flip-on sunshades over their glasses. They drove Lincoln Continentals with back seats roomy enough for Aunt Elizabeth's or Nana Mae's entire bridge foursome. They knew the early-bird specials on every menu in town.

They were nothing like Johnny Magee.

He shifted in his seat, redoubling her awareness of him. She sucked in another breath of his scented male warmth. No, they were nothing at all like Johnny Magee.

He watched the gypsy girl with impassive, sea-colored eyes. Then his masculine hand reached toward her flesh, flesh that was trembling despite the warmth of the fire. Fingertips curled over the edge of her filmy peasant blouse and drew it down, down, down—

That hard male hand shot out to cover hers on the wheel, and jerked left. "Watch out."

She braked, just as a car pulled from a space in Stellar's congested lot and nearly into them if not for Johnny's quick reflexes. "Thanks," she croaked out, her face burning as red-hot as her fantasies. Somehow she'd dreamed all the way to Stellar and almost steered into a fender bender in the process.

She glanced over her shoulder, now even more embarrassed. "I don't know what I was thinking of . . . I meant to stop at the parking valet."

"No problem," he said. "Take the open spot right here."

His hand slipped away from hers but both the sensation of his touch and her self-consciousness lingered as they walked toward the restaurant. He held the door open for her and she brushed by him, raising a prickly set of goose bumps beneath the all-business fabric of her blue suit.

To remind herself that this *was* business, she took the lead at the reservations station, explaining to the inquiring hostess that they were just going into the lounge for a drink. It came as no surprise, though, that while she conducted this short transaction he went ahead and scored the last table in the expansive, but now standing-room-only bar. He was the type who would. With his arms stretched over the back of the cushions behind him, he appeared calm and relaxed as he watched her approach the far corner where he was waiting.

His gaze made her jittery again. As she threaded her way toward him, she couldn't help but wonder what he saw when he looked at her.

A responsible-looking woman, she hoped he was musing. Competent, qualified. Detail-oriented.

And that's what he'd continue to see, Téa told herself. Marching forward, she squared her shoulders and set her spine as straight as a debits column. He wouldn't shake her all-business demeanor again.

Still four tables away, he smiled at her. A lazy smile.

What's she wearing beneath that boring little suit? she thought she heard him say in her head.

His gaze flicked down to her legs.

And she's added to her armor with stockings now. What could she be trying so hard to hide?

Téa's stride hitched. She considered running back to her car. But then a white-shirted cocktail server strode up to the table. With her view of Johnny blocked, she shook her head, jarring loose the silly notion that she'd heard what he'd been thinking. That he'd been thinking anything the least bit personal about her.

This was business.

With that firmly in mind, she reached the chair across the table from him just as the waiter hurried off. "Pinot Grigio okay?" Johnny asked, his expression showing nothing more than friendly politeness. "The place is so crowded I was afraid he'd never make it back if I said I needed more time."

"Pinot Grigio's fine." She settled into her seat, then took a breath, paused.

His head tilted, blond hair brushing his collar. "Is something wrong?"

"No, nothing at all." Téa refused to be derailed by anything this time, so she hurried into the speech that she'd prepared. "I'd like to spend a few minutes acquainting you with my firm and my goals for your project. Then we can move on to your questions. Is that all right?"

He shrugged. "I have your firm's brochure. I don't think we need to go over that information again."

"Oh. Well." She hid her disappointment at losing the opportunity to speak aloud the impressive phrases she'd stockpiled. *"Fresh outlook on mid-century modern,"* (never professionally designed in that style). *"Exclusive attention from the design team,"* (she *was* the design team). *"The firm's calendar adjusted to work with yours,"* (there was no job on her schedule as prestigious as this one). "I guess we can just go ahead with your questions, then."

There was another pause while the waiter delivered their drinks. Johnny took a swallow of his rum and Coke, then cocked an eyebrow her way. "Where were we again?"

Her wine was crisp and cold and if she wasn't careful, it would go right to her head. "I'm ready to answer any questions you might have about the project."

He waved a hand. "I trust your judgment on that. I have few worries as long as you don't go wildly over budget and don't—"

"Undersize the couches and the chairs," she finished for him.

He laughed. "Exactly. So you read minds?"

No! "No." She took another sip from her glass. "It's a common concern."

"What I would like to talk about—" He broke off as a commotion heightened the already loud level of noise in the bar. "Is that Melissa Banyon?"

Téa glanced over her shoulder and couldn't miss the chestnut-haired sultry sex-kitten who'd won an Academy Award for best supporting actress the previous spring. She stood at the entrance of the bar in an electric blue dress and a pair of matching stiletto sandals.

"With her just-as-famous French fiancé, Raphael Fremont, in tow," she said. "They're newly engaged, and they won't be the last celebrities you spot in Palm Springs."

Johnny's eyes were all for mega-star Melissa. *Great tits, fake as forty-four dollar bills, but great to look at all the same.*

"What?" Téa said, staring at him. "What did you say?"

Johnny's gaze returned to her face and he frowned. "I didn't say anything." He raised his glass to his mouth. "Though I was about to ask about you."

"Me?" On the other side of the bar the noise rose again and she ignored it as best she could. "You said you'd looked over my firm's brochure."

"I don't want to know more about your firm, I want to know more about *you*."

There was a smile in his eyes, a friendly enough smile, but all Téa's internal alarms started ringing. Every instinct told her to keep it all-business, all-the-time between them because even at that he could still knock her silly with his all-star good looks and his let-me-take-you-down-to-silk-sheets voice. "I don't think . . . I don't want . . . "

"Hey, no need to be so nervous. I'm not with the IRS."

She tried to smile. "I haven't done anything illegal." Recently.

"I only thought we might work better together if we knew each more . . . personally." He laughed. "Now you look as if I'm asking for your social security and Swiss bank account numbers. Téa, I assure you my intentions aren't as sinister as that."

Of course not. He didn't know sinister like she did.

And then it hit her. Hard.

The birthday party. Her grandfather's impending retirement. Meeting Johnny had pushed them both from her mind. But by the end of the month they'd be big news, and stories of the Carusos' shady activities were going to be hitting the papers again, big-time. She knew Johnny Magee wasn't the type of man who would miss the connection. What she didn't know was if he was the type of man who would overlook it, no matter how strictly law-abiding she was these days.

In the spirit of honesty and full disclosure, she thought with a sigh, she supposed she was obligated to get personal after all, and explain to him she was a mob boss's daughter.

How many clients would the association cost her as the media publicized the mob angle? How many more if she allowed herself to be lured back into the bosom of the family?

"Johnny, I . . . " *I might be kissing this job good-bye.* "I—"

A flurry of sapphire silk and Shalimar swirled near, then dropped onto the cushioned bench opposite Téa and right beside—almost right onto the lap of—Johnny. "Hello, my loves," the actress Melissa Banyon trilled, in her little-girl-lost voice. "Have you been waiting for me long?"

Téa glanced over at Johnny, but he was looking in the general direction of the actress's breasts again. "I, um, don't believe we've actually met," she said.

"We'll fix that right up." She grabbed Téa's wineglass and gulped the contents down. "I'm Missy, and *you* are the most interesting in the room."

Since she was beaming all her A-list power at Johnny while she said this, Téa figured the comment didn't include her. But then the actress aimed her famous violet eyes her way. "Don't you just want to eat him up?"

Téa glanced over her shoulder to where Missy's Frenchman was smoldering from a spot at the bar across the room. "I thought he was wonderful in *The Foreign Legion.* I saw it twice."

"No, no, no." Missy Banyon gave a flamboyant wave of a hand heavy with rings. "Not *him*. He's nothing. He's an imbay-ceel."

Her French accent was atrocious.

"He's your fiancé," Téa thought she should add.

"And so, so stupid." She turned to Johnny and arched her back so her breasts poked out like super-sized cupcakes. "Don't you think?"

He yanked his gaze off those silicone works of art to take in the angry-looking man at the bar. "I think this is where I keep my mouth shut."

Missy didn't seem to mind carrying on the conversation alone. Still chattering away, she clapped her hands together to send the waiter scurrying for more drinks. No one, besides Raphael, of course, seemed the least bit perturbed or surprised that the actress had joined their table.

It was a Palm Springs tradition, this fond indulgence of the Hollywood set that cruised so freely about town. Their presence was, after all, what had put the place on the map, and those who made their living off the rich and famous—which was all of them to some degree or another—regarded celebrities with the same affection as highly paid nannies for charming, yet overpampered children.

Looking at the impossibly lovely Missy Banyon, Téa tried hard to feel accordingly. But it was one thing to let a Hollywood couple be given the best table in the room and quite another to confront one of *People* magazine's Most Beautiful People across your own. Dropping her gaze to her empty glass, Téa tugged on her sleeves, dusted off nonexistent lint, and hoped she appeared as invisible as she felt. As the awkward teenager inside of her started to awaken again, her hand wandered toward the star-shaped bowl of saturated fat nibbles in the center of the table.

Which was whisked out of her reach as the drinks were delivered. In record time, Missy drank down two Cosmopolitans, then used a napkin to pat her overpuffed lips. "If you must know," she said, as if they'd been pressing her for details all along, "Raphael and I are having a terrible argument."

A surfer could ride the waves of animosity rolling from the vicinity of the bar. "You don't say?" Téa responded. "I couldn't tell. It must be all those acting lessons the two of you took together during your courtship."

Missy frowned, Téa's wry tone going right over her head. "Those were PR lies made up by our publicists for the press. During our so-called courtship, I was filming *Neon Nights* in Tokyo. And *that's* what our argument is about." She rounded on Johnny, nearly poking her cupcakes against the lapels of his jacket. "Did your first kiss involve tongue, or not?"

The question must have amused him, because his smile dug a dimple deep in his left cheek. It was one of those masculine, completely uncherubic dimples that made a woman want to cross her legs.

Well, at least it made Téa cross her legs. Missy Banyon moved in for the kill, getting close-up close to Johnny. "Tongue . . . or no tongue?" she breathed.

"Definitely no tongue. I was eight years old and it was the last day of second grade when I screwed up my nerve to lay one on my teacher, Miss Skerrit."

The elementary school reference seemed to lower some of Missy Banyon's heat. She backed off a few inches and then turned to skewer Téa. "You, on the other hand, were seventeen. It involved tongue and you didn't like it."

"Sixteen," Téa corrected, startled. "And if Smelly Kelly O'Hara had cornered you at the parish's Friday night teen dance, you wouldn't like it either."

"I don't know about that," the other woman said, directing her attention back to Johnny. "It's what Raphael's so mad about. He thinks that because I liked my first French kiss, that I'm not pure enough to be a Frenchman's wife. Now, I ask you, does that make any sense?"

Johnny had backed as far into the corner as he could and Missy followed. Over the woman's loose curls he sent a white-of-his-eyes look toward Téa.

Oh, it must be hell to be a handsome man, she thought without sympathy. And she very much doubted that a man like Johnny Magee needed any kind of help in the female department. But then she sighed and pushed herself into the conversation anyway. "I thought your argument was about *Neon Nights.*"

It was good enough to send the actress pivoting toward her again. "It was. It was about my co-star from the movie, who, I mentioned to Raphael, happened to have his first kiss and his first lover at the same age as me."

"Soul-kiss mates," Téa murmured.

"Exactly." Missy beamed a smile that would have made a paparazzo's mortgage payment. "Now he's offended by my sexual history *and* my co-star's."

Téa shrugged. "Sorry."

Missy's eyes narrowed. "Maybe you could go over there and keep Raphael company, you know? You'd have to take off that ugly jacket, but I'm guessing you have at least a C-cup underneath there. Or on second thought, leave it on. He thinks he likes the Puritan type."

"No," she and Johnny said together.

Missy aimed her pout at Téa. "Then at least tell me how old you were when you first had sex."

"What?"

"Never mind." Shaking her head, the other woman picked up her next drink. "It was some time between sixteen and menopause, right?"

"Menopause?" Surely the jacket didn't age her *that* much. "I was—" she broke off, darting a glance at Johnny.

That dangerous dimple was showing again. "Me? Seventeen. She was nineteen and her name was Dawn. Afterward I wrote a rock song for electric guitar in her honor, 'Oh Miss Dawn, You're the Bomb.'"

"I . . . " Téa lifted both palms in defeat. "Can't top that. I won't even try."

Missy gazed upon her with pity. "That's because you waited until some sensible, dispassionate age like twenty-two, twenty-three maybe. Way past the age of consent and composing rock songs."

Téa had been twenty-four and coming off a diet and exercise program that had resulted in a fifty-pound weight loss. The man, an accountant for a small chain of tile stores, had sent her a one-layer box of See's Candies afterward. The chocolate had been better than the sex. To be honest, both had seemed pretty skimpy.

"Well, I'm going to show Raphael what I think of his disapproval," Missy declared, sliding closer to Johnny.

Jesus Christ, Melissa Banyon has her hand on my—

"Johnny?" Over the male voice sounding in her head, Téa called out his name. His attention snapped from the actress to her.

"Yes?" His eyes widened again. "Did you . . . uh, did you say you had to get home?"

Téa swallowed. So that's what he was really thinking. He wanted her to leave him alone with the actress. It wasn't a surprise. She shouldn't be disappointed, and she wasn't, because the beautiful boy jocks always ended up with the thinnest, prettiest girl in the room.

"Right," she said, rising. "I'll be on my way."

Jesus H. Christ, Melissa Banyon has unfastened my—

"But I'm afraid I'm not feeling well, Johnny." Téa found herself plopping back onto her seat. She didn't know where this stubbornness had come from, but there it was. "I think you'll have to drive me home."

"Take a cab," Missy answered for him, sliding closer on the bench seat and wiggling in such a way that her dress drew south another crucial three inches. Johnny's gaze followed the descent.

She's seriously wacked, but the woman bought herself a great pair of tits, just frickin' great.

Téa told herself to leave Mr. Frickin' Great with the woman who was dazzling him. After all, *his* personal life was none of *her* business either. But then, glancing back, she could see the storm cloud that was Raphael getting ready to thunder.

She'd do it for him, she decided, with sudden loyalty. For him, Raphael.

Tonight, she'd refuse to disappear from the bar or into the woodwork in the Invisible Girl moves she'd perfected during her long, awkward adolescence. She'd refuse to leave without Johnny and thus save this stranger's impending marriage.

The Foreign Legion had really been her favorite movie last year.

Reaching across the table, she wrapped her fingers around Missy Banyon's bony wrist—the free one. Téa didn't want to think about where the other had disappeared to. "I'm sorry, but Johnny and I came in together, and we'll be leaving together too."

The famous actress didn't even blink. "We want our own private party, sweetie, so run along."

Tightening her grip, Téa pulled Missy Banyon to meet her halfway across the table. At the other woman's ear she whispered, in a tone that was a legacy of a life around the mob. "If I run out of here alone, *sweetie,* I run right to my grandfather, Cosimo Caruso, *hai capito?*"

It worked like the charm that it was. Téa figured the actress had visited Palm Springs often enough to know the significance of the name. Missy jumped away from their table, bumping against some others to finally land in the safety of the seething, sexy Raphael's arms.

Téa gave Johnny a moment to right whatever the actress had wronged, then slanted a look in his direction. She wasn't going to apologize. If he didn't want to do business with her after blowing his chance to make it with Melissa Banyon, then so be it. A woman had to draw the line somewhere, though granted, it was a strange kind of boundary for someone who had once hand-stenciled life-sized clowns on the walls of a circus-themed kitchen.

"Shall we call it a night?" she asked.

"We can call it whatever you want," he replied, standing. "I owe you, Ms. Caruso, big-time."

She stared up at him. "You mean . . . you didn't . . . "

"I what?" He blinked, then looked annoyed. "You thought . . . I wouldn't!"

His response kept her quiet all the way back to her house. His response and a strange little giddiness bubbling through her bloodstream. Because of her part in saving Raphael Fremont's engagement for another night, she decided. There certainly wasn't any other reason to feel giddy that she could think of.

She braked to let Johnny out by his car. He paused, fingers on the door handle, then turned to Téa. "What did you say to her?"

"Her?"

"What did you say to Melissa Banyon to get her to, uh, loosen her hold on me?"

Téa opened her mouth to give him the truth. She'd intended to tell him of the Caruso connection earlier in the evening, anyway. But that was before she'd shared—thanks to the actress—some other intimate details about her life. Surely those were enough for him to know about her.

It was then that the odd giddiness prodded some mischief to life inside of her. "I told her you were lousy in bed."

His mouth opened. Closed.

"You're welcome," she said before he could speak, even as she wondered, appalled, who this woman was who was talking, and what Johnny would think of her professionalism now.

"You're so certain I'm thankful?" he asked, slowly settling back against his seat. Suddenly he didn't sound the least bit businesslike either. There was amusement and something else, something deeper, in his voice.

She gave a tiny shrug. "What if I told you I *can* read your mind?"

"Then I'd dare you to prove it." He folded his arms over his chest. "What am I thinking right this moment?"

"How much the tabloids would pay for an 'I'm Melissa Banyon's Boy Toy' exclusive?"

"Not even close."

She pretended to mull it over. "It was a surprising, yet pleasant evening and you'll call me in the morning?"

"Nothing nearly that mundane."

"You hope to find a pizza joint between here and home."

"Now you're just guessing."

She made a face at him, knowing he wouldn't see it clearly in the dim shine of the streetlight half a block away. "What then?"

His hand reached out, and that's when it happened. That's when she lost all hope that tonight he'd see her as a cool, consummate professional. Because surely he had to sense the way that giddiness had turned to mischief had turned to flirtation and now had turned to . . . to awareness. Sexual awareness of him. It was a sizzling, sparkling kind of heat that overtook her body, making her pulse thrum and her heart pound. She didn't move, she couldn't move, as he touched her cheek.

The pads of his four fingers trailed along her skin until the tip of his ring finger caught in the corner of her mouth. Her pulse jittered, her skin burned, and beneath her business suit her body went all-woman.

"You want to know what I'm really thinking?"

"Yes." His hand didn't move as she whispered the word. She tasted the salty flavor of his skin.

"I'm wondering how someone who had her first kiss from Smelly Kelly O'Hara could judge a man like me lousy in bed."

Because I'm not, she heard him continue in her head. She figured it was more like wishful thinking than real mind reading, however, because then that inner voice added, *though it seems like a sure bet that sooner or later I'll end up proving it to you.*

He opened the door and climbed out of the car, then paused. "And I'm wondering," he said, looking at her with an unreadable expression in his eyes, "if what's happening here is going to hamper the game or sweeten the pot."

Seven

"Mack the Knife"
Bobby Darin
That's All (1959)

Johnny didn't call Téa the next morning because he had an early, important appointment with someone else. Stanley Thompson had retired as managing editor of the *Desert Bugle* ten years before, at the same time the *Desert Bugle* had retired from existence.

"The newspaper business was booming here after the war," the elderly man said, as Johnny forked over four twenties for two buckets of balls and the privilege to use the practice range at the prestigious Moonridge Country Club. "That's when air-conditioning and the leisure class came to Palm Springs."

They chose two open positions at the near end of the range. Beyond it were acres of carpet-quality grass and sparkling water that made up the playing field of a rich man's most frustrating sport. Johnny acted as caddy for both bags, because Stan Thompson looked as if a sneeze would blow him over, not to mention a full set of furry-headed golf clubs. "Is that when the Carusos came to the area as well?" he asked, placing Stan's bag on a stand.

The old man removed his pale blue fishing hat and squinted in Johnny's direction. "You want to talk about the *Carusos*?"

Johnny had been given Stan's name by the county librarian. She'd assured him that no one knew more about local history, including local mob history, than the old newspaperman. "I thought I mentioned it in the phone call when we set up the meeting."

Stan scratched the liver spots on his bald head, then pulled his hat back on. "You mentioned the Mafia. I assumed you wanted to write another story about Al Capone hiding out in these parts."

Johnny turned his back to set down his own bag. During the phone call, he'd picked up on Stan's assumption that he was a freelance journalist and hadn't corrected him. "I heard the Capone legend's a myth."

Stan shrugged. "Depends on who you talk to. The mob did move in during Prohibition and started some illegal gambling joints. But eventually club gambling was closed down in California and taken to Las Vegas."

"So where do the Carusos come in?" Johnny asked, withdrawing his driver from his bag.

Stan dropped a golf ball to the mat in front of him and used the toe of his shoe to put it in position on the rubber tee. Then he lined up, bony spine and sharp elbows facing Johnny. The swing he took wasn't powerful, but the ball sailed through the air in a smooth arc. The old guy hadn't lost it, Johnny thought, bending his knees and firming his grip to take his own shot. He drew his arms back.

"The Carusos are killers," Stan said.

Johnny's ball flew off his club in a wicked slice. It slammed into the net fencing on his right, then dropped to the ground like a dead man. "I've heard that before," he said to the older man, his gaze on the lifeless ball.

"When the rest of the Palm Springs mob moved on to Las Vegas or were absorbed into what became known as the Mickey Mouse Mafia in Los Angeles, the Carusos stuck it out here and stuck to the old moneymaking standbys—loan sharking, bookmaking, car theft."

They both lined up for second shots. "When did Cosimo Caruso take over the Palm Springs family?" Johnny asked, pitching his voice toward the other man.

Stan's head whipped over his shoulder. "Pipe down." In a maneuver straight out of an old gangster flick, he took sidelong glances in all directions, then let out a breath when he saw that the next nearest golfer was ten yards away. "You can never be too careful."

"Sorry." Johnny's subsequent shot did little better than his first, but he wasn't out here to improve his game. "What can you tell me about . . . you know who?"

Leaning on his driver like a cane, Stan hobbled closer. "He took over leadership of the Mafia in this area in the 1950s, and he did it in the usual manner, by killing the competition. He was young, and it took him time to become as smart as he was tough, but he managed to do it. You'll find few in Palm Springs who don't admire him in some ways."

"That include yourself?"

Without answering, Stan limped back to his place and took a few more drives that made Johnny's look like rookie stuff by comparison.

"You play on the tour, Stan?" he asked.

The old guy laughed, a dry, wheezy sound that mimicked the breeze shuffling the fronds of the many palms that dotted the country club's rolling fairways. "I'm no closer to pro than Cosimo is to sainthood."

"So what's the secret of his success?"

Stan cackled again and watched two Japanese businessmen set up shop a few positions down the way. Then he turned back toward Johnny. "He went legitimate."

"The food company."

The old man nodded. "The gourmet food company, La Vita Buona. Mobsters get sent to prison because they get caught with cash they can't explain. Tax evasion doesn't make as sexy a courtroom drama as robbery, blackmail, and murder, but it puts the bad guys behind bars all the same. With a lawful business, there's all sorts of avenues for money laundering."

"So Cosimo funnels cash through the gourmet food business."

Stan slid a glance toward the businessmen, but they were engrossed in a conversation while cleaning their club heads with cashmere rags. "I didn't say that, exactly."

"But he *has* gotten rich."

"You ever taste that Tuscan sauce they bottle? It's worth the eleven bucks my wife says she pays for it."

Johnny moved to his bag, exchanging his driver for his two-iron. "Cosimo had a son, Salvatore." When he turned back, Stan was at his own bag and Johnny had to raise his voice. "What about Salvatore Caruso?"

Stan glanced over his shoulder. "Long dead," he said, his tone dismissive.

But this was the heart of the information Johnny needed. "Did you know him?"

Stan shook his head.

"Did you know *of* him?" he persisted.

Frowning, Stan turned. "Cosimo briefly passed over the reins of the family to him something like twenty years ago. I forget exactly."

Johnny choked the shaft of his club and tried masking his frustration with an encouraging tone. "The librarian told me you had the best memory in the valley. You couldn't have forgotten."

Stan tipped his basket with his toe and a couple more golf balls popped out to roll idly about the Astroturf surface of the practice pad. "What are you planning to do with this information again?"

"I . . . I'm not sure."

His eyes narrowing, Stan gazed on Johnny. "You don't know what kind of story you're going to write?"

"Maybe about the children of mobsters," he said off the top of his head. "You know, what it's like for the children who try to move out of their family's line of work."

Stan regarded him in silence, then turned back to square up for another shot. "Salvatore had two daughters with his wife. And then there's one in the middle, another girl, that he fathered from his mistress. All three were raised together as sisters after the mistress died."

Johnny knew who they were. Téa, of course, her blonde half-sister, Eve, and the youngest, Joey. "Interesting family setup," he murmured, thinking back to the night before. Interesting *woman*. Such a bundle of contradictions, Téa was, with her strait-laced clothes and her sometimes smart-ass mouth. Lousy in bed, the contessa had called him, a little smirk on her full lips. Then he'd touched her, feeling her velvety skin and her fluttering breath against his fingertips.

The atmosphere in the car had gone from burgeoning sexual awareness to definite sexual combustion in the space of that breath, one of those inexplicable yet unstoppable events that songwriters blamed on the moon and that scientists blamed on pheromones. Johnny didn't know what to blame or what he was going to do about it either, even as he went half-hard just remembering it.

"Later, Salvatore was murdered."

Stan's comment dumped icy water all over him. "Murdered?" Johnny cleared his throat. "I thought the official verdict was that Salvatore disappeared."

Stan gave him another sharp look. "That's right. But if

you're in the California Mafia and you go away one day and never come back—that means you're dead, son. Murdered."

"You don't know any more details than that? I don't mean the kind that come out in court documents or police reports, but the kind that people talk about on street corners."

Stan pulled his fishing hat farther down over his eyes. "Those are old rumors you're asking about."

Sixteen-year-old rumors. "Maybe Salvatore's death was accidental. Did anyone ever look into that? Consider that?"

"A body has never been found, neither here or in Las Vegas. That's the last place Salvatore was seen, gambling at a casino."

"So a hundred things could have happened to him then," Johnny pointed out. "A car accident, a heart attack, a . . . a . . . scorpion bite. It seems strange, don't you think, that everyone jumped to the conclusion that it was murder?"

"Not when a body's missing and the Mafia's involved. In that world, job advancement means getting rid of the man on the ladder one rung above yours—or hiring someone else to get rid of him for you. The way I remember it, the story was that an enterprising young turk decided to rub out Sal Caruso and paid some hit man to do it—he was the last person Salvatore was seen with in Las Vegas. The mob boss's murder started a war on the streets and even more lives were lost until Cosimo got California's Italian underworld back under his control."

Johnny grabbed up his wire basket and tossed the contents to the ground. Golf balls rolled around his feet and he teed them up one after the other, smashing the hell out of them because he couldn't obliterate that same story he'd first heard so long ago.

When the balls were gone, he looked up to find Stan watching him with a trace of alarm. "You gotta take it easy, son. It requires a lot of energy to live a good, long life so you shouldn't use it all up in one day."

"Yeah?" Johnny muttered. "Maybe I'm not so sure about a good, long life ahead." He wasn't sure he wanted one, if it would never include the answers he needed to get a decent night's sleep.

"You might be right about that if you decide to contact them."

"Contact who?" Johnny asked.

"Those Caruso girls," Stan replied. "Cosimo is very protective of those three."

Which got Johnny thinking about Téa again. For some reason, he was starting to feel a little protective of the contessa himself. She was smart, she was funny, she was sexy in a half-exotic, half-innocent way he itched to explore.

He remembered the sleek feel of her lips against the tip of his finger and the way her perfume had bloomed in the car like the scent of hot flowers when he'd touched her. She turned him on. She tempted him. To put it bluntly, he wanted to take her to bed.

That was the hell of it, though, because his Main Street Magee values were starting to nag at him again. While he might not be a man who enjoyed getting close to people, he'd never considered himself a user before either. A player perhaps, but not a user.

And besides sex, he wanted to use Téa Caruso for information.

Jesus, the one he should be protecting her from was *himself*.

And he could. He could go away from Palm Springs. Go back to Vegas or to somewhere else. Delving into the past was all so damn complicated to begin with and the temptation of Téa would only make it more so. Perhaps the best thing to do now was to sell the house and hope that time would rebury the memories.

It hadn't happened in nine months and he didn't think it would happen in another nineteen, or twenty-nine, but he could hope.

He drew the last of his golf balls toward the rubber tee. Fine. As soon as he was done here, he'd drop by Téa's office, he decided. Unless a lightning bolt hit before he got out the words, he was going to tell her the design job was off.

He might never know the complete truth, but then she'd never find out that the man rumored to have rubbed out her father was his. And that the family who ordered the hit that killed Johnny's father in retaliation had been hers.

Eight

"Too Close for Comfort"
Johnny Mathis
Wonderful, Wonderful (1957)

There was a tall and wide white box on Téa's office doorstep. She dropped her briefcase and purse to pick it up, and the slick cardboard felt cool to the touch—proof that it had recently spent time in refrigeration. "Celebrity Florist" was embossed in silver across the lid.

Though the office was still locked up because Téa's assistant was coming in late that day, a delivery person wouldn't have just dumped the package on a doorstep, she thought, glancing around. Even at ten A.M., the morning was too warm to leave flowers unattended for long.

And who would have sent her flowers anyway? If "Caruso" hadn't been inked in tiny letters on one corner, she would have already been walking them toward the insurance company in the next office over. The receptionist there had caught the fancy of a seventy-something taxidermist from Indian Wells. Last week he'd sent her a bouquet of helium balloons anchored by a stuffed coyote. A real stuffed coyote.

Both she and Rachele had heard the young woman's screech of repulsion and come running.

But the only man Téa had had recent contact with was Johnny Magee.

Beneath her oatmeal-colored blouse and skirt her skin prickled, in every place it had no business prickling. Because no matter what had happened last night in her car, no matter what had been said—both real and imagined—he was supposed to be business. Just business.

Yet she could remember that light touch of his fingertips to her face as if they were still there. She could still taste him too, male and salty, on her tongue. Her mind flashed back to that lip-to-lipstick sip that Eve's latest had taken from her drink, and from there it was only a short mental hop to Johnny Magee's mouth. Wide, firm lips made only more masculine by their slight sandpaper edging of golden whiskers.

She wondered what those would taste like against her tongue and her skin reacted again with another round of unwelcome goose bumps.

If he had sent her flowers, then what?

Her fingers tightened on the chilled box. Until she found out for certain, of course, she couldn't make a decision. And though it was girlish and silly of her, she knew, her pulse thump-thumped-thumped in her ears as she used one fingernail to pry open the box's lid. It sprang free.

Cushioning white-and-glitter tissue paper. Glass bowl with an artful arrangement of a dozen apricot roses in water colored a matching hue. A clear plastic prong speared a white card bearing three simple words in distinctive, left-leaning handwriting. *Ritorni, per favore.*

Please come back.

Her fingers went boneless. The box slid out of her grasp.

Glass shattered against the pavement at the same moment that she heard her name called from somewhere behind her.

"Téa?" Johnny's voice. "Jesus Christ, you look like you saw a ghost. Are you all right?"

A hard hand grabbed her elbow and swung her around. She continued to stare down at the ruined box, the broken glass, the scattered roses. The colored water had splashed across her shiny cream-colored pumps and over her stockinged ankles. Orangish droplets dotted the knee-length hemline of her straight skirt.

Johnny took hold of her chin and jerked it up so he could study her face. "What the hell's the matter?"

She wondered why it was that he kept catching her at her worst. Was it mere coincidence or some unique superpower—meet Johnny Magee, MakeHerMessy Man—of his own that destroyed the calm and controlled exterior she presented to the rest of the world?

"Téa? The way you dropped those flowers, I thought they were about to bite. What's going on?"

She hoped she managed a half-smile. "That ghost you mentioned, I guess."

Frowning, he glanced down at her feet. "Who are those from? Is some old boyfriend bothering you?"

"No." But he was going to think she was nuts if she didn't elaborate. "My father used to bring home apricot roses."

From the start of their marriage, her father bought her mother a dozen apricot roses every Friday afternoon. Week-in, week-out. Month-in, month-out. Year-in, year-out. As far as Téa knew, he'd brought roses even during the time he'd kept the mistress he couldn't deny once he'd brought home something else—the daughter he'd had with her. And for as long as Téa could remember, her father would slip one of those Friday roses free of its cellophane wrapping to press the thornless stem into her own small plump hand.

"*Una piccola ricompensa,*" he'd say. A little reward.

A little reward for her little crimes.

Johnny was still looking down at her as if she was un-hinged, she realized, and supposed her explanation left something to be desired. "My father's dead," she offered.

The grip of his hand loosened, but didn't go away. "I'm sorry."

"The roses . . . " and those words in Italian, *please come back*—her grandfather's words, as it was he who had sent the flowers, just more of that emotional pressure he was exerting—had reminded her too much of the prayers she'd broadcast in a fever of grief after her father's disappear-ance. Prayers she'd never stopped sending until her father's crew and then the FBI had turned their house upside down in a fruitless search for the book. "The roses reminded me of him."

Johnny's expression only hardened, making her wonder if she'd struck a nerve. Without thinking, she voiced the ques-tion. "Johnny? Is your father okay?"

"*My* father?" He dropped her arm, stepped back. Beneath his heel, glass crunched, but he didn't seem to notice.

"Is there . . . " she hesitated, trying to come up with a way to put it. "Is there an older Mr. Magee?"

The tension drained from his body and the beginnings of a smile nudged at the corners of his mouth. "Phineas Magee, head of the Physics Department at Central Washington Uni-versity, doesn't care to think of himself as 'older.' "

"I see," she said, bending down to tend to the ruined flower arrangement. Wouldn't you know that Johnny Magee's Nautica-model good looks would come by way of a brainy prof named Phineas? Some people got more than their fair share of that All-American normalcy she'd wished for most of her life. "He sounds like quite the father."

"Yeah."

From the pavement, Téa plucked a couple of roses in one hand and a large shard of the broken vase in the other.

"And what about yours?" Johnny continued. "Was he quite the father as well? Do you miss him?"

Do you miss him? The question stabbed her and she sucked in a breath against the pain. Of course she missed him, she thought, her fingers tightening into a fist. Though Téa supposed every woman had a story about a man she'd loved and lost, it felt particularly devastating when the one that got away was her father.

"Jesus! Téa!" Johnny dropped to a crouch beside her and grabbed one of her hands in both of his. He drew it toward him and pried open her fingers.

In surprise, Téa noted the blood dripping between her knuckles. It splattered against his pants and crimson drops joined the orange dots on her skirt as he flicked away the piece of broken glass she'd inadvertently clutched. With one of his hands cradling her injured one, he pressed his handkerchief against the shallow cut on her palm and pressed hard.

She winced.

He glanced over, then frowned. "You're pale again." Without letting up the pressure on her wound, he slipped an arm around her shoulders and drew her back so they both could sit on the curb of the small planter box lining the short front walk to her office door.

"I'm okay," she protested.

He hitched her closer to him, and the brush of his hard, warm body against hers made her shudder.

"Yeah, right," he said. "You feel cold and you're shivering. You're just peachy."

What was she supposed to do, tell him it was the sensation of his body aligned with hers and not the blood loss that was causing her quivering skin? That wouldn't be businesslike now, would it?

Looking down at the stains on their clothes and the broken mess on the pavement, she groaned and dropped her forehead to her free hand. "Though I'm fighting a losing battle with that good impression anyway, aren't I?"

"What?"

"I've not exactly been a model of poise the past couple of days." From the splash in the pond to the splashes of blood on his slacks, it had been one departure after another from her usual it's-all-under-control and appearances-are-everything self.

"You don't have to pretend with me."

She lifted her head to look at him. "You don't get it. I *don't* have to pretend to present an unruffled image. Usually, anyway. That's who I am, what I am. A calm, unruffled professional."

A smile entered Johnny's eyes like sunlight glinting on sea-blue waves. Heat sizzled through her again. He really had no right to be so beautiful—particularly her personal-hot-button beautiful that had always sent her scurrying for Pop-Tarts or peanut butter cups to subjugate her unrequited cravings.

She frowned at him, because she wasn't going to melt, by God. "You don't bring out the best in me, that's what I think."

Now his mouth smiled too. His fingers lifted from the handkerchief to run once again along her warm cheek. "I might beg to differ."

So she melted. So sue her. Because the living embodiment of her every teenage fantasy was looking at her like she used to look at packages of Entenmann's coffee cake.

"I like this you," Johnny said.

"You do?" It came out breathless, girly. Good Lord. But who would blame her when he was leaning closer and wrapping her in that scent of his that smelled like clean wind and letterman jackets?

"Yeah, I do." His sexy voice hoarsened, darkened, was that by-the-fire seductive whisper that told the story of naked gypsy girls and wild, passionate dances. His fingertips slid against her cheek again. "And you're not so cold anymore."

More breathlessness. "I'm burning."

His palm cupped her face, his fingertips grazing the ticklish skin behind her ear. "I was going to resist this," he said, with a little frown. "I was going to resist you."

She gulped a breath and the top button of her blouse popped open. There was a tug on the barrette at her nape, and then he gripped the freed mass of her hair with his fist and tilted her face to his.

There it was, his mouth, his lips, waiting for her like the last donut in the box or the final French fry on the plate. And willpower, apparently, evaporated in this kind of heat.

He leaned closer and she met him halfway.

It started smooth and warm. Gentle and civilized. Then he touched her bottom lip with his tongue, a polite request for permission, and she responded by opening her mouth. She had to taste him, didn't she?

Except that meant *he* tasted *her*.

His tongue moved inside her mouth, as strong and sure as he was, and desire cracked like a whip through her body. His fingers tightened in her hair and she arched closer to him, wanting more of everything and anything he had to offer. His mouth moved over hers, his tongue played with hers. She pressed against his chest and had the sudden impulse, no *need,* to get naked.

Only then did the tiny hairs on her skin spring high in belated warning.

She pushed her hand between them and broke free. "What was that?" she demanded. It wasn't a kiss, she decided, aware of her unruly hair, her unbuttoned blouse, the morning air cool on her wet lips. It was some sort of locker-room spell handed down from athlete to athlete to ensnare women who wanted to stay well clear of wanton passion. "What *was* that?"

"Lightning bolt," he murmured, shaking his head.

"Mistake."

Johnny raised dark blond eyebrows. Even the ends of his eyebrow hairs were tipped with gold. "You're sure about that?"

"Of course I'm sure. It's the job I'm looking for, Johnny." Her business, her work, the Caruso name that she wanted so much to make over would be here long after the fizzle and pop of one spectacular kiss—not to mention the man—was gone. "I don't want to ruin that."

He froze. "The job."

"That's why you stopped by, isn't it? To discuss the job? We left that unfinished last night."

There was a pause, then he nodded. "You're right, there's a lot unfinished around here. A lot unfinished between us, too." He stood to pace away from her, running his fingers through his hair.

Téa watched him in growing dismay. Eve would know what to do now, she thought. Eve would know how to pretend that kiss had never happened and bring the conversation back around to business. And then, as if Téa had the power to wish people into her presence, Eve's classic Mercedes pulled up to the curb and both her sisters hurried out of the car.

"What's going on?" Joey demanded as she slammed the passenger door shut with a violent clang, her gaze leaping from flowers, to man, to Téa's hand wrapped in the blood-stained handkerchief.

Téa came to her feet. "Nothing. I had a little accident, that's all. And Mr. Magee happened to be here and, uh, lent his help."

Joey shot him another suspicious glance. "Mr. Magee? Who's he?"

Never let it be said that her little sister was one to pussy-foot around.

"A potential client, Joe," Téa said, a soft warning in her

voice. And then, with her sisters' presence lending her an Eve-type talent in man-handling and also some of Joey's own brash brand of bravado, she glanced over at Johnny and took a chance. "A client who, I think, was just about to tell me he's giving me the job."

She held her breath.

His gaze took her in, making her suddenly aware again of her unfettered hair, that unfastened button, the swollen feeling of her lips. The woman that he'd made her.

He looked up at the sky, then back at her. "You really want the job?"

She firmed her voice. "I really want the job."

"Then it's a done deal now, isn't it?" he finally said.

She might have wished he sounded happier about it, but she was glad enough for both of them. Unwilling to let a moment pass without cementing the deal, she reached out her uninjured palm to shake his. "It will be my pleasure."

Both of ours, Contessa, I'll make sure of that, too.

The make-believe Johnny-voice in her mind didn't sound any happier than it had a moment before. She frowned, trying to shake the words from her head as he dropped her hand like a hot potato and reached into his slacks pocket.

"Excuse me," he said, drawing out a cell phone. "I have to take this call."

Eve, Joey, and Téa watched in silence as he walked off to answer the phone. Then Eve looked over at Téa, eyebrows arching above the frames of her black-lensed sunglasses.

"Client?" she asked, skepticism lacing her voice.

"Client."

"Hottie," Joey declared. "Just your type, too."

"I don't have a type," she protested. At least not one that she'd ever confessed to her sisters.

"Any guy who can muss you up like that is your type, Téa."

She was spared from having to answer by Johnny striding

back. "I've got to go, but I'll return this afternoon to . . . finalize things. Ladies." He saluted the three of them with his forefinger to his forehead and started off, but then turned back. His gaze swept the ground and Téa's cut hand, then lifted to meet hers.

"We'll settle other things later, too," he told her, and then he was gone.

"What other things?" Eve questioned, brows once again shooting northward.

Téa ignored her, turning to see Joey purse her lips and send a smacking airkiss in Johnny's direction. *That* she couldn't ignore. "Geez! Joey!"

Not-so-innocent big brown eyes cut her way. "What? It was only because *you* wanted to and wouldn't." Then she clucked like a petite, Italian-American chicken.

Téa sighed. "What do you want?" she asked Eve.

"To take you to coffee." When her sister smiled like that, the angels had to be singing in heaven.

Téa was not so soft a touch. At least not with the promise of Johnny returning in just a few hours. "Can't. Have to work. Big job, big *important* job to discuss this afternoon, so now I have to go home and change." She thought of something else that had to be done as well. "And you should be sure to tell Cosimo I don't have time for coffee or an interest in any more flowers, either. Sending gifts or my sisters is not going to work on me."

Eve studied her face, and then, to Téa's everlasting surprise, shrugged her shoulders. "All right, then."

Joey looked at her older sister as if she'd grown another head. "What? Wait—" But Eve was already dragging her away by the simple, sisterly expedient of grabbing her shirtsleeve and towing her to the Mercedes.

Pleasantly surprised by the quick capitulation, Téa watched after them, smiling. That had gone remarkably well.

Then she turned toward her office, only to face the ruined apricot roses strewn across the concrete. Her smile died and the warm October morning turned chilly.

Or maybe things had gone *too* well. In her experience, nothing came without some kind of price.

Nine

"It Had to Be You"
Doris Day
I'll See You in My Dreams (1951)

Riding in the passenger seat of her father's Ford F-150, Rachele Cirigliano might as well have been on her way to a Brownie Scout meeting or a tap dance lesson. Her father's meaty hands were in their usual ten and two position, the radio was tuned to Rush, and a quartet of empty 7-Eleven disposable coffee cups bounced around her feet like Mexican jumping beans every time the truck hit a bump on Ramon Road.

Except Rachele wasn't six years old and dressed in a scratchy tan dress or toe-squeezing patent leather dancing shoes. She was twenty-one, and the only uncomfortable thing she was wearing were the several sticky coats of vampire-black mascara and the tiny diamond in the new piercing in her left nostril.

"Thanks again for the lift, Papa. My car should be fixed by four, the mechanic said. Téa will take me there to pick it up."

Her father grunted in acknowledgment without glancing

over at her. He never looked at her, not as far as Rachele could tell. Her mother had died when she was four years old and it was probably over-the-top romantic of her, but she figured it hurt her father too much to see the reflection of that love he'd lost in Rachele's face.

Not that her mother had sported eleven piercings and hair freshly colored by a package of Purplesaurus Rex Kool-Aid.

Her boss, Téa, had once gently mentioned that the body and hair adornment might be Rachele's shout for her father's attention. Not hardly. She had her father's attention, all right. She had his overprotection.

But because he never looked at her, in his mind she'd never grown up, and she didn't have the guts to set him straight.

So she wasn't surprised that when he pulled in front of the Inner Life design office he jumped out of the truck to walk her inside. He'd make sure there were no strangers lurking in the nonexistent noon shadows and he'd do a visual sweep to make certain all was well in the reception area, too. Then he'd talk a few minutes with Téa to nail down the exact minute he should expect his only daughter home.

This evening, Rachele would make an antipasto while he grilled steaks. After dinner, she would fold the clothes she'd put in the dryer that morning, then watch TV while turning the pages of a *Jane* magazine. Just another night waiting for whatever force it was going to take to rocket her from her dutiful-Italian-daughter place on the couch and into her own adult life.

"Thank you, Papa," she murmured as he held the office door open for her. Téa looked up from the stack of mail she was sifting through on the receptionist's desk and winced.

Rachele didn't know if it was sympathy for the sore pierced nose or reaction to the muddy-violet hair color. Considering that Téa's personal style icon appeared to be none other than vanilla-flavored First Lady Laura Bush, Rachele didn't let the maybe-criticism bother her.

"What's up, boss?" she asked instead, tossing her neon backpack onto the padded secretary's chair.

"Hey, Rachele. Good afternoon, Beppe." Téa moved around the desk to double-kiss Rachele's dad's cheeks. Then she stepped back, beaming at them both. "Guess what? Johnny Magee said yes."

"No kidding?" Rachele shrieked, jumping toward her boss to deliver a boisterous embrace. "Make-me-throb gave us the job?"

"Hush, *figlia mia*!" Her father said, his voice shocked.

Téa laughed, her hands already at work to undo Rachele's hug damage, straightening her clothing from mussed to its usual neat dowdiness. "Don't try to rein her in, Beppe. You know it's an impossible task."

Her father knew no such thing—

"She's a nice girl," he said, frowning. "And she needs to act like one."

—*see*?

"Of course she's a nice girl," Téa assured him. "Nothing to worry about there."

Ignored by the other two as if she'd left the room, Rachele rolled her eyes. Here she stood, of legal age, wearing outrageous hair coloring, amethyst lipstick, and more stud jewelry than some rock bands, and her nearest and dearest were convinced this particular "nice girl" would never do anything to cause them concern.

It made her want to throw off her clothes and dance naked on the desktop. It made her want to embark on a new career path at some place like Hooters. It made her want to run away with a completely unsuitable man.

Which wouldn't be the least bit difficult, come to think of it. Her father considered *any* man over the age of fifteen and under the age of sixty-two unsuitable. And if they were below or above that range, yet not of Italian descent—fuhgeddaboutit.

But as she trudged toward her chair, she dismissed the wild

ideas. Watching her watusi in her birthday suit would put her father into cardiac arrest, and unlike Téa—who spent a fortune on minimizing brassieres—she didn't have the rack for titty-bar work. As for finding some man to break her out of her rut . . .

Maybe her father's warnings regarding the hairier sex had sunk in over the years or maybe she was waiting for that love-of-a-lifetime feeling she was certain her parents had shared. Whatever the reason, she'd never yet been pricked by Cupid's arrow.

Settling behind her desk, she half-listened to the drone of her father's conversation with Téa.

How was her mother?

Fine.

No, really. How was her mother?

Really. Fine.

The conversation went like this every time the other two met as well. Her father had been Salvatore Caruso's best friend, and he still worried about Sal's widow, Rachele knew. As a matter of fact, her papa worried a lot, seeing bogeymen behind every bush. Sometimes she wondered if it was more than that, though. Sometimes she wondered if his concern for Bianca Caruso was a different kind of concern altogether . . . but no. Her father was as saintly in thought and deed as Rachele wished she wasn't.

Téa drew him into her adjoining office to discuss an upcoming project. Though mostly retired from a landscaping and rockwork business, her father still enjoyed looking at blueprints and home designs. So Rachele was alone in the reception area when the front door half-opened.

One boat-sized black hightop stepped inside. Rachele caught a glimpse of a classic Beatles flop of dark hair.

Both retreated.

Bemused, she watched the door open again and two big feet enter this time. Then followed a lanky body of a male in his mid-twenties. He had a laptop case strapped across his chest, that shaggy mass of hair, a pair of cool, thick-framed glasses, and the shyest, sweetest grin she'd ever seen in her life.

Ouch. A little nick, right over her heart, caught her by complete surprise. Then liquid fuel ignited somewhere inside her, propelling her in one big *whoosh,* right out of her comfort zone. Gripping the edge of the desk, she could only hold on for the ride and stare at the man who, in the space of a step, a heartbeat, a half-drawn breath, had just rocked her world.

"I had to doublecheck the address," he explained, with a self-deprecating shrug. "I have a lousy sense of direction."

Rachele ran a hand through her purplish hair. "You've found the right place," she said over the hip-hop beat of her heart.

He appeared pleased. "I have?"

"Uh-huh." Her certainty wasn't because he carried multiple sets of rolled blueprints, Inner Life's stock-in-trade, under one arm. It wasn't because he'd done that doublecheck of the address. She rose from her chair, comparing her own five-five height to his—six?—feet. Perfect.

With one hand, he worried the frayed collar of his aloha shirt. On a yellow rayon background, men lolled on a beach, watching hourglass-shaped hula girls dressed in red grass skirts and orange coconut shells. "Do we know each other?" he asked.

"Yes."

"I thought so." He nodded, then handed over the blueprints. "Johnny was going to bring these by himself, but he was unexpectedly called back to Las Vegas."

"Téa will be sorry to hear that."

"Téa . . . " he seemed to be searching his memory, then he cupped his hands in a double wave. "Curvy woman, right?"

Perhaps she should have been jealous, but there wasn't a leer in the gesture or in his eyes, though he must possess

X-ray vision to detect Téa's measurements beneath the usual tailored body armor she wore. "Yep."

He nodded again, then reached into his back pocket to pull out a business card and hand it over. "Give her this too, will you? She can reach me on my cell if she needs anything."

Rachele looked down. *Calvin Kazarsky.* "Nice to meet you, Calvin. I'm Rachele Cirigliano."

"It's Cal," he corrected, and if he thought the introduction strange after her assurance that they knew each other, he didn't comment upon it. There was a long pause, in which she could have sworn her pulse synced with his.

"Now what?" he finally asked.

Téa came to stand in the doorway of her office. "Now what, what? Hey, is that you, Cal?"

"Affirmative."

Affirmative? Was that the cutest or what?

"Johnny had to dash back to Vegas," Cal continued. "He said to tell you he'll be in touch very soon."

"Oh." A strange expression—disappointment?—flitted across the boss's face. "I understand."

Cal gestured toward Rachele's desk. "I brought by the original house plans and also those of the previous renovations. Johnny thought you could use them."

Rachele's father shadowed Téa in the doorway. "Who is this Johnny?" Then his gaze lasered in on the younger man and his voice went Papa Bear deep. "And who is this?"

Rachele didn't allow herself a hesitation. "Calvin Kazarsky, my father, Guiseppe Cirigliano. Papa, this is a client of ours."

Her father bustled out of Téa's office to stand between the other man and the two young women. He was shorter than Cal, and his chest only looked more like a barrel in comparison to the younger man's lean body. But his handshake was a white-knuckler, and Rachele was impressed that Cal didn't cry out. Instead, he hung in there, his gaze never leaving her father's. When their grips broke, she let out a breath she hadn't realized she was holding.

"Beppe, come over here. You'll enjoy seeing these." Téa's voice was excited as she spread the blueprints Cal had brought on the long table at the far end of the reception area.

With a suspicious backward glance, he strode away, leaving Cal and Rachele gazing at each other. The younger man adjusted the strap of the laptop case over his shoulder. "Well . . ."

Panic fluttered in her belly. That was a good-bye well. A have-a-nice-life well. A go back to laundry, antipasto, and nothing-more-than-the-occasional-swear-word-for-Father-Mike-to-hear-in-the-confessional well.

Well, no way!

Over her dead body was she going to let Cal run off. Then, thinking of her father's strangling handshake, her stomach dipped, hoping it wouldn't be someone else's dead body that got between them.

But if she wasn't willing to let Cal out of her life so fast, how the heck to make a play with her father sharing the same carpet space? He wouldn't be happy to hear his "nice girl" doing her best to lasso a near-stranger.

Thinking quickly, she dug in her backpack for her cell phone, and quickly dialed the number on the business card, shielding the screen beneath the desktop.

She heard a low buzz, then Cal started and reached under the tails of his shirt for the phone he must have clipped to his belt. He frowned down at the phone's screen.

She knew what he saw.

IT'S ME

Looking up, she made a point to catch his eye and nod. He frowned again, then looked back at the screen.

She rubbed the spot of that wound right over her heart, then took a first step toward living her own grown-up life by sending another text message to him. CU @ COB?

Translation: See you at close of business?

He glanced up at her, then glanced back down. F2F? appeared on her screen.

Face-to-face?

YES

Y MSG?

Wasn't it obvious why she was text-messaging him? She considered how to signal "Overprotective Italian papa bent on protecting only daughter's virginity until menopause is standing six feet away."

She settled for POS, Parent Over Shoulder.

OIC, he replied. His gaze flicked toward her father to show that oh, he saw very well indeed.

OK? She messaged.

Looking up into her face, he hesitated.

She bit her bottom lip.

He froze, his eyes narrowing, and her skin tingled from cobalt-painted toenails to silver eyebrow ring. A hot flush followed.

Did his gaze darken? She only knew for sure that he could text message one-handed and without looking at the keypad.

SLAP showed up on her screen.

Sounds Like A Plan.

Rachele couldn't stop the smile from breaking over her face.

"You're sure?" he said softly.

Her heart leaped toward her throat and seemed to expand there. "You're not?" she said around it.

He grinned, melting it right back down into her chest. "My friends say I'm too smart for my own good."

Rachele sent a warning glance in the direction of her father and placed her finger over her lips.

He nodded, then turned toward the door.

As it closed behind the man of her dreams, Rachele

flopped back against the padded back of her desk chair, stoked with this new feeling, this unexpected infatuation, this . . . love.

She'd always suspected love was going to be easy. And it was. The right guy walked through the door and *bam!* She went from immature and untried to a woman knowledgeable in the ways of the world and men and women.

Her imagination played it all out. With Johnny Magee as their client, there would be plenty of opportunity to run into Cal Kazarsky. And no one—her father—would be any the wiser. A smile played over her face as she watched the future unfurl.

"Oh my God!" Téa's shocked exclamation startled Rachele out of her seat.

"What? What?"

"I just *knew* there'd be more problems." Téa was hugging herself, as if the air-conditioning had suddenly gone arctic. Rachele's father's face was grim.

"What? What?" she repeated, rushing toward them.

In answer, Téa pointed a quivering fingertip at the name on the bottom of one set of blueprints. "Prepared for Giovanni Martelli," it read.

Oh my God. Oh my *God*.

Apparently the house they'd agreed to redesign was once owned by Giovanni Martelli, the Mafia triggerman who reputedly had taken out Téa's father. As quick as it had come alive, Rachele saw her promising new love die a swift, painful death.

The wound over her heart throbbed in unrequited agony. Unless Téa took this job, Rachele would never find a way to get close to Cal Kazarsky. She would be stuck in the purgatory between girl and grown-up forever.

Ten

"I Guess I'll Have to Change My Plan"
Bobby Darin
Love Swings (1961)

Johnny hadn't been to the cemetery in sixteen years.
He would have sworn he couldn't have located it on his own,
but somehow the rented Jag found its way there after his return to the Palm Springs airport.

The "emergency" trip back to Las Vegas the day before
had been nothing more than a bad case of jitters from one of
the syndicate's longtime investors. Johnny had nursed a
vodka tonic at a Bellagio baccarat table, sitting beside the retired CFO of a health care conglomerate. The other man had
dropped ten large bills in less than an hour, all the while
bitching about the business's change of venue.

If the fool had a lick of sense, he wouldn't be playing baccarat in the first place. Somewhere in heaven or hell Ian
Fleming was laughing his ass off at the way his fictional spy
had fueled the fantasies of thousands of James Bond-

wannabes to play a game that was essentially nothing more than calling heads or tails. Two hands of cards dealt. The player bet on which would have a point total closest to nine. Might as well be a damn coin flip. With that, the odds were better.

Johnny had gone to bed in his Las Vegas condo in a lousy mood, got up in a nasty one, and then spent a few hours making the people who worked for him in the penthouse office miserable before catching a plane back to Palm Springs. What a way to cap off the day, he thought, driving through the cemetery's open gates.

But then again, perhaps this was exactly what he needed.

Maybe his subconscious was telling him he'd been wrong and it was returning to the grave, not the house, that would exorcise the demons that had been dogging him since his thirty-third birthday.

In a more determined, if not hopeful, mood, he followed the directions to the grave the cemetery's office had solemnly supplied, along with a stapled three-page listing and map that marked the resting places of such long dead celebrities as William Powell, Sonny Bono, Busby Berkeley, and a handful of Sinatras, including Ol' Blue Eyes himself.

The office had reminded him that any flowers he left behind would be cleared out on Wednesday. Nodding, Johnny hadn't confessed he'd brought nothing for the grave site. He wasn't sure he was going to get out of the car.

But he did. He forced himself to open the door and leave the cool, controlled climate of the Jag. Braced for pain, but hoping instead for some new power to re-inter the memories that had been hounding him, he slowly approached Section A-4, plot #52.

In an area with a billion and six golf courses, the carpet-quality of the grass was no surprise. But his father's grave marker was. Johnny supposed he'd ordered the simple gray granite piece mounted flush to the ground, but he didn't remember it. It certainly hadn't been in place on the day of the burial.

From the foot of the site, he studied the marker as if it was one of Dan Brown's famous DaVinci clues. Noting the words "Loving Father" and the 8×10 black-and-white of a cocky, laughing Giovanni Martelli mounted under clear plastic, he waited for revelation or reaction.

And the only thing he felt was the mundane certainty that it was his mother who had selected the stone. She would have been the one to provide the photo of Giovanni, circa eighteen years old, too.

Johnny focused on it, seeing nothing of himself in the handsome features. While he was 100 percent Italian, the progeny of a Martelli and a Travisano, he had the blond hair and blue eyes of the Northern variety. He looked, as a matter of fact, much more like European mongrel Phineas Magee, the man whose surname he'd used as long as he could remember.

Johnny's parents had been divorced since he was a baby, Giovanni agreeing with Johnny's mother that it created a more stable family if their son used the same name she used, that of her second husband and the little half-brother that came along shortly after that new marriage.

To his credit, Giovanni Martelli had been fully aware that his own life and lifestyle weren't winning any stability prizes.

The devil-may-care tilt of his father's head in the photo said it all. He'd been a kid from a seedy Los Angeles suburb who'd knocked up his girlfriend at sixteen. Yeah, he'd done the right thing and wedded her in the Catholic Church, but then she'd used the brains that had put her on the Honor Roll at the high school for teenage mothers and gotten out of the bad marriage and into college. There she'd met a graduate student who didn't mind the little kid that came as part of her package.

Anna Travisano Martelli might have fallen for Phineas Magee fast, but she fell in love with him for good.

After the divorce, Giovanni Martelli had moved from Los Angeles to Palm Springs and found work doing . . . as a child, Johnny was never sure what. But whatever it was meant there were lean times and there were flush times, and which kind of time it was was evidenced by the digs his father would bring Johnny to during his annual ten-day summer visit.

Sixteen years ago, Johnny's father had been flush. He claimed to be selling cars at a luxury lot and told Johnny there was a special woman he hoped to bring into his life. He said he was out of debt and not playing deep anymore and that he was keeping clear of the "old crowd." As he'd always kept Johnny far away from that crowd, it wasn't until he was dead that Johnny learned from the cops that Giovanni had been hanging around the California Mafia for years.

His gambling habit had been his entrée into the underworld. Rumors were that he'd paid off some of his debts to the bookies with the kinds of favors that cops didn't want to detail to a shell-shocked teenage kid.

But not one of that old crowd or the special woman had shown up at Giovanni Martelli's closed-casket funeral or subsequent burial.

Being gunned down in your own driveway apparently put people off.

Being gunned down by the Carusos in retaliation for your own alleged hit of that family's crime boss *really* put people off.

"Mi scusi!"

At the unexpected sound of the voice, Johnny jolted. His heart slamming like a hammer against his breastbone, he spun around in a semicrouch.

A black sedan idled at the nearby curb, an elderly, hook-nosed little man wearing a straw fedora sitting low behind the wheel. "Excuse me," he said again in Italian, beckoning toward Johnny. There was a shadowy figure beside him, riding shotgun. *"Mi potrebbe aiutare?"*

Can you help me? the old man was asking.

The Boy Scout in Johnny straightened, and took an automatic step forward. "Sì." Then he froze, spooked. Riding *shotgun*. There was a shadowy figure riding *shotgun* in a black sedan driven by an old Italian in a hat.

Dread washed over him like a cold sweat. Hadn't retired reporter Stan warned him of how protective Cosimo was of his granddaughters? What if the Carusos had discovered his identity and wanted to rub him out as they'd rubbed out his father?

Holy Mary, Mother of God, pray for us sinners, now and at the hour of our death. The desperate prayer whispered inside of him, the remnant of a thousand hours in catechism class.

The old man's arm extended out the side window.

Johnny lurched back, expecting . . . what? Then he saw the man held one of the cemetery maps, not a gun.

"Sinatra." He shook the stapled papers as if to make his point understood. "My wife wants to see where Frank is buried," the man said in Italian.

Where Frank is buried. Frank Sinatra.

Of course that's what the wife wanted, Johnny thought, as the dread leeched out of him. To the Italian Geritol set, Frankie's grave would be both Mecca and Graceland rolled into one.

The last of the anxiety drained away, leaving Johnny still shaky yet more certain of one thing.

Jesus. God. Holy Mary, I'm in bigger trouble than I thought.

Revisiting his father's burial place hadn't eased one damn thing, he acknowledged as he walked his still-stiff body forward to direct the elderly couple. It had only made his problem more clear to him. If he didn't get a handle on these—panic attacks, there was no point in pretending they were anything else—he was going to be seeing demons in Disney characters.

And drive himself right over the edge of sanity.

Johnny brooded over the truth of that through dusk and moonlight. As his hotel room clock edged past midnight—he tried to yank the damn thing from the wall, but then found out that even five-star hotels welded their property into the plaster—and closer to his personal witching hour of 1 A.M., he couldn't stand his own company any longer.

At 12:50, instead of crawling out of his skin, he made a call.

"'Lo?" Téa sounded warm and sleepy, and in his mind's eye he saw her perfect skin flushed, the exact shade of those apricot roses she'd dropped to the ground just minutes before the feel of her lips on his had blown off the top of his head.

"How are you?"

"Johnny?" she breathed his name in a way that made him think she was only half-awake. "Johnny, is that you?"

"In the flesh."

"Not flesh." Sheets rustled. "Phone."

"Such a stickler for details," he scolded.

He heard the squeak of bedsprings. "What do you need?" she asked.

Release. Relief. Sleep. "I was thinking about you." And he hoped talking to her would distract him from the dark turn his thoughts always took at this time of night.

"You finished your business?" she asked, her voice still husky with sleep.

"Mm-hmm." He wondered what she was wearing. Flannel? Silk? Skin? In his mind's eye her dark hair tumbled across her naked shoulders and waved over her breasts, playing peeka-boo with her—raspberry-, mocha-, peach-colored?—nipples. "Business all done," he murmured.

"I don't even know what it is you do."

Distracted by the fantasy, he opened his mouth. "I'm a—"
Gambler. Like my father before me, I'm a gambler.

The thought popped that naked-Téa bubble hovering in his
mind. Like his father before him, he mused, scrubbing his
hand over his face. Was that why he hadn't been sleeping
since his last birthday? Was he afraid that following in his father's footsteps meant he was also destined to die at the age
of thirty-three?

But he wasn't a wiseguy. And his father hadn't been one
either, damn it. Sixteen years ago, his father had said he'd
left all that behind and Johnny believed him.

Or he only wanted to.

"Johnny? Are you there?"

He wrenched his thoughts from that shadowy path. His
phone call to Téa was supposed to give him a rest from all
that. He took a deep breath and cleared his throat. "I'm here,"
he said, then remembered her question. "I'm a . . . money
manager."

She made a little noise.

"What?"

"Sounds boring."

That made him smile. "Ouch," he said. "Then I suppose
I'm obligated to prove to you just how *fun* I can be." He
thought once more of her mouth beneath his, warm and wet.
Of the heat of her curvy body beneath yet another matronly
outfit. "Now *boring*, if we're talking about that, are your
wardrobe choices. You shouldn't be hiding behind those
bland colors and schoolmarm suits."

"Now you sound like my sister."

"But I don't kiss you like your sister, do I?"

There was a startled pause, and then she let out an embarrassed laugh. And as if he'd lit a fuse, that sexual time bomb
between them started ticking across the phone lines. He re-

laxed, settling more comfortably against the pillows he'd doubled behind his back. This was more like it. This was why he'd called.

Yes, he'd felt guilty about getting involved with Téa. Yes, he'd come close to bailing on the whole idea. But that mouth-to-mouth outside her office had made one thing perfectly clear.

There was an honest-to-hormones, sizzling chemistry between him and Téa that was too hard to ignore. And why should he? After all, if they'd met in another time, in another place, that potential combustion between them meant he would have done his damnedest to hustle her into his bed.

His conscience had no reason to squeal about him doing that very thing now. If it furthered other goals, so what, right?

He crossed his ankles on the mattress, ready to play the next hand in the game. "And about that kiss—"

"Maybe we shouldn't talk about that."

Oh, but she was already thinking about it, he could hear it in her voice. "I'm with you, I'd much rather repeat it, but—"

"Johnny!"

He had her laughing that scandalized laugh again, and he wondered—

"Are you blushing?"

"I—what? It's dark." She was trying to sound brisk and unaffected, but he didn't buy it for a second. "I wouldn't know."

"Téa. Come on. You don't have to have the lights on and a full-length mirror to answer the question. Are you blushing? Does your skin feel hot? Tight?"

The little catch in her breath made his own skin feel hot. Tight.

"Just slip your fingers between the edges of your pajama top," he coaxed. "Tell me if your heart's beating faster."

There was a pause and he tried to picture a mix of temptation and trepidation on her exotic face.

"What makes you think I'm wearing pajamas?" she finally said.

He grinned. "My imagination says no, but—"

"I also say no." She took a breath. "We are *not* continuing this conversation. At least not like this."

He frowned. "What do you mean?"

"The kiss . . . I need to explain, apologize . . . surely you can concede that it was a mistake."

Right. His tongue in her mouth, her warm body grinding against his was an error. As if he'd let her get away with that.

"I'd been startled by the flowers, okay? And then there was the broken glass and all that blood on my hands . . . "

Blood. Blood on her hands.

Blood on his hands.

Johnny's gaze jumped to the alarm clock. 1:09:09.

The numbers receded, the hotel room receded. Sixteen years vanished.

He ran his fingers through the blond buzzcut that was his hair, knocking askew the headphones blasting The Beastie Boys. Before he could resettle them, he heard the noise.

Pop.

Pop. Pop.

Pop pop pop.

Johnny leaped up, flinging the 'phones away. As tires shrieked against the driveway outside, he tripped over the pair of Air Jordans he'd left out, then ran in his stocking feet along the cool floors through the dark house. After only a few hours in his father's new place, he made a wrong turn, jamming his toes against the leg of a sturdy side table.

"Dad?" he yelled, switching directions and limping as fast as he could toward the front door. "Dad?"

The silence turned his heart into a battering ram. It pounded against his chest as he flung himself through the entry and into the warm night, running down the path and past the newly completed lagoon to the circular parking area by the garage.

"Dad?" Even the insects had been silenced.

His father lay on the ground beside his Cadillac, the driver's door still open. Bullets had shot out the interior lights.

Bullets had left dark holes in Giovanni Martelli's body.

Johnny tried to keep those holes from leaking, pushing hard here, there, and there. Shoulder, chest, arm. But it kept bubbling out. Blood. Life.

He ran for the nearest phone, leaving scarlet prints on floors, doors, walls. The 911 operator told him to stay on the phone, but he threw it aside and went back to his father.

To his father's body.

The knees of his jeans soaked up blood as he begged his dad to open his eyes, to speak to him.

"Johnny? Johnny, are you there?"

The voice yanked him out of the nightmare. "Téa?" he croaked.

"Johnny? What's the matter?"

Like that afternoon at her house, Téa was able to pull him from the vacuum-suck of the past. He followed her voice, holding onto the sound of it, holding onto that feeling of her vital and alive and so damn sexy in his arms when he'd kissed her, letting that more recent memory lead him back to the present. Letting *Téa* bring him back to the present.

The shirt he was wearing was soaked with sweat. His hair was wet with more of it. He smelled fear. He smelled *of* fear.

He couldn't, wouldn't, live like this any longer.

"Johnny, speak to me."

"I'm here." He swallowed, struggling to bring his voice back to normal. "I'm right here."

"Did you hear what I said?"

He swallowed again, and lifted a trembling hand to comb back his hair. "What you said about what?"

"That I have a problem with the job . . . with your house."

Join the club. But he was going to do what he must to exorcise its demons and lay his own ghosts to rest.

"What kind of problem?" The question came out rougher than he liked.

"Maybe we should talk about this tomorrow," she said, her voice puzzled. "You sound as if you need some sleep."

He laughed, a harsh sound. "You've got that right."

"Tomorrow, then."

"Tomorrow." Yeah. He'd face whatever was inside that house tomorrow.

The increasing number and intensity of the flashbacks demanded it. Tomorrow, he'd move into the house. And closer to Téa. She was both a link to his past and a salvation from it. Until he had all the answers he needed, he'd use her for both.

He'd told her they needed to settle things. And tomorrow he would. No more doubts, no more Mr. Nice Guy. He was going to get the truth and he was going to get *her*.

Eleven

"Oh! Lady Be Good"
Ella Fitzgerald
The First Lady of Song (1949)

All good things ended. She already knew that, Téa reminded herself, so there was no reason to feel such sharp disappointment as she arrived—early, of course—for her appointment with Johnny. Unlike her first visit to the compound on El Deséo Drive, this time hers was the sole car in the parking area by the large garage. Like her first visit, as she walked past the lagoon on her way to the front door, a chill crept down her spine.

But the little shiver was chased off as she pushed through the overgrowth beyond the murky body of water and reached the concrete steps leading up to the house itself. This part of the estate had been better cared for than the rest. On either side of the wide, shallow stairs were manicured bushes showing just the slightest shagginess. Beyond them was a sloping, well-watered lawn. As she reached the last step, she took in the smooth concrete walkways that swirled left and right to follow the contours of a generous free-form swimming pool. The water looked turquoise in the morning light, and revealed partially submerged boulders before it took a turn inside the house to flow under a glass panel that delineated one wall of the foyer.

The house itself was stunning too, its flat roof, glass walls, and box shapes seeming to grow out of the low-lying, granite-studded hills surrounding it. Following the curve of the pool, Téa passed tall fan palms and mounds of feathery grasses. At the front door, she turned, catching the breathtaking view that showed the distant and dramatic barren mountain slopes across the valley floor.

"Already?" Johnny's voice said.

Téa jumped, then spun to confront him. He'd come from another direction, around the side of the house. One hand gripped a Starbucks cardboard cup carrier.

"You're early," he remarked.

"I'm always early," she murmured, disappointment piercing her again. Not over the lost design job this time, but over losing him, or her contact with him, anyway. He was every inch the OOD—Object of Desire—that Rachele had once called him, and that based on his voice alone.

Now—in the flesh and in soft-washed khakis and a white silk T-shirt—he was STWSADOI personified. Sex the Way She'd Always Dreamed of It.

"The quintessential good girl, aren't you," Johnny said, plucking a cup from the carrier and holding it out.

She was forced to close her fingers over it. "Thank you. I, well, I . . . "

A redwood trellis above them created diamond-shaped patches of shade, and Johnny leaned against one of its supports to sip from his own coffee. "We've got to do something about that."

But there wasn't going to be any "we," she knew, because

this property had once belonged to Giovanni Martelli, a man the Carusos were rumored to have killed in retaliation for her father's murder.

"Listen, Johnny. There's something I should have told you last night . . . " He was digging in a brown bag centered on the carrier and she let her voice die out as she stared at the shock of golden hair falling over his forehead. Last night she'd been half-asleep during the first moments of the call. Then, later, when she should have told him she couldn't take the job, she hadn't wanted to.

She'd wanted to see him one more time. One last time. That perfect hair, that rangy yet elegant body, those long, strong fingers that had touched her face and cupped her cheek, the mouth that had made her want to strip off her clothes and her common sense to let all her badness out.

Her chest rose on a deep breath, and then she forced open her mouth again. "Johnny, the fact is, I can't—"

He pushed a morsel of something from the bag between her lips.

"—mmf." The taste of buttermilk and cinnamon melted against her tongue, derailing her train of thought. It was good. It was *so* good. She swallowed, the sweetness conga-dancing like a train of wanton women through her system. "What *is* that?"

"Cinnamon scone." He pinched off another piece and held it out to her.

"No." She stumbled back, then quickly righted herself, aware of the pool just behind her. "Thank you, but no. I don't eat sugar."

"No *sugar*?"

"As little as possible." Téa brushed at her tan dress, a bias-cut sheath with a flaring skirt that fell just below her knees, to make sure crumbs weren't clinging. No sense in setting up an opportunity for a traitorous wet fingertip to go looking for them later.

Johnny was staring at her, golden eyebrows raised, still holding the piece of scone between his fingers.

"What?" she asked.

"I had no idea it was this bad," he said, frowning.

"This bad? This bad how?" She wanted to step back again, but there was that pool and she *wasn't* going to sabotage her professional image this time by falling into it. "What?"

He seemed to shrug off the thought. "Never mind."

Oh, yeah, as if she could let it go *now*. "Tell me. What? What's bad?"

"This is more than a typical good-girl thing, Téa. This is some serious self-denial."

She made a face at him and his diagnosis. "Oh, come on. It's watching my weight."

"No." He shook his head. "It's more. You don't allow yourself any of the sweet things in life. Now why is that?"

He had stepped closer to her. Uncomfortably close. Hadn't he?

Because she could see the gray pinwheels in his blue eyes and the way the sun had tipped the very ends of his hair an almost baby-blond. When she took a quick breath, over the roasty scent of Starbucks she smelled a faint tang of chlorine. "You've been swimming."

"Thirty laps in the hotel pool. But you're avoiding the question."

Because she should be avoiding him, and avoiding thinking of his long body stroking through the water, shoulders rearing up, hair slicked back to expose all the masculine angles of his face.

I'd like to back you into that pool and dive in after. Right here, right now. Both of us wet. You getting wetter.

At that imaginary Johnny-voice in her head, her gaze jumped to his face. He was looking down at her, his expression bemused. "What are you thinking now?" he asked.

Not what *he* was really thinking, was it? Of course not.

Blame it on the swimming. She'd had a thing for swimmers since the last summer Olympics. To be truthful, she'd had a thing for the jock Johnnys of the world since she was twelve years old and dreamed of class rings and homecoming dances to escape the reality of missing fathers and FBI raids.

"Téa?"

"This coffee is making me hot." She fanned herself with her free hand.

He lifted a brow and one corner of his mouth turned up. "Téa, Téa, Téa . . . "

Just the way he was saying her name, and smiling, made her want to run screaming for safety. Could he hear her thoughts in *his* head? The mortification!

"You call it coffee," he continued, and this time she knew for sure that he moved closer. "I call it—"

"Maybe we should go inside." Anything to put a little distance between them. Between him, her, and that pool. *Wet and getting wetter.* She cleared her throat. "We can talk in the house where it's cooler."

He stilled, then glanced over his shoulder at the front door. "Not yet. I can't . . . let's not go in there yet."

"Fine. No problem. Sure." There was no reason for them to go inside, not when this job wasn't going to be hers anyway. Glancing around at the beauty of the pool and then thinking of the potential to be found inside the modern-style house, disappointment sliced through her again.

Damn her family for once more standing between her and her dreams.

Anger went on simmer inside her, but she tried ignoring it as she faced Johnny once more. "So you know, I can't take the job."

His eyes narrowed, his gaze a blue laser beam locking onto hers. "Is that right?" he said softly. "You can't or you won't?"

Suppressing a little shiver, she remembered calling his

money manager persona the night before boring. Now she wondered if the occupation might take more steel than she imagined. "I shouldn't, I can't, I won't." She shrugged. "It's really all the same."

"I don't understand."

"You won't want me."

He smiled, making her shiver again. "Téa, you've got to know by now that's not true."

Oh, good God. She was going hot again. Fanning her face, she tried her best to stop thinking about what he'd said and focus on what *she* had to say. "Bad choice of words. My family . . . " Shame and anger edged higher inside of her.

"Your family—?" Johnny prompted.

The right words wouldn't come out. "There was a murder here," she blurted. "Sixteen years ago."

"I know," he said calmly.

She blinked. "You do?"

He nodded. "The realtor told me before I bought the place. But you didn't know?"

He was laser-beamed back onto her again. "No. Not until I saw the blueprints Cal brought over and the name on one of the sets. Giovanni Martelli." The family enemy. The family victim. Both, according to rumor.

Johnny nodded again.

"It doesn't bother you?" Téa asked.

"Not really." His face was smooth, his expression unreadable. "I'm a live-in-the-present, look-forward-to-the-future kind of man."

"That's smart." Why couldn't she live like that? To some extent she tried, it was why she'd refused to move away from Palm Springs, but there were always those whispers following behind her. Those sticky webs reaching out to draw her back to the shadowy world where her grandfather lived.

"It bothers you, though," he said. "The murder."

"No." If Giovanni Martelli had really whacked her father,

wasn't it right that he was dead too? "Yes!" Because being a daughter of the mob didn't necessarily mean she believed in the mob brand of justice. But this ready confusion between right and wrong was just another of the reasons she couldn't live amongst her family again.

Johnny was just looking at her, cool and collected and so handsome that she hated having to tell him the truth.

But she did have to tell him . . . some of it.

"The thing is, Johnny, rumors are that the man was killed on orders from a member of my family." Heat rushed to her face, shame and another sickening wave of anger that she was forced to make such a confession.

"Téa—"

"You don't understand." She gestured wildly with her hand, arcing a spray of coffee onto the pavement. He couldn't understand or he wouldn't be wearing that neutral expression. No man could understand what growing up with a father in the crime business was like. "The Mafia isn't just the stuff of Scorcese movies and Godfather books. My grandfather heads up California's most notorious crime family, Johnny. The Carusos are mobbed up."

"Okay," he said slowly. "But what does that have to do with you? Is your business—"

"No!" Her arm made another wild gesture, splashing more coffee. "My business has never been anything less than legitimate. You have my word on that."

"So then what does the Mafia have to do with us?" he asked, plucking her coffee from her hand and setting both cups and carton on the ground at his feet. He straightened and shoved his hands in his pockets, looking in control and unperturbed.

"With me working on the house, you mean?"

"It's just a house, Téa. My house now."

"Well, yes, but . . . "

"But then what's the problem?"

Her shame of their criminal activities was the problem.

Her embarrassment. And her anger. It was beginning to bubble over the edges now.

"If you want the job, Téa, and you said you did, then why are you turning your back on the opportunity? Life's a lot sweeter if you live it the way you want."

Why did his voice sound like the devil's in her ear? But he was right, of course. There was no real reason to refuse if it didn't bother the client.

Though wasn't working on the house where the man purported to have killed her father once lived weird?

No weirder than her father's family having then killed *him*.

She put her hand to her head, trying to clear her thoughts, trying to tamp down the past that seemed to be rearing its ugly head so often lately.

"Why would you deny yourself something you really want to do?" Johnny asked softly.

He was talking about self-denial again. But it wasn't that. It was bargains she'd made between herself, her conscience, and God. Deals to make up for all the other things she'd done.

But didn't she deserve to have something for herself? And couldn't she, like Johnny, be a live-in-the-present, look-forward-to-the-future kind of person? Doing this design job was that chance for success she'd been waiting for.

It was also her chance to remake the Caruso name. And maybe—just maybe—it was even more fitting to attempt that here.

Coming to the swiftest decision of her life, she held out her hand, palm up.

He cocked an eyebrow.

"Keys," she said. "It's time we go inside."

He reached slowly into his pocket. "Yes," he said. "I suppose it is."

The lock turned easily. She led Johnny across the threshold, never once looking back.

* * *

"If I believed in wishes anymore, this would fulfill every one of them," Téa declared, taking yet another tour between the kitchen and living room.

Johnny followed, as grateful for her final decision to be his designer as he was for her enthusiasm about the house. With her waxing on about the "simple lines flowing from one room to the next," and the glass walls that "brought the indoors out and the outdoors in," he hoped she wouldn't notice the tension that had stretched his nerves and tightened his muscles the instant he'd crossed the threshold. At any moment he expected this first time in the house to force another flashback on him.

Keeping his attention honed on Téa, he watched her turn a circle, the skirt of her dress rising to show off her legs. The sight was enough to tease him with thoughts of her incredible ass, just a few feet higher up. God, he wished she'd stop with the old-maid clothes. Something a little shorter, something a little tighter, and he wouldn't be able to experience a thing beyond this mine-all-mine lust she seemed to bring out in him.

She was chattering again, but she'd moved from the middle of the room toward the opening that led to the bedrooms. The dim hallway beyond snagged his attention, and he peered in the direction of where he'd once slept.

"I studied the blueprints you gave me," she was saying, and now her voice warred with the heavy backbeat of the Beastie Boys' song, "Fight for Your Right to Party," that was playing in his memory. "The original architecture called for just the L-shaped main house arranged around the patio-pool courtyard. The golf course and the lagoon were put in by . . . by the next owner."

The next owner. She meant Giovanni Martelli. The Beastie Boys played louder, never content as quiet background music. The golf course had been playable the summer Johnny had come to visit, he remembered, and the lagoon walls constructed though waiting for water when he'd left.

His palms began to sweat, and he focused on Téa in desperation as she moved to the windows opposite the glass walls that looked onto the pool. "The guest bungalows were built by the second-to-the-last owners, Michigan snowbirds, for the visiting families of their adult children."

The guest bungalows. Okay, the guest bungalows. He could think of them, concentrate on them. "Cal is moving into one of those today," Johnny told Téa.

She glanced at him over her shoulder. "He is? Already? I thought I'd get a chance to—"

"We ordered the bare minimum furnishings to be delivered. Temporary stuff that we'll dispense with once the replacements you order arrive. But we need a place to work and to sleep and hotel rooms get old, fast."

And he had to face the nightmares if he was ever going to make it through the nights.

Nodding, Téa wandered away again, in the opposite direction of his old bedroom. Breathing easier, Johnny followed behind, the Beastie Boys sounding fainter in his head.

"This part of the house is fairly recent construction as well. The Michigan couple wanted a master suite," she said, stepping through the doorway.

Only to make an abrupt stop. He plowed into her, his chest against her shoulder blades, his groin pressed to that glorious swell she tried so hard to hide. His hands palmed her shoulders to steady her. Then, just to make things even, he started to swell too.

And with that, the Beastie Boys put down their instruments and went off to find their own women. This is why he needed Téa, Johnny thought. Somehow she tamed the forces eating away at him, and redirected their malevolent energy into something more earthy, pleasant, *present*.

Téa glanced back at him. "There's furniture in here."

So there was, utilitarian stuff that he wouldn't be sorry to see go when the time came. "Thanks to Cal, I guess. I ordered a bed, a recliner, a big-screen TV, and a desk. All present and accounted for. They promised to deliver early." Someone had even made up his king-size bed, complete with a sleek gold comforter. Probably the housekeeping team Cal had arranged to clean the house and the bungalows before their move-in today.

"You're going to be living *here*?"

"That's the plan."

She swung around, frowning at him. "I mean, *here* here? I thought one of the guest—"

He was shaking his head.

"But we'll be tripping all over each other," she protested. "I'll have to be in and out all the time."

What a punishment, he thought to himself.

Her frown deepened and her sloe eyes narrowed. "Did you—" She broke off, her eyes suddenly shifting upward.

"Oh, my God," she exclaimed.

"What?" The hairs on the back of Johnny's neck jumped on end. "*What?*" Suppressing a cringe, he looked up, half-afraid and half-expecting to see a ghost.

No ghost. Relieved, he let out a laugh and let his gaze roam the sight above them. Oh my God was right, he thought, with a low whistle. Overhead, the ceiling was mirrored. Not with a simple XXX-rated motel, over-the-bed mirror, but with reflecting panels that covered the entire 40×40 space.

"There are people etched into the surface," Téa said, her voice sounding strangled.

Johnny nodded. "Naked people." Lots and lots of naked, life-sized people, some in artful, but odd poses, others doing what came naturally when you were naked and well, well-endowed.

Téa continued to stare upward. With her pretty neck arched, he could see a flush inching up her neck. "Your ceiling, it's . . . it's . . . "

"Orgiastic?" he supplied.

"How elegantly put."

He stifled another laugh, he who never expected to find anything humorous in this house. *Oh yeah, thank you, Téa.* "I'm surprised, that's all. Who would have thought the Michigan snowbirds had it in them?"

She glanced over. "You didn't already know this was here?"

He shook his head. "I told you, Cal must have let the delivery people in early this morning."

Her gaze was back on the ceiling, and she turned to get another view. "I mean before that. Before you bought the house."

Uh-oh. "I, well . . . " She would think it was strange if he confessed to buying the place sight unseen, wouldn't she?

She cast another, sharper look at him. "Johnny?"

The lies were starting to pile up. He gazed upward, hoping for inspiration, and then a grin broke across his face. With any luck, he could distract her. "Check this out," he said, moving toward the bed.

She took wary steps after him.

He flopped down on his back onto the mattress then scooted over to make room for her. "I think I know what those singles in the strange poses are up to," he said patting the free space beside him. "Let me show you."

She crossed her arms over her chest. "Why don't you tell me instead?"

His grin widened as he redirected his gaze skyward. "Okay, but you asked for it. When I lie just like this," he folded his hands behind his head, "that little gal with the open mouth in the kneeling position up there appears to be sucking my—"

"Oh my God!" Her face flushed and she looked up, down, then up again. "You're making that up."

"Try it for yourself." He loved the blush. "If you're squeamish about the girl-on-girl thing, there's a lonely young man right above the recliner in the corner."

He loved the expressions chasing across her face. The good girl trying to deny herself all that sweet, sexual sugar. "Looking doesn't count as calories," he tempted in a soft voice.

She bit her bottom lip.

Oh, man. Even her lips were blushing. They were red and wet and they made him want to whisper naughty things to her while she used them on him just like the etched woman in the mirror overhead.

His cock was semi-erect as she finally scurried to the corner and sat in the overstuffed recliner. "You will *not* tell my sisters about this," she ordered, then pushed down her heels to send the chair into full recline.

He rose up on his elbows to watch her reaction. Her mouth dropped open in a silent scream.

Of shock? Of arousal?

She was so straitlaced he couldn't tell.

"Johnny," she finally choked out, her voice faint. "We have to do something about this."

At that moment, if she wasn't the granddaughter of his enemy, and he wasn't the type who liked to keep things shallow, he might have fallen hard for her. Beneath the surprise, beneath that spinsterish little dress, was the vulnerable note of a woman who saw something she liked and was afraid someone just might guess that fact.

It was a hell of a thing to want to go to bed with a female who was trying to keep her sexual feelings buttoned beneath sand-colored silk.

It was a hell of a challenge.

The kind of challenge that was going to keep him sane while living at this house and searching into the past.

Taking care not to startle her, he rose off the bed and made his way toward her corner of the room. Craning his neck, he saw what intimate act had so caught her attention. And noted it in the back of his mind.

"We better examine exactly what's going on here," he said with authority, lifting her limp hand off the arm of the chair to draw her up. And then, careful not to let a hint of innuendo enter his voice, he took them both on a tour of the room.

At each stopping place, her eyes got bigger. Twosomes, threesomes, there was a whole daisy chain of differing sexual activities above them that they appeared to join, depending upon where they looked up.

It could've been a hell of a lot more fun sans their clothing, but he was pretty satisfied once he had both of them lying on the bed, their shoes on the pillow end, their heads tilting this way and that to fully make out the scene they now appeared to be participating in.

"That can't really be done," Téa scoffed, pointing a finger at the figures above her. "Nobody could hold a pose like that when . . . when . . . "

She couldn't say the words, and her face and neck were still pink with—embarrassment? Excitement?

He rolled over on one elbow to watch her face, which was much more interesting than the lifeless erotica etched above them. Oh, yeah, hustling the contessa into bed was going to be so much fun.

Which reminded him. Now that he was in the house, and even breathing easy, he had another move to make.

"Téa—" he said softly, lifting a stray strand of hair off her face with his fingertip, careful not to touch her skin.

"Hmm?" She angled her head in yet another direction.

He was smiling again. The fact was, she was damn good for him, getting him to smile, getting him to laugh, getting him hard in this place of such bad memories. *It's just a house*, he'd told her, and now he was beginning to believe it.

"I have another . . . small request," he said.

"What's that?"

"My new neighbors invited me over for cocktails tomorrow night. They said I should bring a date. I've only met two women since I've come to Palm Springs . . . "

She stiffened, just the slightest, but he noticed and slapped his ace onto the table.

". . . so it's either got to be you or Melissa Banyon."

Beautiful, exotic dark eyes slid his way, narrowed. "You don't have her number."

He bit the inside of his cheek to keep from grinning. "Missy slid it into my pocket that night. My pants pocket."

Téa's gaze jumped orgy-ward again.

She had to be tempted. She wanted him too. He knew she did. *No more self-denial, baby,* he silently urged.

Her soft mouth pursed. Her fingertips drummed against the comforter. "Well, I guess you won't need that number. As it happens, I'm free."

Johnny smothered any outward sign of triumph. Instead, he lay back on the bed and closed his eyes to savor how well things had gone. He'd made it into the house, no problem. He'd make it with Téa, no problem there either.

Maybe he'd even sleep again.

But then . . . maybe not, he thought with a wry grimace and opened his eyes. With the image of the Kama Sutra players over his head and Téa *in* his head, it was possible he'd only made his insomnia just that much worse.

Twelve

"Tell Me, Tell Me"
Ann-Margret
The Vivacious One (1962)

"You're here early."

Téa froze, midsquat. Her gaze jumped from her own reflection in the mirror to that of her mother, Bianca, standing behind her. Téa's cross-trainers wobbled on the inflatable discs she was standing upon. Instinct made her glance down at her feet to stay balanced, but that only made the wiggling worse. She leaped back to the stable rubber flooring of the workout room at the Kona Kai Resort & Spa.

"I didn't expect to see you either," she told her mother. She'd hoped to avoid the women of her family. She had enough to deal with, like how she could have been so foolish as to allow Johnny Magee to goad her into a date, for example. No doubt about it, the man *was* dangerous.

Her mother studied her, cocking her head so that her sleek chin-length bob slid across her slender jaw. In black, calf-length yoga pants and a matching form-fitting T-shirt, the older woman defied the stereotype of an Italian-American mother. Bianca Sabatino Caruso, now back to plain Bianca Sabatino, was no Mama Boy-ar-dee, responding to crises and death by retreating to the kitchen and the parish church.

Instead, in sixteen years she'd gone from part-time manicurist to manager, then owner, of one of Palm Springs's premier spas. Expansive and completely enclosed by thick, twelve-foot-high walls, the Kona Kai offered the usual health and beauty services, but was also known for its very private and very pricey guest villas to which the famous or just plain rich withdrew to recover from addiction, plastic surgery, or the convenient catch-all, "exhaustion."

Her example of beauty, hard work, and grace under pressure stood firm in the minds of her three daughters. But she rarely cooked. And as far as Téa knew, Bianca hadn't been to Mass in sixteen years. They'd never once seen her cry.

"You look tired, *cara*," her mother said. "Maybe you should have slept in this morning."

Téa grimaced. "I thought I might need a little extra time in the gym to sprain my ankle or pull a hamstring or something."

Her mother's dark eyes widened and she laughed. "What?"

Shaking her head, Téa spun toward the mirrored wall again and stepped back onto the stability discs. "Only in Palm Springs would a cocktail party revolve around a tennis match," she grumbled, sinking into another squat while trying to maintain her balance. "Nobody else in the world still plays the game, do they? Except for Serena and Venus, that is."

"There's Jennifer Capriati."

Téa made a disgusted face. "Oh, thanks for reminding me. Now my 'Italians aren't good with rackets' excuse is shot to hell."

A couple came into the workout area and her mother

smiled at them as they took their places on side-by-side treadmills across the room. Then she returned her attention to Téa. "What's this all about?"

"Maybe you could give me a real excuse," Téa said, feeling inspired. "You know, like the ones you used to write to get me out of Sister Franca's gym class."

"If you don't want to go to this party, then why did you say yes?"

Téa stalled by making herself complete the set of fifteen squats before answering. She'd been egged into saying yes. For some reason, mention of that plastic-coated predator of a woman, Missy Banyon, got under her skin.

Not to mention how that mirrored ceiling had . . . muddled her thinking.

"I accepted for business reasons," she lied.

Johnny wouldn't have reneged on their design deal if she'd refused him. He'd asked her to be his date because he was out to get her into bed. She wasn't so foolish that she couldn't figure *that* out.

But she'd been naïve enough to consider herself resistable to the powerful punch of a purely physical lure . . . and she'd been wrong. So very wrong.

Oh, God. That pulled hamstring was sounding better and better.

Her gaze caught on another guest entering the workout area. Somewhere near fifty, the man had a silver brush of short hair, a deep tan, and a boxer's flattened nose that could benefit from a referral to one of her mother's plastic surgeon buddies. He was very fit, with a flat belly, and the confident way he headed toward the Cable Cross machine made clear he knew his way around a gym.

But then his eyes landed on Téa's mother and she saw his feet trip up. It took him a moment to haul his tongue back in and untangle his Adidas.

Téa smiled and lowered her voice. "Don't look now, Mom, but you just made a new conquest."

Bianca waited a beat, then took a quick glance over her shoulder. She frowned, creating two shallow grooves in the olive skin between her arching brows. Her mother had yet to go under the Botox needle, though she never said never. "That must be the man who checked in late last night," she said. "One of our indefinite stays."

Which could mean anything from another refugee of "exhaustion" to a patient in need of several pre-rhinoplasty consultations.

"He's attractive, Mom." Despite the nose that dominated his features.

Her mother gave an indifferent shrug. "I'm not looking for a man."

Me neither. Téa envisioned her future like her mother's: single, celibate, successful. Because what man without his own rap sheet would want to commit to a woman with such strong criminal ties? And what was wrong with a life without sex anyway? From the looks of things, Eve probably took care of the family's quota all on her own, though Joey undoubtedly hooked up with one of her legion of guy-pals whenever she felt the urge.

"Your sisters stopped by my office yesterday," her mother said.

Maybe mind reading ran in the family.

"Oh?" Téa stepped onto the discs for her next set of squats. Her sisters wouldn't have brought up any Caruso business with their mother. When Bianca had reclaimed her maiden name, she'd cut her ties with Cosimo and company. Everyone had always respected her mother's decision on that.

Téa grimaced at her reflection as her thigh muscles screamed like she wanted to. Why didn't people respect *her* decision on that?

But she wasn't going to think about it. Her focus now was Johnny and how she was going to get out of tonight's date. Common cold? Cold sore? How about just common old cold feet?

"They told me about your grandfather's impending retirement."

At her mother's quiet words, Téa did the whole wild wobble and wiggle as her world once again went sideways. She stumbled away from the discs and looked over at her mother, surprised. "They told you about Cosimo?"

"And the party. And the promise they made to him about you."

Téa backed up until her shoulder blades hit the cold surface of the mirror. Silver Crewcut, on the other side of the room, was watching her. When he saw she'd noticed, he glanced away, as if he felt a sudden fascination for the golden-flowered hibiscus hedge lining the nearby window.

"I don't want to go to the party, Mom." Téa sounded twelve years old, so she cleared her throat and tried a second time. "I'm *not* going to the party."

Her mother waved her left hand. She'd once worn an extravagant wedding set, with a three-carat marquis-cut center diamond, fit for the queen who raised Salvatore's three princesses. When the FBI had confiscated all the cash that was found in the house, she'd sold the ring to pay for their tuition at Our Lady of Poverty, the exclusive and expensive school they'd attended. "It's not the party I want to talk to you about."

Téa pressed closer to the glass behind her, telling herself it was its cold that caused the shiver rippling down her back. Her mother wasn't going to bring up the past, was she? She never discussed the Carusos or her marriage, and Téa figured it was because it was impossible to explain how she'd ended up with a man who was, at best, a philandering criminal.

Téa already knew that love defied explanation.

"We don't need to talk about anything," she said quickly

"You won't remember how it was before," her mother went on despite Téa's protest. "How it was sixteen years ago."

"I remember."

Her mother briefly closed her eyes. "Then I wish you didn't."

Téa remembered everything about that time. Long days and nights without word from her father. Visits from her father's "friends," who wanted to know where Sal might have kept his ledger—the "Loanshark book"—that was actually a handwritten record of all his business activities. Then there were the government-issue cars with the unusual antennas parked near the house twenty-four hours a day. The men sitting inside them, drinking coffee or eating sandwiches, their eyes following Téa, her mother, and sisters as they moved about their own neighborhood.

And that final, frightening and destructive search of the house by the FBI. "I remember exactly how it was."

Bianca took in a deliberate breath. "Still, I want to warn you, *cara*."

More shivers raced down Téa's back. "Can we talk about this another time, Mom?" Another century, when they were both old and gray and the memories and the fears had finally faded away. "I have to get to work and then I have this big . . . uh, thing tonight." She'd walk across hot coals, or even date Johnny Magee to avoid the direction this conversation was taking.

Her mother drew closer and brushed her palm over Téa's hair, the soothing gesture in contrast to her scary next words. "Men will be coming into town."

"Men?" It was hard to swallow the dry lump in her throat. "What kind of men?"

"You know the kind I mean. They'll be coming here soon, and over the next few months, to curry favor with your grandfather, to cement old alliances, to create new ones. They'll be searching for vulnerabilities in the family and looking for ways to take power."

Will they be looking for the book again? Téa pictured its soft, glossy cover and could almost smell the faint scent of the apricot rose pressed between its pages. The book's secrets were sixteen years old, but she doubted their ugliness had diminished. If it came to light, those who had borrowed money, gambled illegally, or had been blackmailed for their peccadilloes would still be embarrassed or exposed.

And others would be implicated.

Her mother brushed her hand over Téa's hair again. "Watch your back, *cara*," she whispered.

The glass behind Téa had been warmed by her body heat, so there was no reason to shudder. But she did anyway, and again, when she found the gaze of Silver Crewcut was trained their way once more.

"What about *him*, Mom?" she said, her eyes flickering over her mother's shoulder. Was it happening already? Was this one of the men her mother was warning her about?

That non-Botoxed frown appeared again between Bianca's eyebrows. "Him? You mean the man who checked in last night?"

"He's staring at us."

Her mother shook her head, smiling a little. "He's a construction manager from Colorado Springs. We don't need to see snakes under *every* rock."

But Téa would feel them around her now, she just knew it, in every dark car that slid around her street corner, in every dark Italian eye that looked her way, in the dark shadows of her very own bedroom.

The opportunity to get out of her house tonight suddenly seemed like manna from heaven.

"The spa has a tennis racket I can borrow, right?" she asked.

Her mother nodded. "Of course."

"And some tennis-y type outfit in the boutique?"

Another nod.

"Not to mention my usual deep discount?"

Her mother laughed and Téa liked the sound of it. Not that she felt like joining in. But at least she was giving herself something else to think about beyond the Caruso problem tonight.

Johnny.

Funny, how in the space of one short conversation, he'd become the least dangerous man in her life.

Thirteen

"The Tender Trap"
Frank Sinatra
This is Sinatra! (1956)

At Johnny's knock on her door, Téa swiped up her purse and the borrowed tennis racket. Then, in the same movement, she opened the door and tried walking past him, already on the way to his car. She was that eager to get out of her house.

"Wait, wait, wait." Johnny caught her by the shoulders and pushed her gently back inside. "I made a mistake about the time. We're not in a rush, actually we're a little early."

The door closing behind him did nothing to calm her jumpy nerves. Tomorrow she'd be better, but today her mother's warning had lurked in her mind. All morning and afternoon she'd imagined villains staked at her corner or stalking past her windows. "I don't mind being early," she said.

He smiled. "You might want to be dressed."

She glanced down at herself—at herself in her enveloping mauve chenille bathrobe—and flushed. It wasn't that she wasn't already dressed for tennis, but the teeny tiny outfit she'd brought home from the spa's boutique might as well have been constructed of wet tissue paper then molded to her skin. The first puff of breeze and the skirt would flutter up to reveal built in "shorts" that hit her legs at hot-pants level. She'd slapped her bathrobe over the getup before too many glimpses of her nothing-left-to-the-imagination figure in the bedroom mirror sent her into hiding forever.

Gripping the nubby lapels, she looked over at Johnny, who appeared manly yet adequately covered in knee-length navy athletic shorts and a white tennis shirt. "Why do men get to wear clothes that are comfortable and loose-fitting?" she demanded. "How would you like to live a life in Lycra?"

One corner of his mouth kicked up again and he flicked a long finger against her nose. "I never win these arguments. So I'll save us both time and apologize right away for everything from Barbie dolls to *Playboy* centerfolds."

"Big apology. They're the same thing."

He laughed, and his finger stroked down her cheek this time. "What's the big Lycra phobia anyway? You afraid to let me see your body, Téa?"

Of course she was afraid to let him see her body, she thought, as tingles skittered down her skin from where he'd touched her. *I'm the fat sister.* The one who battled every calorie from making camp on her hips, her butt, her breasts.

He moved closer, bringing the walls of the room with him.

She tried stepping back, but he'd hooked his forefinger around the thick belt at her waist. At her next inhale, she drew in Johnny's scent, tangy and clean. And then just like that, like a wave, like a whiplash, once again heat whooshed over her body. Desire.

Her heart was tripping all over itself as she tried thinking her way over, through, out of the intensity of it. But her thoughts were as scattered as her breath. She didn't want this! She didn't want this sudden yearning that had to be oozing out of her pores, like steam rising from boiling water.

Because it would control her, and not the other way around.

"Such a coward," he scolded softly, "and still into all that useless self-denial." His head drew closer.

In slow motion, Téa watched his mouth descend toward hers as her body pulsed at her breasts and between her legs. For Johnny, all for Johnny. God, he was beautiful, she thought, the lack of air in the room putting her into a stupid daze. All-American blue eyes and golden hair and tanned skin. The All-American boy most likely to succeed all grown up.

Her fingers uncurled from their place on the robe's lapels and dropped, brushing against hard abs beneath his shirt. He flinched, stilled, then moved in.

Open your lips, Contessa. Let me have you.

His voice inside her head broke through her breathless dizziness and sent a cold bucket of self-preservation over her trembling skin. She jerked back, and Johnny's fingers loosened the tie of her robe. As it slid off, she made a run for the door wearing only the lime-colored V-necked shell and matching tennis skort. "We better go."

A long wolf whistle followed her out her front door.

Johnny didn't.

Taking a deep breath, she turned on the walkway to face him. He was standing in the doorway, staring at her. Tingles ran down her arms and up her legs and she felt the back of her neck go hot beneath the thick braid of her hair.

It wasn't right. It wasn't fair. She wasn't in the market for a man. And she didn't have any practice in dealing with this out-of-control, wild . . . *thing* for one she barely knew.

"What are you waiting for?" she demanded, irritated with both of them.

"A couple of things," he said, rubbing his hand over his chest in an absent gesture. "First and foremost being the ability to think anything beyond 'gimme' when I see you dressed like that."

It shut her up and he didn't say any more until they were both inside his Jag and threading through the late-afternoon traffic on the four-lane section of Palm Canyon Drive. "I'm also waiting for some insight into what you're so afraid of."

Her head whipped toward him. "What?"

He glanced over. "Do I look like the Big Bad Wolf to you?"

"You whistle like him."

He smiled. "If you saw you through my eyes, you'd forgive me for that."

"Is that a compliment?"

"Let's just say Lycra is your friend."

He was grinning, so she wasn't sure she believed him. It was hard to redraw her self-image, just as it was hard to see herself with a man like Johnny Magee. She tugged on the hem of the tennis skirt, secretly loving the bright color, not so secretly wishing it would grow another few inches. Or twelve.

A dark movement in the side view mirror outside her window snagged her attention. A car in the next lane over, nose to their tail. It was a slinky luxury car in the land of slinky luxury cars, but something about the way it stayed even with Johnny's back bumper sent a warning signal down her spine.

Watch your back, cara.

Téa slipped down in her seat, her head turned just enough to keep her eye on that side view mirror. "I know a shortcut," she said.

He frowned. "What shortcut?"

There was no shortcut. But someone might be following them, set on her trail by a rival don in the California Mafia, or even by her grandfather himself. "Just follow my directions, okay? Take a left at the next light."

He maneuvered into the storage lane. So did Slinky.

Téa drummed her fingers against her left thigh as they waited for the green. *Was* someone following her? Johnny reached over to still her fingers and she started, his touch distracting her from the car behind them.

He gave her hand a light squeeze. "You're avoiding my questions again."

The light changed, and he returned his attention to the road, following her directions of four blocks straight—Slinky followed—two blocks right—Slinky followed again. Another right turn, and her neck craned as Slinky continued on without them.

A single driver . . . a man's profile . . .

A silver crewcut? She couldn't be sure. And she couldn't suppress that sense that someone was watching.

They'll be searching for vulnerabilities in the family and looking for ways to take power.

That warning signal edged down her spine again and when Johnny touched her arm, she jolted.

"Téa. I don't get why you're so skittish. Most women like me."

"It isn't—" But it *was* him as well. With her need to keep her distance from the Carusos and every other Mafioso certain to be prowling Palm Springs in the next few weeks, she didn't need another man, another complication in her life.

They hit a stoplight, and while they waited at the red, Johnny dropped her hand to take her chin and turn it toward him.

"Contessa, I'm not asking for your soul."

Then why did it feel as if he was touching it with those hard, warm fingertips?

"I'm not asking for your secrets."

And there. He'd said it. That's what she was truly afraid of, with him, with every man. It scared her to think that some guy could set a match to her one day and burn down all her defenses. That in the throes of wild sex she'd lose her inhibitions and lose all control, setting free God knows what. Secrets, emotions, a badness this mob daughter had been born to but had bargained heaven to keep caged.

"I want nothing so dire," Johnny was saying, his nighttime

voice finding its way inside her like sweet, warm smoke. "Nothing so complicated."

She lifted her gaze to his, finding all that open blue. "What is it you want then?"

"Only where this is already leading to."

Bed. In was in his eyes, in his voice. She was tingling all over again because she wanted that too. Of course she did. But it was such a new force, such a new drive to deal with that she felt confused and conflicted. Because though all the reason inside her brain said it was a bad idea, she couldn't be reasonable when she was looking at him, when he was looking at her and that chemistry between them was bubbling like a high school experiment gone bad. "I still don't think—"

"Don't think then," he said, pinching her chin and letting her go as the traffic ahead of them moved. "If you don't think so much, it will all fall into place."

As they pulled back onto Palm Canyon after their short detour, Téa found herself watching the cars around them again. Then Johnny reached over and put his arm across her shoulders.

His voice was all smoke and sex again. "Relax, Contessa, and you'll discover it's all very, very simple."

Simple? God knows she needed some simplicity in her life, Téa thought, tempted by the notion. She rested her head on his arm, just for a second. A test.

It felt masculine and reassuring and the warnings that had been running down her back were replaced by a wholly different kind of shiver.

It felt good. A good kind of scary. A straightforward kind of scary that was all about sex and nothing about secrets and suspicions. Maybe she *could* do this. And if she did, if she went with Johnny to where this was leading, then tonight she wouldn't have to be alone with the shadows and what might be lingering amongst them.

Fourteen

"Between the Devil and the Deep Blue Sea"
Buddy Rich
Buddy Rich Just Sings (1957)

It had been his dick talking, damn it, Johnny thought as he turned onto the narrow lane leading up to the estate his neighbors had carved into the mountainside next to his property. Not that he didn't want Téa in his bed, and not that it mattered a whit whether it was simple or not. But he couldn't afford to focus on seduction right now. It might distract him from the evening's more important goal.

The neighbors had lived in the same location for thirty years, they'd told him when they'd caught him at the bottom of his driveway to extend their invitation. They'd known all the previous owners. Tonight, Johnny planned on pumping them for every scrap of information they had on Giovanni Martelli.

He braked beneath a piece of arched canvas shading a parking area, then reached into the backseat for his racket. "Ready?" he asked Téa, glancing over at her.

Feathery dark lashes. Apricot skin. She'd forced her mass of dark hair into a long braid. He tried to leave his gaze there, but still it dropped to the tight top that was hugging a spectacular upper curve that would have put starlet Missy Banyon into everlasting envy. That gimme-gimme greediness was already burning through his blood again, and Tea was still sitting on the asset that fascinated him most. When she'd slipped out of her robe to show off the lime-colored tennis skirt riding along the womanly flare of her ass, he'd flashed on SweeTARTS. He could never decide what he wanted to do with the candy first—a delicious suck or one clean bite.

Her eyes widened.

Shit. Was he thinking out loud? Wrenching his gaze away from her, he fumbled with the door handle and stepped into the warm dusk. Téa was out before he could get around to her door.

"Are you ready?" he said again, trying not to stare at her smooth, naked legs.

"As long as you're not expecting an experienced partner."

Was that what made Téa so wary? Lack of experience? *Gimme-gimme-gimme.* He'd be happy to provide all the practice that she needed.

"You're looking wolfish again," she said, poking him in the belly with her tennis racket as he tried stepping closer. "Don't you want to get to the party?"

"Yes." Damn it. She'd meant *tennis* partner, of course, but his little head was doing all the thinking again. Mad at himself, but just male enough to want to take it out on her, he grabbed her free hand and set off at a brisk pace on the pathway toward the house. Voices and laughter made him veer down a set of steps and he towed Téa behind him, refocusing his thoughts on the real reason he was here.

Giovanni. His father. His own memories of what the man had been like before his murder were sixteen years old. Luxury car sales. A woman he claimed to love. Neither went along with a man who one day up and decides to agree to execute a dangerous mob hit, the way the old rumors went. The way the old reporter had told him on the golf course.

A second set of steps led Johnny and Téa to a terrace, where a cabana-style bar was set up along with some tables and lounge chairs. In the distance lay the valley floor and the stark, purple outlines of the Santa Rosa mountains, but here bougainvillea spilled from immense pots and palm trees poked through the flagstoned surface, standing like attendant waiters. A pristine tennis court, with four people standing close to the net, was just another set of steps away.

"Johnny!" One of the players waved an arm. "Come on down."

A flurry of first-name-only introductions followed. Their hosts, Phillip and Doug, he'd already met. From their earlier conversation, it was apparent that the two men were a gregarious, long-committed couple. Wearing deep tans and matching tennis wear, they passed out firm handshakes followed by tall glasses of a whipped drink. The other two people were also neighbors, but fortyish Clark and Megan had only moved in a year before, and so wouldn't have anything to add about the murder.

Doug explained the game they'd planned for the evening. "We thought four of us at a time would play drop ball instead of regular tennis." He explained it was doubles, but court play was limited to the first two squares up close to the net. "The ball has to bounce, so it's about the soft touch and not brute strength. Whoever loses the fifth point will rotate out and one of the waiting players will rotate in. Those that are waiting have bar duty."

Téa's hand went up. "I'm good with ice trays. I can be permanent bartender."

Excellent, Johnny thought. Up on the terrace she'd be out of sight. Off his mind.

"Nonsense," Doug replied. "Johnny didn't bring a beautiful woman all the way here to keep her in a corner."

Yes, Johnny did. Or at least he thought it was the smarter place for her. For him. But he grinned at her. "Don't tell me you don't have a soft touch, Contessa."

Which meant they were partners for the first round. They were facing off against Doug and Phillip, though, just the people he wanted to pump for info. He considered how to bring up the subject as they moved into position. Téa walked past him and his head automatically turned, a hound dog following the scent. God, she had a primo ass.

She glanced over her shoulder. "What?"

He'd lost his train of thought again. "I—" Damn it! He was supposed to be planning how to bring up Giovanni. Then he closed his eyes. Double damn it. With Téa six feet to his left, how the hell could he get away with a casual inquiry of a decades-old murder? He'd already told her it didn't bother him.

"I'll serve," Phillip called out.

Johnny took his racket in a firm grip. No problem, he told himself. It was more than fifty-fifty that they'd bump Téa out at the fifth point, leaving her on ice-cube watch.

Their host's shallow lob dropped on the line between her and Johnny. She lunged for it, and he watched, hypnotized by the way her skirt fluttered with the movement, lifting to reveal her round butt cheeks cupped by tight little shorts.

She missed the ball.

He didn't. Because he was still ogling her body, it caught him full on the mouth.

And because his lip was bleeding, the one who got ice-cube watch was him.

Megan rotated into the game, leaving him with neighbor Clark. Johnny held a cold glass of rum and coconut juice against his mouth and tried making small talk without moving his lips.

His mangled "what is it you do" must have come out "ut is it uu do" because Clark stared at him with a puzzled expression instead of answering.

Johnny tried again. "Ur jod?" *Your job?* Close.

"Your job," the other man said, snapping his fingers. "*That's* how I know you."

"Hm?" Now Johnny was puzzled.

"The World Series of Poker. Champion. Two years running. You're not just Johnny. You're Johnny *Magee.*"

Oh, shit. Like most everyone else who played cards seriously, he went into tournament play with a disguise of sorts. Ball cap and smoky sunglasses to keep his expression as indecipherable as possible. Poker tells weren't only written on the face, but there was a reason that the eyes were called the windows to the soul.

"My God, I recorded your play at the final table last year. I've watched that round a dozen times," Clark crowed. "Damn, and here you are. A professional poker champion."

"You are?" said a new voice. Téa's voice.

Talk about the eyes being the windows to the soul. There was no doubt her soul was surprised . . . and suspicious.

He quickly shook his head. "No' po. Hoddy." When that sounded completely mangled, even to his own ears, he took the glass away from his mouth. "Not pro," he enunciated. "Hobby."

Megan was calling from the tennis court, forcing Clark to leave the terrace and take his turn. Forcing Johnny to face Téa, alone.

My father cautioned me against gamblers a long time ago. She'd said that to him, the very first time they'd spoken.

"Hobby," he said again, wincing as he tasted blood welling again.

Her eyes went from suspicious to concerned and she grabbed up a napkin, then stepped close to hold it against his mouth. "I didn't realize it was this bad."

It was good, was what it was, with her exotic face turned up to his, and her stellar breasts dressed in SweeTART green just a breath away. His free hand moved down to cup her ass, all by itself.

"Kiss it better," he whispered.

Her lashes swept down, feathers against the skin of her cheek that glowed in the lights that suddenly switched on as the evening darkened. "Is this the simple part?"

"Yes," he said. *Whatever she wants to call it. Simple. Necessary. Now.*

She went on tiptoe, the curve of her butt snuggling into the palm of his hand. He set his glass aside and cupped the other sweet cheek, pulling her against him. Her mouth gave him one of those prissy kisses, all tiny smack.

He tightened his fingers. "Don't tease."

Her lashes lifted and her eyes were as hot as he felt inside. She smiled. "I'm trying to be gentle. Earlier you questioned my soft touch."

He groaned. Squeezed his fingers again.

He only got another prissy smack. "So what's this about gambling?" she asked.

Careful, Johnny. Careful, he warned himself. He tried shrugging without losing his hold on her. "I've been living in Las Vegas, Contessa. It's a given. We slip quarters into slot machines like other people put 'em into parking meters."

"Is that right." She slid her tongue across his bottom lip.

Sliding everything but her straight out of his mind. He lifted her higher against him and slanted his head to get himself a real kiss.

A voice called up from the court, stilling his movement. "Johnny? You up to playing?"

Oh, yeah, he was up to playing. With Téa. To hell with sixteen-year-old secrets when until now she'd been hiding that bootylicious butt and let-me-at-'em breasts. He'd play investigator with her all night long.

"Go ahead, Doug," he called back. "I'm still nursing my lip."

"Then we need Téa."

And just like that, the little flirt slipped out of his arms. Smiling, her skirt twitched over her butt as she sashayed off. Maybe he liked her better dressed as a librarian, he thought, downing the damn glass of rum and juice as Phillip bounded up the steps to the terrace.

"Let's whip up another batch," the older man said, smiling as if he hadn't just ripped away Johnny's fun.

For the sake of politeness, though, he pretended an interest as Phillip went behind the bar and pulled fruit juices and booze out of a minifridge. "This is my special recipe," he said, dumping ice in a blender.

"Yeah?" Johnny craned his neck to see how the play was going. With any luck, Téa would be back soon, and in his arms.

"Actually, it came from someone else. A man who lived in your house, as a matter of fact."

"Really," Johnny replied absently, watching Téa bend over to pick up a ball. Her partner Doug was watching her too, and he wondered if the other guy was really gay, or if he might just be straightened out by that one glimpse of such a fine, fine female tush.

Phillip lowered his voice. "His name was Giovanni Martelli."

Johnny closed his eyes, then ground his teeth as the blender pulverized the ice. He'd almost let the opportunity slip away! The blender went silent, and Johnny swung toward the bar. "The Martelli who was murdered at my house?"

Phillip lifted a brow. "You know?"

"California real estate law. Full disclosure and all that."

The other man continued to fuss with the drinks, so Johnny prodded. "Did you know him well?"

"Well enough. He put in that little course and I'd go over

there on Sunday afternoons and play a few rounds with him. Doug, unfortunately, abhors golf."

Phillip wasn't bubbling over with details, but Johnny couldn't tell if it was because he didn't know any more or if he was reluctant to share them. He accepted another frosty glass of the rum concoction, and stared into it. One of his father's other legacies, he thought, besides the mystery behind his death.

He looked up. "This Giovanni, he was a car salesman, is that right?"

Phillip poured out more glasses of the drink. "He appeared to be doing well at a dealership down the valley in La Quinta. Luxury sedans."

Which jived with what Johnny remembered.

"Maybe the motive was robbery then," he wondered aloud, suddenly questioning if the police had thoroughly investigated that angle. At the time, his mother had whisked him back to Yakima, so most of what he knew was secondhand. He'd tried to find the original detective on the case, but the man had long since retired and moved to no-one-knew-where. "Were there other—"

"Nothing was missing," Phillip said, walking nearer. "And we've never had any kind of trouble around here, before or since." Tilting the pitcher, he topped off Johnny's glass. "Is the murder bothering you?"

"No." Not until 1:09:09 that night. "Just curious, is all."

"Me too," Phillip admitted. "Even after the rumors that he was involved with the Mafia and that he assassinated one of their own. I liked Giovanni Martelli. He was impossible *not* to like, especially in the mood he was in during the last few months of his life."

"What kind of mood was that?"

"There was a woman."

Which confirmed what his father had told him as well. "Do you remember her name?"

"I didn't know it. I just knew Giovanni was in love with her."

"Sure doesn't sound to me like a guy who'd take the risk of commiting a crime against the Mafia." *Murder.* That's the part that never seemed to stick. That Johnny didn't want to stick. He couldn't see his father as a murderer.

"Maybe for money? To impress the woman?" Phillip mused. "He was crazy enough about her to do anything, I think. He built her that tiki room on the property you own."

"Huh?"

"The tiki room on your property."

"There's no tiki room on Johnny's property." It was Téa, swinging her racket as she came toward them.

He had the sudden urge to grab her, to hold her, to sink himself into her SweeTART of a body and let it take him away from all this.

"I have all the blueprints," she continued, "and there's no tiki room."

Phillip shrugged, then passed a frosty glass to Téa. "I don't know what to say. Giovanni Martelli told me he was building a tiki room, but I never saw it."

"Giovanni Martelli," Téa echoed. Her gaze cut over to Johnny.

"Phillip was giving me the history of my place," he said, thinking quickly. "As a matter of fact, we were just getting to the snowbirds and their bedroom mirror."

Her gaze dropped. She blushed. And he was pretty certain that one little comment had pushed her concerns about Giovanni Martelli out of her mind.

Leaving him free to lie another day.

But he wasn't going to feel bad about that! There was no reason he should. He had other issues, after all. Though he wished to God it wasn't so, the Mafia connection was no longer coming from some cop with a knee-jerk reaction to an Italian last name. Phillip was someone who had *known* his father and he seemed to believe it was possible.

Meaning Johnny might have to accept his father had been a murderer.

The idea made him want to go to Téa again. He wanted to grab her, hold her, bury his face against her hair and let his dick be the brains of the operation again. But of course, if what he'd learned *was* the truth, she was the last one he should be fucking.

It meant his father had really killed hers.

Not to mention the other lesson he should take away from all this. He may have followed in his father's footsteps and become a gambler, but he sure as hell wasn't going to make Giovanni's other mistake. If Phillip was right, it was a woman who had led Johnny's father to his downfall. So now Johnny had to take extra care not to let a woman be his.

Fifteen

"The Way You Look Tonight"
Stan Getz
Stan Getz Plays (1952)

Though he'd gotten the information he was after in the first forty minutes, the "cocktails and tennis" that Johnny took Téa to turned into cocktails, tennis, conversation, and enough hors d'oeuvres to serve the entire U.S. Davis Cup team. After playing and eating and trying to fill Clark's hunger for knowledge of Texas Hold 'Em and all things poker, it was closing in on eleven P.M. when Johnny drove Téa home and escorted her up her front walk.

At the door, she turned to face him, and he looked down at her, grateful for the shadows that disguised her curvy, follow-me figure. It was only her eyes he could see clearly, their exotic tilt framed by wavy tendrils that had worked free from the long braid hanging down her back.

"I had a good time," she said. "Thank you."

She put her hands behind her back, an action that he knew

would be thrusting her breasts forward. If he let himself think about that. Which he didn't.

"You're welcome. I wasn't expecting the evening to end so late." When he'd picked her up, he'd expected a few drinks, a little information, then long hours in the warmth of Téa's bed. It was optimistic, hell yes, but any good gambler went into the game expecting to win.

Though after what he'd learned from Phillip, Johnny had revised those expectations. It had made the evening hellishly long as he'd watched Téa and wanted her, all the while knowing he wasn't going to do one damn thing about it. But the best gamblers also knew that when the game wasn't going their way, it was time to pick up their chips and leave the table.

Still, it was with regret that he let himself lift one of those liberated wisps of her hair and curl it around his forefinger. "Good night," he said, giving it a little tug.

"Good night?" she echoed, her voice uncertain.

Through his finger, he felt a little tremor run through her. How could she be jittery when he was leaving? He'd thought he was what made her so nervous. "Are you all right?"

She glanced around at the surrounding shadows, then licked her lips. "I thought you might like to come in."

Well, yeah, he might love to, but now it was way too complicated.

Maybe she was reading minds again. Because she went on tiptoe and put her arms around his neck. "Johnny," she whispered. "Show me how simple it can be."

Her mouth was turned up to his, tempting, juicy, and his cock stirred, despite himself. "Téa—"

"I want to forget everything tonight," she said, her body shivering against his as she stepped closer. "I don't want to remember anything but you and me."

Okay, fine, he'd give her a good night kiss. After all his big talk she'd at least expect that. He'd do the perfunctory it's-been-nice smooch, then get the hell out before getting them both in trouble. It might hurt like hell to stop, but nobody ever died of lust.

His hands fell to her waist. Slid around to her ass. Her lips found his and her fruity, warm taste filled his mouth. The tip of her tongue touched the tip of his and he went fully erect and rock-hard.

His hands tightened, tilting her closer to him. He slanted his head, needing the taste, the fit, the heat of her body because the whole night was suddenly so damn hot. She moaned, trying to move in closer, but he held her still, keeping just that fit of pelvis-to-pelvis, mouth-to-mouth, remembering that he was going to have to stop this soon.

Any minute.

She broke from his hold and pressed her entire body against his. Soft breasts against his chest. Her belly to his cock. He lifted his head, thinking he needed air, but instead it was the skin of her neck he needed, the smooth warmth of it against his tongue, the thrum of her pulse beating against him.

His hands raced up her back, encountering that tight club of her hair. He didn't like it. He didn't want any of her bound, fastened, kept away from him. The band at the bottom pulled free and then he sifted his hands through the dark mass, unwinding it as his lips went back to hers.

For just a second or two.

Moving in, he pushed her back against the door and fisted one hand in her hair. Lust and heat were speeding through his system like a car chase, spinning thoughts and sense from his head. He grabbed her left breast.

He grabbed her, he who finessed women, he who had found great success in slow warm-ups and stealthy touches. He who'd enjoyed the kind of foreplay that you could measure in half-degrees.

She arched into his hand, from beneath her bra and the

stretchy knit of her top, her nipple poking into his palm, just as if half-degrees weren't enough. Just as if finesse didn't matter to her.

It didn't seem to matter to him.

He kneaded the softness in his hand, his fingers firm, unable to be soft when his cock was so hard and this need for her was driving him so high.

"Johnny," she whispered, and one of her legs wrapped around the back of his calf. Her smooth skin was rubbing his, any second certain to set off sparks.

His hand slid under that tiny skirt and under those skintight shorts and he grabbed again, cupping real skin, her curvy, silky ass. He groaned, ready now for heaven.

"Inside, Contessa, inside," he said, his voice thick and harsh. There was heat and wet between her legs, he sensed it, just inches away from his hand. "Now. Don't wanna do it against the door."

She froze.

Oh, shit, he thought, replaying his last words. *Don't wanna do it against the door.* Shit! Where was smooth Johnny, cool Johnny, charming Johnny? Women loved his manners, they loved him. *Don't wanna do it against the door.*

"Contessa, I—" But then he realized what had caught her attention. Through her door, he could hear her phone ringing.

"Your machine will pick it up," he said, gentling his hands and letting them fall away, all the while thanking God for the interruption. Though there was no way in hell he was going to stop now—and he'd probably roast in hell or at least under the broiler of his own conscience for it—at least it gave him time to find the practiced lover inside himself, the one who knew how to ease a woman into bed. The lover who did it smooth and slow to prevent any scratches to the surface of his life.

A voice floated from the machine and through the door. "Téa? Téa, if you're there, pick up. It's Eve. The security firm called. There's been a break-in at your office."

Téa stiffened. "Break-in?" she questioned in a frozen voice even as the answering machine clicked off. "Break-in?"

Her eyes moved off his face and into the darkness. "They must think it's in my office," she murmured, sounding faint.

She wasn't making any sense. Feeling a little scared, he figured, and a little startled from having to go from passion to business in the space of a breath. Hell, he was just getting his own breath back. And his sanity, he thought, relief washing through him. Tonight he needed distance, detachment, and with his hands all over Téa and his tongue in her mouth, he'd been speeding in the wrong direction down a one-way street.

"Come on, Contessa," he said, sliding an arm around her shoulders and taking a deep, steadying breath. "I'll drive you over." Even with his big brain functioning again, he couldn't leave her to find her way to her office alone, though he'd be singing silent hosannas all the way that he'd made it past tonight without an emotional scratch.

Her business wasn't far, but the ride was long enough for him to realize that Téa grew tenser with every block that passed. By the time they glimpsed a small crowd ahead, huddled on the sidewalk beside a private security cruiser, she was shivering. He grabbed a front-zip sweatshirt from the backseat and encouraged her to put it on.

"It's baggy, but warm, Contessa," he said, angling into a nearby parking spot. "Come on, honey, wrap up."

She stepped out of the car as soon as he stopped, his sweatshirt a bulky gray paper bag from her neck to her knees. Maybe because she looked like a little kid, maybe because he hated the way the security car's revolving light washed red, red, red, over her face, but something about her made his chest ache.

Ignoring it, he slammed his door shut and grabbed her hand. It was cold and so damn small he took it between both of his and rubbed it as they walked toward the knot of people outside her office.

The circling light flickered across their faces, illuminating some he didn't know, and some he did—Téa's sisters, Eve and Joey, and . . . Cal? What the hell was The Calculator doing at Téa's office?

A small figure in dark goth-wear and facial piercings ran up to Téa. "It's all my fault," she said.

Téa's feet stuttered to a halt, and Johnny pulled her back against him to keep her upright. Damn, she seemed ready to break.

"Rachele," she said. "You didn't have anything to do with this. It's me. I—"

"Didn't need to bother coming after all," Joey finished, charging over. She glanced up at Johnny, calculation gleaming in the red lights in her eyes. "You can blame Eve for that."

Eve strolled up with an elegant older woman who was Téa in twenty years, minus the mouth-drying curves. "You can blame Eve for nothing," the blonde corrected, shaking her head. "Eve is on your contact list if the security company gets no answer at your numbers and the silent alarm goes off."

The older woman—Téa's mother, obviously—reached out to place her fingers against her daughter's cheek and then her forehead. "*Cara*, are you sick?"

Téa struggled to break free of his arms and it took Johnny a moment to release his hold. "Not sick, Mom. I'm fine."

The one who was sick was him! Johnny thought, taking a belated step back. Christ, here Tea was, surrounded by family, and he was pretending to be her pillar of strength. But Mrs. Caruso was looking at him curiously, so Magee manners made it imperative he step toward the women again.

"Johnny Magee, ma'am," he said, holding out his hand. "A client of your daughter's. I was with her when the call came."

Cool fingers shook his. "Then thank you for bringing her over." She smiled.

Johnny stared, aware he was holding her hand moments too long. But when she smiled, the woman beamed beauty rays that age couldn't diminish. "I see where Téa gets her looks," he heard himself mumble.

Joey rolled her eyes, and elbowed the blonde sister beside her. "There goes another one. Doesn't that just make you sick, Eve? Even when you're standing here, with all your Miss Universe appeal, one look at Mom and it's all over for the rest of us lesser mortals."

"Shut up, Joey," Eve and Téa said together.

Then Téa went on alone. "Now tell me what happened tonight. Was there a break-in or not?"

"Or not," Rachele said, fiddling with the ring piercing her eyebrow. "I came by to—to—"

"Get something you left behind you told us," Joey supplied impatiently. "And then you fumbled with the alarm keypad which set off the alarm."

"Which set off the calls to me and to Eve," Téa continued, looking stronger by the second. "So it was all a mistake. But why is everyone here?"

"I was hunting around town for you," Eve said, "so I called Mom and found her and Joey having coffee in the spa's bar."

"Okay," Téa replied, looking at who was left in the crowd, the security officer and Johnny's lead tech-head. She glanced back his way. "That means Johnny called Cal and—" Her voice trailed off as she peered over Johnny's shoulder.

Cal? He hadn't called Cal. He opened his mouth to let her know, when an icy-white stretch limo pulled up to the curb.

"—and Melissa Banyon?" Téa said, incredulous.

"Hell, no!" But it was the actress all right, exiting the chauffeured car, leading with nine yards of legs and those killer fake tits. Still inside the limo, illuminated by the interior lights, was Raphael Fremont, beaming a killer glare at Johnny that didn't look fake at all.

"I just happened by and had to stop once I saw you," the actress said in her baby voice. "Is there something I can do to help?"

The crowd was silent, some stunned, some awed, some annoyed.

"Sign an autograph I can sell on e-bay?" Joey put in, sotto voce.

Since none of the others were taking up the conversation, Johnny felt obligated to step in. "No, no, thank you very much, but we're fine here."

Despite his assertion, she moved like an armored tank with cone headlights, right for him.

Johnny braced himself, wondering what else a man had to go through in one night.

Then Téa stepped in front of him. He thought she bared her teeth.

Melissa Banyon, all six feet and sixty-four ounces of silicone, stumbled. Her gaze fixed on Téa, she lurched back. With a morose little pinkie bye-bye to Johnny, the actress exited as fast as she'd arrived.

Their little group was still silent as the limo glided off and another car took its place. A sleek black car this time. Téa stiffened, her mother backed away, and Eve and Joey exchanged pointed glances.

A tinted window slid down to reveal a dark-haired, dark-eyed man. Not Cosimo, this guy was much too young, but he was definitely a wiseguy. "Téa, your grandfather wants to know if you need any help," he called out.

"No," she called back, sounding falsely pleasant. "I don't need or want anything from him."

Johnny couldn't stop himself from touching her again, his palm stroking the shallow curve at the small of her back, wishing he could absorb some of the tension he felt there.

The wiseguy slipped on an easy smile. "How about an espresso? He has a new machine in his kitchen and he *insists* that you see it tonight."

The asshole was handing out orders now. Johnny took a step forward to get rid of him, but Téa beat him to it. She leaned close to the open car window. "And I *insist* on refusing. You can tell Cosimo I don't drink espresso in the evenings. It gives me nightmares."

She stepped back, bumping into Johnny's body. He cupped the nape of her neck. After a pause, the car moved slowly along.

Then Johnny remembered, so damn slow too, that *he* was supposed to be moving away from Téa as well. With a quick step, he put space between them. She turned toward her relatives, he turned toward Cal. After eliciting a promise from the other man to see her home, Johnny withdrew into the darkness and left.

Sixteen

"Gotta See Baby Tonight"
Louis Prima
Strictly Prima (1959)

Rachele let herself into the house, the low glow from the den letting her know that her father was waiting up for her. "I'm home, Papa," she called out, happiness bubbling over into her voice.

"You have your backpack?" he asked.

Guilt bounced right off her good mood as she walked into the room where her father was settled into his recliner, watching Jay Leno in the darkness. "I have it right here," she said, holding it up. Retrieving the item left at the design office "by mistake" had been her excuse for getting out of the house in order to meet Cal. Her recent little white lies had made time for coffees and ice cream cones and kisses.

From that first day in the Inner Life office when she'd seen Cal, she had known that he was meant for her. Call her crazy, but love had come to her just like that. What she hadn't known was just how sweet and gentle Cal was, his absent-minded braininess dropping away whenever he was with her. Then, the dark-lashed eyes behind his glasses focused, seeming to see past her hair dye, her facial piercings, and her exaggerated makeup to the secret corners of her heart.

A geek with a sensitive side. What more could a girl—no, a *woman*—ask for?

Her father broke into her thoughts. "You took long enough," he grumbled. "I was starting to worry."

Rachele grimaced. *Starting* to worry? Her father had been worried, maybe downright depressed even, for as long as she could remember. "I ran into Téa, her sisters, and mother, and we chatted a while."

Her father's head jerked toward her, the light from the TV giving his face a blue cast. Blue, like her father's perpetual state of mind. "You saw Bianca? How's she doing?"

Rachele slid onto the couch. "She seemed fine." Especially after Rachele had explained her goof-up with the security panel. What she hadn't explained though, was that it was Cal kissing her silly that had caused her to nearly forget the alarm code and then fumble at the keypad. No one had appeared to catch on that they'd been together at the office. "They're all fine."

Except maybe Téa, who had shown up with mussed hair and wearing a baggy sweatshirt. The boss never let herself look so disheveled. She never let a man touch her like Johnny Magee had been touching her either, Rachele thought, remembering how he'd been holding the boss's hand between both of his. She grinned to herself and couldn't help but bounce a little on the tweedy cushion. Love was in the air.

She glanced over at her father, his attention back to the television. On the small table beside him was a framed photo of Rachele's mother. Rachele dusted it herself twice a week, and Windexed it often to keep the protective glass streak-free. Her heart twisted, the exuberance inside her tempering a little.

How lonely her father must feel with his wife forever out

of reach. No wonder he tried to keep his only child under glass and close to him.

But if he knew she'd found her soulmate, wouldn't he relax his hold on her?

"Papa," she ventured, wondering if she could really bring herself to tell her father what was going on in her life, "how old were you when you married Mama?"

"Twenty," he said, still focused on Leno and the NASCAR driver he was interviewing.

"I'm older than that," she replied, not sure he'd believe it. "And Mama was only eighteen, right?"

Her father grunted. "You're stupid when you're young." His voice lowered, sounding almost bitter. "Even stupider when you're in love."

Rachele grimaced, her upbeat mood fast deflating. Sighing, she toyed with the ring in her left eyebrow. Maybe tomorrow she should return to the Palms Piercing Parlor and get another beside it. Or perhaps a colorful tat somewhere on her neck or on her shoulder. Better yet, she could go into the bathroom right this minute and see about adding some peroxide streaks to her purplish, spiky bangs.

But none of those would change her father.

And there was already a man in her life who liked her just as she was.

The laptop computer sat on the coffee table in front of her. She reached for it, then quickly folded her legs Indian-style and balanced it on her knees. The Instant Messenger screen opened in a blaze of colors.

Papa wouldn't approve of her making a call this late at night—nice girls wouldn't!—but she could still make contact with Cal. He'd bring her back to bliss-level.

If he was logged on.

And there he was, YAUN4U—Yet Another Unix Nerd 4U—the #1 buddy on her list.

REHI, she typed, knowing it would show up on his monitor

along with her screen name, ITchick, for "Italian chick." It was hi again, though technically they hadn't even said—let alone kissed—a good night. The arrival of the security cruiser and the Carusos and company had put a kibosh on that.

Her cursor blinked without pause for long seconds. Maybe he'd left his keyboard for a soda or a bowl of cereal or—

HT

His "hi there" seemed less than enthusiastic.

MISS U, she typed quickly, needing reassurance.

The pause was longer this time, and Rachele couldn't hold out against it.

R U THERE? She typed.

HERE, YAUN4U wrote back.

For some reason the four-letter word looked pissed off.

Rachele's fingers flew. WHAT? she wrote.

WE CAN'T KEEP THIS UP.

Her stomach clenched. THIS? she wrote back. WHAT "THIS?"

SNEAKING. HIDING.

PRIVATE! She protested, glancing over at her father. ALONE TIME!

YAUN4U just repeated himself: SNEAKING. HIDING.

Rachele replayed the evening in her mind. They'd met outside the office, and Cal had lifted her up and swung her around in his arms. She'd laughed and run her fingers through his Beatles-mop, then kissed the top of his head. As he'd brought her feet back to the ground, her chin had bumped his glasses askew.

He'd looked so darn cute with them half-hanging off his face that she'd gone on tiptoe and planted a big wet kiss on his smiling mouth.

And like every other time they'd kissed before, she'd felt that Cupid-wound over her heart reopen and spill that perfect mix of exhilaration and certainty through her bloodstream.

But now Cal didn't seem as certain as she.

Was this the infamous electronic dump? A blow-off by e-mail was supposed to be bad, but via IM was ranked the lowest of the low.

R U . . . Her fingers stumbled over the letters. R U SAYING LJBF?

Let's just be friends.

NO. The answer came back with gratifying speed. I'M SAY-ING TELL YOUR FATHER ABOUT US.

Tell her father? Rachele glanced over at him, lost in Leno, so lost to her. Could she break his concentration and break the news that his daughter had another man in her life?

SOON, she typed. Soon she *would* tell him. But how would her father take the news? Would he see her finally growing up as a defection or a natural progression?

She would hate to hurt him. Hate it.

But Cal would hurt *her* if she didn't come clean, because losing him would break her heart. And then she'd be glued to the daughter seat on the den's plaid couch for the rest of her life.

Seventeen

"Let's Sit This One Out"
Vic Damone
My Baby Loves to Swing (1963)

"What the hell are you doing here?"

Standing on the sidewalk outside Johnny's front door, Téa jumped at the sound of his voice. Her fingers slipped off the tape measure's lock. Its long metal tongue, extending more than twenty feet, recoiled, the end whipping back and forth as it was pulled back into its bright yellow housing. "I'm doing my job," she said, trying to sound pleasant while not looking at him. "The one you hired me for."

There was no reason not to sound pleasant, she reminded herself, as she picked up the memo pad lying next to her briefcase to make a notation. Though their "date" on Friday night had ended abruptly—at least it felt that way to her—it didn't have a bearing on this Monday afternoon and their remaining relationship. The professional one.

From the corner of her eye, she saw him across the pool and moving closer. Taking a quick sidestep, she pressed her ankle against her briefcase, keeping herself between him and the secret she'd hidden inside.

The book. The Loanshark book.

All weekend, as she alternated between brooding over Johnny's abrupt abandonment of her outside her office—not to mention nary a phone call to apologize or to explain—and working at her sketchpad on designs for the house, the book had intruded on her concentration. Even now it seemed to call to her in a low, whispery voice.

"And what the hell are you wearing?"

This voice was crabby, abrupt, and much too close by. Téa jolted again, her startled movement knocking over her brief-case and spilling its contents. Pencils, an art eraser, a *Modernism* magazine, and a bulky black nylon makeup bag slid onto the pavement.

Téa crouched to reclaim the items, reaching for the makeup bag first.

Johnny was faster. His long fingers closed over the black nylon as he bent too. "Why are you dressed like that?"

She didn't need to look at what she was wearing. It was a simple, polished cotton shirt dress that was fastened from knees to throat with snaps. So instead she stared at his hand, holding fast to her history, holding fast to her shame. Inside the bag was a Pepto-pink pre-teen diary, the kind that came with a little brass lock and key. Both were ineffective in really keeping away eyes interested in the confessions of a twelve-year-old, but the package made a perfect disguise for the grown-up secrets of a Mafia boss. No one, not in the mob or in the FBI, had ever suspected that the Loanshark book they wanted so badly to find had always been hidden in plain sight—in the room of Salvatore Caruso's eldest daughter.

Conveniently there, because Salvatore had given his eldest daughter the responsibility of all the record-keeping, from the entering of new names to the adding and subtracting of sums. The little job that had made her feel like his most important princess.

"Téa?"

Her heart stuttered inside her chest. She hadn't seen a man's hand holding that book in sixteen years. While she'd prayed for that time to come during the first days of her father's disappearance, she'd prayed just as hard it wouldn't happen in the many, many years since.

"*Téa.*"

Johnny's bark brought her gaze to his face. And from there to the rest of him. She stared.

"What's the matter with you?" he asked. "You're silent, you're jumpy, it's near ninety outside and you're dressed in another of your nun-suits."

He wasn't dressed at all. Elegant, urbane Johnny Magee, the one who she was designing a home for filled with sophisticated decorations like a George Nelson slatted bench and Joseph Blumfeld original wool rugs, had gone jungle on her, wearing nothing more than cut-off Levis, ratty tennis shoes, scruffy whiskers, and a sweat-dotted tan.

"What have you been doing?" she replied, noting streaks of dirt across his arms and chest and a leaf in his hair. If she had to hazard a guess, she'd say he'd been working with the landscapers she'd seen about the property on her way in. In the parking area she'd squeezed her Volvo between two decrepit trucks with GUERRORO GARDENING painted on the doors and plywood walls extending the sides of beds nearly filled with palm fronds and half-decayed vegetation.

But would the urbane Johnny she knew play day laborer? Though this didn't *feel* like the Johnny she knew. Gone were the easy smiles and the facile charm. This man was a tense, bad-tempered stranger who was looking at her as if he wanted to push her away . . . and eat her up whole at the same time.

Her throat closed down, trapping the air in her chest. With

panic fluttering in her belly, she grabbed the makeup bag from him. It didn't matter what he had been doing or what he was doing to *her*. On Friday night, spooked by her mother's warning, she'd considered having sex with Johnny so she wouldn't have to be alone. Dumb. Really dumb. But now she remembered that she had a job to do, that they had a business relationship.

End of story.

Clutching the bag to the chest of her basic black shirt dress, she forced in a breath and aimed a polite smile just past him. "I was hoping to get inside and take some measurements this afternoon," she said. "I warned you that we'd be tripping over each other if you were living here while I worked, but if you want me to come back another time—"

"No," he muttered, running a hand through his hair. "No. You just surprised me, that's all."

"Okay."

He hesitated, ran his fingers over his hair once more. "I haven't been sleeping well. I apologize for . . . *shit*."

He apologized for . . . what? For being rude this afternoon? For leaving her on Friday night? For causing her to go home alone and remember the way he'd kissed her, touched her, and then left her with all the unrequited sexual lust that he'd promised in his devil's voice would be so simple to slake?

She hadn't slept well either. So she'd pulled the Loanshark book off her bedroom shelf and paged through it, studying line after line of perfect Catholic schoolgirl handwriting. For the thousandth time she'd considered shredding it or burning it or burying it deep, deep, deep in her tiny backyard, and for the thousandth time she'd wondered if her father might really be alive. If he came out of hiding, he could use the information inside the book for leverage with the Mafia or with the FBI.

And whether or not she loved him or she hated him, the mob boss's daughter continued to protect him.

It was why she'd decided to carry it with her, instead of leaving it in her empty house all day.

"That's it," Johnny suddenly bit out, pulling on the bag-covered book in her hands to bring her toward him.

"What are you doing?" she said, allowing him to tug her forward because she was unwilling to release the book. But as he drew her too close, she let go and folded her arms against her chest. "What's gotten into you?"

He shook his head. "I don't the hell know. I was just going to . . . I wanted to kiss you again."

"Well, don't." Téa flushed. "I mean, I don't want you to."

"I don't want to want to either," he replied, glaring at her. His hand slashed the book through the air in a impatient gesture. "But then you show up in the butt-ugly dress and . . . *shit.*"

And I want to strip it off you and lick you from your pretty little toes to your hot little tongue.

Oh, no, Téa thought. She wasn't going to let her imagination go wild again. Pretending she heard Johnny's voice in her head only fueled the sexual fire he ignited inside of her. But she wasn't going to burn this time.

"Look, Contessa, the fact is that I'm on a short fuse here, and—"

"You're on a short fuse? *You're* on a short fuse?" The anger she always tried to keep locked away in her mind was rattling its cabinet doors. Her grandfather was trying to rope her back into the family, her business was always on the verge of collapse or the object of public contempt, dozens of dangerous men were moving into town, all who would eagerly, literally, *kill* to find the book that was right now in the hands of the one man who had promised her miracles but paid off in misery.

Sexual misery, the lowest kind of all.

"I'll have you understand," she continued, "that I didn't ask for any of this. I could have gone along just fine, ignoring this . . . this so-called chemistry. I didn't want to know you any better than knowing whether you prefer floor lamps or hanging fixtures. But *you're* the one who told me it was 'simple,' and that I should stop my self-denial and start eating sugar again."

She lunged toward him, meaning to swipe the bagged book out of his hand.

He held onto it. "Maybe I was wrong—"

"*Maybe* you were wrong?" She tugged at the book, but he wouldn't let go. "Then *maybe* you should have figured that out before backing me up against my front door Friday night and then leaving me feeling . . . feeling—"

Realizing what she'd been about to give away, she broke off and went back to yanking on the Loanshark book.

Johnny tightened his grip. "Leaving you feeling what?" he prompted, his voice turning softer. Silkier. "Tell me, I want to know."

"Look, let's just forget about it, okay?" Now that he was gazing at her instead of glaring at her, she wanted to drop the subject.

"Perhaps we should just be honest with each other instead."

"You want honesty?" How ironic the notion was when they were holding her shameful secrets between them. But she managed to stare him straight in the eyes. "Go ahead, Johnny. You start."

He hesitated. For several long, tense moments.

She laughed as his hands relaxed and she was able to pull the makeup bag from his grasp. "It's not as easy as it sounds, is it?" With the book in her hands, she could breathe better. She tucked it back in her briefcase, stuffing it deep, then took pity on them both by doing the same with the personal turn of their conversation.

She stuffed that deep too, and returned to her professional responsibilities. "I'd like to show you some sketches I've prepared. They're preliminary, of course, but I want to make sure I'm on the right track with what you have in mind."

"Fine." He took a deep breath, let it out. "Sure." With another deep breath he strode to the front door and held it open for her.

It was pleasantly cool inside, but their footsteps clattered in the emptiness. Apparently he'd added no more furnishings besides those in the master bedroom, and she couldn't understand why he'd want to live with all the eerie echoes. "I have a few pieces in mind, a chair and a love seat, that I could get in here in a day or so, if you'd like—and if you like them," she said, glancing over at him.

He shrugged.

She crossed to the seat-level fireplace hearth, pushing aside a tall stack of newspapers to make room for them both. "They'll make you more comfortable."

"I doubt it," she thought he muttered, but then he said more loudly. "Would you like some coffee? A soda? I have sugarless."

So he was backing her no-sweets habit now. Téa ignored the little stab of disappointment and shook her head. "Come sit beside me and let me show you my sketches."

"Just a sec."

He disappeared through the front door again. She heard a splash and peered through the glass wall at the pool. But he was out as quick as he was in. In another two minutes he was back in the living room, his hair wet and a blue-and-white striped beach towel wrapped around him from hip to knees.

Certainly he still had on those low-riding Levis, right?

He seated himself on the hearth beside her. She leaned down to pull her sketchpad from her briefcase, her gaze sliding over to his long legs and the damp golden hairs already springing away from his tanned skin. She stared, fascinated, as a lone drip of pool water worked itself from somewhere above and rolled over his knee and toward his ankle.

A flush of corresponding heat rolled over her, and she jerked upright, pulling from her briefcase—the makeup bag.

"Your sketches are in there?" Johnny asked, glancing down at her lap.

"No, no." She dropped the bag like a hot potato and grasped the spirals of her sketchpad instead. With a quick flip, she located her first drawing.

She tilted it to give him a better view of the quick sketch she'd made of the house as seen from the courtyard surrounding the pool. "It's preliminary as I said, but what I propose is to return the exterior and interior walls to the sand color called for in the original plans."

"You know I don't like things around me to be boring."

Like her clothes. Like *her*? Was that why he hadn't brought her back home on Friday night? Téa pushed the thought from her mind. "The color will come from the furnishings and from the outside environment. As a matter of fact, I want to take my cue when it comes to color *from* the outside environment."

He scooted closer as she flipped another page. Her arm, bare beneath the short sleeve of her shirt dress, brushed his cool skin. Setting fire to hers.

She hugged her elbow to her ribs and swallowed hard. "Most of the wood floors in the house can be refinished, but the one here in the living room needs to be replaced. What I was thinking was mimicking the pale turquoise of the pool in a ceramic floor tile for this room. Not only would it visually extend the pool setting into the interior, but it would be cool in the hot months. In the winter, the reflection of a fire in the fireplace against the tiles would be spectacular."

"Spectacular," he murmured. His body shifted again, and his towel-covered thigh pressed against her hip.

"Well?" she asked, glancing over to find him gazing not at the sketch, but at her face. "What do you think?"

I think I want you, right here, right now.

The voice in her head matched the look in his eyes. "Johnny . . ." Her body seemed to sway toward his and, cursing her imagination, she snapped her spine straight, forcing herself upright. With a breath, she focused back on the pad and the pieces of furniture she'd drawn there.

"I can get a couple of vintage pieces from a local shop I know." She pointed her forefinger at the page. "A slat back sofa like this one and a van der Rohe lounge chair similar to this. If you like them, I can have them delivered in a couple of days. Would that make you more comfortable here?"

He traced the back of one finger down her cheek, and those gypsy violins started singing again. She saw the firelight reflected on the blue tile floor and their bodies entwined on a velvety area rug.

"I'm beginning to think only you can make me more comfortable here," he said, his voice husky and low.

"I thought we agreed to take this back to business only," Téa whispered. That's what she'd decided, right? That's what he'd made clear by leaving her alone on Friday night. By not calling on Saturday or Sunday and by barking at her on Monday afternoon. She should have known better than to think that sex would be simple, anyway.

"Business only?" he mused, his finger rubbing against her skin.

Making her look at his skin, miles and miles of golden male skin on this golden male who had told her surrendering to their mutual chemistry would be simplest for both of them.

"Business only?" he repeated.

Hearing it again woke her out of her partial hypnosis. She blinked, then looked away from his chest and the six-pack of muscle disappearing into the blue-and-white striped towel. Averting her face, she avoided another of his seductive strokes.

His hand dropped away.

She cleared her throat and waved the sketchpad in his direction. "So what do you think? To be honest, my concern is that I'm making the look too retro. It's mid-century modern, what you asked for, but does that really suit? You told me you're a man who lives in the present and looks forward to the future. It sounds as if the past might not really be your thing."

He was silent, looking down at her sketches. He stayed silent, and it was then she realized he was staring at her digital watch and not at her drawings at all.

"Johnny?"

He didn't answer. Téa put out a hand to touch him, then hesitated. Though she'd wanted their relationship to return to the impersonal, his attitude seemed much more than that. She didn't think he was hearing her, seeing her, or that he was even aware she was still in the room.

In the tense silence there was only his harsh breathing.

And then new sounds.

Pop.

Pop. Pop.

Pop. Pop. Pop.

Eighteen

"With My Eyes Wide Open"
Dean Martin
Dean Martin Sings (1952)

At the gunshot-like sounds, Johnny started, his body twitching so hard his bare foot jerked, kicking over Téa's briefcase.

"What's that?" he said, his voice low and harsh. "What's that?"

It sounded like backfire to Téa, most likely from one of those clunky old trucks belonging to Guerroro Gardening. She leaned forward, reaching for the makeup bag, which had once more slipped out and onto the ground.

Pop.

Pop. Pop.

Pop. Pop. Pop.

"*No.*" Johnny groaned the word.

Téa straightened, clutching the slick black nylon in her hands as she stared at Johnny. "Are you all right?" she asked.

His eyes looked dazed, and there was a new sheen of

dampness on his face, chest, and arms. "No," he whispered, still not blinking.

"No, you're not all right," she agreed. "What can I get you? Water? Coffee?"

He blindly reached out for her hand, found the Loanshark book instead and closed his fingers over it. "I'll be okay," he said. "I'll be okay in a minute."

Then he stood, with the movement scooping the book from her lap. He started walking, his hands still clutching her property.

Téa couldn't let the Loanshark book get far. She didn't think she should let Johnny get far either. He was moving like a sleepwalker, his head oddly still as his strides ate up the empty floor.

She caught him at the front door, curling her hand around his elbow. "Not there, Johnny." The way he was acting she thought he might walk himself straight into the pool. As a precaution, she tried prying the makeup bag from him, but he was white-knuckling the thing, so for the moment she let him keep it.

"Don't go," he suddenly said, his head whipping toward her. "Please, please don't go."

"I won't," she promised. But she wasn't sure he was seeing her. His eyes still had that dazed look in them and the sweat was now running down his face. She linked her arm with his and turned him away from the front entrance. "Let's get you cooled off."

Too much sun? A sudden flu? Maybe a sudden attack of schizophrenia, although Téa didn't believe for a second that Johnny was crazy. She thought about running to get Cal from his bungalow, but leaving Johnny alone for even that short a time didn't seem like a good idea.

His breath came in short, harsh breaths as she led him toward the master bedroom. With each of his long strides, the towel around his hips slipped. The tail came loose and she inadvertently stepped on it, pulling the material completely away from him. She stumbled over the fallen towel and bumped right into Johnny's backside.

His cool-to-the-touch, bare-assed naked backside.

Her stomach dipped, but he didn't appear to notice his nudity, so she swallowed down a breath, steadied herself, and continued guiding him into the bedroom.

"Why don't you lie down?" she suggested, drawing him toward the big bed in the corner of the room. He was a bed-maker she noted with approval. The satin coverlet was military smooth and the pillows uncreased.

She pulled back the covers and the linens smelled like detergent, dryer sheets, and that tangy scent that belonged to Johnny. With a little shove, she managed to maneuver him onto the mattress.

As she pulled a sheet over him, he found one of her hands with his free one. "It's all right," he said. "It's all right."

"Of course." She smoothed the sheet over his chest and could feel his heart pounding against her palm. A heart attack? "But maybe I should call a doctor."

"No!" He found her fingers, squeezed them again. "Don't need a doctor. Water. Need water. Need you."

She brushed her fingers through his damp hair. His forehead was clammy. "I'll get you water," she promised, then hesitated, staring at her book still squeezed by one of his big hands. She'd get his water and then she'd get her book.

In the attached bathroom, it took her a few moments to get her own breath back. She hadn't made it this far on her first tour, so she hadn't known about the sybaritic tub or the orgy-sized shower, both of which were surrounded by the same kind of mirrors that made up the bedroom ceiling.

Turning her back on the etched X-rated figures, she filled a water glass then wet a washcloth and wrung it out. With one in each hand, she returned to the bedroom.

There she found Johnny rolled onto his stomach, the sheet stretched diagonally across one hip and buttock. Asleep.

The Loanshark book nowhere in sight.

Now what?

She put the glass down on the floor then touched his face, turned in profile against a thick pillow. His skin was warmer now, no longer damp, and he was definitely sleeping, his breath easing in and out in a regular rhythm. His lashes were bristly stubs of dark gold against his cheeks and she could see shadows on his lids and under his eyes. He'd said he hadn't been sleeping, and now that she was really looking at him she could see that it was true.

But even when he was exhausted he looked beautiful.

Her gaze moved from his dark blond hair down the shallow valley of his spine to the tight, round butt that only men possessed but didn't deserve. She put out her fingertip and pressed—just to make sure the muscles were as hard as they looked—and then flushed. Joey would call the action a BL— a body liberty—and Téa had watched Eve take them dozens of times. Little pats on the butt, fingertips sliding inside the open neck of a collar, a proprietary set of nails scratching along the back of a man's hand.

Téa had never thought much about the little maneuvers, had never wanted to pet the men she dated.

But then, she'd never dated a man like Johnny.

And probably never would again.

With that sobering thought, she decided to get her book and get out of his house.

She glanced around the covers to see if he'd left it lying about. No luck. Walking around the bed, she searched to see if it had fallen to the floor.

Not there either.

"What did you do with it?" she whispered at the back of his head.

He stirred, his legs stretching wider and one hand shoving deeper beneath the pillow where he rested his cheek.

Ah-hah. That's where the book had gone, beneath the pillow.

All that she had to do was play Tooth Fairy. Heck, she didn't even need to leave a dollar behind, but she'd be happy to do so if she could get the book and get away.

She circled to the far side of the king-size bed, where his sprawled body didn't take up quite so much room. There, she slipped out of her pumps and then kneed her way from the edge of the mattress toward the pillow he was using.

He muttered something in his sleep. "Don' go. No."

Téa froze as he turned his head on the pillow to face her.

"No," he said again, his eyes still closed but his voice sounding anxious again. "Please, no."

"Shh," she whispered, her hand reaching out to caress his hair. "It's all right."

His eyelids fluttered.

She froze again, not wanting to wake him. Surely he'd be suspicious if he found her sneaking around his bed and stealing under his pillow.

He settled back into sleep with a sigh, and she let out the breath she'd been holding as well. Then she took another gulp of air, trapped it in her lungs, and slid her fingers underneath his pillow.

Her hand found the smooth inner skin of his forearm first.

She kept herself still, not breathing until she was sure she hadn't disturbed him. He didn't move, so she dared to again, inching her fingertips along the line of his arm to his wrist and then to his cupped palm. Watching his face from little more than a nose away, she spread her fingers wide, certain to encounter the edge of the bag.

And only found cool sheet and warm calluses.

She made another surreptitious search, trying to move starfish-slow.

His hand clamped down on hers.

Téa gasped and blinked, but he didn't seem to be any more awake than before. He'd merely latched onto her hand the way he'd latched onto the Loanshark book in the living room.

Great. Just great.

The position was awkward, with her arm trapped beneath the pillow and her butt in the air. Closing her eyes and gritting her teeth, she slowly straightened her legs and then twisted her body so that she was lying on her side on the mattress, mimicking Johnny's pose. His hand would relax in a minute, she thought. Then she'd slip free of him, find her book, and hightail it out of here.

Inhaling a long, calming breath, she raised her lashes.

And stared straight into Johnny's very blue eyes.

Johnny gazed at Téa's exotic face, his heart slamming against his chest, his mouth dry. He was in his bed. Naked. Just awakened from another nightmare. What the hell had happened now?

He remembered finding her outside the house. Remembered jumping into the pool to sluice off his sweat after working with the landscapers. Then he'd been in the living room with Téa, looking down at her sketches and his glance had snagged on the damn time on her watch. 1:09:09.

He'd heard popping sounds and been flung headlong into another of those living, seething memories. *Shit. Shit shit shit.*

Once again, the sounds, the sights, the smells of the flashback and the nightmare that had followed swirled around the edges of his consciousness, swirled around the very edges of the bed, trying to suck him under once again. His body shuddered.

Oh, shit.

Téa scooted nearer, wrapping her free arm around him.

He dragged her even closer and held on. "This is real," he whispered to himself against her hair. "This is real."

But the Beastie Boys were still playing somewhere in his head and a gun was lifting as his father turned off the ignition and stepped out of his car. Johnny shuddered again, trying to resist the dark lure of the memories.

"I'm here," Téa whispered, her warm breath against his face.

But he couldn't believe it without tasting her. He had to taste her to be sure that they were both alive. Rolling, he pressed her flat against the mattress. Then he put his mouth on hers.

Her lips were hot, the wet inside of them even hotter. Johnny thrust his tongue into the heat.

Yes. God, yes.

He thrust inside her mouth again and she moaned, deep in her throat. At the sound, he pushed deeper, his fingers flexing on her shoulders. This was what he needed. Her kiss, her taste, the feel of her that would keep the darkness at bay.

His lips slid off hers and slipped over her chin to the fragrant skin of her neck. Shifting for a better angle, his elbow encountered one of the pillows. With a swat of his hand, he batted it off the side of the bed. Then he pulled the other from beneath her head and tossed it away too. Tangling her hair in his fist, he tugged, arching her neck so that he could lick down the side of her throat. Her pulse beat, fast and alive, against his tongue.

She gasped as he scraped his teeth against the spot.

Reveling in her, he rubbed his cheek along her satin skin, back up to her mouth to kiss her again. Desperate for more, he slanted his head for a better fit and twined his tongue with hers. The sheet seemed to do the same to his legs, so he kicked it free, then shoved the covers off the bed with his foot.

With an elbow on each side of Téa's head, he cradled her face in his hands and let his mouth grind against hers. Her tongue played games with his, jacking up his need, jacking up the crackling heat between them. She squirmed, the slick fabric of her fastened-to-the-collarbone dress chafing his bare skin. Needing her flesh against his, Johnny curled his fingers over the neckline and yanked.

Snaps pulled free with an audible rip. Téa gasped.

Johnny froze.

The scene hit him like a slap. The bed was stripped, the covers and pillows in a drunken heap on the floor. He was sprawled on it, sprawled over Téa, naked and breathing like a racehorse. She was looking up at him with her dark cat eyes wide. There was beard burn on her chin and across her neck and he saw heaving cleavage between the edges of her dress he'd just ripped halfway to her navel.

Where was smooth Johnny Magee? She probably considered the one on top of her a madman. He should lift himself away and give her more air, if not a chance to escape.

Neither thought made him move, however, not when he wasn't done with her yet. Not when just thinking about not being skin-to-skin drew the ghosts closer to their safe oasis. Even now he could feel their cold breath blowing across the bare skin of his back.

He was a mess, God knows he was aware of that, but it was Téa who—no, *sex* that would pull him together again. He couldn't think about all the whys they shouldn't be doing this. Because it was sex that would evaporate the memories, eradicate the ghosts, and hold him in the moment. Sex that would bring the ol' you-only-like-shallow-relationships Johnny back.

He needed her—*it*. He needed it bad.

But he wouldn't go sex-monster on her again. Instead he'd be the slow and gentle lover that experience had taught him would make it good for Téa too.

Taking in a long breath, he set out to soothe, drawing the backs of his fingers down her cheek then brushing his knuckles back and forth across her swollen bottom lip.

She closed her eyes. "Johnny—"

"Shh. Quiet," he said, still rubbing against her bottom lip. "You'll like this, I promise."

I need this. Bad.

He leaned forward and replaced his fingers with his mouth, grazing hers with the lightest, softest strokes. She trembled and he smiled to himself, then slicked his tongue against that same puffy lip.

She trembled again and a burst of need sped through him like a bullet. But Johnny refused to let it drive him. Gentle, he told himself. Slow and gentle. Bending closer, he pressed a series of featherweight kisses against her mouth.

Her hands came up to his shoulders. "Yes," he murmured against her mouth. "Touch me."

Her palms caressed his skin, sliding down his spine.

On the other side of his body, his cock twitched against his belly as if trying to get closer to her touch. But he reminded himself he was a man of style, not speed, and laid another sweet seductive kiss on her.

She moaned, her fingernails biting into his skin.

His cock jumped. His temperature spiked. "Easy," he murmured against her mouth, curling his fingers into fists on either side of her body. "Easy."

Her head swished against the sheet and the ends of her long hair slid across the backs of his hands. He tangled them in the stuff to hold her still and took the kiss just a little deeper.

Téa bit his tongue.

Heat shot up his back. Without his permission, one of his hands shifted, closing over one of her breasts.

They both groaned.

Finesse, Johnny, he reminded himself desperately. *Don't forget finesse.* But the bra she was wearing was some stiff cage of a thing that didn't come close to giving up what he wanted. What he had to have.

He yanked the sides of her dress apart, spotted the front clasp of her bra, tripped the damn mechanism and then, God—*oh my God*—her bare breasts spilled into his hands.

A man with his kind of polish and years of experience shouldn't have been stunned. A man who'd lived in Las Vegas for the last decade had seen hooters aplenty, after all. But Johnny could only stare at the most beautiful, absolutely perfect, how-the-hell-did-she-hide-them-away? pair of knockers he'd ever seen in his life. The tennis dress she'd worn on Friday night had not done them justice either. Only nakedness perfectly suited these beauties.

That speeding bullet of desire shot through his nervous system again as he tried to hold them in his hands. They overflowed his palms, their warm weight soft and fragrant. Her aureoles were a dusky pink that turned to raspberry as he ran his thumbs over her nipples. His cock twitched again as they tightened to his touch.

Her fingers circled his wrists. He glanced at her face and saw her eyes were wide and nervous again. Gulping in a breath, he gentled his touch but didn't take his hands away. "So pretty," he whispered, not wanting to spook her. He ran slow thumbs over the stiff crests. "So damn pretty."

Keeping his gaze on hers, he bent to suck one into his mouth. At the first touch of tight nipple to the flat of his tongue, her eyes closed and her face flushed.

The sign of her desire sent him hurtling over the edge once more.

Forgetting finessing, he sucked her into his mouth. Sucked hard. She made a sound of pleasure and he closed his eyes too, giving himself up to her generous flesh. Heat suffused his body as his tongue circled her nipple, and he played with the other between his fingers. Téa moved one of her legs and his erection had a happy meeting with her outer thigh.

Switching his mouth to her other breast, he pressed himself against her, his hips rolling in the same rhythm that he used on her nipple. She gave another pleasure-moan and one of her hands drifted across his naked chest. Desire surged through him again and he ground his cock against her leg.

Her fingernails grazed across his chest. He bit her nipple and shoved his hand beneath the skirt of her dress.

Then he touched her panties and found them wet.

A hot shudder burned down his spine and he ground harder against her outer thigh.

"That's it," he choked out, lifting his head. "It's now. You're ready, and if we keep this up I'll come on the side of your leg." He barely heard his hoarse voice utter the words and decided he'd be appalled by them later.

There were condoms in the table on Téa's side of the bed. To pull open the drawer, he leaned across her body. She licked his chest.

His hand fell off the drawer pull.

Her little tongue stroked him again.

He managed to hang onto the metal knob the next time, gritting his teeth against the raging lust that her tongue incited so that he could locate the foil-wrapped square with fumbling fingers. Even as he rolled back, he was using his teeth to rip open the package. His hands were shaking, but he covered himself with the condom and French-kissed her at the same time.

For a man in need, it was quite a feat.

Then he kneeled between her legs and went back to her breasts. But those wet panties and what was underneath them couldn't be ignored, so he pushed up her skirt and pulled down the silky undergarment. He only got it as far as her knees before he was distracted by the plump folds, already opening for him.

The uncivilized man that Johnny was today didn't wait for a second invitation. Holding the base of his cock, he insinuated the tip between those wet folds and then pushed home.

She gasped, arching into him with her eyes closed and her mouth half-open. He filled that too, pressing his tongue between her lips. Heat rocketed up his spine.

He rocked between her legs.

It was so good. So damn good.

In a minute he'd slow down. Find the finesse again. Use all the little slow and gentle touches that would please her. He'd know-how her into the most mind-blowing orgasm of her life.

But first . . . but first—

His hand found her breast. The nipple poked into his palm and he slid it between two of his fingers and squeezed it in the same rhythm that he squeezed himself in and out of her tight hold.

She tilted her hips to take him deeper and then did something with her inner muscles that had the hunger in him screaming for mercy. "Fuck," he said, because it was the only thing on his mind, in his mind, the only thing that Mr. Style and Polish could manage to say at the moment that he . . .

. . . came.

"Fuck," he said again, his hips pumping to wring out every last drop of pleasure from the best climax he could remember.

He collapsed onto her warm body, his face buried in her Téa-scented hair.

He'd been right, he thought minutes later, as one cylinder of his brain started functioning again. He'd been a mess, but sex had put him together again. Sex with Téa had most definitely planted him back in the present because he couldn't think of anything beyond her sweet heat and how he was going to get his next breath into his lungs.

Téa.

God, *Téa.* He'd done the selfish sex-monster thing and finished without her. It was something he hadn't done in more than a dozen years, thank you God and the very vocal Linda Bowers, who'd taught him about female anatomy and the joy of giving good sex.

He pushed up, then rolled off Téa. "Contessa. Honey," he said. "I haven't forgotten you. Just give me a second and I'll—" He broke off as he took in the aghast expression on her face.

She wasn't looking at him. She was staring up at the ceiling.

Johnny glanced up to see what had horrified her. It wasn't one—or more—of the etched figures in the mirror, though. Her place on the bed hadn't put her in any of the many possible compromising positions.

Her reflection just showed Téa, her face still flushed, her hair spread around her, a mass of riotous waves. The top of her dress was unsnapped, her stupendous breasts thrusting through the opening. The hem was pushed up toward her hips, showing her splayed legs, pretty sex, and a pair of nude-colored panties circling one knee.

It was enough to get him hot again and his cock started on the rise.

"Contessa," he murmured, running a finger up her thigh.

Her legs came crashing together, rejecting his touch. Her gaze jumped from the ceiling, to his face, to a blank wall on the other side of the room. "I'm a mess," she said, her movements a blur as she jumped off the bed. "A mess."

In the blink of an eye she was gone. He heard the front door slam.

Mess.

He'd wanted to pull himself together from the mess *he'd* been. He'd wanted to anchor himself firmly in the present.

And in doing so, he'd somehow just messed up everything between him and Téa.

Nineteen

"I've Been Too Busy"
Sammy Davis, Jr.
Mr. Wonderful (1956)

Later that afternoon, Johnny did what any self-respecting older sibling would do—he decided to take his lousy mood out on his younger brother. He brought Cal along with him to Michael Magee's bar, The Bivy, in nearby Half Palm. The forty-five-minute trip was much too long a time to be alone with his own thoughts and the man who he glimpsed in the rearview mirror. Johnny didn't recognize himself anymore.

It wasn't yet five when he pushed open the front door of the plain stucco building. This bar wasn't the favored watering hole of the Coachella Valley's wealthy set, it was the place where climbers from around the world relaxed after a day scaling the massive boulders in Joshua Tree National Park or the granite peaks of the San Jacinto range.

A lean, dark-eyed, dark-haired man with a stubbled jaw looked up from behind the bar as they walked inside. He crossed his arms over the ratty T-shirt that he wore with equally ratty jeans and raised a brow at Johnny. "I think you dudes have the wrong joint. Go back out the parking lot, turn left, and your first country club will be on the right, about thirty miles due south."

"We'll take a couple of bottles of Corona first," Johnny replied, hitching up his khakis to slide onto one of the barstools. "If there's a clean glass to be found in a dump like this."

"Only pussies drink their nondraft beers from a glass," the bartender said, plunking a couple of sweating bottles in front of the two men. "So then it must really be you, Johnny."

"It'll be just like old times to kick your ass, Michael." Johnny smiled at his younger brother, his mood beginning to lighten. "I can't wait."

Then they shook hands, each trying to outgrip the other. The battle lasted for ninety seconds before they broke apart, both of them grinning.

"Dog," Michael said, leaning across the bar again to smack Johnny on the side of his arm. "Took you long enough to get over here. I thought I was going to have to mail out an engraved invitation."

Johnny shrugged. "I had things to do." The fact was, he'd been in no hurry to make contact. While he loved his family, he'd always felt outside the little genetic circle of Phineas, his mother, and half-brother Michael.

But after that uncharacteristic, out-of-body episode in his bed with Téa this afternoon, he figured he'd benefit from spending some time with his nearest living male relative. It would remind him of exactly who he was. Smooth, cool Johnny who would never be fixated on the past. Smooth, cool Johnny who would never leave his bed partner flat.

He tipped his beer bottle toward Cal. "This is Cal Kazarsky. Cal, meet my low-life little brother."

They shook hands. "Cool shirt," Cal commented to Michael.

His brother glanced down at his chest and smiled. The slogan of the day read: DON'T WORRY, IT ONLY SEEMS KINKY THE FIRST TIME. "I had to sneak it past Felicity. As much as I love the woman, she has no appreciation for my T-shirt humor."

"How is the new Mrs. Magee?" Johnny asked. His brother had married just a few months before.

"See for yourself." Michael picked up a remote control and thumbed it on. The television mounted overhead blazed to life, displaying the GetTV home shopping channel logo across the bottom and an irrepressible Felicity Charm Magee center screen.

Cal scooted his barstool closer. "Hey, I recognize that woman. I've always liked her."

Michael shook his head in sympathy. "Everybody does. But she belongs to me."

Cal was already engrossed in the details of the product Felicity was selling. Michael glanced at the screen, then Cal, then finally Johnny. "Should we wrestle his wallet from him until she goes off air? She could cost him a bundle."

Johnny shrugged. "He can afford a bundle. He works for the syndicate."

"Still pulling in the dough, huh?"

"You know me." Yes, it had been a good idea to come here, he decided, tilting back his head to take another swallow of beer. Already he was feeling more like himself. Johnny Magee, successful professional gambler. Johnny Magee, who was successful because he was the kind of man who operated in a completely objective and unemotional manner.

That was the true secret to success at gambling. Once you made decisions based on anything but logic, you were already a loser. Pure detachment was the best mind-set with which to play—at gambling and at life.

"Yeah, I know you," Michael said, leaning on the counter behind him and crossing his arms over his chest again. "And you look like hell, Johnny. What's going on?"

Unwilling to let his brother's pronouncement ruin his happier mood, Johnny examined the label on his bottle of beer, running his finger around the edges. "Is it my fault you have no appreciation for good tailoring and shirts that don't come complete with their own raunchy worldview?"

"Oh, you still appear to have walked off page seventy-eight of this month's *GQ*, and Felicity goes ga-ga over those kind of looks so I might have to deck you, but that's not what I'm talking about. There's something in your eyes."

"It's the desert, it's dry—"

"It's serious bullshit you're trying to sell me, brother."

"*Half*-brother." Johnny didn't know what made him say it. No, that was bullshit too. He was warning Michael off, telling him he was getting too close. Johnny Magee, slick, cool Johnny Magee, liked his conversations, just like his relationships, shallow.

"The Heisman isn't going to work on me this time, Johnny."

The expression startled a laugh out of him. He hadn't thought of it in years, the reference to the stiff-armed position of the Heisman Memorial college football trophy that was Magee family code for keeping someone at bay. "How is Phineas, by the way?"

"Dad's a little busy."

"Oh?" Johnny inspected the beer label again.

"Yeah, he's spending a lot of time tying Mom to chairs in order to keep her from flying down here and saving your ass."

He jerked up his head to stare at his brother. "What the hell do you mean by that?"

"You think she hasn't figured out why you all of a sudden picked up your tent and hauled it down to Palm Springs? She's been terrified of your father's mob connections for years."

"We don't know that there *are* mob connections, damn it." Or mob criminal activity, either. The Mafia and his father's murder had rarely been spoken of in the same breath within the Magee household, but it had always been there, just something else setting Johnny apart from the rest of the family.

But he had to face the possibility that there was a real connection, now that neighbor Phillip believed it could be true. It was why Johnny had changed his mind on Friday night about taking Téa to bed. He'd figured she'd never forgive him or herself for making love with the son of the man who'd killed her father. But now he'd blown that scruple all to hell, hadn't he?

Worse, he hadn't done something as civilized as make love to her. He'd lost his mind then lost himself inside her body.

And gave her nothing back.

Michael stepped closer, his gaze on Johnny's face. "Are you trying to tell me this relocation isn't about the Carusos?"

Johnny hesitated. Bluffing was second nature, but lies never came easy.

"He told me we moved here for you," Cal tossed into the conversation, his gaze still glued to the TV screen. "To be nearer to you and your new wife."

This time it was Michael who laughed. "You're too good at this, Johnny. But it won't work with me. You need to save your fish stories for the part of the world that isn't related to you."

"I came to your wedding," Johnny protested. Damn it, that *"you're too good at this"* remark didn't sit well with him. First, it had come out of anchorwoman LaDonna's mouth and now Michael's. It was as if they thought he was only skin-deep.

For God's sake, he only wanted to live that way.

"But you've been little more than a ghost to Mom and the rest of the Magees for at least the past decade."

Actually, for the last sixteen years, Johnny thought. When he'd returned home following his father's murder he'd been numb. Not numb enough that he hadn't noticed his family's worried looks or their attempts to draw him back in. But getting close had meant getting personal, and he hadn't wanted such intimate attachments anymore. Not with people, not to his own emotions.

He sighed. "Listen, Michael. I'll call Mom . . . soon. I'll reassure her that—"

"Oh, that you're *not* looking into your father's death? For God's sake! The Carusos are dangerous. You're the one who told *me* that a few months back. You know what happened to Felicity's cousin."

"The woman doing the interior design of Johnny's new house is named Caruso," Cal piped up again. "Téa Caruso."

Michael groaned. "Johnny—"

"She's pretty hot," Cal added, "Not that I'm interested in her. But I think your brother might be."

Michael groaned again, louder. "Johnny, no. You can't be thinking what I'm thinking you're thinking. I know about those Caruso girls. Felicity went to school with them. If your idea of a righteous vendetta against that family is screwing one of th—"

"I'm not screwing Téa!" Well, shit, the truth was, he had. "I don't *screw* women." Not usually, anyway, which was what made the afternoon's episode with the contessa so unconscionable. Mr. Slick, Mr. Cool Johnny Magee didn't have relationships on the heart-to-heart level, that was certain, but he did a damn thorough job on the body-to-body level. He prided himself on that. That was who he *was*.

Michael stood over him, shaking his head. "These people are killers, Johnny."

"You don't think I know that?"

"You break the daughter's heart and you might get more than your leg broken in return."

"I'm not breaking anyone's heart." But hell, he'd done *something* to Téa. The contessa had stared up into that mirror, aghast, and declared herself a "mess." What kind of asshole let a woman leave his bed with a comment like that?

Especially when she'd looked as erotic and enticing as hell to him. Just the memory made him sweat.

"Damn," Cal said. He'd pulled out his phone and was looking down at it in consternation. "I want to buy that bracelet Felicity is selling for . . . for someone I know."

"There's no cell service in Half Palm," Michael told Cal. "Consider yourself lucky. I know I do. It's how I met my wife."

Johnny polished off his beer, then stood up. "Come on, Cal, I'll take you back to civilization and you can make your call from there." He had things to do in Palm Springs as well, he decided, suddenly certain of his next move. It was time to even the score with a Caruso, all right.

With *Téa* Caruso.

It would be a start on reclaiming his identity that had been on unwelcome hiatus since his thirty-third birthday, the date those nightmares and flashbacks had begun. Mr. Slick, Mr. Cool Johnny Magee knew how to make a woman happy in the sack. He had to prove to himself that while he might be losing his mind, he hadn't lost *that*.

Twenty

"Girl Talk"
Bobby Troup
Feeling of Jazz (1955)

Téa studied the rows of hair styling products for sale at the front of the Kona Kai Spa's beauty salon. Tight Control, Helmet Control, Iron Control, all of them sounded like something she could use . . . and not just on her hair. Frowning, she combed her fingers through the heavy mass and wondered why the pricey straightening process couldn't seem to keep her waves tamed these days.

"Well, well, well," an amused voice—Eve's—said. "This isn't my sister, Téa Caruso, is it, playing hooky on a Tuesday, at eleven o'clock in the morning?"

"I had an hair emergency," Téa answered. Not to mention she was looking for any excuse to keep herself away from Johnny's house today. Forever.

"It looks fine to me." Eve was dressed in something Donna Karan probably dreamed up, her hair in an effortless fall of blonde, her makeup nearly invisible.

"It needs to be straight," Téa insisted, pulling on the ends as she looked back at the pumps and aerosols. "Perfectly straight."

"It *is* perfectly straight."

"It doesn't stay that way," Téa grumbled, then she lowered her voice and told the truth, because if anyone might have some good advice for a woman on the morning-after, it would be Eve. "It doesn't stay that way in bed."

"In bed?" Her sister sounded puzzled.

Téa whispered this time. "In bed with a man."

Eve didn't say anything more, but Téa felt her stunned stare all the same.

She turned to frown at her sister. "Is it so hard to believe that a man would want to . . . to . . . you know, with me?"

Eve blinked. "No, no, it's not that. Not that at all." She put out a hand and touched Téa's arm. "It's that I haven't thought *you* wanted to . . . to . . . you know, in quite some time."

Because Téa had decided it was safer to be like their mother—single, celibate, successful. She still did. It was how to keep her secrets locked tight and her heart locked whole inside her chest. No sense in risking falling in love and wanting to marry because no respectable man would want to wed the Mafia association that would walk down the aisle with her. "It was a mistake, obviously."

"Obviously, why?"

For starters, because she'd gone there that morning with the express purpose of doing business and nothing more. "He manages to get to me somehow. I don't like it."

"Meaning he turns you on in a way that all those great-nephews and grandsons in your dating past never managed to."

"He probably thinks I'm easy," Téa muttered, remembering how she'd looked in the mirrored ceiling. Her dress in disarray, her hair a wild mass, her underwear ringing one leg. She'd *felt* easy. He'd grabbed onto her in an obvious need for comfort and then she'd let that slide into a delirious roller-coaster ride of afternoon delight.

Eve laughed the throaty laugh of a woman who'd loved and left a thousand men . . . and left them wanting more. "We're not fifteen any longer. Forget all that guilt the nuns fed us. Real women experience lust."

Experiencing lust wasn't the problem. Acting on it might be. Téa distrusted the sensation that it was her body taking over and leaving her control and common sense behind. "Anyway, the sex wasn't that good." Not that sex ever was.

Eve raised an eyebrow. "Then you weren't doing . . . you know, with Johnny Magee?"

Téa half-turned back toward the hair products. "What does the *who* have to do with anything?"

"He looks like he'd be good in bed, that's all. There's a certain . . . twinkle in his eyes."

"He *is* good in bed. It wasn't him." She didn't know about the twinkle, but she knew he was long and golden and hard. His mouth set her on fire. When his tongue pressed inside her mouth she melted, just like that, her body ready for him. It had never been like that for her, never. The excitement of the lead-up had been more than she'd ever expected or experienced.

But when it came to satisfaction, she'd always been better off on her own, without a witness.

Eve sighed. "Téa, Téa, Téa—"

"I don't know what to do now, okay?" She swung around to face her sister. If she wasn't envious of Eve's beauty, she would give just about anything for an ounce of Eve's sexual sangfroid. "How am I supposed to look him in the eye and do my job when the last time he saw me I was—" *Flushed and wet and sprawled across the bed.* She shivered thinking about it.

Eve gave her a little smile. "I'll tell you exactly what you should do about it. Listen to Big Sister Eve and I'll clear it all up."

Téa rolled her eyes. "Big Sister Eve is younger than me by four months," she pointed out dryly.

"But decades older when it comes to men. So here's my advice—"

A speeding body whipped through the salon doors. "That's it!" Joey slid to a halt in front of them, the gauzy skirt of her pale green dress whipping around her knees. "I'm buying a gun and I'm going to learn how to use it."

"Shh!" Téa said, glancing around to make sure no one had overheard. "Do you think that's the kind of thing someone with the Caruso last name should go about screaming at the top of her lungs?"

"I don't care," Joey said, sparks snapping in her dark eyes. "If I'm going to be called a kettle, I might as well be black."

"Shh," Téa said again, though she doubted anyone could decipher her little sister's last statement. "Keep your voice down."

Joey flapped her arms, impatient, as always, with any kind of restraint. "You have no idea what just happened to me."

A man strolled past the salon doors, that silver-haired boxer type that Téa had seen the week before in the gym. He glanced at the three of them, and gave a little nod. Though he moved on, the attention made her wary.

"Let's get smoothies from the juice bar and sit out by one of the pools," she said, grabbing each sister by the arm. "We can find someplace private to finish our conversation."

Three skinny berry coolers later, they found a place in the partial shade of a large umbrella. Some spa guests were enjoying the warm sunshine as well—a European couple in matching thong bottoms and suntan oil, a recovering plastic surgery patient in face bandages and oversized sunglasses, a woman drying her wet pedicure while waiting for her next beauty treatment. Téa breathed in the air perfumed by flowers and grass and felt herself relax.

Joey was more docile too, thank God, though she was quieted by the brain freeze she'd experienced with her first hit of icy drink. The girl didn't have a cautious bone in her body, Téa thought, and she was paying for it now. Her eyes scrunched shut, Joey collapsed into a lounge chair, her fingers pinching the bridge of her nose. "What were you guys talking about when I showed up?"

Eve lifted her flawless profile to the sky. "Téa's had you know with Johnny Magee."

"*Eve*."

One of Joey's eyes popped open. "No kidding. I thought you'd sworn off—wait a minute, why are we calling it 'you know'?"

"You know," Eve said, smiling.

Joey nodded. "Oh yeah, because Téa's a prude."

"I'm not a prude."

"Of course you are," Eve replied. "That's why my advice is that you should you know with Johnny some more. Many times."

Joey nodded in agreement again. "Oh, yeah, I think he has great prude-eradication potential. You might even be tardy a time or two after you-knowing your brains out. Would make the rest of us mortals feel a little better about our punctuality habits."

Téa stared at her sisters. "Your advice is that I go right back into the situation that made me feel awkward in the first place?" Then she crossed her arms over her chest, hoping she wasn't sounding as shrill as she was beginning to feel. "And just why, exactly, do the two of you think you know so much about Johnny and his ability to . . . to . . . you know?"

Joey had the answer to that one. "Because any person with eyes can see he's a bad boy, Téa, and a bad boy is *exactly* what you need."

"An elegant bad boy," Eve added, "which is the only kind that can possibly meet your high standards."

And get beneath her defenses.

But she couldn't let him.

"Plus," Joey added, "There's the way he looks at you. Like you're a lollipop and he's one big tongue."

"Eww—" Téa started, then broke off. "Really?"

But honest to God, that's the way Johnny made her feel— sweet, and oh-so-lickable. But her feelings weren't a good reason to get further involved. Anyway, he might not want to, considering the small fact that he hadn't been himself before waking up and finding her holding his hand in his bed. He was likely regretting what happened as much as she.

Joey slid a glance at Eve. "Let's tell her we'll put all her bras in the freezer again if she doesn't agree to you know with him."

Eve smiled. "Let's tell her we'll kidnap her and take her to Grandpa's party."

Téa clunked her smoothie onto the table beside her. She should have known her sisters wouldn't leave that issue alone forever, especially after she'd rebuffed Cosimo's "invitation" a few nights before. "No—"

"Who's that?" Joey suddenly said, shooting up straight in her chair. "That man over there with the silver hair?"

Téa glanced back. The man with the broken nose was across the pool, drying his chest with a towel. He caught Téa's gaze and gave her another little nod of recognition. "A guest. He's been here about a week, I think." Nervous tingles were running up her back again. "Why?"

Joey leaned back in her chaise. "A week? I doubt he's another Fed, then. The rumors about Nonno's impending retirement aren't that old. And with a nose like that . . . he doesn't have a chance of blending in like those other rat-faced bastards try to do."

"I take it those are the rats you're planning to take your target practice on?" Eve asked.

"*Shh*!" Téa said. "Geez. Can't you guys keep it down?"

Joey set her jaw. "I'm ready to tell the world what I think about the Federal Bureau of Ignoramuses. A thug, paid for by yours and mine tax dollars, tried shaking me down in Starbucks today."

"What?" Alarm stiffened Téa's spine. "What are you talking about?"

"I was picking up a latte this morning at my usual Starbucks, at my usual time. I gave my name, and when the barista called out that my drink was ready, a man picked it up before I could. Then he showed me federal ID and let me know that our friends in black have their eyes on us, now that the family leadership is in flux."

Sighing, Eve shook her head. "It's to be expected."

Joey's eyes went round. "It's to be '*expected*'? It's to be *rejected*. We put up with enough hassles after Dad disappeared."

Enough hassles was an understatement, that was certain. They'd been followed, questioned, and followed some more. For three little princesses bewildered by their missing king, it had been cruel.

Téa's stomach clenched, remembering how quickly she'd gone from feeling beautiful in her father's eyes to seeing herself as the FBI must have—as a self-important lump of preadolescence. Just like that, an all-too-familiar sense of chaos began closing in on her. This was what happened, she reminded herself, when she let her mob ties pull tight. Taking deep breaths of the warm, perfumed air, she resisted the frightening sense of disorder, focusing only on the beautiful surroundings.

Wouldn't it be nice to stay poolside at the spa forever? Wouldn't it be nice to be enclosed in a jewel box of emerald grass and turquoise water for all time? No wonder her mother was so content here.

But this wasn't her safe place. There wasn't one, she knew that.

Her cell phone rang, and with her mind preoccupied, she

reached for it, flipped it open, and brought it to her ear without looking at the caller's ID. "Hello?"

"I was hoping I would see you today," Johnny said.

Flushed and wet and sprawled across the bed.

But those were her thoughts, in her voice, that she heard this time in her head. "I . . . I've been working on the designs for your house at my office."

Joey let out another of her unladylike snorts.

"I tried calling you last night," he said. "And this morning."

"Oh. Well." She'd turned off her home phone last night and only powered on her cell phone an hour ago. "Sorry."

"I think that's my line." He paused. "We need to talk."

Oh, God. Talk? Why did they have to talk? What possessed the man to want to rehash something that had made her look—and *sound*—so disheveled and disordered? She didn't need to hear him say it was a mistake, she knew that already.

"Téa?"

"What?"

He sighed. "You wouldn't be hiding from me, would you?"

"Of course not."

"Because you sure as hell surprised me with what you are hiding beneath those librarian dresses and Iron Maiden br—"

"Johnny." He was doing it again, making her all flushed and damp and disturbed. "Does this phone call have a point?"

He sighed again. "The point I want to make involves a person-to-person visit. When will you be by again?"

Téa hesitated. "Maybe . . . maybe not for some time. I've been thinking of giving Rachele, my assistant, a bit more responsibility. She'll be the one you'll be seeing at the house."

On the lounge chair opposite, Joey was flapping her elbows and clucking like a silent *pollo*. Téa pretended not to notice.

"Well. Hmm. That might be a problem. I have something of yours here."

She froze. Something of hers? What? Had she left a piece of clothing behind? But no, while her bra had been pushed up and her panties pushed down, her dress half-opened like a wicked, impassioned woman's, she'd been able to stumble to his front door with everything intact. She'd even remembered to scoop up her shoes.

"It's a little black bag."

Téa squeezed the phone so tight she heard the plastic snap. The makeup bag. The Loanshark book. Oh God. Oh God. He'd made her so muddled she'd run out of his house and left the Loanshark book behind.

She'd been on the hunt for it when he'd opened his eyes and then she'd been lost.

And lost all sense. And sense of self-preservation.

"I need to get that," she said quickly, her voice hoarse. "As soon as it's convenient."

"How about six o'clock tonight?" he suggested, his voice as soft as hers had been rough. "I've found something else you might like to see too."

And though he sounded like the devil again, Téa didn't flinch. She'd put her feet on the road to hell a long, long time ago.

Twenty-one

"The Girl from Ipanema"
Stan Getz/Joäo Gilberto
Getz/Gilberto (1963)

Dusk was overtaking day as Téa climbed the steps toward the deck surrounding Johnny Magee's pool. At the sound of splashing, she hesitated, then forced herself forward. That he was swimming—with or without swim trunks—didn't matter. The Loanshark book mattered. She was going to get it and get out.

But it wasn't Johnny frolicking in the pool. Téa stared at the two twined figures outlined by the greenish glow of the pool light. "Rachele? Cal?"

The pair broke apart. "Oh, hi, boss," Rachele said. She swiped her bangs from her eyes. "You remember Cal."

The man sketched a wave.

"Of course I remember Cal," Téa said. "I didn't realize the two of you were, uh, spending time together." A niggle of uneasiness twisted in her belly as she wondered if Rachele's father had a clue either. But the younger woman was swishing through the water toward Téa, wearing a black bikini and such a wide smile that she didn't have the heart to mention it.

"We're playing lookout for Johnny," Rachele said. Instead of toying with one of her many piercings, her fingers reached up to touch a plumeria blossom poked in her wet purple hair. "He asked us to send you in the right direction."

"I know my way into the house."

Rachele's smile widened. "He's not in the house. You're supposed to follow the path to the guest bungalows and then cross through the golf course. You'll see where to go from there. He has a surprise for you."

The uneasiness in Téa's stomach coiled tighter. "I'm only here to retrieve something I left behind. Maybe you could go get it from him for me."

"He wants you."

"No, he doesn't!" Téa cleared her throat. "I mean, there's no reason for me to disturb him."

"He's waiting for you," Rachele said, then ended the conversation by executing a porpoise dive to the bottom of the pool. In the next instant, Cal was jerked beneath the surface of the water. The couple became a tangle of limbs and young love.

Obviously dismissed and oddly depressed, Téa sighed and headed off as directed. Leaving behind the desert setting of the main house, she walked beyond the guest bungalows and through the golf course toward the green overgrowth that might have been planned as a lush desert oasis but was now an untamed jungle of palms, bushes, and vines. Though neglected, it obviously still received its fair share of the life-giving underground water table that had brought green and golf to the desert.

Rachele's "you'll see where to go" became obvious as Téa spied a burning tiki torch at the far edge of Johnny's Hole 3. The oily scent of the burning citronella beckoned her onto a narrow path cut through the morass of plant life. She followed stepping stones buried in the damp soil and came across another tiki torch, and then another, and then the path opened onto a lone, three-sided structure surrounded by vines and palms and more tiki torches. A nearby pile of plywood sheets explained the absence of a fourth wall.

Inside the one-room building, illuminated by a camping lantern, was Johnny, lounging on a wicker love seat with his feet propped on a matching wide wicker ottoman. He spread his arms to indicate the 20 × 20 enclosure. "Look what I found," he said.

That tiki room they'd heard about at the tennis party, of course. Now that she'd found Johnny, she should just demand her makeup bag and be on her way, but despite her lingering embarrassment, curiosity compelled her to walk inside. She set down her briefcase, then slowly spun to take it all in. The linoleum floor was a natural moss green and the interior walls were covered by simple bamboo screening material accented by fishing nets dotted with blown-glass floats. Here and there hung large framed travel posters for Hawaii and Polynesia. Vintage posters, she recognized right away, and probably worth a bundle.

Besides the love seat and the ottoman, there was an awe-inspiring set of furniture—bar and bar stools—that appeared to be hand-carved. Koa wood, Téa guessed, depicting a squat figure with the bent knees and ET-sized head that was typically tiki. The same little glowering gargoyle was cut into the face of the bar and he also appeared to be holding up the polished seats of the round stools.

Téa drew closer, squinting to get a better look at the pieces in the dim lantern light. Were they ugly or beautiful? "I can't decide if I'm horrified or fascinated," she said.

"Take a look below his waistline and let me know," Johnny replied, rising from the love seat.

Téa glanced over at him, distracted by the movement. In bare feet, putty colored cotton trousers, and a half-buttoned white linen shirt, he looked calm and casual.

Her pulse jumped and she jerked her gaze away from him and back to the tiki man. Below his waist, Johnny had said. She lowered her eyes. "Huuh." The startled sound escaped her lips as she stared at the carvings.

"So what do you think?" Johnny asked from close behind her.

Téa swallowed. "I can't imagine what Tiki-Man is looking so grim about." Because Tiki-Man was hung. In intricately carved detail, he was *well*-hung.

Johnny laughed, then reached past her for two cocktail glasses sitting beside a glass pitcher on top of the bar. His hands stalled as in the distance there was an exuberant male whoop, followed by a flurry of giggles and running feet.

"You can't catch me!" Téa heard Rachele shriek in laughing excitement.

"Just you wait," Cal shouted back.

Johnny cocked his head, a grin tugging at his lips. "Sounds like we're all on the hunt tonight."

Téa froze. The hunt? What did he mean by that?

He picked up both drinks and nudged one into her hand, then tapped the rim of his glass against hers. "To—?"

Apprehension broke out like goose bumps all over her skin as she stared into the fruity scented liquid. "I shouldn't stay for a drink." The hunt, he'd said. Had he really said *the hunt*?

A chill ran over her again. When it came right down to it, she was alone in the dark night with a virtual stranger. A stranger she'd had sex with, but still, a man she didn't know at all well. It was a dangerous situation. And she'd vowed at twelve to stay away from those for the rest of her life.

She cleared her throat. "I came to get my bag and then I'll get out of your way."

"I already tucked it into your briefcase," he said, gesturing over her shoulder. "You have a hot date tonight?"

With her guilty conscience and her bitter regrets. "Well, I, um—"

"Is that why you did a world-record dash out of my bed yesterday? You're involved with someone?"

Women the globe over knew to utter this little white lie when necessary. It's how you got out of lunching with the nice but nerdy engineer behind you in the DMV line or from having coffee with the ex-brother-in-law of your manicurist's best friend. "Are you?" Téa asked him instead.

Johnny raised a brow, and in the lantern light she saw that ghost of a grin curve the edges of his mouth again. "If I was married, don't you suppose you'd be dealing, at least some of the time, with my wife?"

She looked him straight in the eye and told the absolute truth. "My grandfather runs a multi-million-dollar food company, but is also reputed to be the leading California crime boss. When I was three, my father brought home another daughter for my mother to raise. Another daughter, just a few months younger than me, whom he'd fathered with his longtime mistress. Not many years after that, he disappeared one day and never came back. So the truth is, Johnny, when it comes to men I don't suppose anything."

And she'd learned not to give them her heart.

Her mouth dried out by the long-winded answer, she lifted her glass and took a bracing swallow. Then choked. Coughed. Choked some more.

Johnny clapped her on the back as she fought the tears in her eyes. "What *is* this?" she managed to get out, though it was more wheeze than question. It had smelled like fruit juice.

"A zombie mai tai. I found the recipe in the bar along with some sixteen-year-old rum." He picked up the pitcher and topped off her glass.

Whatever it was in the drink that had made her eyes water was blazing a molten path to her stomach. Johnny clinked their rims again, and when he took a swallow, she took a cautious one too, just to make sure it was as lethal as she remembered.

The second sip, however, went down sweet and smooth.

She stared into the glass, wondering if he'd somehow managed to detoxify the concoction, and then took another test swallow.

"So, to answer your question more directly," Johnny said, refilling her glass again. "I'm not married."

Téa licked an errant drip off her bottom lip. "Divorced?" Not that she cared or anything, him being a stranger and all.

Johnny smiled at her. "*Never* married."

"Well. Fine. That's . . . uh, fine." How had this conversation gotten started anyhow? She sipped at her mai tai and enjoyed another warm rush. "But still, I should be going."

"Not so soon," he said, reaching a long arm over the bar. The sound of a guitar and a soft crooning voice washed into the room. A man sang in Portuguese and then the song was taken up by a woman in English. "The Girl from Ipanema."

Téa peered over the bar, saw the sleek boombox that was belting out the mood music, then looked back at Johnny. She might not quite know why this was, but she couldn't pretend not to know *what* this was. "I hate to break it to you, but the music is just about as subtle as Tiki Man's extralarge appendage."

He all-out grinned, then took her glass from her hand and placed both cocktails on top of the bar. "I'm getting desperate. You keep talking about leaving and before you go I want a dance. One dance."

The rum drink was making her rummy, or runny maybe, because looking at him she couldn't muster the steel it would take to walk away. Not when he was gazing down at her with that white smile, not when she could see a slice of his golden skin and hard chest through his half-open shirt.

The back of her neck was hot and she swore she could feel her hair starting to wave in the new, strange humidity of this desert night.

No, she told herself. *No.* But her mouth didn't get the message. "You don't really dance, do you?"

He gathered her close, but not too close. One hand was at the curve of her waist, the other held her fingers against his chest. His naked chest. "My mother thought every young man should have the opportunity to learn the steps and after that we were on our own. In seventh grade, I was forced to take etiquette and dancing from ninety-year-old Mr. Benjamin." Johnny's hips started to sway, and his steps led her feet into a gentle samba rhythm.

To make things even more unfair, a saxophone was playing.

His breath smelled like pineapple juice as he pressed his smooth-shaven cheek against hers. She closed her eyes because that mai tai melt was affecting her resistance, her muscles, her sense of self-preservation.

Remember Téa, she thought, he's a stranger. You really don't know this man.

"And speaking of my family—" he murmured.

Had they been? She had to snuggle closer to hear him. "Yes?"

"I visited my brother yesterday. He does business in the area."

"Hmm." Johnny could really dance. With just the slightest pressure of his knee between hers, he was shifting their positions, moving them farther from the bar and closer to the love seat.

"He was recently married. He mentioned that his wife knows you and your sisters."

"Really?" She blinked up at him, and the reflection of the lantern light in his eyes dazzled her. She stumbled a little, and he squeezed her waist to help steady her.

"His wife is Felicity Charm."

"*Really*?" Téa remembered Felicity well from her school years at Our Lady of Poverty. The other woman was now a star on GetTV. "I always liked her."

One of Johnny's dimples deepened. "Everybody does."

And she'd married Johnny's brother. Wow. Maybe he wasn't such a stranger after all. The idea made her smile. "It's a small world, isn't it?"

"More than you know, Contessa." His head lowered.

He was going to kiss her. Téa swayed back, one last instinct not yet under his spell.

"Trust me," he whispered. "Trust me."

Twenty-two

"I'm In the Mood for Love"
Julie London
Julie is Her Name (1955)

Trust me, he'd said.

The two words struck Téa like a one-two punch. It was her most well-defended yet most tender vulnerability, that longing to trust a man. And here was Johnny Magee, the embodiment of all her teenage fantasies, whispering it to her like a hot promise.

She shivered, and he drew her closer. As he shifted their bodies to the rhythm of the music, his thigh brushed the pad of her sex. Heat spread across her pelvis and between her legs. She had to clutch at his shoulder to keep from stumbling again.

He rolled his chin across the top of her head and put his mouth by her other ear. "One dance," he said again, an apparent expert in stereophonic seduction. "Trust me."

Despite the goose bumps breaking out all over her body, Téa managed to hold onto her sanity and then look up and catch his gaze. "Johnny. Trust a beautiful man on a warm night when he's plied you with alcohol and has his hands all over your body? They make afterschool specials and Lifetime Movies of the Week about moments like this. They'd call it something like 'Her Secret Seduction.'"

He froze, and she tripped over his suddenly still feet. "I don't know how you do this," he said, his voice half-exasperated, half-amused. "Every time I think I have a handle on things between us, you derail me."

"I do?"

"You do. Knock me right off my feet and onto my egotistical ass." He sighed and pushed her a little away. "You are the most infuriating woman."

"Now, see, I like the sound of that." It sounded as if she had the upper hand. Well, if not the *upper* hand, at least *some* hand on this situation.

Sighing again, he pulled her close once more and resumed dancing, his cheek resting on top of her head. "Afterschool special," he grumbled. "I must be losing my touch."

Relaxing into his embrace, Téa smiled against his shirt. She rubbed her face along the linen and then found herself flesh-to-flesh with his bare chest. Another wave of hot prickles rushed over her skin and she felt his heartbeat kick into a higher gear. His hand tightened on her waist.

"Téa—"

She didn't want to lose contact with his naked skin. "Hmm?"

His movements slowed and his thigh found its way between hers. He lingered there, his hard muscle a presence against her sex, his erection tucked against her belly.

And Téa didn't want to lose that contact either.

"Answer a question for me," he said, moving his head so they were cheek-to-cheek. The ends of his hair tickled her ear. "Is it still seduction if she sees right through it?"

Seduction, she thought, closing her eyes as another hot

shiver trembled through her. He wanted her, Johnny Magee wanted *her*, and it was still hard to grasp the idea in her mind. It was a fantasy as old as the one about trust—a fantasy shared with a hundred pints of Ben & Jerry's and a thousand batches of undercooked brownies. The beautiful blond boy across the room, the dance floor, the playing field, shedding the cheerleader hanging onto his arm to take up with Téa Caruso.

She'd shed fifty pounds and still never believed the fantasy could come true.

"Téa. Contessa." He kissed the corner of her eye, then the corner of her mouth. "What's going on in that busy head of yours?"

That she could have *this* fantasy. That she could *choose* it, unlike the interlude the afternoon before that had happened upon them both. If she knew that's what it was, a fantasy— and not a threat to her heart or her secrets—if she kept it clear in her mind that the only thing she was trusting here was how her body responded to his, then maybe she could know what it was like to bed the captain of the varsity team after all.

If there was a wicked, groupie-sex kind of feel to the idea, she was going to ignore it. This was Johnny, who she now knew wasn't a stranger and wasn't some anonymous sports star or celebrity. This was Johnny, whose desperate kisses and hot hands had turned her wild the day before.

It wouldn't change who she was or what she'd done, but she could feel that again. Though this time while keeping her decorum about her.

She looked up at him, enthralled by his golden looks for the hundredth time. "What's going on in my head," she said, excitement starting to hum beneath her skin—*I am really going to do this!*—"is that I've always wanted to dance in the dark."

Then, leaning toward the nearby lantern, she turned it off.

The good thing about varsity-level lovers is that they caught on immediately. Johnny laughed softly, then danced her around the room to extinguish the flames of the two torches at the tiki room's entrance. Then with the room almost pitch-dark, he drew both of her arms around his neck and wrapped his around her waist. Pulling her close, he left nothing between their bodies but clothes. He swayed with her in the kind of slow dance that had gotten her sister Eve sent home early from every parish teen mixer.

Téa flashed on her own misery during those Friday nights. The corners she'd found, the anxious yearning she'd felt each time a boy came her way, the humiliation when he'd looked right through her.

"Contessa."

Johnny's nickname for her. Johnny's voice. Johnny. Pushing away the memories, she pressed even closer to him, her nose against his bare chest so she could breathe in the scent of his hot skin. Reality was not allowed to intrude. This was her fantasy night.

And this time, in its darkness, she would be the graceful and elegant lover of her dreams.

"Contessa." Johnny slid his mouth from her ear to her lips.

She tilted her face to meet his kiss.

His tongue slid into her mouth, hot and sure. Her fingers clenched the strands of hair at his neck and she hung on as he drugged her with his taste and the slow penetration and retreat of his tongue. His fingers flexed on her hips, and at his urging, she tilted her pelvis into his body.

He slanted his mouth over hers, making a tighter fit, and she opened her lips wider to take the more-urgent thrust of his tongue. One of his hands slid up, under the loose cotton of her sweater. His fingertips touched the small of her back, and she jerked against his wide chest, startled by her sensitivity.

His palm flattened along her spine, pinning her closer than ever. When he tore his mouth from hers, their bodies heaved against each other as they fought for air. She loosened her fingers from his hair and ran her hands along his neck to his shoulders, needing to touch his skin too. He inched back and she drew her fingers down his chest until she found the first fastened button.

He sucked in air as she pushed it through the hole, freeing more of his skin for her touch. His breaths sounded loud in her ears as she finished unbuttoning the soft linen, then pushed the edges out of her way. He gave a graceful shrug, and in the darkness she saw the white fabric float to the ground behind him.

She covered his pectorals with her palms, cupping the heavy muscles, and pressed her mouth to the center of his chest, intending to give him the most gentle of kisses. But his wind-and-lime scent went to her head and without thought, she widened her mouth to flatten her tongue against his flesh and taste.

His harsh groan reverberated through her palms.

The sound, the sensation, jolted her back to awareness. Her hair felt damp. Her skin was on fire.

Her elegant fantasy was already unraveling.

Johnny speared his hand in her hair and pressed her face back against his chest. "More," he said, his voice hoarse. "Do it again."

The dark tone turned up the heat inside her body and evaporated her good intentions. She rubbed her mouth over the light fur on his chest until her lips found one of his nipples. Her tongue licked there too.

Johnny groaned again, and his hands moved quickly to cover her breasts. He squeezed them once, then released the catch on her bra and took them into the palms of his hands. Her eyes closing at the wild pleasure of his touch, Téa sucked on his nipple as he flicked his thumbs over hers.

Then Johnny took his hands off her and jerked back. "No," he muttered. "Not this time."

"What?" Téa blinked in the darkness, disoriented and dizzy without his body against hers. "What?"

"Not this time," he said again.

She sucked in a shaky breath, the heat on her face turning from desire to embarrassment. "I'm sorry," she said. Her dignity disappeared when Johnny touched her. "I'll . . . I'll go."

"Not on your life," he said. "Jesus, Contessa, don't you see that you get me so hard and so high so fast, that I—never mind." He grabbed her wrists in one hand. "It only means that the one to go up in flames this time will be you and the one who gets to do all the touching is me."

With that, he hauled her close again and found her mouth with his. Téa sank under a fresh wave of desire as he rubbed his tongue against hers. Still gripping her wrists in one of his hands, he used his free fingers to slide beneath her sweater again and pluck her nipples.

Though she swallowed her moans, she couldn't help but twist against him, trying to get relief for the building ache in her breasts. He pulled on one nipple, playing with it with his fingers until she thought she might go mad.

She crowded her hips with his. He lifted his head and laughed softly, the sound both satisfied and sexy. "Now if you'll promise to keep your hands to yourself, I'll take off your top and have my way with your beautiful breasts."

Téa bit her lip instead of pleading as she wanted to. Thank God he went ahead with his plan anyway. In the space of a breath she was standing in front of him, topless. Heat washed over her skin and she thanked God for the camouflaging darkness too.

Still, she saw Johnny's head bend toward her and when his wet mouth latched onto her, she couldn't hold back her moan. Her hands went to his hair again, but he caught her wrists and held them to her sides as he sucked on first one nipple and then the other. His tongue licked over her tight flesh and then he drew back to blow out a cool breath. Her fingers tightened on his restraining hands and he laughed again.

"You like that?"

Of course she liked that. But she wasn't going to risk opening her mouth and shouting it to the rooftops. He had to be accustomed to elegant, accomplished lovers and she was barely hanging on to her silence.

Johnny pulled her against him again, the wet tips of her breasts meeting the hard, hot skin of his chest. At the contact, air hissed from between his teeth, covering up the little moan she only half-swallowed. Then he kissed her again, his body swaying in another slow dance as he grabbed her full, lightweight cotton skirt in both fists.

Téa bowed back as his kiss burned through her. He followed the movement, keeping their chest-to-breast contact as his hands gathered up the material of her skirt, slowly baring her legs. His mouth broke away from hers to slide to an ear. As he bit her lobe, he tucked the rolled ends of her skirt in her back waistband.

"Mine," he said, cupping her buttocks in his palms. "Oh, God, all mine."

Téa buried her face against his skin. What must she look like, bare on top and her skirt ruched up to leave her— Johnny's hands moved again—

—bare on the bottom too.

His whisper was hot in her ear as he pushed her panties all the way off. "Step out, Contessa, step out and dance with me."

She kicked off her sandals and walked out of her underwear, leaving them on the floor with Johnny's shirt. As she began to follow his lead in the dance, her skirt worked itself out of the waistband and fell free.

As he had earlier, Johnny looped her arms around his neck, pressing her fingers together. "Hold there," he said. "Don't let go." Then he pulled up her skirt and cupped her bottom again.

Her skin goosebumped from the heat of his hands. She closed her eyes and rubbed her face against his chest. Then his fingers wandered to the crease between her cheeks and thighs and he slid them toward her wet heat.

She froze, riveted by the graze of his fingertips.

"Keep dancing," he said. "Let's keep dancing."

His hoarse voice was impossible to disobey. As she shifted one foot, he found the access he'd been seeking. Two fingers thrust up inside of her.

Téa cried out, pleasure breaking over her body. "Johnny," she breathed, closing her eyes. "Johnny."

"Keep dancing." His voice was tight and he rubbed his cheek against hers. "Move with me."

He took the lead, still swaying, still forcing her to shift and to move while impaled on the stiff length of his fingers. With every change in her posture, she could feel him touching a different place, exploring a different angle inside her body.

The beat of the music was the beat of her blood. Her head dropped back as he covered her breast with his free hand and set his mouth over the throbbing pulse on her neck, his tongue flickering in time with his thrusting fingers.

He controlled everything about her.

The thought pierced the smoky delight, her mind sharpening enough to feel the dull prick of fear. Her eyes popped open and suddenly frantic to get away, she wriggled and squirmed and . . .

. . . came.

The orgasm shook her body. She could only hang onto Johnny as it overtook her, could only suck her bottom lip into her mouth to hold back whatever wanton sounds were trying to break free.

As the tremors tapered off, he gathered her closer with one arm. Then, with his fingers still inside her, he set his mouth over hers. She was too dazzled to do anything but accept the heavy thrust of his tongue. Then his fingers moved again, his thumb shifting on the outside to touch the still-throbbing knot of nerves between her folds.

He circled it, rolling it in her own wetness again and again. Then his other fingers thrust once more, deep inside.

And again she danced to his tune. This time she was pretty sure she screamed.

But it was impossible to know for sure, because her mind wasn't working any longer. She was just a body, an elastic collection of torso and limbs that made Johnny laugh softly as he drew her toward the love seat.

Somehow she found herself naked on his lap, and he was naked too.

"That zombie mai tai made me tipsy," she told him. She was slurring her words.

"You're drunk on sex."

"Oh." She watched him arrange her legs on either side of his lap. "*Oh,*" she said again as he drew her down onto his erection. "Are we going to lap dance now?"

He groaned. "I'm sorry, baby, but this might be more of a race than a dance. You make me so damn hot." His hips thrust high.

She moaned.

His fingers found her clitoris again as he began to move. "Come on, Contessa. Winner takes all."

They were both walking like drunks, Téa thought later, as they made their way along the path back to Johnny's house. He snuffed the tiki torches as they passed, and she was glad for the darkness that concealed her face if not her rubbery knees.

What might it reveal?

Bliss? Wonder? A silly grin because she'd lived out her fantasy . . . and loved every minute of it too?

Johnny extinguished the last torch, then twined his fingers with hers as they headed across the golf course in the direction of the house.

"You're quiet, Contessa."

In the tiki room, she hadn't managed to keep perfectly quiet and perfectly civilized, though she hoped the darkness had covered up most of that, too. "Just enjoying the night," she said, tilting her face to the sky. The stars seemed ready to rain down on them, they looked that bright and close.

"You're all right?"

"Of course." *It was perfect. My perfect fantasy with my fantasy lover.* And she could leave it behind now, like a pair of outgrown sneakers.

Right?

Johnny halted, and pulled her into his arms to place another kiss upon her lips. Gentle and sweet.

Téa leaned into him. Maybe reality didn't have to intrude quite yet. For a little while longer she could forget she was a mob boss's daughter.

The grass beneath their feet seemed to agree. *Shh-shh shh-shh* it said as they continued on toward the house.

They took the steps to the pool deck. The house was dimly lit, but the empty pool was glowing. A plumeria blossom floated across its surface. Téa thought of Rachele as she'd seen her last, an amusing yet charming goth wahine, diving beneath the water.

Ah, she thought, smiling. *Now that's young love.* It didn't seem so bittersweet, not after her fantasy night in the tiki room.

"Johnny—"

He stopped beside the pool, looking down at her. The uplight cast shadows on the planes of his face and her heart jumped, dazzled once more by his masculine beauty. Maybe it didn't have to be a one-night fantasy, a beguiling voice whispered inside her. And then she heard Johnny in her head, too.

It's not enough, Contessa. I want inside you again. And again and again and again.

It sounded so real. She studied his face. Swallowed. "Johnny, are you thinking—"

Behind him, a massive shadow detached from the side of the house. A man.

Téa's heart seized. She screamed.

Johnny spun. "What?" His voice sounded harsh as he pushed her behind him. "Who are you? What do you want?"

The book, Téa thought, going cold. It was someone after the book. From a rival family or even from her grandfather. She clutched her briefcase to her chest and hoped there wasn't a radioactive glow emanating from it.

"*Mi scusi.* I'm sorry for disturbing you."

"Beppe?" Relief made Téa's voice squeak. Dear, harmless Beppe. She hastily combed her fingers through her hair then ran a palm down her skirt, hoping her clothes didn't show what she'd just been doing.

Rachele's father walked into the light cast by the pool. "Yes, yes. *Sto cercando mia figlia.* I'm looking for my daughter."

"She's not here," Johnny said. His voice still sounded tense. He pulled Téa forward, his fingers icy on hers. "I believe my associate, Cal, was going to drive her home when she finished her—" he hesitated, "—measuring."

"She said she had some work to do here today," Beppe replied. "Is that right, Téa?"

"Sure. Yes. I'm giving her more responsibility. Rachele's such a hard worker, you know." It wasn't up to her to spill the news that his darling daughter was in love. Not to mention, as Joey had pointed out so often, she was chicken.

Rachele's father grunted. "Then maybe she went back to

the office to do something there. I was worried when she didn't get home for dinner."

"I'm sure she'll be there any moment, Beppe."

He nodded, then looked from her, to Johnny, then back again.

Téa took the hint. "Johnny Magee, this is Guiseppe Cirigliano, Rachele's father. Beppe, this is one of my clients, Johnny Magee. Beppe recognized your blueprints, Johnny. He did the rockwork that created your lagoon before he retired."

The two men shook hands. Johnny cleared his throat. "I'm certain Cal will see your daughter home safely."

The older man nodded. "Then I shall return the favor and see Téa safely to her car, since her . . . measuring here appears to be done as well."

Hello, reality.

"Good-bye, Johnny," Téa said.

No sense in being silly, anyway. This wasn't going further between them. One dance, he'd said. Meaning her one night with him was over.

Twenty-three

"Just One More Chance"
Dean Martin
Dean Martin Sings (1953)

It took Johnny a few days to make it back to the tiki room.
He'd sent the cleaning crew to retrieve the barware, but he'd avoided the place himself.

He didn't know why he was here this afternoon, he thought, sliding onto one of the stools. But he'd been restless and distracted since the night Téa had left him.

She hadn't been back either.

Rachele had come by, ostensibly to take additional measurements and to show him some sample books, but more accurately to flirt with Cal. Their relationship had this curious clandestine vibe to it.

The night Rachele's father had startled the bejesus out of Johnny, he'd covered for the young couple without really thinking about it. Téa had too, he remembered now. Maybe he would have asked her about it if she'd come within shouting distance.

She hadn't.

And he didn't know what to do about it. He didn't know what he *wanted* to do about it.

There were all the same reasons not to get further involved with her. And the other night he'd achieved his goal of recouping a measure of his self-respect by making her come before he did, like any gentleman would. So he could leave things as they were in good conscience.

Not to mention she appeared to want nothing more to do with him.

It didn't rankle.

"Johnny?"

He swung around to find Cal lurking at the entrance, a sheaf of papers in his hand. He was wearing baggy flowered shorts, a plaid shirt, the ubiquitous black hi-tops, and . . .

"Is that a *tan?*" Johnny asked. He couldn't have been more surprised if the other man had shown up with an eyebrow piercing like his girlfriend's.

Cal lifted an arm and squinted at it through his glasses. "Maybe. We haven't been working as much as we usually do."

Guilt gave Johnny a little jab. For a few hours each morning, he'd been reading the sports pages and perusing the tech-heads' reports, but without his usual attention to detail or requests for additional data. Though he'd daily been calling in the bets his people were to play, the fact was he'd been sleepwalking through the decisions.

With a sigh, he looked at the papers in Cal's hand and gestured him inside. "Is that what you have there? Work?"

Cal stepped into the tiki room, blinking as his eyes adjusted to the dimmer light. "Holy Don-the-Beachcomber, Batman," he said, handing over the stack of reports. "So this is the hidden room you found."

His father's hidden room. Johnny spread the papers on top of the bar and pretended to be interested in them. His father had supposedly built this room for a woman he'd claimed to love. A woman unknown to Johnny, who might be able to tell him for sure if his father had become a hit man for the mob.

He still couldn't believe it was so. Though they'd only had those annual visits, Johnny was sure he'd known his father. He thought his father had loved him. Could a man love his kid and be a killer at the same time? Could a kid love a man who was a killer? Jesus. No wonder he couldn't sleep.

He didn't know anyone else plagued by such hellish questions, except . . .

"Téa," he thought, murmuring the name aloud. "Téa." Maybe that was the source of their chemistry. Maybe that was why he couldn't get the woman out of his head.

"About her."

Johnny jerked his gaze toward Cal. He'd forgotten the other man was in the room. "What? What about Téa?"

"I remembered what your half-brother said."

Half-brother. More guilt poked at Johnny. He'd been an asshole to Michael that day at his bar. "My brother doesn't know anything about Téa."

"He told you to be careful of the Caruso connection. I asked Rachele about it."

Johnny slid a look at Cal. He was wearing a dogged expression, the one that said he'd swum up from his usual realm, fathoms-deep in nanodigits and quartiles. It meant he wasn't going to be put off easily. "Yeah? So?"

"The Carusos are the first family of the California Mafia," Cal said. "But I guess you know that."

Johnny shrugged.

"And maybe your brother was right to warn you off an involvement with Téa."

He had no "involvement" with Téa. She wasn't even speaking to him, damn it.

"Especially now that the leadership is in question."

"What?" Johnny stared at Cal. "What are you talking about?"

"Rachele told me Téa's grandfather is the head of the family, but he's announcing his retirement soon. Rachele also said that in the last few days Palm Springs has been crawling with mob goons jockeying for position in the coming new order."

Johnny rolled his shoulders. None of this mattered to him. It was the Mafia of the past that concerned him, not its future.

"They've been dropping by the design office."

"What?" Johnny frowned. "Who?"

"The goons. They come in and try kissing-up to Téa." He plucked his cell phone from his belt and peered at the screen. "Rachele sent me a text message a few minutes ago and told me another couple of them were hanging around even though Téa said she was busy."

Johnny half-rose from the stool, then forced himself back down. She was a big girl. And not *his* girl, so it was none of his concern. He shuffled the papers in front of him. "We've got work to do."

Cal came closer and slipped one sheet from the rest. "These are the games we have to decide on today."

"Right, right." He tried focusing on the list of Sunday matchups and their current odds while Cal wandered about the room. Which ones should the syndicate put their money on?

The Raiders vs. the Chargers, the Chargers favored by 13½ points.

Johnny might have managed to find out about Cosimo Caruso retiring, but he'd been brooding for the last few days instead of doing anything to uncover the truth about his father. Not to mention that he'd let Téa slip through his fingers. Téa, his hunch, Téa his one and only real connection to the California Mafia.

From the corner of his eye he saw Cal come around behind the bar, and he bent his head over the papers and tried to concentrate again.

The Jets vs. the Dolphins. Would the home field advantage give the New York team at least a 10-point win over Miami?

"Hey, a boombox," Cal said.

Johnny glanced up to see him reaching out a skinny arm. "No—" But it was too late.

"The Girl from Ipanema." Guitar strings plucking out a samba beat. The silvery sound of a metal brush stroking a snare drum.

And then Téa. He was getting damned good at this flashback thing. Because suddenly she was in his mind, in his arms, her skin hot, her mouth molten, her sweet ass full and pushing into his hands. Thank God for that darkness. If he'd seen what he'd touched he would have been lost once again, too impatient to wait for her. He would have taken what he wanted.

What he wanted now. Again.

Johnny scooped the papers into a pile. "Cal."

The other man was frowning down at his cell phone. "More goons," he said.

Johnny stood, the legs of the stool screeching against the linoleum. Goons kissing-up to Téa. His hunch. His woman. "I'm going over there."

Cal's voice caught him halfway across the room. "The matchups, Johnny. You have to decide on which matchups."

Sighing, he stalked back to pluck the handful of mechanical pencils out of the other man's pocket protector. "Now hold the list against the wall," he told Cal.

To give his friend credit, he didn't quibble or quiver as Johnny aimed for the makeshift dartboard with the pencils. All five found a place on the page, held fast by the bamboo lining the walls. "Now you have your matchups," he said, turning again to leave.

With the exception of one private matchup that he was going to play today.

Magee vs. Caruso.

He was betting on himself to win.

Twenty-four

"Oh Me! Oh My! Oh You!"
Doris Day
Tea for Two (1950)

Téa barreled out of the front door of her office and into a man's arms. She gasped and clutched her purse tighter. Not again. She'd just sent one pair of long-lost "cousins" packing and she wasn't yet ready to steady her nerves and steel her spine to face another Italian male who wanted something from her.

She forced herself to look up. *Oh.* "Johnny." Relief sluiced through her, then she remembered the last time she'd been in his arms. *You're drunk on sex,* he'd said.

Just looking at him brought it all rushing back. Face going hot, she stepped away, and tried to tell herself it didn't matter that she was wearing a very casual long denim skirt, chambray shirt, and her scuffed clogs. "What are you doing here?"

He blinked as if he wasn't sure of the answer, then forked a hand through his blond hair. "I . . . wanted to see you."

She gestured with her hand. "I'm on my way out." Before

anyone else could corner her in her office. Her mother had warned her the wolves would come sniffing and they had done more than that. Every day a Dominelli or a LaScala or a Pastorino dropped by and then set up camp in her reception area until she made it forcefully clear she wasn't saying yes to breakfast/lunch/drinks/dinner or whatever else they suggested as a way of *conoscerci*—getting chummy. Either her estrangement from her grandfather wasn't widespread news within the ranks of the families of the California Mafia or the dark-haired, dark-eyed men trying to get close to her didn't believe it. "Can we make an appointment for another time?"

"It's not an appointment I want with you." His hand scraped through his hair again.

Huh? Téa tilted her head, trying to figure out what he meant. Now would be a good time for her mind-reading imagination to kick in. But it didn't, and then, over Johnny's shoulder, she saw a car cruise the street, a black, ominous Escalade. There was no concrete reason—other than her Mafia "cousins" seemed to go more for show than subtlety—for her heart to trip and tumble, but better safe than sorry.

She brought her purse to her chest and crossed her arms over it. "Look, Johnny, I'm sorry, but I really have to go."

"Can I give you a lift somewhere?"

She shook her head. "I'm going to the swap meet in Riverside," she told him, then instantly regretted it. A trip to a swap meet wouldn't sound urgent to him, she was sure, but to her it was imperative that she get out of town for a few hours. She needed a break from the unpleasant sensation of the wolves' hot breath on her back.

Johnny frowned. "A swap meet?"

See? She'd known it wouldn't make sense to him. She licked her lips, and then tried to sound reasonable and professional. "It runs on the weekends as well, but today's the day for the best selection at the music dealer I want to visit.

I'm going on a search for your project, as a matter of fact. He usually brings an extensive collection of exotica LPs."

Johnny nodded. "Rachele showed me your new sketches."

Téa had proposed framing vintage album covers for the room that was to be his office. "She said you approved the idea."

"I did. I like it."

Then why wouldn't he get out of the way so she could get *on* her way? Something was up with him and she couldn't fathom what it would be. His posture was stiff and he was staring at her mouth as if . . . as if . . .

No. She wasn't going to read anything into his sudden appearance or his odd tension. They'd had their "one dance" and that's all there was to it.

That's all he'd said he wanted.

Movement down the street caught her eye and her head jerked right. Damn. The Escalade was back, cruising slower this time. She had to get out of here before she pulled the Loanshark book out of her purse and confessed all to the next mobster who showed up on her doorstep.

"I have to go, Johnny." Okay, so she sounded like a kid with a bathroom issue, but that wasn't so far from the feeling of anxiety building inside her.

His hand took hold of her elbow. "Then we'll go together." Already he was guiding her toward his silver Jag, parked on the street just a few feet away.

"What?" Frowning, she looked up at him. "Why?"

His expression was as indecipherable as before. "I'm the client, aren't I?"

Before she could even think of a way out of the situation, he had her in the passenger seat and was pulling away from the curb. As she gave him the requested directions, she tried to figure out why she felt hustled. And she tried to figure out why he wanted to accompany her to a swap meet, of all places. Johnny Magee wasn't a swap meet kind of guy, not in those European-cut slacks and that collarless shirt.

Sliding a glance his way, she caught him sliding one at her. Their gazes caught. A hot flush washed from her hairline to her toenails.

I want you again. I want you drunk on what I can do to your body.

She swallowed hard and clenched her thighs together. It sounded like Johnny's voice, it looked like that's what his gaze was saying, but it couldn't be. He'd wanted that one time. He'd said so. And she'd promised herself to be content with that. Plenty of women survived one-night stands.

They didn't feel the need the day after, and the day after that, to be in their lover's arms again, his hot palms cupping her bare behind, his hard chest beneath her lips and tongue. She squirmed against the leather seat.

"Did you always want to be an interior designer?" he asked abruptly, his gaze shifting back to the windshield.

Téa blinked. "What?"

"An interior designer. How did you hit upon that as a career?"

Well, that just went to show how inexperienced she was in the ways of men and mornings-after. Or, more accurately, days-after. He wanted to talk about her work. She flounced against the seat, annoyed with herself. It drove a woman to think about starting to date again. Even if it meant more grandsons and great-nephews, at least she might gain a modicum of expertise on this whole man-woman thing.

But the grandsons and great-nephews wouldn't be Johnny and it would be a waste of time, anyway. Her mob past meant she wouldn't be getting serious with anyone.

"Téa?"

"Yeah, yeah, yeah," she muttered.

He shot her another unreadable look.

She pretended not to notice. It was a waste of time trying to interpret it.

"Téa?"

"My job. I know, I know." With a silent sigh, she leaned her head against the backrest and thought back. "Before I even knew anything about a career in the design business, I was driving my sisters nuts by rearranging our bedroom."

"You shared?"

"Always. My mom's idea, I think, as a way for the three of us to feel, no, to *know* we were sisters. Equal sisters. When Eve came to live with us, my mother accepted her with her whole heart and she wanted to make sure that none of us ever forgot that."

"Special woman, your mother."

"I see that now, of course. But the truth is, I don't remember a time without Eve, so whatever difficulties there were at the beginning—if there were any—I don't know." Because though her mother *was* special, she was private, too. They all kept their pain and their secrets well hidden, every single one of Salvatore Caruso's women.

"So you were shoving beds and dressers around the room from the tender age of—?"

"About nine, I'd say. And also sewing curtains and bed-covers whenever a new whim struck."

"You *sew*?"

She shot him a baffled look. "It's not a disease."

He was shaking his head. "You don't strike me as the sewing type. Women who sew are . . . I don't think I've ever met a woman who sews, actually."

"I feel a stereotype in the offing," she said dryly.

Though his attention was still directed out the windshield, he grinned. "Sorry. But my idea of a sewing woman is a plain-Jane homebody wearing pincushions on each wrist and who spends her nights with one of those dressmaker dealies instead of a date."

"They're called dummies. Dressmaker dummies." She owned two. One in the plus size she used to be and one with the more streamlined curves she now laid claim to. And, as humiliating as it would be to admit, she *was* a plain-Jane homebody. Though Johnny didn't seem to think so.

She sat up a little straighter. "So I, um, don't fit your image of a woman who sews, is that right?"

"Contessa, you made your very own mold the night you danced in my arms."

That hot flush once more warmed her skin. Again, she wiggled against the leather seat.

"Stop doing that," he said softly, "or I'll go insane."

Téa froze. What did that mean? Her eyes swiveled his way, but his gorgeous face might as well have been carved in stone. "I can see why you're good at poker," she murmured under her breath.

They were on the freeway heading out of the Coachella Valley now, and he set the cruise control then looked over at her. "What did you say?"

She cleared her throat. "I, uh, asked if you always wanted to be a—what did you call it?—money manager?"

"I . . . well . . . " Johnny hesitated, one hand reaching up to rub his chin.

All at once, there was a new thread of tension between them.

"You don't have to tell me," she offered quickly. "It's none of my business."

"No," he said. "I want you to know about my work. Maybe you'll think I should have told you about it before."

Téa frowned, alarmed and curious at the same time. "Really, Johnny. As long as your checks clear, that's good enough for me."

"It's nothing illegal."

She already felt a thousand times better. Not that she'd really believed he was involved in criminal activity, but hearing him say it was a relief. Given her family history, who would blame her?

"I told you that my playing in poker tournaments is a hobby."

"I remember. I have a friend who holds a monthly girls' poker night and she's always inviting me. Maybe I should get you to give me some lessons first."

He smiled, this one creasing a sly dimple in the side of his cheek. "It would be a pleasure. It *could* be a pleasure." His voice held that dark undercurrent that always sent her imagination soaring.

She cleared her throat, trying to rein it in. "But you were saying . . . ?"

"Poker's my hobby. Gambling's my job."

"Huh?" She blinked, trying to understand. "I don't get it."

He drummed his fingers against the steering wheel. "Let me go back for a minute. Have you ever heard of the group of MIT students who cleaned up in Vegas several years ago?"

Not that she wanted to admit to it, but she'd caught a *Dateline NBC* rerun last summer when she was home on a Saturday night spending time with—what else?—her dressmaker's dummy and her sewing machine. "Maybe . . . " she said, trying to sound uncertain. "Didn't they have some sort of card-counting scheme?"

"Yes. And if you use just your brains to win at the game, that's not illegal either. But the casinos don't like their clientele so smart. They finally sniffed them out and put their photos in the Griffin Book—an encyclopedia of sorts used by the biggest security firm in Vegas that the casinos hire to catch not only cheaters, but habitual winners. Whenever someone in the book shows up at one of the places they protect, the transgressor is politely, or not so politely, shown the door."

"So you were part of this group from MIT?"

He shook his head, then shot her a little grin. "That group

was caught. I was part of a different group from UC Berkeley. It's how I made my seed money to invest in the syndicate I now run."

She supposed she admired his youthful talents, but she still didn't understand about this syndicate. "Which means you do exactly what?"

"I'm no different than any other kind of fund manager, meaning I direct the dollars of our group of highly capitalized investors. Rich men. But instead of investing the money in mutual funds or stocks and bonds and betting we'll turn a profit from them, our group bets on the outcome of sporting events. Usually the three biggies, football, basketball, and baseball."

"There's real money to be made doing that?" According to the Loanshark book, there was only debt and more debt. Many of the men—and women—her father had given money to had needed the high-interest loans to meet their gambling obligations and then to make more of them.

"There's big money to be made doing that, *if* you know how."

"And you do," she said it slowly, trying to determine what she felt about the revelation.

"I do, with the help of brainiacs like Cal who provide statistical analyses and a whole team of what we refer to as 'legs'—the people who walk up to the casino windows and actually place the bets. Believe me, it's very profitable. I'm on the IRS's list of favorite sons. The business's quarterly checks could fund a small country."

An unusual occupation, but not an illegal one. He regularly paid his taxes. Okay. "But why are you telling me this?"

He sent her another of his unreadable glances. "I want you to know more about me before I suggest something else."

"Suggest what?" She had no clue.

His long-fingered hand rubbed over his chin once, then moved back to its calm grip of the steering wheel. "Moving the business and my primary residence is more . . . stressful than I expected. I think I could use a distraction from my obligations and responsibilities. I'd like something in my life that's just pure pleasure." His eyes glinted as he aimed one of those sly-dimpled smiles her way. "And I think, Téa, that could be you. Interested?"

Twenty-five

"Mad About the Boy"
Jackie Gleason
Lonesome Echo (1955)

Téa's first reaction: surprise. Second reaction: excitement.
Third reaction: anger at her own inexperience.

All those years wasted on the grandsons and great-nephews left her unprepared for this kind of male-female ne-gotiation. An offer for another early-bird dinner date was easy to field—and to refuse. A request to be a man's "pure pleasure" was something else entirely.

A request to be *this* man's pure pleasure was mind-boggling.

But he didn't seem to think it was as outlandish as she did. God, how thrilling was that? Despite the three reasons that would make her say no—M, O, and B—it was still a flatter-ing proposition.

He ran his forefinger down the side of her hot cheek. "I didn't shock you, did I?"

"Of course not," she scoffed. What an actress she was. "But you mentioned that uh, one dance, so I thought it was all you were interested in."

"I decided to put my money where my mouth is. I told you self-denial was a waste of time and so I stopped trying to deny myself from being with you again."

Oh God, how ultra-thrilling was that? But a man like Johnny wanted more than a puddle at his feet, she felt sure of it, so she held herself together and suppressed her sudden urge to burst into one of Eve and Joey's silly high school cheers. So she couldn't have him. That he wanted her was enough—wasn't it?

He must have taken her silence for hesitation. "I realize running your own business takes a lot of your concentration and energy. But how about spending some . . . social time with me?"

That "social" sounded more like "sexual" and her face flushed hotter even as everything south of there had its own clench-and-release reaction. She was thankful he couldn't notice, though, because they'd reached the grounds of the swap meet and he was following the hand signals of the parking attendant into a nearby space.

It gave her much needed moments to cool down and think clearly. As he came around to help her out of the car, she opened the passenger door for herself. He looked down at her, his eyebrows raised. "Well?" he asked.

Well, he was her teenage fantasy and the lover who'd blown away her "better without witnesses" rule about sex all rolled into one. She'd be a fool—no, she wouldn't be a woman—to refuse him.

Except she had those three good reasons. Though Johnny knew of her mob background, he didn't fully understand the taint she carried from it. There wasn't going to be any more pure pleasure between Johnny and Téa.

"Well?" he asked again.

She stepped out of the car. "I'm thinking about it," she heard herself say.

Because her mouth rebelled against a flat-out refusal. And because it was exciting to have the upper hand with him for once. For once, to play it cool.

Okay, it might be playing a game, but . . .

She slid a look at him from under her lashes as they headed for the swap meet entrance. Could she think of this as a game between them? If she did, then she wouldn't get too serious about it. Certainly the blond varsity god walking beside her wasn't interested in anything more than an amusing diversion. That's what he'd *said* he wanted.

What if she could see it as a temporary, amusing diversion too?

Though the temperature was cooler here than in Palm Springs, the sun's rays reflected off the asphalt of the huge parking lot. The atmosphere only got hotter as Johnny managed to appropriate her hand. He was even able to guide her direction of walking once they were past the swap meet's entrance gate.

"Hey, look here," he said, tugging her toward a set of tables filled with sunglasses. "Try these on."

He pushed a pair of oversized hot pink plastic frames onto her face. Humoring him, she peered at herself in the mirror. "I don't think these are me, Johnny. I'm all dark lenses and a mouth."

"And what a mouth it is," he murmured, handing over a five-dollar bill for the glasses even as he leaned in for a kiss. "I like you . . . in . . . hot . . . *hot* . . . pink," he murmured against her lips.

She supposed she should have protested, or at least found a pair of sunglasses as cheesy to purchase for him, but when he lifted his head and towed her onward, she was too dizzy to make such a decision. Besides, the sleek, expensive pair he wore suited him to perfection.

Damn, she thought. This wasn't going to work as even a temporary amusement. He was way, way out of her league.

Though not that you could tell by some of his shopping selections. Before they'd made it past two of the dozens and dozens of rows, he'd bought a set of miniature wrenches, a leg-sized bag of kettle corn, and a package of athletic socks. He halted again as they came upon a booth of Jamaican products. His hand hovered over a crocheted Rasta cap in black, red, and yellow stripes as he sent her a speculative glance.

"No, no, no, no." She put her hands over her very expensive, very difficult-to-maintain straight hair. "That won't look good with my new sunglasses."

He listened. And bought another in gradated shades of pink that he clapped onto her head without a by-your-leave.

"I thought men didn't like to shop," she grumbled, checking out her bizarre, but slightly rakish reflection in another mirror.

"Do you really mind so much?" he asked, putting his hands on her shoulders and giving them a gentle squeeze. "I want to bring some color into your life, Contessa."

"How do you know that I'm not perfectly happy with my neutral tones?"

"Because you're not some anemic mouse, as much as you seem to be comfortable in the wardrobe of one."

She frowned at him. "I might take offense at that."

"Don't." He smiled. "I just think you look best in bright, warm colors."

"I'm a designer, Johnny, I'm aware of it." She couldn't let him think she didn't know her business.

His hands busied themselves adjusting her cap. "Then why the mouse-wear?"

She shrugged, looking away from him. "Maybe because I gave up on competing with Eve a long time ago. It seemed easier to disappear into the woodwork." It was part of the reason. Sort of.

"You don't seem the jealous type."

Because she hid her passions as well as she hid her secrets. She clutched her purse beneath her arm, realizing she hadn't thought about the Loanshark book or the Mafia wolves since climbing into Johnny's Jag. Imagine that. He already *had* diverted her. Grateful, she rose on tiptoe to give him a quick peck on the lower lip. "Thank you."

His arm curled around her waist and held her there. "For what?"

She could feel the thrumming of his heart through both their shirts. Steady but fast, and it made her feel bold and almost beautiful. "For the sunglasses, the hat . . . "

For this unfamiliar type of confidence taking root inside of her. Téa Caruso with Johnny Magee. She was a good daughter, sister, designer, but it was something new to feel she could be good with a *man*. This kind of man. She broke free. "For that tempting offer I think I really am considering."

He smiled. "Take your time, Contessa. Take your time."

But as if to belie his words, he started up a subtle yet insistent pressure. As they browsed the aisles, he stayed close beside her, always a hand on the back of her neck or on the small of her back, his mouth a whisper away from her ear. Her skin seemed to be lifting toward his touch, nerve endings quivering in anticipation of his next stroke or his next breath.

And trying to play it cool only heightened her sexual tension.

He bought her more things. A glittery tube of lip gloss. A goofy necklace with her name spelled out in fluorescent bead blocks. When he drew her hair to the side to latch it on, he also unfastened the top button of her chambray shirt to loosen the collar. The second button popped free of its own accord, but when she reached up to fasten it, he grabbed her hand.

"Don't," he whispered against her fingers. His lips were warm and soft.

Swallowing hard, she jerked her gaze away from his and

glanced down at what the loosened buttons revealed. Nothing even R-rated. Only a hint of cleavage that rose and fell with each of her ragged breaths.

She left it alone, but had to move quickly away before she forgot her cool and begged him to touch her, taste her, have his way with her. She hadn't decided yet that she could risk that again.

But the wanting to didn't get any better when they happened upon a vendor selling candles and bath products. He picked out half a dozen pillars in various heights, lining them up and looking them over with a critical eye. "What do you think?" he asked her.

"What do I think about what?"

"I want candles in my bedroom. How many? What color? Which sizes?"

She stared at him, her imagination leaping up to paint the scene. The big bed, surrounded by flickering flames, illuminating their reflections in the mirror overhead. Her skin burned, her womb clenched.

"Téa? You're the designer. What do you think?"

Blinking, she pulled out of the fantasy. Johnny was watching her, his own face expressionless. Clearing her throat, she wiped her damp palms on her jean skirt and then commanded her fingers to remain steady as she pointed out possibilities. As the saleswoman wrapped them in tissue paper, Johnny picked up a small sample vial of scented oil.

He sniffed it, then pressed his fingertip on the top to collect a drop. His hand found hers.

She tried pulling away, but he held fast and turned her arm to expose the paler underside. Her gaze couldn't leave his hand as he stroked the oil on her inner wrist. The scent of bergamot and citrus bloomed between them. "What do you think about this?"

She stared at the wet line he'd painted on her skin. *I think I'm in trouble!* How could she manage to hold her own against someone so much better at the art of seduction? She was supposed to be playing here, not losing her head. The ridiculous bead necklace was already halfway to stealing her heart.

No. Of course it wasn't.

His fingertips tickled up her forearm to the bend in her elbow. "It says it's called 'Heat of Passion.'"

Téa licked her lips and was glad of the oversized sunglasses shielding her eyes from him. "It smells . . . heady."

"So do you, Contessa."

She shook her head, knees weak. "You're too good at this."

He froze, then his touch slipped away from her skin. Pivoting toward the saleswoman, he accepted the bag of candles and then set off down the aisle.

Perplexed by his abruptness, Téa started after him. "Johnny? Johnny, wait."

He hesitated, then paused to let her catch up. "Sorry."

She tried to determine what had gone awry, but he wore that damned detached expression so well there was no clue to be found on his face. "I didn't mean to, but it was the wrong thing to say, wasn't it?" The knowledge that something she said might actually affect him had its own special pull.

"Don't worry about it. It's nothing I haven't heard before." He strode off again, then halted once more to confront her. "I want to have you, Téa, but I don't want to hurt you."

Her fingers flew up to the bead necklace, already warm from her skin. She didn't like that rough note in his voice. She didn't like him mentioning her name and "hurt" in the same sentence. "I thought you said you wanted a distraction. That doesn't sound serious enough to cause either of us any pain, Johnny." It was the only reason she was remotely entertaining the possibility.

"Yeah." He spun back around. "Of course. Let's find those albums you're looking for."

Lauer's Music, thanks to Murphy's Law, was set up in the

farthest corner of the swap meet. On other visits she'd browsed through the files of vintage albums just for fun, never with today's particular intent. Johnny's sudden dark mood didn't make her job any easier. He stood off to the side, arms crossed over his chest, watching her flip through the albums.

The stall was sheltered from the sun by a blue tarp that, combined with her new sunglasses, darkened her vision. She pushed off her hat and put it aside with the glasses as she continued her search for albums in the musical subgenre known as "exotica."

It referred to a type of music from the 1940s and '50s that was a fusion of instrumental pop, Latin jazz, and unusual percussion. It was also known for its sophisticated, sexy album covers. They epitomized the slant she was taking with Johnny's mid-century modern design. His wasn't going to be a sterile, industrialized type of home, but one with clean lines and deep colors that said unique, urbane, and very sensual.

Like Johnny himself.

And she wanted him.

Despite all the reasons she shouldn't, Téa suddenly decided that this good girl wasn't going to deny herself any longer either. Instead, she was going for it. Why shouldn't she take of him what she could get? Johnny had given her enough confidence to accept his proposition to be each other's amusement, diversion, pure pleasure. She only had to remember that's all it was.

But was he having second thoughts? Téa took a deep breath and inhaled that deep, complex note of bergamot. It was on her arm, it was on his fingers. They smelled like each other, just like that night when they'd made love. Her skin prickled as she remembered going to sleep in her bed with his scent on her hands and in her hair. She hadn't wanted to wash it away.

Téa glanced at him over her shoulder. He was watching

her again, and gone was all that practiced detachment. This time, she felt him smoldering.

Catching her on fire.

Taking another breath, Téa gathered together a selection of albums she liked. "Come look at these," she said. "Tell me what you think."

She'd found a dozen that were not only in good condition, but were in the right tone and color scheme. He grunted at each as she displayed them for his approval. "These are my favorite three," she said, reaching the last of the group.

First, the George Shearing Quartet's *Velvet Carpet*. On the cover, crystal chandeliers hung over a dark-haired, dark-eyed woman in an evening gown, her body stretched out on red velvet. Téa drew a finger across the carpet. "We can echo this color in the armchairs. Maybe not red velvet, but something as deep and rich as this."

He moved closer, and she felt his warmth at her back. Good, she thought. He was close again.

"I like it," he said. "Nice call."

Next, she showed him the cover of Jackie Gleason's *Velvet Brass,* which depicted two women in '50s cigarette skirts and tight sweaters, hips caught in an orgasmic sway while surrounded by the brass instruments apparently responsible for their wild delight.

Téa shuffled back a fraction, so that her bottom brushed Johnny's hips. He didn't move away. Turning her head, she glanced over her shoulder at him. "Do you like this one?"

He'd removed his sunglasses too, and his eyes appeared almost black in the shaded light. His body shifted—an accident?—the movement pushing him against her bottom again.

"I like all the velvet," he said softly. One fingertip found that line of scented oil on her inner arm and stroked, up and down. Up then down.

Her shiver caused her body to rub against his, just the tiniest bit. His skin temperature went from warm to hot. He reached around her to flip over the Gleason album and reveal the final one she'd selected.

Music of the African Arab, from Mohammed Al-Bakker and his Oriental Ensemble. The album cover showed an olive-skinned, bare-breasted woman dancing in a red vest and diaphanous harem pants. Johnny stilled, his inner arm pressed against her outer arm. With his other hand, he continued to stroke her skin, up and down. Up then down.

She licked her lips. "Too risqué?"

His lips found their way to her ear. "What do you think?"

She shrugged.

"Coward," he said.

Not today. Maybe not anymore. Temporary diversion. Pure pleasure. She leaned back into Johnny's body. "I thought it might remind you of our dance."

His indrawn breath was quick and sharp. "Is that your answer?"

She turned so that she was caught between his body and the table of albums. "My answer is yes."

How they made it back to the car, she didn't really remember. Johnny paid for the albums; she was pretty sure, at least, they didn't steal them. Then he dragged her through the swap meet to the parking lot and stowed their purchases in the Jaguar's trunk.

He slammed the lid shut, then leaned against it and pulled her into his arms, widening his stance so that she was nestled against him, his long inner thighs pressing against her outer ones. His mouth was hot and eager and when his tongue sank deep between her lips, she moaned.

She would never regret this. Never.

And she would remember that cool was overrated. Because heat was consuming her now—Johnny's hot mouth, his hot embrace, the passion inside her body that was rising to meet him. It was glorious. It was the way a woman was supposed to feel.

It was the perfect way to forget everything that was worrying her: the Loanshark book, the wolves, her grandfather's upcoming birthday and all that his retirement might mean. Johnny was proving to be an excellent, effective distraction.

He ended the kiss, dragging his mouth off hers. Then he pressed her head to his shoulder and she sagged against him. They were both breathing hard and she reveled in the certainty that they were both as strongly and passionately affected.

"Contessa?" he whispered against her ear.

"Hmmmm." She drew it out, every part of her feeling languid and loose, ready for him to mold and penetrate and make his.

His fingernails bit harder into her scalp and his voice went rougher. Quieter. "Is there some reason a man would be following you?"

Twenty-six

"More Than You Know"
Count Basie Orchestra
The Jubilee Alternatives (1943–44)

As Johnny drove back to Palm Springs, Téa made him explain what had aroused his suspicions fourteen times. "There was a man in jeans and a windbreaker. Gray hair, early fifties, maybe. I first noticed him at the sunglasses table, then again when we bought your Rasta hat. He was hanging around the music stall and followed us out to the parking lot. I had the impression he was watching us."

On the seat beside his, her knees were pressed together and she held her purse in a protective embrace on her lap. "There is absolutely no reason for anyone to be following me. The idea is preposterous."

It was also ridiculous, ludicrous, outright absurd, and ten other adjectives that made clear the notion had truly rattled her.

The traffic was a bitch in both directions, a typical Southern California rush hour, but Johnny took his hand off the wheel long enough to stroke his palm over her dark hair. It was wavy and wild around her shoulders, just the way he liked it. "Give it a rest, Contessa."

She toyed with the new bead necklace at her throat. "I don't know what you're talking about." But then she swiveled her head, canvassing the vehicles stacked in the lanes around them. "Did you see what kind of car he was driving?"

Shaking his head, Johnny sighed. If he didn't get her back on track, he wasn't going to get her any later.

And that's what he was after. Sex with Téa. He'd been honest with her about needing the distraction and she'd seemed willing enough after he'd given her the time at the swap meet to think about it.

Though her "you're too good" had almost derailed *him*. When anchorwoman LaDonna had made the declaration, he'd felt nothing. When his brother Michael had thrown the same comment in his face, he'd shrugged off any remorse. But Téa—when she said the same words they struck him like an accusation.

"You're too good" sounded too much like *you're all charm and no substance*.

"You're too good" sounded too much like *you're unfeeling*.

"You're too good" sounded too much like *you're uncaring*.

Funny how he'd always considered those last two attributes, and they were, in the business he was in. When gambling, the best mind set was unemotional and completely objective. But when it came to Téa, damn it, he was being sincere. He wanted to have her but he didn't want to hurt her either. It would only be good between them if they both regarded the relationship in the same way.

Distraction, diversion, amusement, you name it, as long as it didn't have an emotional component.

He smothered the little devil in the back of his head whispering the reminder that he wanted her for another reason as well—the Caruso connection. Fine, there was that too. Shit, maybe he was unfeeling and uncaring, because he wasn't, *wasn't* going to feel guilty about wanting her and wanting her connection to Cosimo as well.

But he also wasn't going to be stupid. Aware that she was still looking over her shoulder despite the dark and the unidentifiable headlights all around them, he didn't head straight for his house.

She needed time to loosen up.

So he took her out to dinner. They landed on Palm Canyon Drive, in the heart of the downtown district, at the Coyote Café. He opted for the patio because he wanted to see her in the starshine of the fairy lights strung around the trunks of the palm trees.

He hadn't considered how slow the service might be on a weeknight. But it was high tourist season after all, and he counted them lucky they'd snagged a free table close to the wrought-iron fence separating the outdoor seating area from the public sidewalk. Though the desert night was cool, the day's heat still radiated from the asphalt and the walls. Patio heaters stood ready, but unnecessary. The scent of tortilla chips in hot oil made his mouth water.

The waitress brought their drinks quickly. That's when he learned not to order "large" when it came to margaritas at the Coyote in Palm Springs. His whiskey arrived in the requisite rocks glass. Téa's tequila and lime concoction came in something sized like a fruit bowl.

She blinked at the drink when it was first set before her, but it was testament to her ongoing case of nerves that she lifted the salt-encrusted glass with almost eagerness.

It was testament to his horniness that watching her lick the rim with her pink tongue brought his cock to full alert.

He wasn't going to feel guilty about that either.

But as he watched her frequent sips of her drink, he wondered if he shouldn't. She hadn't eaten a kernel of the popcorn he'd bought at the swap meet, or the hot dog she'd shuddered over later. Her stomach had to be empty, and so far she was filling it with a potent brew that, by the glazed look in her eye, was mostly alcohol.

Getting her drunk to get her into his bed didn't lead to blame-free mornings.

And the way she was looking at him from those smoldering sloe eyes told him the margarita was loosening her inhibitions. She'd let her blouse stay two-button open. She was showing honest-to-God cleavage and it was such plump, centerfold-quality cleavage that he felt his cock twitch in its direction.

Wearing a small smile, she continued to play with the necklace he'd bought her on a whim. The way her fingers worked over the beads made him think of her fingers working on him, and looking at her flushed face and lips reddened by the icy glass, he had the sudden urge to see how far he could push her. Would she take off her panties if he asked? He drop-kicked his conscience off the playing field and leaned across the table.

"Téa," he said, needing to touch her. Needing to feel her vibrancy beneath his hand.

As his fingers found the back of hers, her chin jerked up. "There's my mother," she told Johnny, looking over his shoulder. She waved a wild hand toward the sidewalk that was crowded with tourists gathered in knots around the celebrity plaques that studded the Palm Springs Walk of Stars. "Mom! Over here!"

Johnny snatched back his hand as Bianca skirted a bronze star on her way to greet her daughter. Her eyes widened as she took in Téa's relative state of dishevelment and her neon-beaded necklace and then her gaze dropped to the half-full, bucket-sized margarita on the table.

"You look like you're having fun," she said to Téa.

Téa beamed a smile that was a little sloppy around the edges. "Oh, I'm planning to."

Damn. She might as well be wearing a flashing sign declaring "I'm going to be fucked later." Her mother's gaze flicked to Johnny's face and he leaned against the back of his chair, trying to look suave and sinless at the same time. Surely she couldn't read on his face the sexual dare she'd interrupted. But damn, she was giving him the uncomfortable and indisputable mother-eye.

"We've ordered dinner," he offered, to prove he wasn't just trying to get her darling daughter drunk. Then he cleared his throat and poured on the charm, because no badass Vegas gambler was going to let a mama scare him off. "Please. Join us."

"No." The word came out in stereo, as both Téa and her mother spoke at the same time. Téa blushed.

Bianca shot a knowing look at her daughter, then laughed. "No, I can't stay, thanks. I'm meeting someone down the street."

Téa tucked her hair behind her ears. "See, I knew that," she said, then ducked her head to take another deep draw from the straw in her margarita.

Her mother laughed again. "I'll leave you two alone then. It's been good seeing you."

"It's been good seeing you, too." Johnny hoped the devil's snicker sounding inside him didn't show on his face.

Téa's mother started to turn, then she hesitated, frowning. "You remind me of someone."

He stilled, newly alert. His physical resemblance to his father was remote and his coloring completely different. But might she see a similarity? It hadn't even occurred to him that she could have been acquainted with Giovanni sixteen years before. "Is that right?"

Bianca nodded her head. "Someone I've recently met."

"His brother lives in the area," Téa supplied. "Maybe you've seen him."

"Perhaps that's it," her mother said, and then with a little wave, she was gone.

Johnny downed the dregs of whiskey, chasing away the last of his tension. Over its rim, he watched Téa use her fingertip to pick up grains of coarse salt from the edge of her glass then bring them to her mouth. Oh, yeah. With her mother out of the picture it was back to the game.

"Now, where were we?" he asked softly.

She froze, her lips around the end of her forefinger. Her gaze met his and the flickering light on the table showed the new flush washing up her face.

Though it was obvious she hadn't wanted her mother to join them, it was up to him to remind her why. Reaching out, he took her hand from her mouth, then brought it to his own. He sucked in her wet finger.

She made a little sound. "Johnny," she whispered. "Johnny, I don't think I'm hungry anymore."

He licked the end of her finger and released her hand. "I'll pay the bill."

She nodded, then drew her margarita closer to take another big gulp of the frozen drink.

Johnny closed his eyes. Damn it. Damn Téa's mother, his mother, his boring but unbreakable Main Street upbringing. All three of them were conspiring against him. "We need to eat first, Contessa. You need food."

Thank God the waitress was at that moment bearing down on them with enormous platters, an enchilada combination plate for him and a spinach-and-cheese quesadilla for Téa. They'd eat, they'd leave, they'd fuck. Since he was giving her food, his conscience had nothing to complain about.

It didn't take long for the meal to affect Téa's mood. Gone was the dizzy look in her eyes. She pushed the margarita away though it was still one-third full. The sexual flush on her face faded and she stared at her plate instead of at him.

Johnny cursed his own scruples.

"Second thoughts, Contessa?" he asked. It looked as if her earlier acquiescence was gone and that he'd be going home to an empty bed. He didn't want to think how difficult it would be to get to sleep tonight.

She looked up. "What? Uh, um, no. Not really." An embarrassed blush bloomed on her cheeks and she clapped her palms over them. "This feels so awkward."

Second thoughts would have killed him. Awkward, he could handle. Smiling at her, he leaned forward to take one of her hands in his. "Maybe I should have gone ahead with my first inclination. I promise you wouldn't be feeling awkward right now."

She narrowed her pretty dark eyes. "What inclination was that?"

He lowered his voice. "I wanted to dare you to take off your panties during dinner."

Her fingers bit into his. "Johnny." She sounded scandalized. Almost tempted.

"Téa," he countered. "Would you have agreed?"

Her primo ass squirmed against her seat. "Of course not."

"No one would have to know," he whispered. "Just you and me. Our little, sexy secret."

She squirmed more. "Nooo. No."

He grinned, certain that panty-less or not, she was feeling that way right now, as if she was naked beneath her skirt and that he was the only other one who knew it.

"You're evil." She frowned at him.

"I try." He wiggled his eyebrows. "Come on, Contessa, do it."

She hesitated. God, he almost had her.

"It'll be our sexy little secret," he whispered again, sliding his fingers along the smooth insides of hers and shutting his conscience away for good. Tonight he'd have her in his bed, tomorrow he'd talk his way into an introduction to her grandfather.

Biting her lip, she looked away. "Speaking of secrets," she said. "I have to be honest with you about something."

What? Honesty? Now?

Johnny sank against the back of his chair. "We don't need to talk any more tonight." His gaze darted around the court-yard, looking for the waitress so he could signal for their check.

"This is important, Johnny. It's . . . it's about that man who might have been following us."

He wanted to stand up and kick the table, the chair, his own butt for mentioning the man to her in the first place. His as-sumption had been the guy was a bodyguard type sent to watch over Téa—retired newspaperman Stan had warned him of how protective Cosimo was of his granddaughters—but apparently it was without her prior knowledge or approval.

"You need to know what you're getting into when you get involved with me, Johnny."

You need to know what you're getting into when you get in-volved with me. Shit. The devil in his head and his guilty con-science were both laughing their asses off at him now.

"If this has something to do with your grandfather and your family—"

"It has everything to do with them and everything I won't do to cooperate with them."

"Huh?" Johnny had thought he already knew what she was going to say, but this wasn't it. "What do you mean?"

"I'm estranged from the Carusos, Johnny. At least from my grandfather and his . . . men."

"Huh?"

"My grandfather still keeps his eye on me, I've always known that, but recently he's been upping the pressure to bring me back into the fold. It's been little stuff until now—my sisters, the flowers, that invitation to espresso, but it could get worse."

She's estranged from the old man. She's estranged from the old man.

"So, if we're . . . together . . . we might find ourselves followed on occasion. Or Cosimo himself might try to make contact. I'll understand if it creeps you out. Frankly, it creeps me out."

She's estranged from the old man.

"Johnny?"

He wrenched his gaze off the tablecloth to stare into her face. "What?"

"I understand if the situation means you've changed your mind about . . . being social with me on a more regular basis. But so you know, I'm never going to be around him again."

The waitress slipped their bill onto the table. Johnny automatically reached for his wallet and fished out plenty of cash to cover it. He didn't check the numbers because he didn't think his brain had the focus for anything but . . .

She's estranged from the old man.

Suddenly, he laughed out loud. Téa looked at him as if he was crazy, and he felt a little that way too, but he continued laughing as he pulled her up from the table and walked her to his car. Oh, the irony.

Yet his mood continued to lighten on the drive to his house. As he tugged her toward the front door, Téa tugged back, her feet slowing. "Johnny, are you sure about this?"

The catch in her voice made him catch her in his arms. Oh, yeah, with Cosimo out of the picture he was really, really sure about this. There was no reason to hesitate. "Aren't you?" he whispered against her lips.

In the bedroom, he remembered he'd wanted to have candles. Téa naked in the candlelight and spread out for his hands and for his tongue. But he didn't want to trek back to the car, not when she was warm and heating up.

She made him keep the lights off.

He knew she was thinking of the mirror overhead and that made him laugh again. It turned to a groan as she pushed his shirt off his shoulders and spread her fingers across his chest.

She made little noises as he made love to her. He thought

she was biting back the sounds and he promised himself he'd make her really let go soon. But now he fought hard for his control too, making sure that he played her with his fingers and felt her come before letting himself inside the tight wet glove of her body.

He was going to pull out and taste her, he promised himself, just two thrusts more . . . just one. Now. But then she tilted her hips and her sleek inner thighs slid along the outside of his.

Without skill, without suavity, without any of the finesse he'd honed for years, he came. His rough thrusts slapped his belly against hers. He couldn't help it.

When he collapsed on top of her, she cradled his head in her palms. "I'll move in a second," he promised.

She murmured something that sounded already half-asleep. They dozed.

Johnny came awake in a rush. There was a fragrant pillow . . .

Téa. He smiled to himself and gathered her close, two spoons in the cozy drawer of his bed.

"Johnny?"

"Shh. Go back to sleep."

Her arm shifted against the one he had tucked beneath her breasts. The movement must have pressed the backlight button on her watch, because the businesslike face blinked on. It was 3:12:37.

For the first time in months, he'd slept through the witching hour.

Twenty-seven

"I've Grown Accustomed to Her Face"
Johnny Mathis
Warm (1957)

Rachele danced around the kitchen, preparing the evening
meal for herself and her father. Over the weekend, she'd
made a big pan of lasagna and then frozen it in individual
squares. Two were warming in the microwave. A little bread,
a little salad, and her father would sit down to one of his favorite dinners.

Little did he know it was eggplant that gave the pasta dish
its heartiness. The tomato sauce was purely vegetarian as
well, with grated carrots, honey, and the juice of a fresh
lemon to balance the flavors. Her traditional Italian papa
didn't know how untraditional the Ciriglianos could be.

She caught sight of her reflection in the stainless steel
toaster and grimaced. You'd think one look at her dark
makeup and nose and eyebrow piercings would drive the
point home, but no.

A few minutes later, with a full, fragrant plate in front of him, her father didn't even appear to notice when she seated herself across from him. It didn't wipe the smile off her face. It couldn't.

"Why are you humming?" her father asked, his attention still focused on his lasagna.

Humming? "I am?" She had been, she realized. One of Dean Martin's signature songs, "On an Evening in Roma."

You could put Usher in an Italian girl's iPod, but you couldn't take Dino out of an Italian girl's mental music files. "It was a good day at work, I guess," she said.

Her father grunted what might pass for an, "Oh, yeah?"

She decided to accept it as such. "First, Téa—"

"How's her mother?"

"Fine, I guess."

His head came up, his gaze fixing somewhere over her left shoulder. "When's the last time you saw her?"

Rachele frowned. "Let me think . . . last week? She stopped by with a new product for Téa to try. She's been moaning that her hair refuses to stay straight."

"Bianca has been moaning?"

"No, *Téa*. Her mother seems just fine."

"Fine?"

Rachele sighed. "Just fine."

"That's good. That's very good." Her father's head dipped back toward his food.

Rachele frowned at the top of his head. Did he really have the jones for Téa's mother or was the suspicion just a hangover from the bubbly atmosphere that had been floating around the design office in recent days?

"Téa's got a boyfriend," she blurted out.

Her father's fork paused between his plate and his mouth. He appeared to study the bite of lasagna.

Maybe he was noticing the eggplant for the first time in seven years. But then he shoveled it into his mouth without comment.

"As long as I've been working for her, she's only dated these fuddy-duddy fix-up guys, but this time she found a man all on her own." And Rachele couldn't have been more surprised if her father had commented upon the midnight-black shade of her fingernail polish. "She's been coming into the office *late*."

Her father grunted again, so Rachele felt obliged to tell the whole truth.

"Well, it was only once and she blamed it on a blow-dryer malfunction." Since Téa's hair had been a wiggly mass of waves lately, it was sort of hard *not* to believe her. But there'd been something that looked an awful lot like a case of beard burn on the underside of her chin. Rachele smiled to herself and rubbed a finger along her own jaw. Cal kept a close shave, but there was the teeniest rough edge to his skin that made his kisses only that much more exciting.

"Who's this man?"

"Cal . . . " Rachele started, then caught herself. "You mean Téa's . . . uh, man? His name is Johnny. Johnny Magee." And when he came into the design office, sometimes he'd hang in the reception area and lean against the wall, looking Rat Pack-cool if you didn't take into account the way he gazed through Téa's office doorway and just *watched* her working at her desk.

As if she was a present he'd never asked for and didn't deserve, but that he wouldn't ever, ever give back.

The thought was kinda weird, but Rachele wondered if it was the way her mother might have watched *her* when Rachele was a little girl. As if the other person mattered in a totally unexpected way.

"Johnny Magee owns the property on El Deseo," her father said between bites.

"Yes," Rachele answered. "I told you about that job."

"I've been there," he said. "Looking for you, but you'd let this Johnny's associate drive you home."

Rachele gripped her fork. Was this the right moment to talk to her father about her new relationship? She'd put it off time and again, and she knew Cal was getting impatient with her excuses. "His name is Cal. Cal Kazarsky."

"Well, it doesn't matter what his name is, because I don't want you going over to that house anymore." Her father didn't look up from his food. "And I don't want you going home with some stranger."

"Cal's not a *stranger*, Papa." A tense little laugh escaped from her mouth. "And I didn't go home with him, he drove *me* home."

"No matter." He waved his fork. "You won't see him again. You will not go back to that house."

She stared at the man across the table. He was in his mid-fifties, still handsome, she supposed, with a full head of salt-and-pepper hair. But he was her father, not her keeper, and Cal was right. If she didn't come clean, he would continue to treat her like a child. She'd kept her secret for too long already.

"You don't even know Cal," she said.

He waved his fork again. "Neither do you."

"Yes, yes I do." She swallowed. "I've been seeing him for a couple of weeks. We're . . . we're dating. Like a couple."

Her father frowned at his plate. "A couple? No. I didn't give you my permission to date."

His flat tone started her pulse thumping. She set down her fork and clasped her hands in her lap, trying to stay calm. Trying to sound calm. "Papa, I'm a grown woman. Twenty-one years old. I don't need your permission to do anything."

"You are my daughter," he said. "And you will do as I say."

She swallowed again. "Let's try this one more time. Papa. I don't need your permission to come and to go, to do my job, and especially not to . . . to fall in love."

His head jerked up. "I forbid you to use that word."

"Love?"

"I forbid you to use it."

She stared at him. "I don't understand."

"I forbid you to use it!" he repeated, his voice rising as he shoved back his chair. He stood, his hands in fists at his sides. "I forbid you to make mistakes or to be hurt or to have your heart broken. Do you understand me?"

"Papa—"

"There's to be no more discussion of this."

Rachele rose to her own feet, her legs shaky. She started backing away from the table, not afraid of her father, but afraid of what they might be about to sever. "We need to discuss this. This isn't a field trip you're forbidding me to go on. This is about my becoming my own woman. A grown woman."

"There will be no men in your life," her father asserted again. "And there will be no mistakes or hurt feelings or having your heart broken. This is for your own good."

She still couldn't believe what she was hearing. She'd expected him to be worried, but not to out and out refuse to be reasonable.

"Papa, I care for this man. I have feelings—"

But he couldn't concern himself to listen to them. "Defy me in this, Rachele," he declared with such conviction that she could only believe him, "and you are no longer my daughter."

Cold washed over Rachele's skin as she stared at the man who had raised her. Was this really her father? Was he really the kind of person who could dismiss her feelings, dismiss her, so easily? For years she'd thought it was grief that kept him at a distance, but now . . . now she could see that it was indifference. She was an obligation and a responsibility, but not a person to him.

"Then I guess I'm no longer your daughter," she said slowly. "Because I am going to defy you."

"You will do no such thing—" Then her father blinked, and blinked again, his expression growing bewildered.

"What is that on your face, Rachele Maria?" His forefinger touched his nose, his eyebrow. "What have you done to your face? You don't look like my daughter anymore."

And she realized that for the first time he was seeing her.

"*How could you do that to your face?*" he asked.

Her father was really seeing her. But he still hadn't heard a word she'd said. Rachele felt a wild urge to laugh.

Because it was too late for him to finally open his eyes.

It was too late to keep her from Cal.

It was too late to keep her from falling in love.

And, she thought, looking at the father who was, she realized, the true stranger in her life, it was too late to keep her heart from breaking.

He'd already done the job.

Twenty-eight

"I'm Confessin'"
Kay Starr
Rockin' with Kay (1958)

Téa sat at a table on the patio outside of the Kona Kai
Spa's small bar, a glass of wine in front of her as she waited
for Johnny to arrive. It should have been a peaceful place to
wait, because a mid-October late afternoon in Palm Springs
meant the air was a perfect 75 degrees. Palm fronds created
spiky shade across the pebble-paved patio, and twenty feet
away, a swimming pool refreshed the eyes. The scent of
blooming gardenias in a nearby terra-cotta pot wafted by in
the slight breeze. Behind her, water trickled from a wall-
mounted fountain into a clam-shaped bowl.

But though Téa appreciated her environs, they didn't bring
her a measure of peace. Ten days had passed since she and
Johnny had decided to become each other's "distraction."

Ten days that had felt so right she was now convinced that
something was about to go very, very wrong.

Her growing dread had only been exacerbated by the certainty that eyes were watching her every move. With her stubborn refusals, she'd managed to discourage the mobsters roaming around town from hanging about her office, but when she was driving the streets and particularly when she was with Johnny, she sensed a stranger's scrutiny. It had to be someone sent by her grandfather.

She refused to think anyone guessed she possessed the Loanshark book. The watcher was Cosimo sending her a message, she insisted to herself, staring at the straw-colored liquid in her glass. He was sending a signal just as clear as the one that had come with the apricot roses. He wanted her back in the family fold.

Footsteps sounded behind her, paused. Not Johnny, she would feel him in the air, but this presence set the hair rising on her arms in an entirely different way. She didn't look up, even when olive-skinned fingers gripped the back of the chair beside hers. Coarse black hairs curled between scarred knuckles.

"I've been looking for you. I have a message."

She hadn't spoken to him in years, yet she recognized his voice. "Is that right, Nino?" Nino Farelle. She glanced up. He was in his thirties now, but he was still as darkly handsome as he'd been when Eve had fancied herself in love with him eight years ago. Before he'd given her the black eye and the split lip.

Téa met his gaze. "I couldn't have been that hard to find since you've been following me all over town for more than a week." At least now she knew who the watcher was, and that her instincts had been right. Nino worked for her grandfather.

His expression didn't flicker. "Sorry, sweet cheeks. But it hasn't been me on your tail until about thirty minutes back."

Sweet cheeks. Téa tried hard not to let that old nickname he used get under her skin. Eight years before, she'd tried to tolerate him for Eve's sake, though his snide "sweet cheeks" had only made her feel more fat and undesirable. "Nino, I know you, or some other of Cosimo's minions, have been watching me for days."

His face flushed ruddy. "I'm no minion anymore. I've moved up in the ranks. Way up. And nobody's been clocking you, sweet cheeks. Your grandfather ordered the kid gloves . . . " his voice took on a threatening tone, "until today."

"Oh wow, Nino. Now I'm scared." But she was. If it was true and her grandfather had been keeping his distance, then who had been stalking her and Johnny?

Johnny. She took a quick glance around. She didn't want him, or anyone else for that matter, to see her with a man as nasty as Nino Farelle. It was the kind of association that wouldn't do her business any good and it only served to remind her of all the things she wished to forget. "What is it you want, Nino? Spit it out quick."

He smiled, and that felt threatening too, even as he slid his hands in the pockets of his ash-colored slacks. "I knew I could get you to come around. Told Cosimo I have a special touch with you girls."

"I know all about your 'special touch,' Nino," she said, her stomach starting to churn. "So you better stick to the message and then get going."

His eyes narrowed. Apparently he hadn't known she was aware of the beating he'd given Eve and how it was her sister's promise not to tell Cosimo that kept Nino away from her . . . and him, most likely, alive. "Your grandfather wants to see you at his party, *va bene?* He's feeling his age and wants to have all his family around him on his special night."

Out of Nino's mouth, this argument had even less chance of plucking her heartstrings than when it came from her sisters. "Maybe I'll send something from Hallmark, but I won't be coming to the party."

Nino took her refusal less well than they had. He glowered at her. "Your grandfather says it won't be a celebration unless—"

"Come on. He doesn't need me to help blow out the birthday candles. I'm not buying it, Nino."

"*Merda!* Fine. It's more. It's to show unity within the family at this time of change."

She'd known sentiment wasn't driving Cosimo. Still . . . "He's done just fine without me all these years. I'm confident he'll continue to do fine without me the next few months."

Nino's dark brows drew together in frustration. "He's expecting me to bring back your word you'll come."

"Then you're going to disappoint him, because I'm not offering it."

He set his jaw. "Sweet cheeks—"

"And don't call me that either, or maybe I'll have something to say to Cosimo after all."

"Say you'll go to the party." His hands were balled into fists inside his pockets.

"Over my dead body."

"Don't be so flip," he retorted. "There's unrest in the families. Your grandfather doesn't want to see you hurt. It's another reason he wants you close."

Though that thought had her heart pounding, she couldn't let a bully like Nino think he'd gotten to her. She tried to sneer. "So he's willing to scare me into it? Tell him that won't work either."

He stared her down for a long minute, then shook his head in disgust. "I'm out of here."

Not soon enough for her. "Nobody's stopping you."

But Nino was already turning back, a predator's smile on his dark-angel face. She should have known he wouldn't let her have the last word. "By the way, sweet cheeks, tell your sister Eve I'll be keeping my eye on her, too."

Téa held her hand over her stomach as he walked off, then

she downed half her glass of wine in one quick gulp. God, Nino gave her the creeps. But he was gone. Thank goodness he was gone. And any minute Johnny would be here.

Johnny, her temporary sex buddy. The appearance of Nino made it even more obvious there was nothing else it could ever be between them. At some point, involvement with the progeny of a notorious crime family and all that it entailed would turn too intrusive or just plain too ugly for Johnny to deal with.

No man ever stayed.

Even before her confrontation with Nino she'd known this. That's why, aware the end had to be rushing upon them, she'd suggested meeting Johnny at the spa today instead of somewhere more private. Privacy equaled intimacy and it was smarter for her to keep their relationship less personal than that. It was also why she'd made up her mind not to go to bed with him that night . . . for the first time in more than a week. She shouldn't be getting quite so cozy with a temporary sex buddy.

Because the sex . . . oh, the sex *was* personal. And intimate. She continued to insist on the darkness and knew he thought she was being unnecessarily prudish. But in the dark she managed to hold her responses back. In the dark she felt some measure of protection from him. Some measure of control. A voice broke into her thoughts.

"Well, if it isn't the little Puritan."

Great. Another unwelcome visitor.

Téa reluctantly raised her head. Melissa Banyon stood in front of her, decked out in one of the spa's white robes and a ridiculous pair of marabou-trimmed sandals. A stretchy white turban covered her hair. Beside her, Raphael Fremont projected more of that brooding sensuality that had so captivated Téa in his starring role in *The Foreign Legion*. But with his dusty uniform replaced by a satiny robe that matched his fiancée's, his smoldering stare seemed something between overdone and overwrought.

Téa let out an inward groan. Her mother hadn't mentioned that Melissa Banyon and pouting boyfriend were in residence, but then her mother never did mention the names in her registration book. Complete discretion was one of the prime attractions the Kona Kai offered. Guests, particularly celebrity guests, were able to be as private as they liked, and most would gnaw off their right arms before striking up conversation with near strangers—

"Where's your handsome friend?"

—unless they had a gorgeous, sexy provocation like Johnny Magee.

Fiancé Raphael shot Melissa Banyon a sharp look and his smolder jumped several more degrees. Téa stifled another groan. All she didn't need was dealing with this couple's troubles too.

"Téa's friend is right here." Johnny emerged from the French doors leading to the bar, carrying a glass of wine in one hand and a martini in the other.

She swiveled to watch him cross the patio. In a blue silk shirt, open at the neck, tan slacks, and distressed-leather loafers, he looked like Palm Springs had been made for him. His sleeves were rolled up, and as he set the glasses on the table beside her, the waning rays of sunlight glinted off the golden hair at his wrists.

He bent to catch her mouth with his. "Contessa," he murmured against it, "I missed you."

That one kiss had her forgetting everything. He stretched toward the potted gardenia and picked a perfect bloom, then leaned close again to tuck the flower behind Téa's ear. Tingles burst from curve to lobe and goose bumps sprinted down her neck.

A "distraction" wasn't supposed to make her forget! A

"distraction" wasn't supposed to make her feel so desired and so . . . *enjoyed,* she thought with a sense of panic. This was just another reason why she had to cool things between them—starting tonight.

And Melissa Banyon appeared ready to help, Téa could see, as the other woman fiddled with the lapels of her robe so that the inner curves of her sili-cones were exposed. "So good to see you again," she said to Johnny in her annoying, little-girl voice. "Would you mind if we joined you?"

Raphael looked from his fiancée to Johnny, and though Téa would have sworn the desert air couldn't get any drier, it crackled. Then the actor's eyes flicked to Téa's face, and lingered there.

"Oui," he said slowly, his body shifting in her direction. "I see. Yes. It could be fun to join with you."

Téa couldn't believe what she'd just heard. Or she couldn't believe the double meaning she was reading into what she'd just heard. Was the actor really suggesting a ménage-a-quatre?

Johnny's hand stroked the top of her hair. She looked up.

One of his eyebrows rose and she caught a hint of that wicked dimple in his cheek. *It's up to you, Contessa.*

Heat rushed up her face and she stared into her glass of wine. "We—" Her voice squeaked, and she had to clear her mind and then her throat before starting again. "We'd rather be alone, if you don't mind."

She didn't look back up until she heard Melissa and Raphael move off and Johnny's chair legs scrape against the patio. Through her lashes, she tried to gauge his expression.

"I see you peeking at me," he said, grinning. "I'm disappointed in you, Téa. I thought for a minute you were going to agree."

"I was not even tempted."

"Liar," Johnny said softly.

She laughed. Amazing. Even after her chat with Nino, even after an almost-foursome with a famous Hollywood couple, she was laughing. Johnny made it so frighteningly easy to feel happy. "If I said I was tempted, then I'd have to admit you're not keeping me satisfied, now, wouldn't I?"

His eyes narrowed and his nostrils flared. "Is that the way it is?" He found her bare skin beneath the hem of her straight skirt and cupped his hand along her inner thigh. "Go in the bathroom, take off your panties, and I'll satisfy you right here, right now."

The lightning that had been in the air a few minutes earlier flashed over Téa's skin. *Talk about being tempted . . .*

But no, no! She was supposed to be pulling back from him. Starting tonight. Starting now.

Remember Nino and the Loanshark book and how quickly happiness could die. Remember why she hadn't wanted to meet in private with him. She couldn't afford to get too intimate.

Taking a breath, she opened her mouth to make clear they were having this drink together, and that was it. "Johnny—"

"Téa." Rachele rushed through the French doors and onto the patio. "Téa, I hoped I'd find you here."

Maybe they would have been better off in private after all, Téa thought in resignation. Then she looked into her assistant's face and jumped to her feet, alarmed by the girl's expression. "What is it, Rach? What's the matter?"

"I've just run away from home." Rachele burst into tears, her thick mascara causing black tracks to course down her cheeks.

At that, wouldn't most men have made themselves scarce? Téa had expected that Johnny would and been glad of it. She'd been in desperate need of a reason to keep her panties on and their relationship less personal.

But as she put an arm around Rachele and tried to understand her choked-out explanation about an argument with her father, Johnny had a word with a roving cocktail waitress. Within minutes, Téa's mother was on the scene with a steaming mug of tea and keys to one of the private suites on the spa property.

He was still around half an hour later when Eve and Joey arrived in the cottage. By this time Rachele's face was clean and she was wrapped in a spa robe and propped in the corner of one couch. Johnny had appointed himself mini-bartender and hailed the newcomers with mixed drinks and fifteen-dollar bags of mixed nuts.

Téa's sisters accepted with polite smiles for him and raised eyebrows for Téa. She could only shrug.

They all waved off Bianca, who murmured she had a previous engagement she couldn't break but who kissed Rachele's forehead and assured her she could stay as long as she liked.

Once the door had shut behind her, the rest of the group turned their gaze on the young woman. Gone was Rachele's usual cheeky confidence. Instead, she looked sad and lost and about twelve years old.

Téa remembered exactly how that felt—and suspected Rachele had always been hiding a fragile heart behind her goth-girl mask.

Johnny handed her an icy glass of what looked to be ginger ale. "Would you like me to call Cal for you?" he asked.

Rachele's head jerked up. "No. I don't want him to see me like this."

"He cares about you. If you're hurting, he'd want to be here."

"No," she repeated.

Téa understood the need to protect her vulnerability from the man in her life and sat down beside her. "We'll take care of Rachele."

Joey and Eve took their places in matching easy chairs. "That's right," they said together.

Perhaps he saw it as a challenge to his manliness, because despite those assertions he *still* stuck around. After a time and a few more mini-bar beverages, the other three seemed to forget he was in the room.

Téa didn't forget, because he'd moved a straight chair behind her spot on the sofa and was amusing himself by playing with her hair. The gentle swish of his fingers made it nearly impossible to concentrate on the conversation between her sisters and Rachele. It was nothing kind of talk, actually, because Rachele seemed to want it that way.

Joey suddenly turned toward Johnny. "So why are you still here?" she asked, in her usual impatient manner.

Eve rolled her eyes. "My God. It's as if you're six instead of twenty-six. Let me show you how this is done, little sister." She put on her angel-singing smile. "Johnny, how are you enjoying Palm Springs?"

You could hear the returning smile in his voice. "What's not to enjoy?" He plucked the gardenia from behind Téa's ear and stroked the petals against her cheek.

She tensed her muscles so as not to show her shiver.

Eve continued to use her party-circuit voice. "And how's the design of your house going?"

"Your sister's a cross between a miracle worker and a slave driver. Demolishers are demolishing. Painters are painting. More furniture arrives every day."

Pride warmed her from the inside out to meet the tingles that his touch started on her skin.

"Then you've learned one of her secrets," Joey said.

"What's that?"

"She's bossy." Joey grinned. "Not to mention overly worried about what she looks like and what other people think."

Téa sent the younger woman an "I'm killing you later" look. Tonight she was supposed to get less personal with Johnny, not more.

"I think I'm glad I don't have sisters," he murmured, bending closer to her ear.

But Joey heard it. "No sisters? Brothers then?"

"One brother. We're not that close."

"Ah," Joey said, nodding. "But we're Italian, which means we call 'em like we see 'em. We don't play the nicey-nice WASP game."

"Well maybe we could try," Téa protested.

"Hey, I'm no WASP," Johnny said. "I'll have you know I spent my formative years in catechism at St. Charles parish church," Johnny said.

Every Italian eye in the room focused on his face.

"You're Catholic?" Rachele replied. "No way."

Johnny shrugged. "I can still remember the seven gifts of the Holy Spirit that were awakened at my confirmation." He ticked them off on his fingers. "Wisdom, understanding, right judgment, courage, knowledge, reverence, and fear of Our Lord."

"Give the man a St. Christopher's medal," Eve said. "He knows more than I remember after thirteen years of parochial school."

Téa's neck prickled. Catholic? She didn't care if he was Buddhist or Baptist, but somehow, finding out he was Catholic made her wonder what other things he'd been keeping from her.

"This is the worst day of my life," Rachele suddenly whispered, squeezing shut her eyes.

Téa reached over to rub her arm. Had the mention of parochial school made Rachele remember "Honor thy father?" Téa had experienced problems with that one herself, after Salvatore had disappeared and left them to face the FBI alone.

Maybe the minds of her sisters had gone in that direction too. Eve looked off into the distance. Joey scowled.

"Those FBI SOBs gave me the worst day of my life," she said.

"No, Joey," Téa whispered. Not now. Not more secrets tonight. Not with Johnny so close to her.

Johnny's hand stroked down the length of her hair. She wanted to move up, move away, but she couldn't let him guess how tense she was.

Eve frowned. "The FBI are showing up at your Starbucks again?"

"No." Joey's eyes were gazing at a place in the distance. In the distant past. "Remember that day they burst into the house? I was hiding under my bed."

Johnny's hand stilled in her hair, midstroke.

Eve sounded offhand. "Of course I remember. We all remember, Joe."

Téa let out the little breath she'd been holding and felt Johnny's hand resume its soothing stroke.

But then Eve spoke again, her voice lower. "They pulled you out by your ankles. I'm sorry, Joe. I should have stopped them. I hate that I'm such a coward."

Damn it, Téa thought. This wasn't the time or the place or the people she wanted to discuss this around. But *she* hated hearing the guilt in her sister's voice. Anger started rattling its cage inside her again as images shuffled in Téa's mind. Memories. "You were in the closet, Eve. You didn't know they were dragging her out by her feet."

Rachele made a muffled noise. Johnny's hand moved to rest on Téa's shoulder.

The touch renewed Téa's resolve. "But let's not talk about this tonight," she said, mustering all her big-sister bossiness. Maybe at some point they should have talked about the events that changed their lives, but their mother had started the silence they all still kept.

Except for Joey, who now couldn't seem to keep her mouth still. "They didn't care about us or our feelings," she said. "They only wanted to find the stashes of cash they were sure we were hiding, no matter who they had to grab by the ankle or pull by the hair."

"Damn," Johnny muttered near her ear, apparently repulsed.

But the sisters kept on talking. "And the Loanshark book," Eve added. "They wanted that too, but they only found the cash and left us with nothing."

"God. Damn. It." Johnny spit the words out. His hand pulled away from Téa's shoulder. She could feel his disgust.

And almost, almost, could laugh about it. She'd wanted to cool things between herself and Johnny. She'd wanted to put him off before she got hurt. The funny thing was, it only took getting more personal, more intimate with him to find the way to make that happen.

Now that he knew more of her secrets, her heart was safe.

Not surprisingly, the subject of the FBI raid put the final damper on an already depressing evening. Rachele, who looked exhausted, assured all of them that she'd be fine alone. Certain that their mother would check in on the younger woman later, Eve left, then Joey, then finally Téa and Johnny.

It was a silent walk to the parking lot.

He hadn't said a word since his muttered, "God. Damn. It," and she hoped he'd leave it that way.

She had no need of platitudes. He didn't need to say, "Hey, maybe we'd better take a break from this distraction thing," for her to read the writing on the wall. FBI, stashes of cash, the Loanshark book. A man wouldn't want to be mixed up in ugliness like that.

She didn't expect him to understand what it was like to have a father like hers. Who would? Thinking she could be anyone's "distraction" or anything more than that was just a silly dream. Her father, her family, her past would always bubble up and give any good man sensible, second thoughts.

So, letting her relationship with Johnny die this quick, sudden death was all right with her.

Her hand was in her purse, scrambling around for her keys when he spoke, his voice rough and abrupt. "Where were you hiding?"

"Huh?"

"If Eve was in the closet and Joey under the bed, then where the hell were you?"

She swallowed, the memories coming alive again, a slide show of anger and fear. "You don't want to hear about that."

A white Cadillac cruised past them, its headlamps bathing their legs in light. It turned into a spot farther down the lot. The night air carried the sound of the Caddy's doors opening and a couple's conversation as they walked closer.

"Yes, I do." Johnny turned to the Jag and unlocked the passenger door. Holding it open, he nodded toward her and then the seat. "Get in. Get in and tell me."

Bristling, she glared up at him in the darkness, angry at his insistence and angrier still at the memories that had been poked alive by Joey and Eve, and now by him. She didn't like remembering them.

"Damn it. Get in and *tell me*."

Fine. He thought he wanted to know? Téa marched toward the car and ducked into the seat. Then she would tell him. Maybe he needed the words in order to feel less guilty about breaking things off. Certainly what she had to say could only tarnish the "pure pleasure" he claimed he wanted with her.

But when he was settled in the driver's seat beside her, he had to prompt her again. "I gather the FBI raided your house—after your father's disappearance?"

She took a breath, nodded. "They came in wearing bullet-proof vests and carrying sledgehammers and crowbars. At least a dozen of them. They pounded on the door and then didn't give us a chance to answer. They poured into the house like cockroaches."

Her mother had been frozen for days, ever since it was clear that Salvatore wasn't coming home. She'd watched the agents invade with dead eyes. "My father had been missing for more than a week."

"Where did they find you, Téa?"

She laughed, the sound dry and bitter. Scornful. "I wasn't hiding, if that's what you're asking." She'd still thought of herself as royal then. And loyal. So stupidly loyal. "I stood in the foyer and told them to get the hell out."

It seemed to take him a moment to absorb that. "How old did you say you were . . . twelve?"

"That's right. Twelve years old and I thought I could order them off the premises."

"Jesus." Johnny forked his hand through his hair. "Did they have a search warrant?"

She laughed again. "I don't know. Do you think they would have bothered to show it to me, Salvatore Caruso's little bitch of a daughter?"

"They called you a little bitch." Apparently he recognized the direct quote.

"Only when I bit the hand of the agent that shoved me out of the way."

That surprised a laugh out of him. "I would never have guessed you're a biter, Contessa."

"Oh, you don't really know me, Johnny." And he never would. Strange how sad and glad she felt about that at the same time. "You don't really know me at all."

He let the comment go, staring straight out the windshield as if he found the dark street fascinating. "They found cash then?"

"Wads of cash. I remember this one agent getting a little giddy as she scooped handfuls of twenties from a space behind the shelving in a linen closet. I read all about it in the newspapers. There was over $130,000 found in various places around the house. They confiscated every last dollar bill."

"It's no crime to have an aversion to Citigroup and B of A."

"I wish I'd thought to mention that when they smashed our piggy banks. I'm fairly certain that's what cemented Joey's hatred for the Federal Bureau of Investigation."

"Jesus," Johnny said again. "Jesus." With a jerky movement he started the car and then slammed it into reverse.

"Wait, wait." Bewildered, Téa put her hand on his arm. It was stiff and tense beneath her fingers. "My car."

"We'll get it tomorrow."

"You're driving me home?"

He glanced over. "What? I thought we were going back to my place."

"I . . . I don't want to go home with you." She cleared her throat. "I mean, you can't want me to go home with you."

"Why the hell not?" He was already racing down the street.

"Because . . . " She wanted to cool things between them. Because he had to be disturbed by what he knew about her family.

"You can't think this changes my attraction to you, Téa."

Of course she thought it changed his attraction to her! She was counting on it! Panic started to flutter in her belly again. Her family wasn't known as part of the Mafia because they were Italian and liked their pasta. It was because the FBI had found inexplicable sums of cash in the walls . . . and because of the Loanshark book.

"You don't understand. You don't know everything," she heard herself say.

He sped through a stale yellow light. "What don't I know?"

"Don't kid yourself." She'd done that, of course. But not

anymore. "My father didn't have an aversion to banks, Johnny. He had a business that dealt in cash. An illegal business that was documented in the Loanshark book."

"Eve mentioned this Loanshark book. But if it was never found, then how does anyone know what it actually documented?"

Johnny was already pulling into his driveway. In another couple of minutes they'd be in his house and in his bedroom and she didn't know if she'd be able to deny herself another night with him . . . or where another night with him might take her heart.

So she had to tell him the truth now—or at least most of it, she thought, desperate. Get it out, so that he'd have his eyes opened about who she *really* was. Then certainly he'd be done with her.

"*I* know what the Loanshark book actually documented, Johnny, because I did all the record-keeping for my father."

Twenty-nine

"I Didn't Know What Time It Was"
Bobby Darin
Love Swings (1961)

Johnny screeched to a stop in the apex of the circular parking area adjacent to his garage. "What? What did you say?"

"I've never told another soul." Téa found herself whispering it, as if the night might now be listening. "I'm trusting you not to tell anyone either."

"You kept the books for your father's business? A high-interest, unsecured loan business, I assume." He sounded both puzzled and upset. "Why the hell did he have you do that?"

"The business was loan-sharking, bookmaking, a little blackmail." She gave a shrug, trying to play it nonchalant. "And I did it because I was good with numbers."

"Jesus, Téa! You were a kid, a little girl." In the moonlight she saw him squeeze the steering wheel as if he was throttling it. "Your father should be shot."

"He probably was," she said.

"Oh, shit." He rubbed both hands up and down his face. "What a fucking mess."

"It's *my* mess. My mess, my family, my sin."

"Your sin." He rubbed his face again. "My God, Téa. My *God*."

Which only reminded her of that bargain she'd made so long ago—that if she would stay away from trouble, then He would let her get away with her crimes. Johnny, with all his golden good looks, had dazzled her, rendering her blind to reality. *He* was trouble. He had to be, right? Because she'd just confessed to him her past.

"None of this is your fault," he said. "None of it."

She wouldn't let him sugarcoat it. "I knew what I was doing, Johnny, don't think I didn't. I saw the names, the sums, the payments made and the debts enlarge. I wanted to help my dad and I wanted to do something for him that my sisters couldn't. I didn't care what that entailed or whether it was right or wrong. I only knew he was proud of me, and that I was special for the secret we kept together."

"But you didn't understand—"

"Of course I understood it was wrong." It made her feel sick to say it, but that was the truth. She took a breath. "And later, I admitted to myself that I was wicked."

"*Téa.*"

"Now if you'd drive me home, I'd like to get on with the rest of my life." Her voice was steady but her body was trembling. She wrapped her arms around herself to stop her bones from rattling like a skeleton's. "I hope none of what I've told you will affect our professional relationship, but I'll understand if you think it does."

"If you expect I'll walk away from you tonight, after this—"

"I don't need a hero, Johnny."

He laughed, short and harsh. "You'd be out of luck if you did."

"Look, who we Carusos are, what I am and what I did, I can't pretend them away." She'd thought she could. Her arms pressed tighter to her ribs. "I can't ask you to pretend them away either."

"I know who you are, Téa."

"No—" Yes.

Yes. She'd just told him, hadn't she? She'd just told him something she hadn't shared with anyone, not her mother, not her sisters, not the FBI. Her bones started rattling again.

Johnny reached out to touch her face. "Sweetheart, you're ice cold and shaking."

"I'm just . . . it's just . . . " Her voice was shaking now too. "Please take me home."

"Not before we talk this out."

"I don't want to talk about it anymore." She wanted to go back home to her dressmaker dummies and her TV shows. There, she could stuff the past and her memories, her shame and her anger, into the mental compartments where they'd resided for the last sixteen years. "Please take me home."

"Not until we've warmed you up."

Despite her protests, he pulled her from the car, and wrapping an arm around her, propelled her back to the house. The heat of his body burned against her skin, but couldn't seem to penetrate.

Inside, the entry and living room smelled of fresh paint and the new sofa, chairs, and coffee table were pushed to the center of the room and covered with drop cloths. Téa struggled to muster a professional interest.

"I should check on the painters' work," she murmured.

"Jesus Christ, Téa," Johnny said, sounding irritated. "Turn off the good girl for once, please." He propped her against a kitchen counter and then pressed a half-full brandy snifter in her hand. "Drink up."

But her trembling fingers made it difficult to bring the rim to her mouth. Johnny muttered another swear word, then covered her wrapped hands with his and helped her bring the glass to her lips. He tilted it too far, and though she took a hasty gulp, some of the alcohol spilled and dribbled down her chin.

His gaze on her face, he made a soft groan. Then he dipped his head and tongued the brandy away.

Now heat spread over Téa's skin, moving from her lips to her breasts to between her thighs. She pressed her spine against the countertop even as his mouth moved and pressed a kiss on hers. He freed the snifter from her hands and set it aside, then cupped her face between his big palms.

"Contessa." He kissed her nose, then each corner of her lips. "Sweetheart."

Oh, she liked that. And oh, she still wanted him. But she closed her eyes instead of succumbing to that warm comfort and that tantalizing sizzle. "You should take me home."

"Téa?"

Her lashes lifted. He was a nose-and-a-half away, his gaze direct. "Is that the good girl talking again or is that the real you?"

"You don't understand—"

"I know you now. We don't have to be in the dark anymore."

"That's not why—"

"I think it was, Contessa."

She shook her head. "You just want more sex," she said, trying to stay strong. "You know I see right through your smooth talk."

A corner of his mouth kicked up in a rueful smile. "You're right. But now I think I see through you, too."

You could recognize charm and temptation and still be swayed by it, Téa thought. But this was never going to last! As a matter of fact, she'd been certain it was over half an hour ago. Yet now . . . now . . . oh. He did know her now.

He knew her.

As no one else did.

· She reached blindly for the brandy snifter and brought it to her mouth and swallowed more down.

Now, she had nothing to hide and no reason not to indulge while she still could.

And she must be truly wicked, because she couldn't muster any more reasons to deny herself. It was going to end sometime, of course, she knew not to dream of forevers, but it didn't have to end tonight.

Going up on tiptoe, she took Johnny's mouth.

He gave it up without a fight.

She realized she liked that in a man.

Without her crimes or secrets between them any longer, Téa felt free. Not too free, she was quick to remind herself as she stroked her tongue against his.

She would open herself to passion and nothing else.

He speared his fingers in her hair and slanted his head to find a new fit. She took the initiative next, moving her head, moving her mouth, letting it roam from his lips over his chin, to the hot skin of his neck.

She bit him.

He grunted, and his hand sped down her back to pull her against his hips. His erection was hard and heavy against her belly.

It made her breasts feel heavy too, achy, and she pressed them against his chest while she licked down his skin to the notch of his collar. Her fingers fumbled with the buttons of his shirt, and then she had the sides open. She rubbed her cheek on the skin she'd bared, until she found the hard point of his nipple.

He groaned when she bit him again.

His fist wrapped in her hair and he pulled back her head. His eyes glittered like blue ice. "Don't push me," he whispered, his voice rough.

The gypsy girl stamped and whirled, freed by the wild mu-

sic and the heat of the flames. She would push him, tease him, take him because letting go meant he'd let go too.

Rising to her toes, Téa bit Johnny's bottom lip.

He grabbed her shoulders and held her mouth to his. Their mouths met in a feast of wet and heat and tongues. Her head fell back. He curled his fingers in the stretchy fabric of her knit pullover and yanked it down her arms to below her breasts. With her elbows trapped at her sides, he jerked his mouth from hers and stared down at the cleavage revealed by her bra, his chest heaving.

"A boy's fantasy come true," he said. "I'm weak just looking at them."

A boy's fantasy? Something about her was *his* fantasy? The idea rushed through her blood with another jolt of arousal. Leaning her hips against the counter, she took a centerfold pose, feeling strong and powerful and womanly. "Tell me you're not just going to be looking at them."

A flush edged high on his cheekbones. "Maybe you are wicked," he whispered, then bent his head.

Wicked. The word was swept away in the sensation of his mouth running over the thick fabric of her bra. Now she cursed the figure-minimizing style with its no-see-through styling. Her nipples felt trapped behind the material, the points hard and desperate to feel his fingers, his mouth, his tongue.

"Take if off," she pleaded. "Please, Johnny, take it off."

He glanced up and met her eyes. "You want to be naked?"

Before, she'd always managed to keep something on—her shirt, his shirt, some piece of clothing to cover her in case the darkness wasn't adequate camouflage.

He cupped his hands around her bra, lightly squeezing her breasts. "You want to be naked for me?"

"Anything," she heard herself say, because the darkness had been lifted from her. He already knew her worst. "Yes. Please. Now."

He popped the front catch free, brushed the bra straps from her shoulders, and then cupped his hands beneath her breasts to hold them up for his inspection.

Then for his mouth.

She arched into him as he sucked on one hard nipple and pinched the other between his fingers. "So good," he said, his voice guttural. "So good."

His sleek hair tickled the inside curves of her breasts, sending goose bumps skittering down her belly and between her legs. She struggled to free her arms, and he helped her, pulling down her top until it was caught at her waist, even as he continued to mouth her with slow, steady pulls on her breast.

Too slow, too steady, too not enough.

Not naked enough. Not free enough.

With one hand she held the back of his head against her, with the other she tugged and pulled at her knit skirt until she could shimmy it down her hips into a pool at her feet.

His hands slid around to cup her bottom. "Take these off," he said, giving a little snap to the elastic of her panties at the crease of her thigh. "Take everything off."

Then he moved away to watch her, his eyes narrow, his body tense. Sexual.

She stood in front of him, her shirt a band at her waist, her panties the only real protection she had left. He remained dressed, his hair messed by her fingers and his shirt open and rumpled, but still much more covered than she.

I'm free, she reminded herself. *Wicked, and passionate, and free.*

Squeezing her eyes tight, she caught her thumbs in her stretchy shirt and then in the top band of her panties and slipped them both over her curves and off her body.

She heard his harsh intake of breath, and savored that proof of his arousal. Then she felt the bite of his hard, hot hands at her waist. In a quick move, he boosted her onto the countertop.

It was cold beneath her bare bottom, but she had only a brief moment to register the sensation. Then he was pushing her knees apart to stand between her thighs.

"Open your eyes, Contessa," he said, his voice rough, "and watch. Because I'm not going to just look at this either."

Surprise and excitement gave her another hot jolt as he knelt between her splayed legs. "Oh, God," she whispered. Her breaths went no further than her throat.

The silk covering his shoulders brushed against the insides of her thighs. Johnny stroked through her folds with his fingers, opening her to his gaze. She knew she was slippery and could see her wetness already coating his fingers. Embarrassment started edging in on her arousal, but he glanced up, as if sensing her mood.

"I see you, Téa," he said. His breath brushed against her wet flesh. "All of you."

His fingers slid over her aroused flesh again. "I taste you, Téa." He sucked two of the fingers into his mouth. "All of you."

"I want you." He ran his palms up the inside of her thighs, opening her wider. "All of you."

Then he put his mouth there and wrenched away the last of her control and the last of her inhibitions.

She fell back to her elbows. She would have screamed if she could have found air, but the room was devoid of it. Instead there was only the soft-rough sensation of Johnny's tongue exploring her sensitive flesh, the incredible sight of his blond hair against the olive-toned skin of her thighs, the curling, twirling, climbing path that he drove her along as he encouraged her, cherished her, laved her toward orgasm.

She was almost there, his tongue had found that perfect spot and he fluttered against it.

"Johnny Johnny Johnny." Her muscles were tense, everything inside her clamoring for relief.

"All of you," he said against her wet flesh. "Everything."

Then, catching the bit of flesh between his teeth, he slid long, hard fingers inside her.

Her body shook with powerful spasms. Her head fell back.

She heard a distant *thunk* and saw only stars.

"Téa. Sweetheart." Johnny was standing up and she was in his arms. His palm was gentle against the back of her head. "Are you hurt? You hit the top cabinet pretty hard."

"No wonder I saw fireworks." She leaned into him, feeling satisfied, relaxed, and yet still very, very sexy. Her hands stroked up his bare chest, over his shoulders, then down the sleek muscles of his back. "Johnny, I think I need to lie down."

He looked into her face, and she saw the faint alarm there evaporate into something else entirely. His nostrils flared as her hands came back up his chest and her fingertips found his nipples. "Let's get you to bed then," he said.

In the master bedroom, he suggested lighting the candles he'd bought before, claiming they'd help her "headache."

She played along because . . . well, because she felt like playing.

And she did. In the candlelight ringing the bed, with their reflection flickering in the mirror overhead, she watched him make love to her. She watched herself make love to him.

Without shame. There was no shame in this.

Her hair rippled in untamed waves down his wide chest. It swirled around his lean thighs as she swirled her tongue over his erection. It draped both their faces as she straddled his waist and rode him.

Groaning, he gripped his fists in the wild stuff. "Contessa. God, Contessa."

She straightened, changing the angle, changing the pleasure. She shook her hair back and undulated. She *was* a contessa. A princess. No, a queen.

His hands circled her waist and held her down against him. She undulated again.

He palmed her breasts and groaned again. "I can't hold on anymore, Contessa."

"I don't want you to," she whispered, from her place above him. The beautiful man between her thighs was her serf of passion, her slave of sex. Hers to command.

She cupped her hands over his. "I order you to come."

And as he did, so did she.

She awoke a long time later. The candles on the floor around the bed were guttering in their holders, with wide puddles of wax around their bases that looked as warm and formless as she felt. Johnny lay sprawled on his back; she was curled on her side, her head pillowed on his arm.

I know who you are.

He'd said that. Oh, God.

He knew who she was.

Her heart tripping, she tried to shift, but then realized a swathe of her hair was trapped beneath his bicep.

She couldn't get away from him.

Her heart tripped again. Maybe her tension woke him, because his eyes suddenly opened. His head rolled toward hers and in silence he studied her face. As usual, she was unable to read his expression, but his searching look set her to trembling again.

She wanted to hide, but there was nowhere she could go.

Then he smiled.

And she remembered begging to be naked for him.

But telling him her secrets had already done that. She'd bared her soul and he'd bared her body and if being a good girl meant never knowing this . . . this lightness of being combined with this heaviness of passion, then she planned on being very, very wicked for as long—or as short—as Johnny would have her.

Johnny traced Téa's features with his eyes. "You're made for candlelight," he said, his voice still raspy from their burning, bruising bout of sex. He stroked his hand over the velvet warmth of her face, the edges glowing as if they'd been dipped in gold. Her sloe eyes were mysterious pools, framed by the mass of dark hair that winked with just the slenderest threads of bronze and copper.

"Such a smooth-talker," she chided.

"Truth-teller. I'm too exhausted to be charming right now."

But she deserved charm. And rose petals, and every other beautiful thing he could think of for her. Instead he'd lost control again, the sight of her body rising above his, with its womanly breasts and tiny waist, the curvy hips that took him in, had shoved everything from his mind but getting it, having it, getting her, having her.

"I left you behind again. I'm sorry."

A crease appeared between her dark brows. "No you didn't. You just didn't notice my, uh, response when you were so caught up in your own." Her lashes swept down and she peeked at him from beneath them. "Besides, you were at my command."

Her command. That should scare him. *She* should scare him, now that her sensuality was coming out from under all those tailored wraps.

But there wasn't room in their bed for regrets. Not tonight. Unless . . . "What time do you think it is?" It felt like the midnight hour plus one.

She shrugged. "Does it matter?"

He hesitated. "Not really." Then he rolled over on top of her, loving her little squeak of surprise.

Thirty

"Embraceable You"
King Cole Trio
Vocal Classics (1955)

Johnny had never felt any ghosts in the tiki room, but maybe that was because he and Téa had made the place their own the first night they'd danced there. Tonight, she was snuggled against him on the love seat, their legs tangled on the matching ottoman. The tiki torches flickered at the entrance, the light from their orange flames licking color over Téa's naked flank and shoulder.

He ran a possessive hand over the smooth curves of both. His to touch. His to lick. His.

He focused on that alone, he focused on Téa alone, just as he'd been doing for the past few days since they'd been in his bed by candlelight. There was no hell to pay, not yet, and he wasn't going to anticipate future trouble or dwell on the ugly past when the present was sleek and warm and scented like his contessa.

It was supposed to be a man thing, this inability to concentrate on more than one task at a time, and he was damn grateful for it.

He was grateful that he'd been sleeping well, too, and even now let his eyelids drop though it couldn't be later than 10 P.M. "Maybe we should head back to the house," he murmured against her hair. "Get into bed before we doze off out here."

"Why don't you ever watch sports?"

His eyebrows rose and his eyelids reluctantly followed. *She* didn't sound the least bit tired. He rallied his brain, not liking the sense of being caught off-guard. "You don't really want to talk about football now, do you?"

"No." She stacked her hands on his chest and propped her chin on them to look into his face. "I want to talk about you."

"You know about me." *All I ever want you to know.* With his palm, he stroked her hair back from her forehead. "You know I like dark-eyed, dark-haired women with great asses . . . and sulky mouths."

"I'm not sulking, but if I was, it's because you're trying to avoid the subject."

Fine. I like dark-eyed, dark-haired women with great asses and who are too smart for my own good. So he shrugged. "I don't watch the games because I'm not an action-hungry fan. I manage money, I don't personally care about the teams or the outcome of the seasons."

"Why do you manage gambling money, then? Why not do something more mainstream? Wall Street or something like that?"

"Because . . . " He struggled for words. He didn't know why and he didn't care to examine it either. It probably was some weird impulse to follow in his father's footsteps, but then beat the game that had gotten the best of Giovanni so many times. Johnny couldn't tell Téa that, though. "Do you know how early you have to get up if you're a West Coast trader? I'm not a morning person."

His prevarication smelled like bad fish apparently, because she pushed off his chest. "I think I'll go home."

"No." *Shit.* He watched her scoop her fallen clothes off the floor. "Can't we just enjoy each other? Enjoy the moment? Why do we have to talk?" It was the masculine lament of all shallow assholes, he was acutely aware of that, but he couldn't seem to help himself.

"You're right," Téa said. "We don't have to talk."

Which meant, of course, that *unless* they talked there'd be no more nookie for Johnny. He ground his back teeth together and tried reminding himself that she didn't know what she was asking for. Getting to know more about him was only going to get *them* into trouble.

He groaned, and shoved his legs into his boxers and then his pants. "Contessa, hold on."

But she was already dressed and reaching for her purse. It took him another second to realize her cell phone was ringing. Oh, yeah. Good. It would give him time to come up with an explanation or an excuse or some sort of conversation to make her happy.

He didn't want to sleep in his bed without her.

Not now. Not yet.

"What?" she said into the phone, then sank down on the cushion of the wicker love seat. "Of course I'm okay. But what about everyone else? Joey? Mom? Grandpa?"

Grandpa? Did she mean *Cosimo*? The Caruso connection was just something else he'd put from his mind since embarking on this affair with Téa. He'd been surprised, amused, then finally relieved to discover that she had cut her ties to her grandfather and that part of her family. It had quieted some of his guilt and sex had tranquilized the rest.

Johnny sat down beside her and rubbed her back with a light palm. She propped her elbows on her knees and held her forehead in one hand. "He told you he has extra security with him now? That's good, that's good. No! Don't let Joey call the FBI. She'll only make matters worse. Well, sit on her until I get there if you have to. Eve, you've dated five men at a time. Surely you can manage one pesky little sister. Yes, yes, I'm on my way."

She flipped off the phone and stood up. "Now I really have to go."

"What happened?"

"Just another day in the life of your average Mafia family. The resort where my grandfather's birthday party was to take place at the end of the month burned down tonight. It's pretty clear that it was arson . . . and pretty clear that someone's sending a message to my grandfather."

"A message saying what exactly?"

She shrugged. "I don't know. I'm sure he does."

"But he's all right?"

"Yes." She raked her fingers through her hair. "I shouldn't care. I shouldn't worry—"

"But you do." He rose and took her hand and was glad when her fingers automatically tightened on his. It was a sign of trust. "Come on, where am I driving you?"

"I don't need—"

"*I* shouldn't care, *I* shouldn't worry, but I will, unless I'm with you. Let's go."

Her sisters were at her mother's house, located on the spa property. Téa was quiet on the drive there, and Johnny kept his mouth shut too. The silence between them was only broken by the directions she gave to a side street closer to the entrance to her mother's place. Once he pulled to the curb, her fingers went to the handle of her door. "Thanks," she said. "I'll see you later."

He flipped the switch for the universal lock. "Not so fast."

"Listen, Johnny. We'll talk . . . or not talk, later."

Teeth-gnashing wasn't making him any points. "I'll walk you to the door."

The narrow street was dark. On one side was a lot, empty

of anything but sand and some clumps of scrubby brush. On the other was the western border of the spa property, delineated by a twelve-foot-high wall covered with bougainvillea to keep out prying eyes and the sounds of traffic. Not that there was any traffic to speak of. The area around them was deserted.

The back of his neck prickled as he took Téa by the hand. Swinging her purse over her shoulder, she glanced behind her as if she felt something or someone watching too. He tightened his grip on her fingers and tugged her toward the arc of light shining from a nearby street lamp.

Then movement exploded behind them.

Thudding footsteps. Téa gasped a breath as a stocky figure reached for her. Johnny yanked her against him and their assailant grabbed the strap of her purse. He pulled it from her arm and threw it aside.

With a cry, Téa broke from Johnny's grip and chased after her tumbling purse. Johnny started after her.

And plowed into a ham-sized fist.

It caught him under the eye, and sent him reeling back. "Run!" he shouted, stumbling as he regained his balance. "Téa, run!"

A hand gripped his shoulder and swung him around. Johnny flowed into the movement, then ducked his head and drove his shoulder forward.

"Whoof," the other man said. This time he was the one who stumbled back.

Johnny pressed on, still leading with his shoulder, and shoved the man back another few feet. He landed against the vine-covered wall with a thump that sent him bounding back toward Johnny.

The man's gray hair glinted in the meager light and his face was set in grim lines. He took another swing that caught Johnny under the chin. Johnny's head snapped back. He jerked it forward, ignoring the rubbery feel of his neck. That fist was coming at him again, determined to flatten him.

But with Téa in danger, there was nothing and no one more determined than Johnny. Adrenaline honing his focus, he ducked the next punch, then closed in. He shoved the guy back, then shoved him back again. The guy's shoulders smacked the bougainvillea. Without hesitation, Johnny jammed his forearm across the other man's throat.

Blows rained on his face and head. He ignored them, grunting as he applied greater pressure to the assailant's windpipe. The man lifted his knee as if to get in a kick to Johnny's groin, but he didn't have the oxygen for it. His standing leg crumpled and Johnny lifted his forearm. The other man dropped to a heap on the ground.

The thug lay there, breathing harshly. Praying like hell that Téa was safely away, Johnny backed off and nearly tripped over her.

"No more," she said to the crumpled man, her voice high and breathless. "You leave him alone. I have it. I have it right here."

"Shit," the man wheezed out, going very still. "She has a gun?"

Johnny glanced back even as he pushed her more fully behind him. "Damn it," he barked out, fear and his heartbeat ratcheting up again. "I told you to run." The only weapon she had was her purse. She held it chest-high, her hand thrust inside the opening.

The older man lifted his palms. "I'm not carrying and nobody told me either of you would be."

Carrying? *Carrying a gun.* Jesus.

"Get out your cell and call the police," Johnny ordered Téa, staring the bad guy down. "Don't move, you son of a bitch."

"Who do you work for?" Téa demanded, though she still

sounded scared. She wasn't getting out her cell phone. "One of the rival families? The Dominellis? The LaScalas?"

"Cell phone," Johnny commanded again. He'd pull out his own, but he wanted his hands and his attention distraction free. His left eye was already closing and there was the salty taste of blood in his mouth.

"Or was it my grandfather?" Téa continued to talk. "Is he paying you to scare me back into the fold?"

The thug was looking at Téa like another man might eye a snake, obviously still worrying about that alleged gun she was holding on him. "I'm here for him," he said, jabbing a finger in Johnny's direction. "For Gianni Martelli or Johnny Magee or whatever he calls himself."

Johnny started, blinking his one good eye. "For me?" *For Gianni Martelli or Johnny Magee or whatever he calls himself.* The adrenaline-induced numbness was wearing off and his face was starting to pulse like a giant toothache.

"Look, look." The other man held his hands up higher and took a deep breath. "I don't want any more trouble. I'm a P.I. from Hollywood, okay? And I got two kids in braces and the daughter wants tickets to a Nelly concert for her birthday. When Fremont added a little extra to the latest assignment by asking me to rough you up for five large, I thought, what the hell?"

"Fremont?" Téa stepped forward.

Johnny shoved her behind him again. "Raphael Fremont? Why would he give you five thousand dollars to beat me up?"

"Because he's an overpaid, petty little prick who's obsessed with that big-jugged bimbo of his. He wanted me to mess with your face so she wouldn't think it's so pretty. He pays me to get the goods on every guy she ogles, which is why I could afford to start my kids in braces to begin with. But then Dr. Perfect Smile says it's gonna take two phases. Two phases!"

The root canal that was Johnny's head started pounding harder than the P.I.'s fists. "Get up and get the hell out of here," he said wearily. "Tell Fremont that you did your job."

The older man didn't move. "Not until she takes the gun off me," he said, nodding toward Téa.

Johnny swung around so he could look at her with his one good eye. God, with that fierce expression on her face, he *could* believe she'd been a biter. "Let him go, Contessa."

She slowly took her hand out of her purse and lowered it to her side. "My mother's going to kick the bimbo and her boyfriend out of the spa tonight," she muttered, then raised her voice to a vicious threat. "And I don't want to see you around town ever again."

The P.I. didn't bother with further conversation. He scrambled up and limped toward his car, parked about half a block from Johnny's Jag. He must have followed them here, but Johnny had been so preoccupied with Téa that he hadn't noticed. As the sedan took off down the street, he sank onto the curb beneath the streetlight.

Téa hurried to sit beside him. "Let's go into Mom's and clean you up."

"Later." *Never.* He turned his head, tilting it to stare her down with his good eye. She looked as shaky as he felt. "Next time I tell you to run, you damn well better do it. *Capisci?*"

She didn't seem to notice his use of Italian as she brushed his hair off his forehead. Wincing, she examined his swelling face. "You must be hurting."

"You should've seen the other guy," he said dully.

"Where'd you learn to be so tenacious? He just kept whaling on you while you were holding him against the wall."

"Water polo and basketball in high school, rugby in college."

"You're a hero."

He laughed, and it hurt his lip, just as it should. "Keep on believing that for as long as you can, sweetheart."

"Well, at least now we know who's been following us, and why."

Johnny grunted.

"But frankly, I don't think Raphael got much of a private investigator for his money. At first, I thought he might be the same man who recently checked into the spa, but I've never seen him before. You, however, spotted the guy following us a while back. And then, he didn't know your real name from the name of someone who lived in your house ages ago."

"You caught that, did you?" He'd known she would. Hadn't he thought earlier this evening that she was too smart for his own good?

"Mm-hmm. He called you both Johnny Magee and Giovanni Martelli."

"Johnny Magee or *Gianni* Martelli." He wished he was the kind of man who could continue scamming her. Without the P.I.'s intrusion, he didn't know how long he would have been able to ignore the outside pressures and live in the highly-sexed and highly pleasurable present with her, but now it was definitely over, baby, over. He was Gianni Martelli as well as Johnny Magee, and the latter had been raised to treat well the ones who trusted him.

He remembered her fingers curling around his in the tiki room tonight.

Téa trusted him.

She had, anyway.

Run, Téa, run, he whispered to himself. *Get away before this ends ugly.*

"Johnny Magee or Gianni Martelli," she repeated, her voice puzzled. "I don't understand."

He looked at her again and could see the wheels turning in

that bright and beautiful head of hers, but he knew she couldn't possibly see this coming.

"That's who I am. The name on my original birth certificate, anyway. Gianni Martelli. Giovanni was my father."

Thirty-one

"Frankie and Johnny"
Lena Horne
More Than You Know (1946)

Téa stared at the stranger she'd been sleeping with.
Minutes ago, she'd thought someone was out to hurt her to
get the Loanshark book, but this—this was so much worse.
"Giovanni Martelli is your *father*?"

"Yeah." He lifted his hip to pull a handkerchief from his
back pocket and then daubed it against a cut on his lower lip.
"But my parents were divorced when I was a baby. I went by
Magee after Phineas married my mom."

She still didn't understand. "Why did you move to Palm
Springs? Why would you move to *that* house?"

Johnny, no *Gianni*, looked down at the handkerchief in his
hands, then back at her. One eye was nearly swollen shut, the
other was its usual unreadable blue. "I have questions about
my father too, Téa. His murder has gone unsolved for sixteen
years."

She recoiled as she started to make sense of what he'd revealed. Though Giovanni Martelli's murderer had never been caught, the common belief was that he'd been killed in retaliation for the hit on her father—killed in retaliation by someone associated with the Carusos.

"You thought *I* would know something about your father's death?"

He frowned, and his lip started bleeding again. "Of course not. What happened sixteen years ago has nothing to do with you. I said that—the day you came to the house and told me about the family connection."

A connection he'd already been fully aware of.

"That's why you contacted me about the job, isn't it?" Not because she'd impressed him with her credentials or was swayed by her design ideas. "You thought somehow I'd help you find those answers you want."

"I didn't know. I thought . . . maybe."

Rising to her feet, she wrapped her arms around herself, holding her purse to her chest. Not only had she shared with this man, this *stranger*, her secrets, she'd shared with him her body and her passion.

What should she feel? Horror? Revulsion? Instead she was numb. There was a block of ice in her belly and its cold was moving outward through her blood and to her limbs. Already her heart was frozen.

"So you went to bed with me, knowing my family probably murdered him." She took a step back. "You went to bed with me, knowing that the rumors say that your father murdered mine."

"I don't believe that," he said quickly. "He was no killer."

His words barely penetrated as she took another step away. "You went to bed with me, knowing that the rumors say that your father murdered mine and that then my family murdered yours."

He closed his open eye and rubbed a hand over his hair. "It's a little like Shakespeare, isn't it?"

Her voice sounded cold now too. Icy. "It's a lot more like betrayal."

"Téa." His good eye popped open and he moved, reaching toward her, but she shuffled back.

"Don't touch me. Don't talk to me." The ramifications of what he'd done and what she'd let him do to her were swirling in her head. How could she take it all in? Not here, not now, not when she was anywhere near Johnny.

"I don't ever want to see you again." She'd become expert long ago at hiding humiliation, but even she wasn't up to this. Her feet stumbled back another few steps. "I never, ever want to see you again."

With that, she whirled in the direction of the spa, and escaped. He didn't try to stop her.

Her mother's living room was a feminine haven. The peach and vanilla upholstered chairs and sofa had been picked out by her mother. Téa had spent a Saturday with blue painter's tape and two different cans of paint to create the walls striped in mocha and cream. Tonight, the room was filled with the scent of hot tea and the voices of her sisters and her mother.

Téa slipped into the room, managed a brief greeting, then poured herself a cup of tea and took a seat in the farthest corner. Apparently Eve had redirected Joey's anxiety about the arson with an argument over what the fire meant to their eightieth-birthday-party plans. Eve wanted to cancel the whole thing, while Joey refused to consider the possibility.

"Carusos never back down," she declared.

Téa tuned out the discussion, cupping the teacup in her palms and wishing the heat could warm her. Or maybe not. Maybe this frozen, numb state was preferable to anything else.

Johnny had lied to her. He'd surprised, shamed, shocked, and betrayed her.

He was Giovanni Martelli's son. My God.

Giovanni Martelli's *son*.

And she was Salvatore Caruso's daughter.

Maybe it *was* a little like Shakespeare.

"Téa? What do you think?" Joey appealed to her from across the room.

She blinked. "What do I think about what?"

"Party or no party? We'll have to find a different location, but hey, it's just a matter of finding some outdoor space where we can set up tents like we were going to do at the Desert Star. How hard can that be in golfing's world capital?"

"It doesn't matter to me whether you go ahead with the party or not. I told you I won't go."

"But it's different now," Joey insisted.

"Different how?" Téa asked. *I'm different now. I know what it can be like in a man's arms. I know what it can be like when you really let go.* When you let go and lost control of your heart. She shook off the thought. "Nothing's different now. Nothing."

"More's at stake. We need to show the world the Carusos stick together. Mom said even she might come to the party if we decide to go ahead with it."

Téa's gaze jumped to her mother. "Mom?"

She gave a little shrug. "Cosimo's retiring. Maybe it's time I retired my . . . discomfort too."

This wasn't right, Téa thought. Everyone around her was either changing their minds or changing their spots.

Her mother was willing to associate with the Carusos.

Her Johnny was Giovanni Martelli's son.

How can that be?

How can that *be*?

Giovanni Martelli's son.

All at once, anger exploded inside her. It melted the ice and evaporated the anesthesia that had been affecting her emotions. The teacup dropped from her hand, shattering against the hardwood floor.

"Are you all right?" Her mother started forward with a napkin.

Seething, Téa stared down at the mess and wondered what they'd think if they knew she'd let go of the thing in lieu of throwing it. "No, I'm not all right," she said. "Not nearly all right."

Something in her voice must have warned them all.

Her mother halted mid-stride. Eve's head jerked sharply toward Téa. Even Joey stopped talking, her mouth hanging open.

Téa was not all right. She was furious.

She'd lost the design job that was a wonderful artistic opportunity.

She'd lost the chance to build her professional reputation into something to be proud of.

She'd lost the man she might have loved.

She hated him now. Hated him!

His face popped into her mind. Full of humor as he laughed with her. Tender as he leaned down to kiss her. Battered by the Hollywood P.I.

She should have hit him herself.

He'd wanted to get close to the Carusos, so he'd found a way to get close to her.

Bastard.

She rose to her feet and the anger rose with her, starting at her toes and filling her with an unyielding strength until she felt a hundred feet tall. Powerful. Royal.

A woman determined to find a way to pay back the man who'd done her wrong.

"Téa?" Eve said softly, in a voice you'd use on a wild animal. "Do you want to tell us what's going on?"

I lost my father, I lost a man I could have loved, but I'm not going to lose anything else.

"Joey said it," Téa told her sister. "Carusos never back down."

"Oh-kay. And that means . . . ?"

She wasn't sure. Not yet. But then—

Yes. Oh, *yes*.

"Joey also said you'll have to find another place to set up the party tents. And that some place like a golf course would do?"

Eve narrowed her eyes. "A golf course would do fine."

The course at Johnny's had always been well-maintained and the new landscaping team had done wonders with the rest of the property. She could put a rush on the inside workers and get a lot more of the interior finished in the next ten days. If they held Cosimo's party at Johnny's, she'd make sure the press was given a tour to show what her firm had done to the house. Mid-century modernism was a pet love of Palm Springs, of all Southern California these days, and was certain to get attention.

The publicity would be the kind of advertising she couldn't afford, and enough of a plus to overcome the downside of the Mafia association.

The association was what she'd always worked to avoid, but what Johnny had done made it clear that she would never escape the Caruso connection. So now, by God, she was going to use it to her advantage.

If only he would agree. If only she could face him again, and again and again, until the job and the party were over.

"Carusos never back down," she murmured to herself. She'd been doing that for years, backing down, backing away, hiding her true nature and turning from what she'd learned from her father.

But she was going to embrace his ruthlessness now.

She could face Johnny. And if she did, she knew he'd agree.

He wanted to get up close and personal with the Carusos

after all, and here was his chance. Not to mention the fact that he was a gambler by trade.

Surely he would see that, in this game, everybody won. •

Téa had turned into Boss-zilla, Rachele thought, watching the other woman supervise the placement of an Eames leather lounge chair and ottoman in Johnny Magee's new home office. Though it was amazing what a little intimidation could do. In the past nine days she'd gotten out of the workers twice the hours and four times the labor. The only part of the property that wouldn't look its best by party night was the murky lagoon with its crumbling retaining wall. Téa said she didn't like the water feature anyway, and had ordered some temporary trellises to obscure it from view.

Maybe her astonishing results had something to do with way she looked. Gone were the dull and drab suits, and though rumor was that she'd been evening gown-shopping with Eve, her day wardrobe had gone in the other direction. Each morning she arrived on the job in a T-shirt and overalls and within minutes was elbows-deep in whatever project needed an extra pair of hands. Right now, a red streak slashed across her forehead like war paint and her usually perfect hair was a wiggly mass she'd tied back with a yellow twisty from a bread-bag.

"Rachele!"

Rachele jumped and hurried over to Boss-zilla's side. "You roared?" The good thing about this manic Téa was that her mood kept Rachele too busy to get into her own over her father. She was still in a suite at the spa, and though Téa's mom, Bianca, had told her dad where Rachele was living for the time being, she'd yet to make any long-term plans for herself.

The fact that her father had so readily accepted her absence made it pretty clear he didn't love her. Now she figured he'd never loved anyone.

"Rachele, go get Johnny," Téa said, tilting her head to look at the chair from another angle. "It's time we settled the issue of that mirrored ceiling in the bedroom." Then she glanced over at Rachele and grimaced. "Please."

Sighing, Rachele turned and marched off. Being in the same space with Johnny and the boss was bound to give her more than something to think about. It was going to be a headache, because the tension between the two of them was as thick as cheesecake. Though not nearly as sweet.

Two weeks ago they'd clearly been lovers. Now it seemed as if they were enemies.

It made her wonder if her father wasn't right about lo—

No! She didn't know what had happened to sour her father on the emotion, or if she ever would know, but she wasn't going to let his attitude ruin hers.

Entering Cal's cozy bungalow only made her more determined to remain upbeat. He smiled at her from behind the gaggle of monitors on his desk. She smiled back, then jabbed her thumb in the direction of Johnny, who was stretched out on a recliner and reading from a stack of papers piled on his chest.

Though the bruises on his face had faded to a barfy yellowish-green, he still looked model handsome. No wonder Téa was in a nasty mood.

"The Steelers in four," Rachele called out.

He didn't look up. "Steelers aren't playing this weekend."

"The Diamondbacks then. I'm getting a vision that they're going all the way to the championship."

"Not in football," Johnny replied. "They're a baseball team and this year's World Series is over. Now boogie, kid. We're busy. You can flirt with Cal later."

Since she already had out her cell and was phone flirting with him that very instant—HI QT—she ignored the dig. "I'm here for you, old man. Téa requests your presence in your house."

He grunted. "*My* house? It hasn't been my house in days.

That woman has completely taken over thanks to the damn birthday party."

Which she'd somehow leveraged Johnny into hosting. Rachele didn't know how or why, but it must be juicy if their attitude toward each other was any judge. "She's talking about getting rid of the mirrored ceiling in the bedroom again."

The recliner went erect in one mighty *thwump,* scattering newspapers to the floor. "I'm going to end this discussion once and for all," Johnny declared. "I have very fond feelings for that ceiling and she's not gonna talk me into removing those mirrors. This time, the victor of the battle will be me."

Unwilling to miss the show, not even for the migraine that might ensue, Rachele sent a last message to Cal—BFN, bye for now—and hurried in Johnny's wake.

Thirty-two

"I've Got You Under My Skin"
Perry Como
Como Swings (1959)

Cal peered through the open bedroom doorway as Johnny worked at his bow tie. "Why do you have curtains on the bedroom ceiling?"

Johnny glanced over at the other man, surprised and amused to see him in dark slacks and a white dinner jacket. The ubiquitous black high-tops didn't look that out of place with them either. "I think Téa called them draperies. Since I was grinding my teeth at the time, I can't be sure."

Cal seemed to accept the explanation. "They frisked me at the gate when I came back from the newsstand. A couple of goons with dark shades and metal detectors."

"Security. They'll be checking everyone." He looked at his assistant again. "You didn't have to come tonight."

"*Both* of us could still boogie out of here and go for pizza."

Johnny shook his head and straightened his black bow tie, then shrugged into his own white jacket. "I have things to do here." He was scheduled to give reporters a tour of the new interior of the house and he was planning on being all-out poetic in praise of the job done by the design firm Inner Life and its owner, Téa Caruso.

He owed her that.

And she'd been happy to tell him so, the day after he'd revealed he was Giovanni's son. Frankly, he'd been shocked as hell to find her on his doorstep that morning, and then he could only admire her for cornering him so neatly.

The man who'd betrayed her trust couldn't say no to her—not about hosting the party, not about covering those memorable mirrors with the ridiculous drapes—even as he couldn't come up with any good excuse for the betrayal in the first place.

All the rationales he'd dredged up for himself during the past few weeks had never rung true, not even to himself. There wasn't one legitimate reason that he'd gone so far as to take Téa into his bed. He was probably as pissed at himself as she was.

Angry at him or no, the amount of work Téa had accomplished in the last week and a half astonished him, from the gleaming turquoise-blue tiled floor in the living room to the lush yet simple red velvet armchairs in the office. She'd been at the house eighteen hours a day, rushing here and there in a flurry of flushed cheeks and wild hair that sent his imagination spinning toward sex.

Of course, she'd always sent his imagination spinning toward sex. Maybe that was why he'd B.S.'d his way into an affair with her in the first place. Thinking only with his little head.

Damn his own weakness. Badass gambler and all-around ultracool bachelor Johnny Magee knew that operating from detachment and logic was the only way to win. It didn't make sense that he'd forgotten that.

But he remembered now. So he was going to keep his dis-

tance from her tonight. He'd play the hand she'd dealt him—
taking care of the reporters and ensuring the good publicity
she wanted—but he'd stay at the periphery of the party and
away from her.

"You gonna talk to that grandfather of Téa's?" Cal asked.
"That Cosmo?"

Johnny adjusted the cuffs of his white shirt and fastened
the top button of his jacket. "Cosimo. And no, I think I'll
leave the old man in peace on his eightieth birthday."

Johnny's fact-finding mission into his father's life and
death was as over as his relationship with Téa. Short of de-
manding a confession from a Mafia don regarding a crime
without a statute of limitations, there wasn't anything else he
could do. In any case, his questions had always been about
what crimes his father had committed rather than those committed against him.

He'd wanted to believe his father wasn't a killer. Without
definite proof to the contrary, he still could if he wanted to.

And that's just what he'd do, Johnny decided, letting out a
long breath. Tomorrow, next week, very soon, he'd shake the
sand of this desert paradise off his shoes and go someplace
else. He might wake up in a cold sweat at 1:09:09 for the rest
of his lousy life, but when he woke up he'd tell himself his father was innocent. Damn it, he *knew* he was.

"Let's go check out Party Central," Johnny said to Cal.
"Make sure that the last details are done."

Dusk was settling into night as they made their way to the
long, wide fairway of the golf course's first hole. Three tents
were set up there, one for drinks, one for dinner, and one for
dessert. A large catering staff bustled about each. "Forty-five
minutes until the first of the guests arrive," a dark-suited man
called out to the bartenders in the first tent. "Get that glass-
ware polished."

Johnny and Cal came to a stop between the second and
third tents, where a large wooden dance floor had been laid

out. Fairy lights were strung from a central pole in the dance surface then looped to a lower framework that ran around its edges, creating a "roof" that twinkled like stars. A nine-piece band was already setting up music stands and opening instrument cases.

"Oh, there's Rachele," Cal said, in that besotted tone he usually saved for his latest iMac laptop.

She was emerging from the third tent, a clipboard in hand. A slinky green dress, resembling the satin lingerie of some silent-era Hollywood star, petaled around her knees like a mermaid's tail.

Johnny gave her an admiring once-over as she approached them. He elbowed his favorite tech-head. "Who's this beautiful dame deigning to talk to us, Cal?"

The younger man shot him a puzzled glance. "It's Rachele. I just pointed her out to you."

Johnny shook his head, even as Rachele dimpled in a smile. "Thank you, sir," she said, and twirled for the two men. "Do you notice the emerald streaks I put in my hair to match my dress?"

"Excellent choice," Johnny answered, noticing the effect was a much softer look, now that the rest of her hair was a more normal-looking—perhaps natural?—chocolate-brown. Her makeup was more subtle tonight as well. "And I like the little jewel dangling from the eyebrow ring too." Because Rachele wouldn't be Rachele without her little fashion quirks.

"Téa gave it to me," she replied. "A thank you for all the overtime I'm going to be charging her for—which consequently means will be billed to you." She looked so pleased with that remark, that Johnny wondered if the contessa had spilled his duplicity to her assistant.

He shrugged away the guilt, even as he wondered for the hundredth time what impulse had pushed him past good judgment and into a flaming affair that he'd known could only end in ashes. "Does she need any further help from Cal or . . . me?"

Rachele glanced over her shoulder. "Why don't you ask her yourself?"

Johnny followed the direction of her gaze. From the same tent that Rachele had recently emerged, another woman strolled into the night.

She was taller than Téa. Wearing a painted-on-her-body, full-length, sleeveless dress that scooped over spectacular breasts, hugged a narrow waist, licked over curvy hips and thighs to end in a frothy swirl from knees to ankles. A red dress. Cherry red. Flame red. Brand-him-through-his-flesh red.

This woman spotted them, hesitated, then started forward again, graceful in pin-sharp high heels. Her neck looked incredibly long and graceful too, with her dark hair piled on top of her head. One long, wavy lock was freed at the front to flirt with the outer arc of her eyebrow and the outer curve of her red, pouty lips.

She wore rubies in her ears, and from a gold chain around her neck hung a ruby-encrusted heart. Now that she was close enough for him to see her jewelry, he also recognized her one-of-a-kind, exotic face.

Jesus Christ. It was Téa.

Looking taller thanks to heels and hairdo. Looking more voluptuous than ever, thanks to the second-skin dress. Looking more like the damnedest mistake he'd ever made in his life when she flicked a cool glance at him from her sloe eyes.

"Cal," she said, with a little nod. "Johnny."

He nodded back. God knows where his tongue had disappeared to.

Rachele helped out. "They wanted to know if you need any assistance," she said.

"Like I could taste-test the food," Cal offered.

Téa laughed. "If you're hungry, go help yourself, Cal. You too, Rach."

That left Johnny alone with the contessa. "You look beautiful," he said, managing to reclaim his powers of speech as the younger couple walked off.

"Always so charming," she murmured. "Thank you."

The response set his back teeth to grinding again. Her "always so charming" held the definite ring of "always so insincere."

"You're welcome," he said in a wry tone. "I'll be on my way then."

"Wait." She put out her hand, stopping just short of touching him. "I do need to talk with you." Her expression said she wished like hell she didn't.

He crossed his arms over his chest. While he'd given her good reason to hate him, it was starting to tick him off that she'd taken him up on it. Okay, it wasn't rational, but Téa in flame-red was burning rational right out of him.

"So shoot," he said, then grimaced. "Bad choice of words. I don't want to give you any ideas."

The nostrils of her slender patrician nose flared and her eyes narrowed.

Now he should feel bad for needling her. But he didn't. Not when the way her body fit into that cinnamon-hot dress was making his palms itch. That he could look but couldn't touch was irritating him much more than his comment could possibly irritate her.

She inhaled a breath. "I want to discuss my grandfather," she said. "Are you . . . are you thinking of talking to Cosimo tonight?"

Though Cal had asked the exact same question, Johnny didn't feel like answering so directly this time around. "Why shouldn't I? There's no secrets between you and me anymore."

The ruby heart of her necklace rested in the shallow depression at the base of her throat. He watched it tremble with the racing beat of her pulse. "There are other secrets," she said, looking away. "I haven't told anyone about the connection this house has to Giovanni Martelli."

His eyebrows rose. "Ah. Of course you haven't," he said slowly, realizing what a spot that would have put her in. "Some of the guests might have balked at attending a party where the enemy once resided, dead or not."

Her spine straightened and she lifted her chin. "Right."

"Screwing your whole little ploy for publicity."

"Right again."

"What about Cosimo, though? Doesn't he remember?"

"He hasn't said."

Johnny studied her face. "Meaning you still haven't spoken with him, have you?"

The flush that crawled up her perfect neck was a paler shade of red than her dress. "That's none of your business."

He ignored that fact. "I know you Téa. You're still feeling guilty, and you shouldn't. What you did as a little girl—"

"Shh!" She gave an abrupt shake of her head, then took a hasty look around. Her fingers bit into his forearm and she backed up so that they stood alone on the dance floor, under the canopy of sparkling lights. "No one else knows about that either. No one."

"In any case, it has nothing to do with who you are and what you have become, Téa. It's not logical for you to let the past affect you like this."

She stared at him. "And I should listen to you?"

"Why not? I—"

"*Why not?*" She seemed to grow another inch taller and her spectacular breasts almost popped out of her dress as she took a quick, angry breath. "I know you too, Johnny."

"What's that supposed to mean?"

" 'It's not logical to let the past affect you like this,' " she quoted back to him, every word as harsh as a slap.

He shoved his hands into his pockets and struggled to retain his usual savoir faire. "And your point would be?"

"Why the hell did you come to Palm Springs, Johnny? Because of the past. Why the hell did you come on to me, Johnny? Because of the past."

No. That wasn't why he'd come on to Téa. He'd come on to her because . . . he didn't have a sensible explanation for it, that was the trouble. "We're not talking about me."

"Well, maybe we should, now that you're no longer trying to hide from me behind a different name."

The musicians were warming up their instruments, their individual notes clashing to create a discordant soundtrack to their conversation. The noises bored like drill bits into his skull. "You're the one trying to hide. Don't think I can't see what all those boring tailored suits were about, Téa."

She whirled as if she were going to run from him. He might drop dead before she got five feet. The siren's dress didn't stop with the mind-blowing front. The back plunged too, cutting so deep that her spine was left naked to the dimples of her ass.

The tension in his body went from half-angry to near-full alert. Fine. Okay. He'd admit it. He'd gotten involved with her because her face and her body were so fucking beautiful that he couldn't think straight around her.

It had always been lust, pure and simple.

Then she whirled back. Her eyes were hot, her cheeks were flushed, her breaths were ragged. "You're starting to make me mad and I'm not going to let you get away with it."

"Oh, I'm paying already, baby. I've been paying since you left my bed empty of anything but your memory."

She looked as if she didn't believe him. "I'm sure you'll find another woman to fill it fast enough. But first you're going to admit something to me."

The drummer behind him spit out a riff that ended with a cymbal crash. "Admit what?"

"That I'm not the only one ashamed of my past and my family."

The drumming riff. The crash of cymbals.

"I'm not ashamed of anything." *Except that I hurt you.*

"Afraid then. You're as afraid as me."

"I'm not afra—"

"I *know* you, Johnny. I told you that. I know you, too. You're just like me, worried that inside of you is some darkness, some shadow that our fathers left behind like a fingerprint."

"No." The drummer was hitting the cymbals again. Crash after crash. *Bam. Bam. Bam.*

"Yes. Maybe it's not logical. But it's true. And until you admit it to yourself, then the doubts are going to keep you from having a real, honest relationship with another person. You'll be too afraid to let anyone in because that might mean letting something else—that darkness—out."

Bam. Bam. Bam.

Then, the metallic sounds still echoing in his head, she turned from him. She didn't run away, she walked, graceful and certain.

But certainly wrong.

Certainly wrong.

But he'd been wrong too, he realized, his gaze unable to move off her. So wrong, he thought, as he watched her leave him in that flame-red dress.

He'd thought lust had driven him to take her to bed. And he'd thought he could scratch the itch he had for her and then somehow go on with his life.

But she'd scratched back. Scratched him, and then found her way beneath his cool, slick surface, and from there, beneath his skin.

She'd made it all the way to his heart.

Damn the woman, damn the woman, damn *the woman.*

In his head, the curses crashed like cymbals.

Now he knew exactly why he'd gone against his conscience, his common sense, and his Magee Main Street morality. As fucking ironic as the truth was, he now knew exactly what had led him to betray Téa.

It was because he'd fallen in love with her.

Thirty-three

"Bella Notte"
Peggy Lee
Songs from Walt Disney's Lady and the Tramp (1955)

Rachele sat with Cal at a table out of the reach of the party lights. The band was playing a golden oldie that had the dance floor filled. The guest list had been something over three hundred and she'd be astonished to find out there was a single no-show. Drinks continued to flow, but dinner had been served—prime rib, lobster, and a selection of pasta dishes that even she couldn't have improved upon. All that was left was to light the birthday candles and consume the four tiers of layer cake.

"Which one is Téa's grandfather?" Cal asked. "I was hoping to meet a real live Mafia man."

"You've already met some real live Mafia men tonight," Rachele replied. "Remember Dom, Nick, and Brandon? They were the ones in the first tent shoving unopened champagne bottles under their coats when the bartender wasn't looking."

"They were Mafia? The ones yammering about their own private party later? They looked like your average young dudes."

Rachele shrugged. "Rumors are they're part of the Caruso crew."

"So you're not going to introduce me to the grandfather?"

She gazed around the party grounds, trying to spot Cosimo. "He's over there, with the police chief and the lady in the blue sequined dress."

"The white-haired woman with the shocked look on her face? Must be some conversation."

"Around here we call that woman's expression 'Palm Springs Surprise.' It's not the conversation, but the bill and the latest procedure from her plastic surgeon that has her all wide-eyed like that."

Cal grinned. "Hey, you're funny."

But she didn't feel so funny when she spotted her father in the crowd. Her heart clenched as she watched him move alone through the party, a champagne glass held awkwardly in his meaty hand. He wore his one dark suit and she knew for a fact that his white dress shirt wasn't pressed. Without her around, she doubted his socks matched.

He was getting closer, but she couldn't face any unpleasantness tonight.

"Let's go for a walk," Rachele said, jumping to her feet. She grabbed Cal's hand. "I want to be alone with you."

"You want to be away from your father," Cal said, after they were well clear of the celebration.

"I stayed with him too long as it was," Rachele said. All that time telling herself he loved her, when all that time he hadn't wanted love and hadn't wanted to give love back. What a fool she'd been.

"Let's think of something else," she said, tugging Cal down another path. "Let's think about the future. You can help me pick a career. What do you think I should do? Radio

DJ? Chef? Or should I fall back on my childhood dream of becoming a professional in-line skater?"

They'd reached the man-made lagoon that Téa had partially shielded with trellises to hide the crumbling retaining walls. Filled with nervous energy, Rachele jumped on top of the rock ledge and wavered to keep her balance. Cal grabbed her hand to steady her.

"Téa fell backward into the water here the first time Johnny and I met her," Cal said, squeezing her fingers. "You don't want to fall in her footsteps."

She smiled down at him. "Now you're funny." Then she sighed. "But to tell the truth, I'm actually thinking of *following* in her footsteps."

"How so?"

Twin moons reflected in Cal's glasses. Rachele hesitated. With her father's true colors now revealed, she hated the idea of losing the only other man in her life. She drew in a breath, let it out. "I've been thinking about going to design school in L.A."

The moonglow in Cal's lenses made it impossible to read his expression. "That's what Téa did?"

"Yeah." She started walking atop the ledge of the lagoon, and Cal walked beside her, his feet on solid ground.

"It would be hard to leave Palm Springs," Rachele continued, "and . . . everyone here." The valley had cupped her in its warm hands all her life.

"It's not far," Cal pointed out.

"A world away, if I lived on my own. Right now, though I'm out of my father's house, I'm practically living with Téa's mom, and she and her sisters are around all the time."

"They'd still be there for you when you need them." Cal walked a few more steps alongside her. "*I'll* still be there when you need me."

Rachele's heart bobbed down, then back up. "Really?" she whispered.

"Really."

"Do you think I should go?"

"I think you should do what you want. What will make you happy."

"But what if something goes wrong? What if I fail? What if I end up losing . . . " She wanted to say *you* but didn't have the guts.

"I'm a gambler by profession, Rachele. I make my living by calculating odds. Nothing's one hundred percent fail safe. You know that."

They were words that could have set her free. Should have set her free. Her father's love and his assumed loneliness had tied her to Palm Springs. But now that she'd seen his true indifference to her, she should be taking chances and making tracks from the place in order to make her own life.

But without any kind of tether she worried she might float away and never find her way back. Could she count on Cal or Téa and her family to be the anchor she seemed to need in order to fly free?

Her shoe wobbled on a loose stone. She wavered, then felt the ledge beneath her feet crumble. With a little shriek, she lost her balance. Cal caught her against his chest as rocks tumbled to the ground around his high-tops.

He felt solid and warm and she hung onto him. With her mother gone from this world and her father gone from her life, she probably clung too hard. Cal stiffened in her arms and she flushed, embarrassed by her neediness. She loosened her hold and struggled to get free of his clasp.

He swung her outward so that she landed safely away from the now-broken ledge. "Oh, God," he said, turning his back on her to look down at the destruction. "Oh, God."

Rachele frowned. "It's all right. Johnny has to have the lagoon repaired if he wants to keep it, Téa said. I didn't break it or anything."

When Cal didn't move, she put her hand on his arm.

He jumped, then spun toward her. "Let's get out of here, Rachele." His hands grasped her shoulders and he pushed her backward.

"What's the matter?" His shoulders were broad and she had to lean around him to assess the damage to the lagoon.

It didn't look any worse than it did on the far end, where other rocks had fallen as well. She squinted, something odd catching her eye.

"Oh, God," she said, echoing Cal.

Thirty-four

"Please Don't Talk About Me When I'm Gone"
Doris Day
Lullaby of Broadway (1951)

Joey threw herself into a seat at the table where Téa was sitting alone. "Why are you looking so gloomy? The food's great, the party's rocking, no one's died."

Téa shook her head. "Not yet." She couldn't shake the feeling that something might still go wrong.

Eve sank into the chair on the other side of Téa's, looking like an untouchable blonde statue in silver sequins. "Worrywart," she declared. "I talked to a couple of the journalists. They were impressed with the house tour. The *L.A. Times* reporter is going to contact the editor of the Homes section. Johnny must have done a hell of a sell job for you."

"Oh, I'm sure he did," Téa said. "He's got great lines."

Joey glanced around. "Where is your B.F.? He should have had you out on the dance floor by now."

"B.F.?" She laughed. "He's not my boyfriend." Not only hadn't she shared with her sisters that he was Giovanni

Martelli's son, she hadn't told them her brief fling with the man was over.

Eve frowned. "What did you do *now,* Téa?"

Joey was looking at her with the same disapproval in her eyes.

Téa avoided their gazes by transferring hers to the dance floor. "Look, there's Mom dancing with Beppe. Maybe she can talk him into calling Rachele. The poor kid seems lost since she moved out of his house."

"You can't keep turning your back on the men in your life," Joey said. "You didn't even wish Nonno a happy birthday."

Téa held onto her temper. "I found a new venue for his birthday party, didn't I?"

"Where, despite all your fears, the guests include the eminently respectable, such as several politicians, the police chief, heads of three local hospitals—"

"Not to mention the dozen or so too-slick types who complained about the security check at the gate. Apparently they can't really get down and party without carrying a piece."

Joey waved a hand. "You make too much of all that."

Téa bit back her reply. By never revealing the secrets of the Loanshark book, she'd protected her sisters from the gritty reality of their father's life. They could still think it was all just rumors and innuendo, and there was no sense in tarnishing the crowns of Salvatore's youngest princesses now.

But they didn't let the argument go. "We want to be a family again," Eve insisted.

"And you're the one who's making that difficult," Joey added. "Can't you just forget about the past so we can get on with the rest of our lives?"

Heat rose like tiny hairs on the edges of her skin. She'd tried so hard to be good, she'd tried so hard to make up for what she'd done, that she'd let her sisters and everyone else pass judgment on her without a defense or demur. But the anger was breaking free of its bonds now. It expanded, filling her up, and she rose from the table as it rose like lava inside a volcano.

"Don't think you know what I should do," she spit out, shaking with emotion. Her voice was too loud, but she didn't care. "Don't presume to tell me how I should live my life."

They were staring at her as if they could see steam pouring from the top of her head. "You don't know me," she told them, almost shouting. The words shook too, made heavy with molten emotion. "You've never known me."

Then she spun away from them.

And found herself against Johnny's chest.

His hands closed over her upper arms. "Just the woman I wanted to dance with," he murmured, then took a step back that brought them to the edge of the dance floor.

She was rigid under his touch. "I don't want to dance. I don't want to be near you."

"You don't want to cause a scene either, Contessa," he said, bringing his mouth against her ear. "But people are looking and I somehow doubt you want to undo all that positive publicity you brought to yourself and your design firm tonight."

"I thought you told me not to be a good girl anymore."

"Ah, but you have to pick your moments. Save the fight you want to have with your sisters for another time."

Téa couldn't stop her limbs from trembling, even as she glanced around and noticed the curious glances directed her way. Tears of frustration stung at the corners of her eyes. "I've tried to do the right thing," she said fiercely. "I've tried to make up for what I did."

Johnny pressed his hand to her head, urging it against his shoulder. "Deep breaths, Contessa. Long, deep breaths."

All the deep breaths in the world weren't going to fix this. Her sisters would never understand her unless she betrayed her father. The only person who *did* understand her, the one she was in love with, had betrayed her.

Her head jerked up to stare at the man who held her in his arms.

Oh, God. Oh, God. She'd done the unthinkable. The stupid. The thing she'd feared from the beginning. She'd gone ahead and fallen in love.

She was in love with Johnny.

Her heart stuttered. Her knees went soft as air caught in her lungs and found no way out.

He just looked at her with that noncommittal expression on his handsome, varsity-captain-of-heartache face.

She opened her mouth to gasp in oxygen and then another wave of anger and despair washed over her, tumbling her heart and her stomach in its wake. He'd made her vulnerable. And weak. Oh, God.

"How I hate what you've done to me," she whispered. "How I hate you."

His eyes closed. "No, Téa. Please. We've got to find a way around all this—our fathers, my mistakes."

There was no way around the fact that by making her fall in love with him he'd won. And she'd lost.

Control. Pride. Power.

Stepping back, she moved out of his embrace. But he grabbed her hands and held them so she couldn't get away. "Contessa, please. I—"

Then Cal was on the dance floor, grabbing Johnny's arm and breaking his hold on her. The lanky man muttered something near the older man's ear.

Then, without looking back, Johnny hurried away from her.

She stared after his retreating form, glad to be rid of him. Glad. With any luck, she'd never see him again.

But no, she wasn't glad, she thought, those frustrated tears pricking her eyes once more.

Because he wasn't the one who got to walk away! His didn't get to be the last words! Maybe that was how to turn this evening into a true triumph. She'd take back her heart and her life by making clear how totally she despised him.

Her gaze on the direction he'd taken, she followed.

Téa found Johnny near the lagoon, standing by a section of collapsed retaining wall. Cal was at his side with a flashlight, while Rachele stood a ways off, one hand over her mouth, the other playing with her eyebrow ring. Her head jerked toward Téa.

"Boss!" she called out, darting a glance toward the men. "You shouldn't be out here."

Johnny and Cal spun toward her, and then Johnny sprinted to her side and took hold of her arm. "Contessa, go back to the party," he ordered.

"What?"

His mouth was set in a grim line. "Go back to the party."

"Why?"

He was breathing fast and rough, as if that sprint had been miles instead of a few yards. "Because . . . " His free hand wiped down his face. "Because, I need you to do as I ask. Please."

"Right." She wrenched her arm from his and stomped toward the lagoon and the broken wall.

The other three converged on her, blocking her view. "You don't want to see this," Rachele said, her voice pleading.

Something cold tiptoed down the back of Téa's naked spine. She'd never liked this part of Johnny's estate, but now it and Rachele's desperate voice were out-and-out spooking her. "What is it?"

Cal looked at Johnny. He rubbed his hand over his face again, then gave a weary nod. The other man handed her something he held, then trained the flashlight on the object.

It was a wallet. The black leather was moldy around the edges of the trifolds, and it felt chilled and damp beneath her fingers. "You found a man's wallet."

"It's your father's," Rachele whispered.

Téa's grip tightened for a minute, then she watched herself unfold the edges. The plastic sleeves inside were a little moldy too, but she recognized what they held as she flipped through them with her fingernail. A California driver's license. Expired American Express and Visa. ATM card from Palm Springs Savings. A snapshot of Téa's mother in a wedding dress and veil, looking young and achingly optimistic.

Then the last photo. Téa almost smiled. The three little princesses, at ages four, six, and six, wearing white velvet dresses and gathered around a Christmas tree. She ran her fingertip over the plastic covering the picture. Her father must have taken it, she was sure, because each daughter wore identical expressions of smugness and joy. *I know I'm your favorite,* the three little faces seemed to say.

Her father had been so good at making them believe in fairy tales.

She looked up at the trio gathered around her. "So you found my father's wallet."

"There's more." Johnny took a breath. "We think we found your father's . . . "

"What?" Knowledge was buzzing around her like an annoying fly, but she batted it away. "What else did you find? His keys? His handkerchief? A pair of sunglasses that he dropped into the water on some long-ago visit here?"

It had to be one of those things, right? Something innocuous. Innocent. Though she hadn't thought her father and Giovanni Martelli had a social relationship, there must have been one, or else his belongings wouldn't have shown up at Giovanni Martelli's house.

"Téa . . . " Johnny's voice drifted off again, and he squeezed the bridge of his nose between his fingers.

She stared at him. Were those tears in his eyes? Her heart jolted, but she quickly seized back control. She wouldn't go soft. She hated him.

By some sort of tacit agreement, Rachele and Cal each took one of her arms and drew her away from the lagoon. Johnny followed, and they didn't stop moving until they'd put the trellises she'd ordered between them and the murky water. Rachele took a seat on a smooth boulder and tugged Téa down beside her.

Johnny crouched in front of her. For a second, she had the wild thought he was getting ready to propose.

"Téa, there's no easy way to say this." His voice was hoarse. "We think . . . we think we found your father's remains."

Her father's remains?

My father's remains.

Of course my father's remains, she thought, as her brain seemed to pull away from her body. When she'd seen the wallet, when they'd said they'd found something else as well, she'd known it had to be that. Her father's remains. She hadn't wanted to believe it.

"Are you sure? You're certain it's him?" She looked at the faces around her.

It was Cal that nodded. Calvin, "The Calculator," wouldn't make that kind of mistake.

Her father's remains.

Her father was dead.

Odd, how strange it sounded when she'd been certain she'd accepted it so long ago.

Johnny glanced up. "Cal, go back to the lagoon and make sure nobody else stumbles upon . . . what you did."

"Will do. Rachele and I saw some young guys with champagne bottles looking to hold a private bash and we think we sent them on their way, but I'll keep an eye out."

Rachele rubbed her palms up and down Téa's chilled arms. "Are you breathing, boss? You gotta keep breathing."

"My father's dead. My father's really dead."

"Oh, baby." Johnny gathered her hands in his, then bent

his head over them. Téa had the weirdest feeling that he was praying. "I'm sorry."

She stared at his thick shiny hair, the thick shiny hair of the man she love—no, hated. He looked up, and this time she was certain there were tears in his eyes.

"I'm so sorry my father killed yours."

Thirty-five

"You're Breaking My Heart"
Vic Damone
Angela Mia (1959)

Johnny was sorry that his father had killed hers. Téa just blinked at him. He thought finding the remains here, at Giovanni Martelli's former house, was proof positive that his father was a murderer.

"I didn't want to believe it," he said. His fingers dropped hers and he shot to his feet and rubbed both hands over his face. "I'm such a fucking fool. Everything that I did, every time I was with you, every time I touched you, teased you, took you to bed, I told myself it wasn't so bad because I'd find out that my father had nothing to do with the death of yours."

Rachele clutched Téa's arm. "What's he talking about?"

Téa closed her eyes, her emotions reeling. "He's Giovanni's son. Rachele, meet Gianni Martelli, aka Johnny Magee."

Rachele rose to her feet and sidestepped to stand between Téa and Johnny. "I don't understand what's going on."

"He seduced me under false pretenses." *Why pretty it up?*

"Shit," Johnny muttered. "I think I'm going to be sick." He ran into the nearby tangle of vegetation.

Rachele stared after him. "This is seriously cracked."

"This is a serious mess." Téa put her face in her hands. "We're going to have to call someone, the police or—"

"Let me take care of that," Rachele said. "You stay here and keep breathing and I'll go get . . . I'll figure out who and I'll tell them what they need to know."

Téa couldn't muster the energy to do anything else. She watched Rachele hurry off, her thoughts refusing to coalesce into anything meaningful. Instead, her mind replayed snippets of earlier conversations.

Can't you just forget about the past so we can get on with the rest of our lives?

We've got to find a way around all this.

I'm so sorry my father killed yours.

In the distance, faraway strains of a song caught her attention. The band. That's right, she thought dully, there was a party tonight. They were celebrating while her father's remains were being uncovered.

Then, closer, came other, more violent noises.

Pop.

Pop. Pop.

Téa's body jerked straight.

Another *pop*, followed by the wild whoop of a young man.

A final phrase echoed in her mind. *Rachele and I saw some young guys with champagne bottles looking to hold a private bash . . .*

Still uneasy though, Téa came to her feet. "Johnny?" She took a step in the direction she'd last seen him take. "Johnny? Where are you?"

When silence was her only response, she took a few more unsteady steps, her heartbeat stumbling as well. "Johnny! *Johnny!*"

He materialized like a ghost between the trunks of two palm trees. His face was moonlight pale and his eyes looked flat. Lifeless.

She hugged her body so that she wouldn't go to him. "Are you hurt?"

He moved, and immediately stumbled too, his momentum taking him forward until he found the boulder she'd been sitting on. He put out his hands, feeling for it as if he were blind, then sank down onto it.

"Johnny, what's the matter?"

"It's all the blood," he muttered.

Now she ran to him, patting him to find his injuries. "What blood? Where are you hurt?"

He caught her hands. "Contessa," he murmured. "This is real. You're real."

"Of course I'm real." His fingers were icy on hers. "I'm real and I'm right here. Are you hurt?"

Squeezing her hands, he shook his head. "Not hurt." His chest rose in a long, deliberate breath. "Talk. Talk to me."

"You're scaring me," she said. "I need to know what's the matter. Johnny! What's the matter?"

He shook his head again, as if he were trying to shake off a blow.

She'd seen him like this once before, she remembered. That first day they'd made—had sex. "Are you sick?"

"Sick in the head, maybe." He sucked in another breath, shook his head again. "You're real. You're real."

She knelt so she could look into his face. "Johnny, it's Téa. I'm here, I'm real. What's happening to you?"

His eyes were squeezed shut. Slowly, he opened them, his fingers biting into hers. He let out another breath, this one easier. He took in another, blew it out. "I'm all right now. I'm okay."

She tried to move away, but he wouldn't let go of her hands. "What's going on?" she asked.

"Flashback," he muttered. "The mother of all flashbacks. Probably because of the body. And then those sounds. Like gunshots."

The pops. That other day there'd been gunshot-like sounds too. Backfires from the gardener's truck. "Flashback to what?"

Now he released her hands, and stared down at his own. He took in another breath, let it out. "Flashback to the night of my father's murder."

She frowned. "Why—" *Oh, no. Oh, no, no, no.* "Were you here when it happened? Oh, God, Johnny, were you *here*?"

"Annual summer visit. First night. Last night, too, I guess."

She backed a step away from him. "You never told me."

He laughed, a harsh, tired sound. "As you well know, I didn't tell you a lot of things."

"Tell me now." When he hesitated, she strengthened the words. "Tell me all of it now."

He glanced at her, then looked back at his hands, his voice low, but clear. "My parents divorced when I was a baby. My mom remarried Phineas Magee. But every summer I'd spend a couple weeks with my real dad, Giovanni Martelli. When I was seventeen, I flew from Washington state into the Ontario Airport and my dad picked me up on his way back from Vegas. He brought me here, to this house." A half-smile quirked the corners of his lips. "Which I thought was pretty cool, even then. Didn't know mid-century modern from a rat's ass, of course."

His dad had picked him up on his way back from Vegas. Téa latched onto that piece of information and played it over in her head. His dad had picked him up on his way back from Vegas. "And that first night . . . "

"I heard the gunshots. I ran down to the garage and found my father's car . . . and my father. I tried to keep him alive, Téa," he said, his voice roughening. "He was bleeding everywhere. All that blood. All that blood . . . "

She put her hand on his shoulder. "Stay with me."

His hand covered hers. "I called for an ambulance and they took him to the hospital. He went into surgery and came out, but then he died shortly afterward."

A new voice cut through the shadows. Joey's voice, cold and hard. "And you expect Téa to feel bad about that? He died as a consequence for killing *our* father, Johnny. Or do you prefer Gianni?"

Johnny let go of Téa's hand and leaped to his feet. They both swung toward Joey and took in the knot of people who'd arrived on the scene with her, presumably mustered by Rachele, who stood to one side, worrying her eyebrow ring.

Téa's mother, Joey, Eve, Beppe Cirigliano, and . . . Cosimo Caruso.

Téa's grandfather.

Eighty didn't look a day over sixty-five on him. Maybe it was his Mediterranean diet. Or good genes. Or a criminal conscience. He was upright and lean in his dinner jacket and dark slacks, his full head of silver-threaded hair brushed back from his face with its Roman nose—the masculine form of her own—and sharp, black eyes.

He addressed his first words to Johnny, his voice soft and holding only the slightest of accents. "My son has been found?"

"Yes," Johnny replied, his voice and poker face at their noncommittal best. "Interred, I suppose you'd say, in the wall of the lagoon."

"By *your* father," Joey said, taking a step forward.

Eve caught her arm. "Stay put, little sister."

"Are you all right, Mom?" Téa asked, her gaze traveling from vibrating-with-emotion Joey, to the older woman who was now clutching Beppe's wrist as if she needed support.

"I don't know," she whispered.

Joey sent another venomous look toward Johnny. "See what you've done," she said. "See what you and your father have done."

He flinched. "Forgive me," he said. "I'm sorry for bringing this back to all of you."

Téa almost laughed. It had never left them. Never left any of them.

"You'll get nothing from us," Joey spit back. "Nothing."

Téa understood her sister's fury. God, she'd felt it herself, hating whoever had taken her father away from them, hating her father for being the kind of man who *would* get taken away, hating her grandfather for his part in bringing them into this kind of life.

But she'd never hated Giovanni Martelli, because she'd always suspected he wasn't the one responsible. And now she was certain he wasn't.

My dad picked me up on his way back from Vegas. She could tell what she knew . . . or she could keep it to herself.

Johnny had done her wrong. He admitted that. He had betrayed her with his lies. And leaving him with the image of his father as murderer was the perfect revenge.

She was Caruso enough, ruthless enough, to enjoy the poetry of the payback. She'd given Johnny her body, and—though she was going to have to fight to get it back from him—her heart. He'd betrayed her and she could have her vengeance by giving him coin in kind.

Oh, yeah, that sounded really, really right. Really bad.

Wickedly good.

She could link arms with her sisters right now and walk

away, leaving Johnny with his pain and herself with the smug warmth of the perfect reprisal. Salvatore's crown princess having herself a royal good time at Johnny's expense.

But . . .

"He didn't do it," she heard herself say aloud. "Giovanni Martelli didn't kill our father."

Johnny stared at Téa. The night was only turning more surreal. The damn party, the grisly discovery of Salvatore's remains, the suffocating flashback, this surprise confrontation with the Caruso family.

He wanted to disappear, go away, forget his time here and go back and accept the sweaty nightmares and the paralyzing memories because they seemed infinitely more bearable than this endless night. If only he'd never met the dark-haired, sloe-eyed contessa that could wound him with only the tragic expression she was wearing on her beautiful face.

"Giovanni Martelli didn't kill our father," Téa said again.

Wound him with a sentence. Of course his father had killed hers. Giovanni had been a murderer because Téa's father was truly dead. Bile splashed against the sides of Johnny's empty stomach.

"Oh, right," Joey scoffed. "Giovanni is innocent and you know this how?"

Johnny heard Téa take a breath. "I know," she continued, "because of the book."

His gut roiled. Not—

"The Loanshark book?" Eve said, asking the question for him. "That book? What does it have to do with this?"

Tension radiated from Téa's body. Standing this close to her, he could see the way her fingers twined and tightened upon one another. "I happen—"

Johnny grabbed her shoulders, and yanked her around to face him. "Don't, Contessa."

She was ashamed of her part in that cursed thing. He

couldn't imagine why she was bringing it up now, but he wouldn't let the shock of their finding her father's remains lead her to make admissions that would only hurt her. His conscience couldn't take the added weight of that too. Tears stung the back of his eyes and the bile churned inside his belly.

"Johnny—"

"*No*, Téa."

Impatient as usual, Joey called out again. "Well, if somebody has something more to say, they better say it right now now."

It was Beppe Cirigliano, Rachele's father, who spoke up first.

"I killed him. God help me, it was an accident, but I killed my best friend. I killed Sal."

Thirty-six

"You're Nobody Till Somebody Loves You"
Dean Martin
This Time I'm Swingin' (1960)

Rachele rocked back as if her father had struck her with his fist. "Papa?"

He took a step toward her, then halted. "My little girl. My Rachele. I never wanted you to know I killed Salvatore."

Téa's mother, Bianca, tried to put her arm around him. "Beppe, you must not be feeling well."

He spun away from her touch, his lumbering movements making him look like an overwound mechanical bear. "It's true, Bianca. I killed Sal."

"Beppe?" Old Mr. Caruso could have been carved from stone. His voice was hard too. Cold and hard. "*Calmati.* Get ahold of yourself."

Rachele's father laughed. "I haven't had ahold of myself in sixteen years."

Rachele crossed to her father. He didn't know what he was

saying. He *must* be sick. "Let me take you home, Papa. After a good night's sleep—" She reached for his hand.

He jerked away from her and she froze, stung by the rejection. But he'd been rejecting her for years, she reminded herself. She'd just been too immature to see it clearly.

"It's been eating at me all this time," he said, looking at Téa's mother. "I know you won't understand, Bianca, but I thought I was helping you."

"By killing Sal?" she answered, her voice faint.

Eve moved to stand beside her mother, but Joey seemed transfixed, all her earlier attitude gone. Mr. Caruso's stiff posture gave nothing of his emotions away. Rachele felt as frozen as Johnny and Téa looked.

"I was working on the rockwork around the lagoon," her father said, his gaze still on Bianca. "It was getting dark and I'd sent the other laborers home, but I had cement mixed in my wheelbarrow that I wanted to use before I called it a day. Then Sal showed up. He'd been in Vegas the past week and said he'd stopped in at your house, but you and the girls were out shopping so he came here."

He looked down and shook his head. "You know Sal. Couldn't stand to be alone with his own company. Always had to have some action going—somebody to talk to or something to do."

His head came up and he looked over at Cosimo. "Remember that, Mr. Caruso? Sal was always the life of the party. Hell, he *was* the party. I always loved that about him."

"I remember, Beppe," Mr. Caruso said, his voice soft. "I know you loved him. So what happened that day?"

"Night," Beppo corrected. "It was almost night. I'd been working a lot of hours because the house seemed so empty with my Maria gone. Rachele was invited to a friend's for dinner. There wasn't any reason for me to hurry." He stared off into the distance. "The house seemed so cold and empty without Maria."

Her mother would have been dead for about a year, Rachele thought. Taken by pancreatic cancer that had been as quick as it was deadly. Rachele's only real memory of her mother was a white face on a white pillowcase. Pale lips, pale, chapped lips, that had smiled at Rachele even while her eyes had filled with tears. "Take care," she'd whispered. "Take care of Papa." And Rachele had tried to live by that promise.

"Beppe, we know you were hurting over Maria," Bianca said. "Sal and I both worried about you."

His head swung toward her and he smiled. Rachele couldn't remember the last time she'd seen him smile. "You were so good to me, Bianca. To me and to Rachele. Always. It's why I couldn't stand what Sal was doing."

"What was he doing?" Cosimo Caruso asked. "What bothered you, Beppe?"

His smile faded away. "I don't want to say."

"It was a woman," Bianca said, her voice matter-of-fact. "I always knew when there was another woman."

"But they didn't mean anything to him," Rachele's father protested quickly. "That's what made me so mad. He was hurting you without good reason."

Hurting Bianca. And that was what had bothered her father, Rachele figured out. With her mother gone, her father had found himself another woman to love. Bianca Caruso. Rachele had always suspected it was more than mere concern he felt for his best friend's widow.

He'd loved her sixteen years ago.

Perhaps he loved her still. She wondered if he realized.

"I talked to him about it that night," her father said. "I told him he shouldn't be so foolish. I told him maybe you'd get angry and fed up enough to file for divorce and take the girls away from him."

"What he'd say to that?" Téa asked. She was still standing near Johnny, but she'd put a bigger distance between them and was hugging herself.

"He got angry. If there was one thing that Sal cared about more than a good time, it was you three little girls. When I said your mother might take you away from him, he went a little crazy. He swore at me, and when I said it again, he came after me."

Rachele's father shifted his gaze to Bianca and Cosimo. "You know what a hothead he was. I was only trying to defend myself. I was standing by the wheelbarrow, stirring the cement with a hoe, when he went for me. I held the hoe across my body." He pantomimed the scene, showing how he gripped the handle of the tool chest-high.

"Sal ran into it and then stumbled back. He tripped over the rocks I had piled up and he fell, his head slamming against the section of the ledge I'd just finished. He was gone. It only took a few seconds for the whole thing to happen. But he died the instant his head hit. The instant. I swear that on Maria's grave."

"But why didn't you call an ambulance—or at least the police?" Téa asked.

Rachele's father blinked. "I couldn't risk it. What if they didn't believe me? Who would take care of my little girl? She didn't have a mother, so how could I possibly put her in a position of losing her father too?"

What? Had Rachele heard right? He'd hidden the accident because of her?

Rachele felt the freaky numbness that had overtaken her begin to wear off, pins and needles pricking her skin and then her heart. Perhaps her father had confronted Salvatore Caruso because he'd loved Bianca, but afterward he'd kept quiet about what happened out of his concern for Rachele.

Oh, Papa.

"So you buried him here, Beppe," Cosimo said. "And his car?"

"I drove it home and put it in my garage. A few days later, I took it out to a desert wash I know about and torched it."

"So that's what happened to the damned Loanshark book," Eve murmured. "Up in flames."

"I felt sick when someone else got the blame," Rachele's father went on, looking over at Johnny. "But I didn't know he had a son. Giovanni Martelli's murder only made me more determined to keep my mouth shut."

There was a long moment of stunned quiet.

"I'm sorry," Beppo said again, and his shoulders bowed as he aged before Rachele's eyes. "I'm so very sorry."

It was Joey who next found her voice. "What now?"

"Now . . . " Cosimo Caruso inhaled a long breath. Then he looked around the small group. "Now I put some men to stand guard down here and we go back to the party. We've been away too long already."

"Back to the party?" Joey started to protest. "But—"

The old man cut her off by holding up his hand. "We'll deal with this tomorrow. Tonight, there's too much at stake. We need to show happy faces. Happy, strong, united faces. *Avete capito?* Do you understand?"

Rachele shivered at the steel beneath the words. This was the Mafia don in control, the CEO of crime who had ruled California for decades. Tonight they had a reprieve, some time for these new facts to sink in. But tomorrow, her father's fate would be in the mob boss's hands.

Rachele moved to her father and slipped her arm through his. He didn't pull away this time. "Papa, let me drive you home now."

He let her take the lead. When she stopped in front of Cosimo Caruso, her father seemed not to notice. "He's a good man, Mr. Caruso," Rachele said, remembering her promise to her mother and pinning the old man with her gaze. Her heart pounded and the spit in her mouth dried as she gave her voice its own edge of steel. "What happened to your son was an accident and I expect you will treat it as such."

The head of the California Mafia dropped his neutral expression. For an instant he looked surprised, then admiring, then—nothing again. Perhaps she'd imagined it. But he nodded his head at her. "All will be handled fairly, Rachele."

"Is that a promise?"

His dark eyebrows rose. "Must you ask?"

"Yeah, I think I must."

"Le donne!" he remarked, the tiniest of smiles crossing his face. "Then it's a promise."

Giving him her own dignified nod, Rachele set off, keeping her father close to her side. She didn't know exactly what would happen now. Maybe she and her father would finally talk, adult to adult. Maybe her father was going to break her heart all over again. But not because he'd never cared for her.

Her father knew how to love. Perhaps he'd even loved too well. He'd cared enough to try to intervene in his best friend's marriage. He'd cared enough about his best friend's wife to stick up for her. He'd loved Rachele enough to keep a secret buried here and in his conscience for the last sixteen years.

She *had* been immature.

Before now, she hadn't known that bad things could happen to good people. She hadn't known that good people could do bad things in the name of love.

Because it wasn't simple or easy. Love wasn't the bam-slam lightning bolt that made all things possible. After what her father had done, she couldn't believe that anymore.

She saw Cal in the distance and gave a little wave. He'd be there tomorrow when she needed him, she didn't doubt that. She still believed in love; her father's actions had proved its very real power, too.

Perhaps she was finally, truly, growing up.

Thirty-seven

"The Best is Yet to Come"
Frank Sinatra
It Might as Well Be Swing (1964)

They were in a collective state of shock, Téa decided, as they followed her grandfather's order and returned to the party. It was the only explanation for why they stayed silent and obedient.

Her father was really dead.

An accidental death, kept secret by his best friend for the last sixteen years.

It was going to take a while to process that.

But until then . . . hey, it was time to pa-a-arty!

Johnny disappeared somewhere between the lagoon and the tents. She couldn't imagine what he was feeling right now, though she hoped he was as numb as she.

Her family had murdered his father for no reason. Because of what she knew was in the Loanshark book, the timing had always made her suspect about Giovanni Martelli's involvement. Of course, that was before she'd known about his son.

That his son had been close by at the time of the hit.

That she was in love with his son.

Her mother took a place at an empty table near the dance floor and Téa and her sisters followed like automatons. Cosimo linked up with a couple of his ubiquitous lieutenants—Nino and another man she didn't recognize—and proceeded toward the bar.

She could really go for a zombie mai tai herself right now, Téa thought. She wanted to nurse this numb feeling for as long as possible.

But there was only time for the wish, as the bandleader suddenly signaled for attention with a crash of cymbals. Then came the familiar tune of "Happy Birthday." Cosimo strode back out of the tent as the dance floor cleared and the three hundred or so partygoers sang along. He smiled and nodded as if he hadn't a care in the world, then walked to the bandleader and murmured something in his ear.

The musicians segued into a new song, "My Way," as the bandleader leaned into the microphone. "Ladies and gentlemen, tonight's guest of honor will lead off the next dance with his eldest granddaughter and the desert's rising star of interior design . . . Téa Caruso."

The crowd applauded as Téa's grandfather approached her. The desert's rising star of interior design didn't know what to do.

Cosimo gave her a small bow, then held his hand out for hers.

She swallowed.

"Per favore, cara," he said, his hand still extended.

She didn't want to talk with him, let alone dance with him. But even if she could find the energy to stamp her feet and scream at the top of her lungs, she couldn't make a scene in front of all these people. Old habits died hard. Old bargains were impossible to forget.

And there was information she needed from him.

So she put her hand in his. It was warm and dry. The skin felt thin, fragile even.

Cosimo, fragile? The notion sent an odd sympathy through her. But then her sandal strap caught in the hem of her long dress, and his grip tightened. His steely hold steadied her. No, Cosimo—nickname the Cudgel—would never be fragile.

On the dance floor, he took her in a loose embrace. With her high heels they were almost eye-to-eye. "Desert's rising star of design, eh?" he said.

"Don't try that on me. You told the man what to say."

Cosimo sighed. "You were always so smart."

In silence, he led her into a stately fox trot. They had danced together when she was little at other birthdays, weddings, holidays. Always patient, always willing to slow down for a little girl's short legs. While her father would grow restless at such a pace and end up snatching her off her feet and dancing her around the room like a rag doll, Cosimo would bend himself to accommodate her size.

Téa used to think of her father as a dazzling comet and her grandfather as the calm and quiet moon. But, of course, even the moon or the *il capo di tutti cappi*—the boss of bosses of the California Mafia—didn't remain in the sky forever.

She looked up at the twinkling canopy of fairy lights. Their brilliance caught in the sequined dresses of the women ringing the dance floor, causing them to flash like a thousand tiny cameras. They were surrounded by hundreds of gazes too, and Téa could feel their weight and the questions behind them.

Would the old man really retire?

Who would he name to take his place?

And who would battle to take that position away from the new leader?

My family, Téa thought, with a wry inner grimace. *My ordinary family.*

She closed her eyes. "How could you, Grandpa? How could you have lived this life?"

He was quiet a moment. "You know, *cara*, I used to dance with your grandmother on Saturday nights at the Chi-Chi Club. She'd make a little sound—a little gasp—whenever she spotted her favorite celebrities like Frank Sinatra or Ava Gardner or Cary Grant. I could live a month on one of those little gasps, but it took more than that to feed and clothe all those who relied on me."

"There were other ways to make a living," Téa pointed out. "Legitimate ways."

His shrug was elegant, yet resigned. "My friend Henry once said, 'The illegal we do immediately; the unconstitutional takes a little longer.' As I have told him before and will now tell you, the legitimate can take a man's lifetime."

"Who's this Henry?"

Her grandfather smiled. "Kissinger. Mr. Henry Kissinger."

Téa's jaw dropped. "You're friends with Henry Kissinger."

He shrugged again. "A friendship forged long ago, *cara,* even as the choice of this life was made long ago as well."

"You should have unchosen it before it became our life too."

"If only it were that easy."

"But look at what happened! Giovanni Martelli murdered by mistake."

He acknowledged it with a small bow of his head. "It is unfortunate. Regrettable."

"Regrettable!" She took a breath and asked the question that had brought her onto the dance floor. "Do you know who murdered him, Grandpa? Did . . . did you?"

He was already shaking his head. "It was an action off the record—meaning I did not sanction it, nor did any of my lieutenants. We're never so hasty. A young one went ahead on his own to—how do you say it?—make points."

Téa didn't know whether to believe him. "Who is this young one? And was he properly rewarded?"

"You might think so. He died a decade ago when he made another hotheaded decision."

The dance was coming to an end. Cosimo's gaze left her face to take in the people surrounding the dance floor. She wondered if he could feel the dark undercurrent surrounding them as well. But of course he did. How else had he survived as boss of the California Mafia throughout the years?

His hand gave hers a gentle squeeze. "Tell your friend his father's killer is long dead, *cara*. It may bring him some comfort."

He walked her back to her table to a smattering of more applause. Then Téa watched him stroll amongst the guests, one of his men at each elbow. He paused to shake the hand of another crime boss based in Florida, a woman who headed a Hollywood studio, the governor of California. Perhaps Henry Kissinger was somewhere in the crowd.

Tell your friend his father's killer is long dead.

It may bring him some comfort.

Téa slumped against the back of her chair. If she faced Johnny again, what was going to comfort her?

To Téa's mind, the habits she'd established later in life had been hard-won and were therefore the hardest to break. It was why she walked away from the party when the wedges of creamy-iced Italian rum cake were served. It was why she couldn't ignore her clamoring conscience and so made her way up the path to Johnny's house.

Apart from the oasis-like vegetation of the rest of the estate, it stood out against the desert setting as it always had, elegant and sophisticated. The pool lights were on, and the water glowed turquoise. The house itself was dark, but she smelled the scent of burning mesquite and as she neared the front door, she could see through the glass wall that logs were burning in the screenless living room fireplace.

In the light of the fire, she saw Johnny too, sprawled on the wide sofa, his tie unfastened, the top button of his shirt undone. Her breath caught. Not because he looked golden and beautiful, but because he looked so cool and detached.

How could he not be seething with rage? Her numbness hadn't lasted this long and he had far more to be angry about.

As she watched, he plucked a playing card from the stack in one hand and with an expert flip of his long fingers, spun it into the fire. Then he did it again. And again.

She wanted to run away, as she had all her life.

But it was time to face up to what her family had done. What she had been part of.

Raising her hand, she rapped on the door, then opened it without waiting for his permission. She was afraid he'd give her a chance to back out. He glanced over his shoulder as she walked into the living room, then returned his attention to the fire.

"I didn't think we'd see each other again so soon," he said. His voice gave nothing of his emotions away.

But she knew he hated her family, and by extension, her.

Who could blame him?

Yet Johnny sounded as composed as ever.

She perched on the chair adjacent to the sofa, cradling the item she'd brought in her hands. Her tongue felt too big for her mouth and she swallowed, trying to moisten it before speaking.

He flipped another card into the fire and she watched the ace of spades burn. Its edges singed and then it curled into itself in a fiery fetal position.

She swallowed again. "I know I'm sorry isn't—"

"Then don't say it."

Téa squeezed her eyes tight. "This I have to say. My

grandfather claims he didn't order the hit on your father. The man who did it, on his own, has been dead himself for over a decade."

Johnny didn't twitch. His dispassionate expression didn't falter. Without a tremor, his fingers flipped another card. The jack of clubs sputtered, then caught fire.

Watching his smooth movements, she wondered if the Carusos had killed off yet another man tonight. At the very least, Johnny must have ice water in his veins.

Her hands squeezed on the item she'd brought with her. She looked down at it, tracing with her eyes the cartoon image of the pony-tailed girl pictured on the front. It was all she had to give Johnny. Piss-poor payment, but all that she had.

When she rose and held it out to him, the one thing she'd thought she would never give up, it felt as if she was offering him her heart.

Which was ridiculous, because he already had that.

"Take this," she said.

He glanced at the object, then her face. "What is it?" he asked, lifting another card from the stack in his hands. The queen of hearts.

"The Loanshark book."

His fingers stilled. "What?"

"I have it." Téa had saved the book and kept its secrets for sixteen years as a reminder of her own complicity, as a touchstone to her guilt, as tangible proof that giving your love to a man could leave you holding only ugliness. "I've always had it."

"You told me you kept the records for your father—"

"And I kept the book, too. It wasn't in his car. It always sat on a shelf in my room. The FBI didn't look twice at a little girl's diary."

Johnny gave a disbelieving shake of his head. "Why didn't you get rid of it?"

She shrugged her shoulders. "I thought . . . I thought someone might need it someday. It seems that someone is you."

"What the hell would I want with it?" There was a new, tight note in his voice.

"For one, it does exonerate your father. There's something in it that I always wondered about. When you said your father picked you up at the airport on his way back from Las Vegas, the pieces of the puzzle fit. The last entry in the book was written by *my* father, and it indicates Giovanni Martelli paid off the last of his loan a few days before."

"I don't get it."

"Beppe added another piece that cleared it up. He said my father stopped by our house after returning from Las Vegas before heading out again. I wasn't home, so he wrote that last entry in the Loanshark book himself and then went to visit Beppe. On that day, Giovanni was still in Las Vegas. It was a few days before he picked you up." She held the book closer to Johnny. "Here."

"I don't need the book. I know my father's innocent."

"But mine isn't," Téa replied. And neither was she. At least that was how she'd always felt. Handing over the book to Johnny, though, was the way to finally separate her adult self from the actions of the child she'd been. "You can use the information here to prove that to the police and to the FBI. A fitting revenge, don't you think?"

A scene from the recent past popped into Johnny's head. The Las Vegas penthouse office. Cal and Johnny at their desks.

Who said revenge is a dish best served cold?

Johnny stared at the thick, bubblegum pink book in Téa's hands and watched one of his own reach out to take it from her. The plastic cover was squishy and the cartoon character on the front stared up at him with big-lashed wide eyes. Inside was years of secrets, details and names that he knew would be powerful even after all this time.

Who said revenge is a dish best served cold?

And he felt cold. From the moment he'd understood his father was innocent of murder, that he'd died without reason, Johnny had felt fucking frigid.

His blood was cold enough that he could take this innocuous little diary and pay back the California Mafia for what they'd taken from him and the hell they'd put him through in the last months. For every minute that he hadn't slept, he could keep a member of the Caruso crime family awake.

He would be their very own nightmare.

Ah, revenge would taste so very, very sweet.

The FBI would put him up for a fucking medal.

The same FBI who'd referred to Téa as Salvatore's little bitch of a daughter.

But who cared about that? Who could blame the Feds or anyone else for hating a member of the family that could lay claim to crimes, and pain, and death?

Holding onto the book and caressing it with his thumb as if it was the One True Ring and he was some overgrown Frodo Baggins, Johnny looked up at Téa. Those beautiful sloe eyes of hers were steady on his, but the ruby-encrusted heart was once again trembling at her throat.

She'd just handed him her past, he realized. To do with what he would.

"You love me." It was a statement of fact. "You're in love with me." That's why she'd given it to him.

That heart stopped trembling. He didn't think she was breathing. "What does it matter?" she finally choked out.

"I want to hear you say the words." He sounded as cold and deadly as Cosimo.

She made a choppy little nod. "Fine, then. You can have

that, too, though I don't know why you'd want an admission like that from a Caruso, from *me*. But I am in love with you." Her voice faltered. *"Ti amo, Gianni."*

Ah, yes. That did make it all the sweeter. At the same time, he could break the California Mafia and break its first daughter's heart. Wouldn't that be fine? Wouldn't that be fitting?

Logical, too. This wasn't just about emotion. This was about truth and justice for all. He'd turn the Loanshark book over to the authorities and—

They would know that Téa had participated in her mob family's business. They wouldn't prosecute or even blame her, of course, she'd been a little kid, but . . .

They would know Téa's shame.

The shame she'd hidden from her mother, her sisters, her friends. The shame she'd hidden from everyone but him.

So what? Screw that. Screw logic, too. He didn't need another reason beyond the fact that her family had been responsible for his father's death and somebody had to pay.

He remembered thinking just a few hours ago that he'd come to Palm Springs because he needed to know what crimes his father had committed, not those committed against him. But with the ghosts on his back again, their dank breath ruffling the hair at the nape of his neck, he had to admit that was a lie. He wasn't satisfied knowing his father hadn't killed anyone. His father had been wronged. Murdered.

And somebody has to pay.

But it shouldn't be Téa, a voice inside him said. *It shouldn't be Téa.*

He hesitated.

And then despised himself for it.

Because he knew the voice was right and that he was wrong for wanting to punish her. It wasn't his Main Street morality taking him to task, though. It wasn't Phineas Magee's adopted son remembering the Boy Scout rules.

Giovanni Martelli had raised Johnny to be a better man than this. The dark, icy mix of fury and grief Johnny felt inside himself right now was not his father's legacy. No, the only fingerprint Giovanni Martelli had left on Johnny's soul was how to treat the people he cared for. Giovanni had sacrificed living with his son, even letting him use another man's name, for his former wife's happiness and that son's security.

Though Johnny had spent sixteen years trying not to care about anyone that way, now he found he couldn't sacrifice Téa's happiness or security for anything.

"Fuck," he said, breaking the ghouls' stranglehold to fling them from his back, "No."

And then he heaved the book into the fire.

Téa jumped as the Loanshark book hit the flames and sparks burst like fireworks.

"Damn it." Johnny shoved to his feet and stalked toward her. The playing cards scattered to the floor.

Téa scuttled back.

"Damn it!" He grabbed her by the shoulders. "Hold still."

She'd never seen him like this. Emotion had broken free of its ice-encasing and he seemed wild with it.

"It almost happened," he said, his eyes flame-blue instead of blue-cool. "Do you realize how close that was? We almost let it happen."

"I—I don't know what you're talking about."

"Our fathers. Their mistakes. They almost ruined us."

She didn't know about Johnny, but she didn't feel "almost" ruined. She was the whole way gone. He had her heart, he had her love, and she was never going to get them back.

While she might free herself from the past, she was never going to free herself from loving Johnny.

I love you, Contessa.

It was her imagination again, pretending she could read his

mind. She stumbled back, out of his hands, and put the sofa between them. "I'm leaving now, Johnny."

"Like hell you are. I love you, Téa. I'm in love with you."

Her heart fell to the pit of her stomach. "No," she whispered. "I won't believe that. We're enemies."

"We're our own worst enemies if we let the past get in the way of what we could have together."

She put out her hand to steady herself on the sofa back. "This is a trick—"

"No." Johnny glanced over at the smoldering fire. "Didn't I just prove that you can trust me, Contessa?"

Oh, God. She stared at the flames as they consumed the Loanshark book and her shameful secrets. Trust him? "But my family, what they did, what they do, no man could—"

"This man could. I *can* understand who you are and how you feel. I *do*. Giovanni wasn't a complete innocent, Téa. But he didn't leave darkness on my soul either. You were right, I was afraid of that, and afraid that connecting with people would connect me to emotions I didn't want to feel. But I'm not afraid anymore. His legacy to me is other things. I'm beginning to believe that one of them is you."

But she couldn't believe. Because finding Johnny, loving Johnny but not having him, wasn't that the final yet necessary restitution for her "little" crimes? Wasn't that part of the bargain she'd made with her conscience and with God?

It made her angry, furious really, but didn't it have to be that way?

"My father taught me how to take a gamble, Téa," Johnny said softly. "And I've laid myself on the line here. What did your father teach you?"

To be ruthless. To keep good records.

Yes. But he'd taught her more, hadn't he? He'd taught her that she was the smart sister. No insult to Eve and Joey, but he'd been right about that. So she couldn't turn away from the one good lesson her father had ever taught her, could she? That the smart princess should always use her brains.

And it was her brains as well as her heart that were telling her, had been telling her from the beginning, whispering, shouting—*here's the one!* The one worth risking it all for. The one who she didn't have to fear would discover her secrets and her shame because he was the one man who could understand them.

The man who loved her. She looked at the Loanshark book, burning in the fire. *The man I can trust.*

She thought she leaped over the sofa to find her way to Johnny's arms.

It didn't matter how, because she was there, in his embrace, feeling his heart pounding against hers. "I trust you, I trust you. I do trust you."

"Téa," he said against her mouth. "Be my love. Be my life."

And oh, she would. She'd be his love, his life, his contessa, his princess, his queen.

Varsity men deserved no less.

They couldn't get enough of each other. Or close enough. She popped the buttons on his shirt to get to his naked skin. He pulled pins from the updo until her hair swept her shoulders. His chest was bare and his pants unfastened when he pushed her a little away. "How do we get you out of this dress?" he said, his voice rough.

"Right here, right now?" Téa glanced over at the fire. Oh yeah, right here, right now. The gypsy girl was going to dance right here, right now, with the man she loved. Already the violins were singing, their voices rivaling the angels'. She smiled at Johnny. "It's sort of a peel and eat kind of gown."

He groaned. "Then show me where to start peeling, Contessa."

He was very efficient, until he realized what was missing. "No panties?" he croaked out, his hands stilling. "You're not wearing panties?"

She shrugged. "Where was I going to put them?" she said, as she arranged herself on the rug before the fire.

He dropped down beside her. "I love you," he said. "Oh God, how I love you." His body joined with hers.

All playfulness evaporated in the heat of the fire and the heat between them. This wasn't sex, but lovemaking—life-affirming, love-securing, love the way she'd always dreamed it would be. Téa closed her eyes against the rush of tears that burned in them.

They were tenderly moving against each other when something made her eyelids rise. Johnny's golden face was above hers, but then her gaze caught on the scene outside the glass windows. A knot of people stood by the pool, apparently transfixed by the sight of them entwined before the fire.

Her fingers tightened on Johnny's shoulders as embarrassment washed over her. What would people think? What would people think about how this looked? Punctual, proper, puritanically dressed Téa Caruso now naked and doing the wild thing for all to see!

But then she remembered.

She was beautiful.

She was loved.

And she was wicked too, or at least very, very bad, because it occurred to her that in their position, the audience had a clear view of only one person. Johnny. Johnny and his bare naked, quite outstanding butt.

So, assured her own privacy was semi-safe, she smiled to herself.

And drew Johnny's mouth to hers, closing her eyes to everything but their future.

Epilogue

"More"
Bobby Darin
From Hello Dolly to Goodbye Charlie (1964)

A week after the big birthday bash, two of Salvatore Caruso's three daughters sat on plush chairs in the elegant spa waiting room at the Kona Kai. Wrapped in luxurious robes, their new pedicures drying, they were lost in thought.

Men were on both their minds, Eve Caruso guessed. Her older sister Téa might be mooning over her Johnny, who was on business in Las Vegas for a few days. Or maybe she was thinking of Beppe Cirigliano. His daughter, Rachele, had stopped by earlier and told them it was definite—her father was cleared of anything more than an accidental involvement in the death of Salvatore.

It was a relief, Eve thought, just as she was probably supposed to feel relieved to finally know, once and for all, what had happened to their dad. So what that she'd always been secretly convinced he was safe and alive in the witness protection program somewhere? It had been a childish fantasy, she saw that now.

"You're brooding," Téa suddenly said. "That's not like you."

"Brooding?" Eve tried to scoff. "I don't brood. I'm the party girl, remember?" Palm Springs's favorite society columnist didn't have time for gloom, not when the social season was just beginning to swing. Not when her old way of life was slipping like sand through her fingers.

"Where's your Mercedes?" Téa asked. "In for repairs? That old Hyundai you're driving looks like it won't make it to the dry cleaners and back."

It had made it to the designer consignment shop and then to the spa, just fine. "I sold the Merced," Eve said, leaning over to pick up a glossy magazine instead of looking into her too-smart sister's face. She didn't want the family who had taken her in to know that her pride was one of the few things of value she had left. "I'm going to be getting a new model." If she ever had the money again.

She flipped a page, staring at the spread of fancy jewels. Too bad she didn't have any more of those to cash in as well. Damn the CEO she'd been dating and her own stupidity. His lousy stock tip had sucked away every last dollar she had. "Just so you know, I have my condo on the market too."

"Looking for another upgrade?"

Eve shrugged.

Téa sipped from her glass of ice water and lemon slices. "Maybe Johnny and I should take a look at it. We need to find a bigger place—another house, but until then . . . "

"The two of you aren't comfortable at the El Deseo property?" Of course they weren't. It was where both their fathers had been killed.

"There's bad memories . . . and good, but we need to find something that's just our own."

Her dour mood lifting, Eve smiled. Something, some secret, had held her sister back for years, but she seemed free of it now. "You know I'm glad for you. I'm so glad you've finally let a man into your life."

"I recommend it." Téa slid a glance at her. "Anyone capable of stealing your heart, Eve?"

"You know I won't let that happen."

"I know you like to tell us that."

"It's true." Eve hoped to God it was true. Since she'd lost everything else, she had to hang onto her heart. "But in my case that doesn't mean I turn my back on men. They have their uses." Just don't count on them for sound financial advice.

Téa gave a sly smile. "I'm beginning to figure that out."

"Sex, the new antidepressant."

Her sister shook her head. "You mean love."

"I do not—"

"You do not what?" Their younger sister Joey walked into the room on her heels, keeping her still-wet toes in the air. Her arms were filled with a stack of magazines.

"Téa's going gooey on us." Joey would understand where Eve was coming from. Their little sister had more men friends than any other woman she'd met, but she didn't romanticize her relationships with them either. They were golf partners or tennis partners or sex partners, but the younger woman didn't look for anything more than that. "I'm afraid Téa's going to start dotting her *i*'s with little hearts."

Joey made a face. "I thought it was you that did that. Remember? Seventh and eighth grade."

Eve felt her cheeks grow hot. "You're thinking of someone else."

"It was you," Téa confirmed. "In seventh and eighth grade and then again when you had that crazy infatuation for Nino Farelle."

She didn't want to talk about Nino Farelle. She didn't want

to think about him, because that made her remember that she'd caught sight of him far too often lately. After that one beating she'd realized he was the first of her stupid mistakes about men, but she swore now that the CEO whose stock tip had siphoned away her money would be her last. "Well I've learned my lesson now," she said. "We'll leave the hearts and flowers to Téa, eh, Joe?"

A funny expression crossed her little sister's face. "Yeah. None of that mushy stuff for you and for me."

"So what are those magazines?" Téa asked.

A blush was crawling up Joey's neck now. "Oh, just, uh, some issues I happen to have."

"Issues of what?"

Their little sister hesitated. Then, with a scowl, she stomped forward and dumped the stack onto the table in front of Téa and Eve. The magazines fanned out. Issue after issue of *Bride, Bridal, California Wedding, Down the Aisle, Of Veils and Vows.*

Stunned, Eve and Téa shared a glance. Eve found her voice first. "You, our sister, you, Joey Caruso, collect bridal magazines?"

"I don't *collect* them. I happen to have them." Joey crossed her arms over her chest. "I thought they might come in handy for someone and now they are. We need to plan a wedding— Téa's wedding." Her gaze moved to their older sister and her scowl deepened. "Thank me, Téa."

"Thank you, Joe." The words sounded faint.

Eve snickered. She couldn't help herself. Joey, straight-forward, no-nonsense, unsentimental Joey, was a closet nuptials geek.

Téa started laughing too.

Joey slumped into a third chair, then hid her face behind one of her precious magazines. Her shoulders shook.

It was good to hear them laugh, Eve thought. Despite their father, despite their individual secrets, despite the trouble brewing thanks to their grandfather's impending retirement, they could still laugh.

She picked up one of the magazines and ran her fingers over the cover model's frothy veil. Her life was in shambles, but she could put off thinking about it for a while. She glanced over at Téa, and saw that her big sister was already turning pages, her eyes dreamy, her face glowing with happiness. Definitely mooning over her Johnny now.

"We *do* have a wedding to plan," Eve said. "Let's get started."

About the Music . . .

*It started with a man! My music-major-turned-math-*teacher husband has a huge and ever-growing collection of vinyl albums and CDs. It's an eclectic mix coming out of our stereo speakers, and there was one memorable month when it seemed to be all Dino (Dean Martin, of course) all the time.

Then I was infected by the Rat Pack, convened by Frank Sinatra for what he called a "summit of cool." After that, it was a sweet and easy journey to the other swank artists and forms of mid-nineteenth-century popular music. From space-age pop to swing to exotica, there's something for every crazy-cat bachelor and bachelorette (not to mention hip married couple) in what we think of today as the lounge or martini sound.

Garage sales and grandparent giveaways are a good source for the originals, but remastered compilations on CD are easy to find as well. They're a must-play for those nights when the mood is sophisticated and the man is sexy. Sleuthe out your own favorites, but here are some that especially appeal to me:

Dino: The Essential Dean Martin
The Rat Pack: Boys Night Out
Ultra-Lounge series (especially Volume 5, which has all
    vocal tracks)
Cocktail Mix series
Music for a Bachelor's Den series

Enjoy with three olives!

"I need a hero!"

Imagine that you are the heroine
of your favorite romance. You are
resilient, strong, intrepid.
You rule a country, own a business,
or, perhaps, run a drafty country house
on a shoestring budget. You *can* do it all . . .
and, usually, you do.

But every now and then a gal needs
some help—someone to vanquish
the enemy soldiers,
keep your business afloat . . .
or just plain offer to keep
the servants in line.

Sometimes you need a hero.

Now, in three spectacular new romances by
Kinley MacGregor, Samantha James and
Christie Ridgway—
and one delicious anthology
by Stephanie Laurens, Christina Dodd
and Elizabeth Boyle—
we meet heroines who can
do it all . . . and the sexy,
irresistible heroes who stand
by their side every step
of the way.

May 2005
Experience the passion of
Kinley MacGregor's

Return of the Warrior
The unforgettable second installment
of the "Brotherhood of the Sword"

Queen Adara has one mission: to find her wayward
husband and save their throne! But handsome warrior
Christian of Acre doesn't seem to care much about
ruling his kingdom; he clearly doesn't even consider
himself married! All he wants to do is travel the countryside, helping the poor and downtrodden. But it's
Adara who needs his help right now, and she'll do
anything—even appear in his bedroom naked and
alluring—to get him to rule with her . . . forever.

"Well?" Queen Adara asked in nervous anticipation as her
senior advisor drew near her throne.

Xerus had been her father's most trusted man. At almost
three score years in age, he still held the sharpness of a man in
the prime of his life. His once-black hair was now streaked
with gray and his beard was whiter than the stone walls that
surrounded their capital city, Garzi.

Since her father's death two years past, Adara had turned

to Xerus for everything. There was no one alive she trusted more, which didn't say much, since, as a queen, her first lesson had been that spies and traitors abounded in her court. Most thought that a woman had no business as the leader of their small kingdom.

Adara had other thoughts on that matter. As her father's only surviving child, she refused to see anyone not of their royal bloodline on this throne. Her family had held the royal seat since before the time of Moses.

No one would take her precious Taagaria from her. Not so long as she breathed.

Xerus shook his head and sighed wearily. "Nay, my queen, they refuse to allow you to divorce their king. In their minds you are married and should you try to sever ties to their throne by divorce or annulment they will attack with the sanction of the Church. After all, in their eyes they already own our kingdom. In fact, Selwyn thinks it best that you move into his custody for your own welfare so that they can protect you . . . as their queen."

Adara clenched her fists in frustration.

Xerus glanced over his shoulder toward her two guards who flanked her door before he drew closer to her throne so that he could whisper privately into her ear.

Lutian, her fool, crept nearer to them as well and angled his head so that he wouldn't miss a single word. He even cupped his ear forward.

Xerus glared at the fool.

Dropping his hand, Lutian glared back. A short, lean man, Lutian had straight brown hair and wore a well-trimmed beard. Possessed of average looks, his face was pleasant enough, but it was his kind brown eyes that endeared him to her.

"Speak openly," she said to her advisor. "There is no one I trust more than Lutian."

"He's a half-wit, my queen."

Lutian snorted. "Half-wit, whole-wit, I have enough of them to know to keep silent. So speak, good counselor, and let the queen judge which of the two of us is the greater fool present."

Adara pressed her lips together to keep from smiling at Lutian. Two years younger than she, Lutian had been seriously injured as a youth when he'd tumbled from their walls and landed on his head. Ever since that day, she had watched over him and kept him close lest anyone make his life even more difficult.

She placed a hand on his shoulder to silence him. Xerus couldn't abide being made fun of. Unlike her, he didn't value Lutian's friendship and service.

With a warning glare to the fool, Xerus finally spoke. "Their prince-regent said that if you would finally like to declare Prince Christian dead, then he might be persuaded toward your cause . . . at a price."

Closing her eyes, she ground her teeth furiously. The Elgederion regent had made his position on that matter more than clear. Selwyn wanted her in his son's bed as his bride to secure their tenuous claim to the throne, and the devil would freeze solid before she ever gave herself over to him and allowed those soulless men to rule her people.

How she wished she commanded a larger nation with enough soldiers to pound the arrogant prince-regent into nothing more than a bad memory. Unfortunately, a war would be far too costly to her people and her kingdom. They couldn't fight the Elgederions alone and none of their other allies would help, since to them it was a family squabble between her and her husband's kingdom.

If only her husband would return home and claim his throne, but every time they had sent a man for him, the messenger was slain. To her knowledge none of them had ever reached Christian and she was tired of sending men to their deaths.

Nay, 'twas time to see this matter closed once and for all.

"Send for Thera," she whispered to Xerus.

He scowled at her. "For what purpose?"

"I intend to take a lengthy trip and I can't afford to let anyone know that I am not here to guard my throne."

"Your cousin is not you, Your Grace. Should anyone learn—"

"I trust you alone to keep her and my crown safe until I return. Have her confined to my quarters and tell everyone that I am ill."

Xerus looked even more confused by her orders. "Where are you going?"

"To find my wayward husband and to bring him home."

June 2005
It's a special treat

Hero, Come Back

Three unforgettable original tales
Three amazing storytellers:
Stephanie Laurens, Christina Dodd, Elizabeth Boyle

Imagine, the return of three of the characters you love best—Reggie from Stephanie Laurens's *On a Wild Night* (and *On a Wicked Dawn*)! Jemmy Finch from Elizabeth Boyle's *Once Tempted* (and *It Takes a Hero*)! And Harry Chamberlain, the Earl of Granville, from Christina Dodd's *Lost in Your Arms*!

Now you get to meet them all over again in this delicious anthology of heroes who were just too good *not* to have stories of their own.

Lost and Found
Stephanie Laurens

Releasing Benjamin, Reggie looked at Anne. He'd recognized her soft voice and all notion of politely retreating had vanished. Anne was Amelia's sister-in-law, Luc Ashford's second sister, known to all family and close friends as highly nervous in crowds.

They hadn't met for some years; he suspected she avoided tonnish gatherings. Rapid calculation revealed she must be twenty-six. She seemed . . . perhaps an inch taller, more assured, more definite, certainly more striking than he recalled, but then she wasn't shrinking against any wall at the moment. She was elegantly turned out in a dark green walking dress. Her expression was open, decided, her face framed by lustrous brown hair caught up in a top knot, then allowed to cascade about her head in lush waves. Her eyes were light brown, the color of caramel, large and set under delicately arched brows. Her lips were blush rose, sensuously curved, decidedly vulnerable.

Intensely feminine.

As were the curves of breast and waist revealed by the tightly-fitting bodice . . .

Jerking his mind from the unexpected track, he frowned. "Now cut line—what is this about?"

A frown lit her eyes, a warning one. "I'll explain once we've returned Benjy to the house." Retaking Benjy's hand, she turned back along the path.

Reggie pivoted and fell in beside her. "Which house? Is Luc in town?"

"No. Not Calverton House." Anne hesitated, then added, more softly, "The Foundling House."

Pieces of the puzzle fell, jigsawlike, into place, but the picture in his mind was incomplete. His long strides relaxed, he retook her arm, wound it with his, forcing her to slow. "Much better to stroll without a care, rather than rush off so purposefully. No need for the ignorant to wonder what your purpose is."

The Matchmaker's Bargain
Elizabeth Boyle

"Oh, this cannot be!" Esme said, bounding up from her chair. "I can't get married."

"Whyever not? You aren't already engaged, are you?" Jemmy didn't know why, but for some reason he didn't like the idea of her being another man's betrothed. Besides, what the devil was the fellow thinking, letting such a pretty little chit wander lost about the countryside?

But his concerns about another man in her life were for naught, for she told him very tartly, "I am not engaged, sir, and I assure you, I'm not destined for marriage."

"I don't see that there is anything wrong with you," he said without thinking. Demmit, this is what came of living the life of a recluse—he'd forgotten every bit of his town bronze. "I mean to say, it's not like you couldn't be here seeking a husband."

The disbelief on her face struck him to the core.

Was she really so unaware of the pretty picture she presented? That her green eyes, bright and full of sparkles, and soft brown hair, still tumbled from her slumbers and hanging in long tangled curls, was an enticing picture—one that might persuade many a man to get fitted for a pair of leg-shackles.

Even Jemmy found himself susceptible to her charms—she had an air of familiarity about her that whispered of strength and warmth and sensibility, capable of drawing a man toward her like a beggar to a warm hearth.

Not to mention the parts, that as a gentleman, he shouldn't know she possessed, but in their short, albeit rather noteworthy acquaintance, had discovered with the familiarity that one usually had only with a mistress . . . or a hastily gained betrothed.

He shook that idea right out of his head. Whatever was he thinking? She wasn't interested in marriage, and neither was he. Not than any lady *would* have him . . . lame and scarred as he was.

"I hardly see that any of this is your concern," she was saying, once again bustling about the room, gathering up her belongings. She plucked her stockings—gauzy, French sort of things—from the line by the fire.

He could imagine what they would look like on her, and more importantly what it would feel like sliding them off her long, elegant legs.

When she saw him staring at her unmentionables, she blushed and shoved them into her valise. "I really must be away."

The Third Suitor
Christina Dodd

Leaning over the high porch railing, Harry Chamberlain looked down into the flowering shrubbery surrounding his oceanfront cottage and asked, "Young woman, what are you doing down there?"

The girl flinched, stopped crawling through the collection of moss, dirt and faded pink blossoms, and turned a smudged face up to his. "Shh." She glanced behind her, as if someone were creeping after her. "I'm trying to avoid one of my suitors."

Harry glanced behind her, too. No one was there.

"Can you see him?" she asked.

"There's not a soul in sight." A smart man would have let her go on her way. Harry was on holiday, a holiday he desperately needed, and he had vowed to avoid trouble at all costs. Now a girl of perhaps eighteen years, dressed in a modish blue flowered gown, came crawling through the bushes, armed with nothing more than a ridiculous tale, and he was tempted to help. Tempted because of a thin, tanned face, wide brown eyes, a kissable mouth, a crooked blue bonnet and, from this angle, the finest pair of breasts he'd ever had the good fortune to gaze upon.

Such unruliness in his own character surprised him. He was, in truth, Edmund Kennard Henry Chamberlain, earl of Granville, the owner of a great estate in Somerset, and because of the weight of his responsibilities there, and the additional responsibilities he had taken on, he tended to do his duty without capriciousness. Indeed, it was that trait which had set him, eight years ago, to serve England in various countries and capacities. Now he gazed at a female intent on some silliness and discovered in himself the urge to find out more about her. Perhaps he had at last relaxed from the tension of his last job. Or perhaps she *was* the relaxation he sought.

In a trembling voice, she pleaded, "Please, sir, if he appears, don't tell him I'm here."

"I wouldn't dream of interfering."

"Oh, thank you!" A smile transformed that quivering mouth into one that was naturally merry, with soft peach lips and a dimple. "Because I thought that's what you were doing."

Julianna felt herself tumbling to the floor. Jarred into wakefulness, she opened her eyes, rubbing her shoulder where she'd landed. What the deuce . . . ? Panic enveloped her; it was pitch black inside the coach.

And outside as well.

She was just about to heave herself back onto the cushions when the sound of male voices punctuated the air outside. The coachman . . . and someone else.

"Put it down, I s-say!" the coachman stuttered. "There's nothing of value aboard, I swear! Mercy," the man blubbered. "I beg of you, have mercy!"

Even as a decidedly prickly unease slid down her spine, the door was wrenched open. She found herself staring at the gleaming barrel of a pistol. In terror she lifted her gaze to the man who possessed it.

Garbed in black he was, from the enveloping folds of his cloak to the kerchief that obscured the lower half of his face. A silk mask was tied around his eyes; they were all that was visible of his features. Even in the dark, there was no mistaking their color. They glimmered like clear golden fire, pale and unearthly.

The devil's eyes.

"Nothing of value aboard, eh?"

A gust of chill night air funneled in. Yet it was like nothing compared to the chill she felt in hearing that voice . . . So softly querulous, like steel tearing through tightly stretched silk, she decided dazedly.

She had always despised silly, weak, helpless females. Yet when his gaze raked over her—*through* her, bold and ever so irreverent!—she felt stripped to the bone.

Goose bumps rose on her flesh. She couldn't move. She most certainly couldn't speak. She could not even swallow past the knot lodged deep in her throat. Fear numbed her mind. Her mouth was dry with a sickly dread such as she had never experienced. All she could think was that if Mrs. Chadwick were here, she might take great delight in knowing she'd been right to be so fearful. For somehow Julianna knew with a mind-chilling certainty that it was he . . .

The Magpie.

Dane Quincy Granville did not count on the coachman's reaction—nor his rashness. There was a crack of the whip, a frenzied shout. The horses bolted. Instinctively, Dane leaped back, very nearly knocked to the ground. The vehicle jolted forward, speeding toward a bend in the road.

The stupid fool! Christ, the coachman would never make the turn. The bend was too sharp. He was going too fast—

The night exploded. There was an excruciating crash, the sound of wood splintering and cracking . . . the high-pitched neighs of the horses.

Then there was nothing.

Galvanized into action, Dane sprang for Percival. Leaping from the stallion's back, he hurtled himself down the steep embankment where the coach had disappeared. Scrambling over the brush, he spied it. It was overturned, resting against the trunk of an ancient tree.

One wheel was still spinning as he reached it.

The horses were already gone. So was the driver. His neck was broken, twisted at an odd angle from his body. Dane had seen enough of death to know there was nothing he could do to help him.

Miraculously, the door to the main compartment had remained on its hinges. In fury and fear, Dane tore it off and lunged into the compartment.

The girl was still inside, coiled in a heap on the roof. His heart in his throat, he reached for her, easing her into his arms and outside.

His heart pounding, he knelt in the damp earth and stared down at her. "Wake up!" he commanded. As if because he willed it, as if it would be so . . . He gritted his teeth, as if to instill his very will—his very life—inside her.

Her head fell limply over his arm.

"Dammit, girl, wake up!"

He was sick in the pit of his belly, in his very soul. If only the driver hadn't been so blasted skittish. So hasty! He wouldn't have harmed them, either of them. On a field near Brussels, he'd seen enough death and dying to last a lifetime. God knew it had changed him. Shaped him for all eternity. And for now, all he wanted was—

She moaned.

An odd little laugh broke from his chest, the sound almost brittle. After all his careful planning that *this* should occur . . . But he couldn't ascertain her injuries. Not here. Not in the dark. He must leave. Now. He couldn't afford to linger, else all might be for naught.

The girl did not wake as he rifled through the boot, retrieving a bulging sack and a valise. Seconds later, he whistled for Percival. Cradling the girl carefully against his chest, he lifted the reins and rode into the night.

As suddenly as he had appeared, the Magpie was gone.

August 2005
We're going to make you
an offer you can't refuse in
Christie Ridgway's

An Offer He Can't Refuse

The first in her delicious new Wisegirls series

Téa Caruso knows what everyone thinks about her
family . . . her very large, very powerful family. After
all, she grew up in the shadow of her grandfather—
The Sun Dried Tomato King—and her uncles, with
their mysterious "business." And, of course, there
are her aunts, who don't ask too many questions.
She's spent a lifetime going legit, and now her past
comes back to haunt her when she falls for Johnny
Magee. He's a professional gambler, the worst kind
of man, one who'd make the family proud . . . or
is he?

Téa Caruso had once been very, very bad and she wondered
if today was the day she started paying for it. After spending the morning closeted in the perfume-saturated powder
room of Mr. and Mrs. William Duncan's Spanish-Italian-
Renaissance-inspired Palm Springs home, discussing baby
Jesus and the Holy Mother, she emerged from the clouds—
both heavenly and olfactory—with a Chanel No. 5 hang-

over and fingernail creases in her palms as deep as the Duncan's quarter-mile lap pool.

Standing on the pillowed limestone terrace outside, she allowed herself a sixty-second pause for fresh air, but multitasked the moment by completing a quick appearance check as well. Even someone with less artistic training than Téa would know that her Mediterranean coloring and generous curves were made for low necklines and sassy flounces in gypsy shades, but her Mandarin-collared, dove gray linen dress was devised to button up, smooth out, and tuck away. Though she could never feel innocent, she preferred to at least look that way.

The reflection in her hand mirror presented no jarring surprises. The sun lent an apricot cast to her olive skin. Tilted brown eyes, a slightly patrician nose, cheekbones and jawline now defined after years of counting calories instead of chowing down on cookies. Assured that her buttons were tight, her mascara unsmudged, and her hair still controlled in its long, dark sweep, she snapped the compact shut. Then, hurrying in the direction of her car, she swapped mirror for cell phone and speed dialed her interior design firm.

"She's still insisting on Him," she told her assistant when she answered. "Find out who can hand paint a Rembrandt-styled infant Jesus in the bottom of a porcelain sink."

Still on forward march, she checked her watch. "Quick, any messages? I have lunch with my sisters up next."

"Nikki O'Neal phoned and mentioned a redo of her dining room," her assistant replied. "Something about a mural depicting the Ascension."

The Ascension?

Téa's steps faltered, slowed. "No," she groaned. "That means Mrs. D. has spilled her plans. Now we'll be hearing from every one of her group at Our Lady of Mink."

A segment of Téa's client list—members of the St. Brigit's

Guild at the posh Our Lady of Mercy Catholic Church—
cultivated their competitive spirits as well as their Holy Spirit
during their weekly meetings. One woman would share a
new idea for home decor, prompting the next to take the same
theme to even greater—more ostentatious—heights.

Three years before it had been everything vineyard, then
after that sea life turned all the rage, and now . . . good God.

"The *Ascension*?" Téa muttered. "These women must be
out of their minds."

But could she really blame them? Palm Springs had a
grand tradition of the grandiose, after all. Walt Disney had
owned a home here. Elvis. Liberace.

It was just that when she'd opened her business, filled with
high artistic aspirations and a zealous determination to make
over the notorious Caruso name, she hadn't foreseen the pitfalls. Like how the ceaseless influx of rent and utility bills
and the unsteady trickle and occasional torrent that was her
cash flow meant she couldn't be picky when it came to
choosing design jobs.

Like how *that* could result in gaining woeful renown as designer of all things overdone. She groaned again.

"Oh, and Téa . . ." Her assistant's voice rose in an expectant lilt. "His Huskiness called."

Her stomach lurched, pity party forgotten. "What? *Who*?"

"Johnny Magee."

Of course, Johnny Magee. Her assistant referred to the
man they'd never met by an ever-expanding lexicon of nicknames that ranged from the overrated to the out-and-out
ridiculous. To Téa, he was simply her One Chance, her Answered Prayers, her Belief in Miracles.

Carnival Pride℠
April 2 - 9, 2006.

7 Day Exotic Mexican Riviera Itinerary

DAY	PORT	ARRIVE	DEPART
Sun	Los Angeles/Long Beach, CA		4:00 P.M.
Mon	"Book Lover's" Day at Sea		
Tue	"Book Lover's" Day at Sea		
Wed	Puerto Vallarta, Mexico	8:00 A.M.	10:00 P.M.
Thu	Mazatlan, Mexico	9:00 A.M.	6:00 P.M.
Fri	Cabo San Lucas, Mexico	7:00 A.M.	4:00 P.M.
Sat	"Book Lover's" Day at Sea		
Sun	Los Angeles/Long Beach, CA	9:00 A.M.	

ports of call subject to weather conditions

TERMS AND CONDITIONS

PAYMENT SCHEDULE:
50% due upon booking
Full and final payment due by February 10, 2006

Acceptable forms of payment are Visa, MasterCard, American Express, Discover and checks. The cardholder must be one of the passengers traveling. A fee of $25 will apply for all returned checks. Check payments must be made payable to **Advantage International, LLC** and sent to: **Advantage International, LLC, 195 North Harbor Drive, Suite 4206, Chicago, IL 60601**

CHANGE/CANCELLATION:
Notice of change/cancellation must be made in writing to Advantage International, LLC.

Change:
Changes in cabin category may be requested and can result in increased rate and penalties. A name change is permitted 60 days or more prior to departure and will incur a penalty of $50 per name change. Deviation from the group schedule and package is a cancellation.

Cancellation:

181 days or more prior to departure	$250 per person
121 - 180 days or more prior to departure	50% of the package price
120 - 61 days prior to departure	75% of the package price
60 days or less prior to departure	100% of the package price (nonrefundable)

US and Canadian citizens are required to present a valid passport or the original birth certificate and state issued photo ID (drivers license). All other nationalities must contact the consulate of the various ports that are visited for verification of documentation.

<u>**We strongly recommend trip cancellation insurance!**</u>

For complete details call 1-877-ADV-NTGE or visit www.AuthorsAtSea.com

---

For booking form and complete information

go to <u>**www.AuthorsAtSea.com**</u> or call **1-877-ADV-NTGE**

Complete coupon and booking form and mail both to:

Advantage International, LLC,
195 North Harbor Drive, Suite 4206, Chicago, IL 60601

GCRB 0805